HELL GATE

HELL GATE

LINDA FAIRSTEIN

Little, Brown

LITTLE, BROWN

First published in the United States in 2010 by Dutton,
a member of Penguin Group (USA) Inc.
First published in Great Britain in 2010 by Little, Brown

A CIP catalogue record for this book
is available from the British Library.

Hardback ISBN 978-1-4087-0081-5
Trade Paperback ISBN 978-1-4087-0082-2

Typeset in Janson Text
Printed and bound in Great Britain by
Clays Ltd, St Ives plc

Papers used by Little, Brown are natural,
renewable and recyclable products sourced
from well-managed forests and certified in accordance with
the rules of the Forest Stewardship Council.

Mixed Sources
Product group from well-managed
forests and other controlled sources
www.fsc.org Cert no. SGS-COC-004081
© 1996 Forest Stewardship Council

FSC

Little, Brown
An imprint of
Little, Brown Book Group
100 Victoria Embankment
London EC4Y 0DY

An Hachette UK Company
www.hachette.co.uk

www.littlebrown.co.uk

To the women and men of the special victims units of the Manhattan District Attorney's Office and the NYPD – past and present – who have always worked on the side of the angels . . . with respect and gratitude

Resignedly beneath the sky
the melancholy waters lie.
So blend the turrets and shadows there
That all seem pendulous in air,
While from a proud tower in the town
death looks gigantically down.

— Edgar Allan Poe, *The City in the Sea*

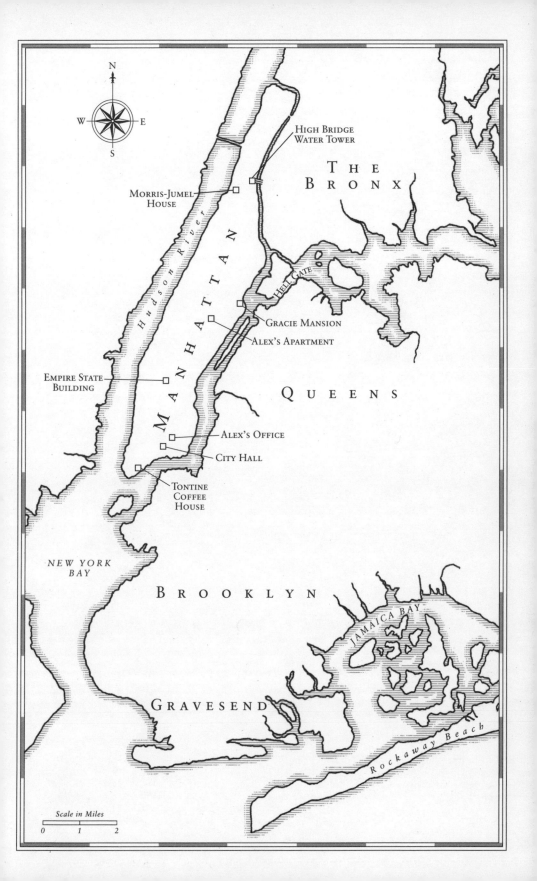

N

W E

S

HIGH BRIDGE
WATER TOWER

THE
BRONX

MORRIS-JUMEL
HOUSE

Hudson River

HELL GATE

GRACIE MANSION

ALEX'S APARTMENT

M A N H A T T A N

Q U E E N S

EMPIRE STATE
BUILDING

ALEX'S OFFICE

CITY HALL

TONTINE
COFFEE
HOUSE

*NEW YORK
BAY*

B R O O K L Y N

JAMAICA BAY

G R A V E S E N D

Rockaway Beach

Scale in Miles

0   1   2

ONE

"How many bodies?"

"Six, Ms. Cooper. So far we got six dead. But there's a mean rip and a swift current out there. Anybody's guess what's going to wash up by the end of the day."

I was walking toward the ocean behind a cop sent to escort me from my car, following him on the path that had been formed in the dunes by the first responders who had tracked across it two hours earlier, at daybreak.

"One woman?" I asked.

"What?" The cop cupped his hand to his ear as he turned to look at me. The gust of wind that blew a clump of damp sand against the side of my face also carried off my words.

"The news is reporting that one of the victims is a young woman."

"We got two now. Girls, really. Teenagers at best. Four men and two girls."

I stopped at the crest of the dune and scanned the horizon. Dozens of police officers were scattered along a quarter mile of beach, their blue uniforms a deeper color than the rough Atlantic. Detectives in windbreakers and all-weather jackets looked slightly less incongruous in this unlikely setting, some scouring the shoreline while others gathered around the survivors who had been brought to land.

"That's it," the cop said, pointing at the rusted freighter that was grounded on a sandbar about three hundred yards out to sea, listing to port, as police launches and Coast Guard boats darted around it. "*Golden Voyage.* That's the name of the ship they sailed on."

"*Golden Voyage* my ass," Mike Chapman said, coming up beside me, adjusting his sunglasses as he spoke. "It must have been the crossing from hell. Happy New Year, Coop."

"Same to you, Mike. Although this doesn't get it off to a particularly pleasant start."

"I got her from here, pal," Mike said, dismissing the cop. "You warm enough?"

"I'm fine. Battaglia called me at home this morning," I said, referring to my boss, the district attorney of New York County. "Did you just arrive?"

We were both dressed in jeans. I had a cashmere sweater under my ski jacket, with gloves and a scarf to protect myself against the brisk January day. Mike wore a white turtleneck beneath his trademark navy blazer. The winter cold never bothered him, any more than the sight of a corpse.

"Nope. Human trafficking—you don't get worse scumbags than the guys who deal in flesh. All the squads got called in right away. Every borough," he said. "I was doing a midnight so I shot out here from a crack den in Harlem. Just went back to the car now to get my shades. The glare on the water's a killer."

Mike was one of the best detectives in the city, assigned to Manhattan North Homicide, which handled every case from Fifty-ninth Street to the northern tip of the island. We'd been professional partners—and close friends—for more than a decade.

"Where do you want to start?" he asked me. People were swarming across the beach like armies of insects. "The tent over there to the left on that paved area—that's the temporary morgue.

The group in the middle, we've got more than a hundred victims off the wreck so far, trying to get them in dry clothes. The commissioner is due in by chopper any minute now."

"Who's in charge?" I asked.

"Feebies, kid. The feds are running the operation. Your buddy from the task force, Donovan Baynes. His group is trying to set up a command center on the right. Hardest thing," Mike said, starting down the slope, "is holding the press at bay. Roping them off on the street is easy, but keeping the helicopters and power boats away is more of a problem, now that news has spread. C'mon."

"Take me to Baynes, okay?"

"Battaglia doesn't let go, I'll give him that. Rockaway Beach— the Irish Riviera—this is Queens, for Chrissake. That parking lot where the morgue is, it's over the line in Nassau County. What makes him think he has jurisdiction here?" Mike's loafers made a crunching sound as they pounded the sand while we toured the scene. His straight black hair, gleaming in the sunlight, was blowing wildly as he walked into the wind.

"Global and mobile. That's how he likes to think of himself. He's been DA for so long he doesn't believe there's anything that limits him," I said. "That's why he fought so hard to get me on the task force."

Human trafficking, a modern-day form of slavery, wasn't even on the books until federal laws addressing it were enacted in 2000. Before that, prosecutors had patched together local legislation to attempt to punish the handful of individuals who could be linked to efforts to transport victims across borders, coercing them to work at everything from agricultural labor to child prostitution.

"Good morning, Counselor," a detective greeted me as we approached the group of men encircling Donovan Baynes. "Chapman, how many interpreters did you call for?"

"A boatload. Why? How many you got so far?"

"Two. Only two have showed up."

"What language?" I asked, trying to process the sight of scores of dazed victims who were wrapped in blankets, staring out at the shipwreck, undoubtedly looking for family members and friends.

"Ukrainian," Mike said. "Why? You ever do a Ukrainian, kid? A little pillow talk and your Ukrainian could be almost as good as your French."

I had just returned from Paris two days earlier—on Monday—where I spent the New Year holiday with my lover, Luc Rouget. The more about my personal life I kept from Mike, the more he needled me. "No surprise. Since the Soviet collapse, Ukraine leads Eastern Europe in the number of trafficking victims."

"What do you want me to do about it, Chapman?" the detective asked. "We got to move these guys off the beach before they freeze their balls off. Sorry, ma'am."

"Nobody's gonna freeze today. It's almost fifty degrees," Mike said, not breaking his stride. "Send some cars over to Little Odessa. Go to a few coffee shops and grab anybody who's sitting still."

"Where's that?"

"Brighton Beach. Right next door, in Brooklyn. You're like Coop—you need a road map to the Outer Boroughs."

Brighton had been built as a local beach resort in the 1860s, named for the English coastal town in a contest held by its developers. In the 1970s, it was nicknamed Little Odessa because of the large concentration of immigrants from that Black Sea city, once one of the great ports of Imperial Russia.

Donovan Baynes waved as he saw us approaching. I'd known the forty-one-year-old since his days as a federal prosecutor in the Southern District of the U.S. Attorney's Office. He was surrounded by four men, three of them agents I recognized from our task force meetings. "Hurry up, Alex. Glad you're here. I think you know everybody."

I shook hands and introduced myself to the unfamiliar man. He appeared to be in his early fifties, barefoot and dressed in a wetsuit that was sculpted to his well-muscled body. "Hi, I'm Alexandra Cooper. Manhattan District Attorney's Office."

"Stu Carella. Used to be homicide, NYPD. Guess you don't remember me, but we met at a few crime scenes when I was still on the job. The dancer at the Met, the broad who was kidnapped at Fort Tilden," he said, then nodded at Mike. "I see she's still stalking you, Chapman."

"My order of protection expired, Stu. I asked the judge to keep her three hundred feet away and to tell her to stop stealing my underwear, but she's out of control again. Be careful, man, Coop's a sucker for guys in tights."

"Let me bring you up to speed, Alex," Baynes said, ignoring Mike's chatter as he put his arm around my shoulder. He'd been around the two of us enough to know this was standard operating procedure for Mike. Behind us were the high-rise buildings of the Rockaways—mostly nursing homes at this end—and the smaller residences that bordered the beach. "About five of the vics have been debriefed. The ship left Sevastopol more than a month ago, with close to three hundred people on board, mainly men, but at least thirty women and children."

I looked out at the decrepit cargo ship, amazed that it had made it here from Europe.

"Smugglers find the villagers living the most desperate lives, promise them jobs and a better life in America. Take every nickel they've managed to save, claiming to use it to feed them on the trip. Bribe officials. You know all that. They trucked these folks from small towns all over their country and loaded them into sweltering holds on board the ship, then began dodging immigration police throughout the Mediterranean."

"They got all this way only to run aground here and die within sight of land," I said. The stories I'd heard from trafficking victims were heartbreaking, but at least those who were rescued by law enforcement agencies often had a second chance.

"It wasn't an accident," Baynes continued, turning to his deputy. "The leader of the operation in New York—well, what do you call a snakehead in Ukrainian?"

"A friggin' snakehead, Donny," Mike said. "You brainiacs got to go to law school to figure that out? It's the same in any language."

Ages ago, the Chinese perfected the ugly practice of smuggling human beings, called snakes, for slave labor. Ringleaders of the inhumane syndicates had long been known as snakeheads.

"The boss of the operation is somewhere in this city. When the captain got close to shore just after midnight, he radioed his contact, who was supposed to send a small fleet of speedboats out to pick up the passengers," Baynes went on. "Two, three hours went by and no sign of escorts. Apparently, the anxiety level of the immigrants who'd been pigeonholed for weeks went over the top. The first handful of men had been brought up on deck to be unloaded, and one of them got frantic when he saw a vessel with government markings coming toward them."

"Coast Guard?" I asked.

"We haven't gotten that far, Alex. No agency we know of has claimed yet that they tried to intercept the ship."

Mike picked up the story. "That first group just went berserk and staged a mutiny, according to two of the guys who made it ashore. They locked the captain in his cabin with a few of the other managers. Some of the men were in such despair about being caught by immigration that they started jumping overboard to swim in."

"That water must be frigid," I said.

"Frigid? Don't go showing off your area of expertise, Coop. That's why we hauled Stu out of retirement."

"Like I was just telling Donovan," Carella said, "I'm in the Polar Bear Club here at Coney Island. We swim every Sunday, all winter long. Just had our big New Year's party five days ago. Not so bad for the Atlantic. Forty-three degrees. Some hypothermia, maybe. Everybody will be watching out for that today. Cold water doesn't have to be fatal, Alex."

"But at least six people have died."

Carella shook his head. "Probably drowned."

"Drowned? The ship is so close to shore. The water isn't even that deep."

"Panic kills, Coop. Everybody who works on water knows that."

"Panic?"

"Can you believe it? Not all the peasants in Europe grew up with a pool in the backyard like you did, princess."

Shouts went up from the crowd of victims and several of them broke through a line of cops, running almost thirty yards eastward to the water's edge. Stu Carella dashed after the frantic young men and passed beyond them as he dove into the surf, where something that looked like a large rag doll was lifted again and flopped around by a tall wave that kept licking at the sand. He and three cops in scuba gear grabbed and carried another body onto the beach. One of the men immediately crouched in an effort to resuscitate the limp corpse.

I started after them and Donovan Baynes pulled me back. "Let it be, Alex. They know what they're doing."

"How many do you think jumped ship?" I wanted to make myself useful, but all the specialized squads of the NYPD were well-trained for this kind of disaster.

"It's impossible to get an accurate count at this point. One fellow they've talked to explained that when the mutineers began to struggle with the captain, he tried to steer the damn thing away from shore, back out into the open sea. Making that turn, he ran the ship aground on a shallow sandbar. Some of the victims figured they were so close to the beach they could reach land—even several who didn't know how to swim. Maybe twenty jumped. Maybe forty. Nobody seems to know yet."

"The men you've talked to, do they know where they thought they were going?" I asked.

"Nobody told them the truth, Alex. It's the usual scam," Donovan said. "You've been there—people who don't see a future for themselves and want to believe in a dream, but wake up in the middle of a nightmare. Countrymen were supposed to meet them right here in Queens and bring them into their homes until they're placed in jobs—mostly agricultural ones—in farms upstate and in the Midwest. Those would be the men, the lucky ones."

"The young women would become your territory," Mike said.

I had seen this time after time in my role as chief sex crimes prosecutor in the DA's office—girls abducted from their homes in Thailand or Montenegro, running away from abusive parents and desolate lives in Sri Lanka or Serbia, smuggled across borders in car trunks or leaky boats, often following their brothers or school-mates, hoping that hard work and physical labor would eventually gain them the freedom of a new life in the States.

But the girls rarely made it to farmlands and fields. The sex trade had become a huge transnational industry, as lucrative as it could be deadly. The teenagers on the *Golden Voyage* were doubtless bound for basements and brothels, to be broken in by their owners for the months and years of prostitution that awaited them in the promised land.

"Is there any way to identify these victims?" I asked.

"No better than usual. Each one is supposed to have a piece of paper with his or her family name and town of origin in their pockets when they ship out," Baynes said. "Most of them tossed or swallowed the paper as the police launches arrived. The brother of one of the dead girls is among the few who are talking. He dove in and she tried to follow."

A lanky man sat at the corner of the tented morgue, with a gray blanket covering his head and upper body. I couldn't tell whether he was shaking from the cold or because he was crying so hard.

Stu Carella was making his way back to us, refusing the offer of an NYPD sweatshirt that one of the cops thrust at him.

"Another kid gone," Carella said, throwing a tuft of algae at the ground in disgust. "Probably drowned in three feet of water, unable to handle the pull of the rip."

"From his hand?" Mike knelt down and picked up the slimy green vegetation with the tip of his pen.

"Yeah."

Mike whistled and the closest cops looked up. He signaled one, who jogged to us. "Carry this over to the medical examiner. Goes with that latest body."

The fact that the victim had been clutching algae, and I'd bet a handful of sand, as he was dragged across the ocean floor meant that he had been alive when he went into the water. Drowning, I had learned over the years, was a diagnosis of exclusion. A complete autopsy would be necessary for each of the Golden Voyagers who had washed up on the windy beach, despite how obvious the circumstances appeared to be to us.

"What do you plan to do, Donny?" I asked. "I mean, with the survivors."

There was no good answer to this question. It was commonplace for these individuals whose lives at home were already overcome with despair to risk everything for this run to freedom, only to find themselves handcuffed in the backseat of a patrol car to begin the next leg of their ugly journey. A few might eventually be granted political asylum, some would be deported, but the majority would wind up in immigrant detention centers somewhere in the heartland of America.

Baynes stammered as he surveyed the bleak scene stretched out across the waterfront.

"I—I haven't had an operation of this size since I—uh—since I was appointed to the task force. Frankly, I don't know what becomes of these poor souls."

The noise overhead was a police helicopter, probably carrying Commissioner Keith Scully, whom Donovan, Mike, and I all knew well.

"Not jail," I said. "We can't let them rot in jail while we sort it out."

"Scully's too smart for that," Mike said.

"You'll have to start working with the women right away, Alex," Baynes said. "We'll have them checked out medically and then each one needs to be interviewed. You've got backup?"

"The senior people in the bureau will be on it with me." I had a great team of lawyers assigned to my unit by Battaglia, experienced in the courtroom and compassionate in their interactions with traumatized victims.

I could hear wailing now, a cacophony of voices that seemed like it could carry for miles. Cops were trying to move a small cluster of bedraggled survivors toward the dunes, to the vans waiting in the street that would shuttle them to whatever police facility Scully designated. The men were refusing to separate from their comrades despite prodding—all still focused on the others being ferried ashore, all still searching the waves for signs of missing friends.

"C'mon, Coop. You'll rerun this movie in your brain all day and all night," Mike said, taking my arm to turn me away from the sight. "You got what Battaglia sent you for. Donovan's not doing anything on this case without your input."

My feet were firmly planted in the sand. "I want to talk to Scully, Mike. Let go."

"Scully's running late."

My head whipped around as I recognized the voice of Mercer Wallace. I squinted in the sunlight and shaded my eyes with my hand to look up at him. His six-foot-six frame towered over my shivering five-foot-ten-inch body.

"Good to have you here, buddy," Baynes said, shaking his hand. "We've got a monster of a problem on our hands."

Mercer was one of the only African American detectives in the city to make first-grade. He was my best ally at the Special Victims Squad—a former partner of Mike's from his days in Homicide—and I had urged Donovan to include him on the JTTF—the Joint Trafficking Task Force, assembled to combat the increasingly desperate fight against human trafficking into the New York area.

"I'm waiting on the commissioner to land," Baynes said, staring as the chopper banked and circled out over the freighter. "We'll fill you in."

"You sleep in today or what?" Mike asked Mercer. "Half a tour?"

"Scully's not making it here, guys. I've been with him for hours," Mercer said, sipping from a cardboard cup of coffee.

"Where at?" Mike said. "Anybody think to tell him this slave ship just capsized in his very own territorial waters?"

"The commissioner knows all about it, Mr. Chapman. He's got his hands full with some other business."

"The mayor won't want to be stonewalled on this one," Baynes said.

"He and Scully are together as we speak," Mercer said, offering me a slug of his coffee. "Counting on you to hold this down, Donovan, till they get on it."

"Something more important than this, huh? Lemme guess," Mike said, tugging at the fringe on the end of my scarf. "You got a mayor who wants to be president and a commissioner who wants to be mayor. Ship of fools gets trumped by what? A whiff of political corruption with maybe a dollop of sex. Am I warm? Somebody passing money to a cross-dressing candidate in the stall of a men's room at Grand Central Station?"

Mercer was taking in the panorama of disaster that spread out before us. He crossed his arms and walked off to the side. "You're not too far wrong."

"Give me a hint."

"Ethan Leighton."

Mercer Wallace had everyone's attention with the mention of the name of the forty-two-year-old congressman from Manhattan's Upper West Side.

"What's he complaining about now?" Mike asked. "That guy's been a whiner since he was born."

"Ethan's a good guy. You know we were classmates at Columbia

Law," said Donny Baynes. "His dad's always had big plans for him, he's under a lot of pressure."

"Yeah, well, either way, this time he's on the other side of the complaint," Mercer said. "Leighton's the perp."

Donovan Baynes seemed blindsided. I knew he and Ethan had even worked together after law school in the Southern District. "What are you talking about?"

"Ethan Leighton flipped his car on the FDR Drive at three thirty this morning. Hit a van before he plowed into the railing. The two guys in the van broke some bones, but they'll make it. The congressman was intoxed. Maybe *tanked*'s a better word," Mercer said. "Where do you want me to start? DWI? Reckless assault? Leaving the scene?"

"Is Ethan hurt too?" I asked. He was a rising congressional star who hoped to be New York's next governor. In all likelihood Donovan Baynes was one of his closest advisors.

"A few bruises. Dead drunk, and somehow he fled the scene— or staggered away from it—before the cops got there. Tried to have one of his former aides take the weight."

"I don't believe it," Baynes said, squaring off against Mercer. "Ethan's such a straight shooter."

"I guess he had a rough night with his girlfriend," Mercer said. "The baby was sick, spiking a really high fever, and they fought about whether to rush her to the emergency room."

"That's nonsense," Baynes said. I'd never seen him so agitated. "Where did you hear that crap? It can't be true. There's no sick baby. Ethan doesn't have a girlfriend. Just because the mayor's got a grudge against his old man—or, or he's looking for some bait to get the paparazzi off the scene of this shipwreck—you're buying into that? Who's peddling these lies?"

"There's apparently more than enough fodder to go around," Mercer said, breaking away from Baynes as he headed in the direction of the morgue. "Ethan's got a girlfriend, all right, and what the tabloids will undoubtedly call a love child."

"Who fed you this story?" Baynes said, charging after Mercer, challenging him to answer. "I want to know where you picked that up."

Mercer turned and put his arm out to bring Donovan to a stop. "You got a sea of misery right here, Donny. Let's deal with that. Don't be getting in high dudgeon over Leighton."

"He's my closest friend, Mercer. I need to know where this is coming from."

"It's Ethan's wife who told me, okay? I heard every sorry detail from Ethan Leighton's wife."

TWO

Shouts went up from the beach as a small speedboat nosed into the sand, the driver lifting and tilting the engine as he came to a stop. Five guys stepped out of it into the shallow surf to the roaring cheers of their friends, and one of the rescuers hoisted a young woman over his shoulder and carried her in. When he reached a dry spot at the foot of a low dune, he lowered her onto her feet, steadying her while she caught her breath.

A man broke loose from the group and ran to embrace her. Before any cops could reach them, both dropped to their knees and began praying together, the girl's body wracked by sobs.

"Cooper! Give me a hand," one of the homicide detectives yelled to me as he tried to break them up.

I took off running and Mike jogged beside me until we reached the terrified pair. The girl picked up her head and noted the dozens of people staring at her. She dissolved in tears again as I knelt beside her.

I stroked her back and tried to calm her. "The interpreters, Mike, get me one *stat*."

"Is okay, lady," the male said to me. "I speak little English."

The girl looked back and forth between our faces, fearing that I was the enemy.

"My name is Alexandra. I'm a lawyer for the government," I said, "and I'm going to help you."

He repeated my words to her, but the idea of government and help in the same sentence didn't seem encouraging to either of them.

"Are you related to her?"

"Is girlfriend. Is my girlfriend."

This was not the time to break investigative rules. One victim, one friend or relative, should not be translating for another. There was nothing I could ask her about her ordeal in his presence that she wouldn't try to filter as she answered questions through him.

"What are your names?"

"Cyril," he said. "Am Cyril. Her is Emilia."

I looked back over the beach to see whether any other shelter had been put up, but the only covered area was the morgue.

"Let's get Emilia warm first. Let's make her more comfortable," I said. Then I whispered to Mike. "Find a place where I can talk to her without the boyfriend."

"We're waiting on buses to take all of them to the hospital to be examined."

"Good. I'll ride with her. Get her alone. See what she knows, where she thought she was going."

"I don't mean ambulances." They were known in police parlance as buses. "I mean big yellow school buses that can take groups of them at a time."

"What's that building behind the cabanas?" I asked, pointing past the morgue. "What does that sign say, Sun and Surf?"

"Yeah, it's a private beach club, all closed up for the winter. They'll be calling it Surf and Turf if any more dead meat washes up in front," Mike said. "Wait till she's been examined and treated. Then you'll have her by herself with all the support you need."

Cyril had wrapped his own blanket around Emilia's shoulders. A strong gust of wind blew the woolen cover off and revealed a large, raw patch of skin on her forearm.

"What happened to her, Cyril?" I shouldn't have asked him the question but I worried about particles of sand becoming embedded in the open wound.

"Was so crowded below docks—decks? What you call it in the boat? Decks. She was burned against one of the engines in boiler room." He raised Emilia's arm so that I could see the injury.

"Please tell her she'll be examined by a doctor in a few hours." I could only imagine the inhumane conditions during the ocean passage.

I wanted the travelers to be made safe and I wanted the criminals behind this operation to be identified as quickly as possible.

Plainclothes officers were setting up folding tables at the foot of the dunes as a food station. Others were carting coffee urns and passing snacks out to the bewildered victims.

"Yo, Chapman," one of the new arrivals called out, his gold shield case hanging out of his jacket pocket. "You want a shot of vodka with your coffee? A little hair of the dog?"

"The dog didn't bite last night, Rowdy. Didn't even lick me. Why, I look hung over to you?"

"Nah. I thought maybe you stopped for a few pops with the congressman."

"You heard about Leighton already?" Mike asked. "I never drink with guys I can't stand. Irritates my throat and my mood. Didn't know word was out."

"The parking lot's buzzing," he said, jerking his thumb over his shoulder. "The reporter from the *Post* wants to clone himself so he can get exclusives on that story without missing any of this one. You look like you've seen a ghost, Alex."

"Sorry, Rowdy," I said, feeling the blush running up the side of my neck and coloring my cheeks. We had a professional history together, history I didn't relish reliving. "I didn't know you were back."

"Never left. Just hit a bump in the road that had me sidelined for a while. The department kept me rubber-gunned for eighteen months but restored me full blast in the fall," Rowdy Kitts said, the right side of his mouth drawing back into a grin. "And that paragon of congressional virtue—Ethan Leighton—was one of the people who made my life stink."

"Am I interrupting a personal reunion here? What's your problem, Coop?"

"No problem at all."

"I think she's still peeved at me 'cause the jury tossed one of her unit's cases when I got jammed up. The judge threw out my testimony. Didn't find me credible. Can you imagine that?"

"Coop doesn't hold grudges, Rowdy. She takes body parts," Mike said.

The last time Rowdy and I had worked together it hadn't ended well. He was a smart cop who had chosen the wrong professional allies and paid a price for it. I could never tell if the chip on his shoulder was permanent or a result of his political troubles on the job.

Roland Kitts had been an active rookie in a rough neighborhood in Washington Heights, with a great record for getting guns off the street that earned him the nickname Rowdy and led to his promotion to detective after only four years on the job. While working on a special antiterrorist project after 9/11, he caught the attention of Bernie Kerik, who was commissioner at the time.

Kitts was glib and self-promoting—like Kerik—and it was no surprise to most cops who knew him that the brash, freewheeling commissioner chose him to serve on his personal detail. A few years later, when Kerik was charged with accepting tens of thousands of dollars in illegal gifts while serving in office, the feds cast a wide net, which landed the young hotshot back in uniform during the lengthy investigation. He'd only recently been able to work his way up again.

"You remember that case, Alex?" Kitts asked.

"Let's not go there now," I said. "We've got enough real grief right here."

"We start moving these folks off the beach before we bring everyone in safe or there'll be a riot," Mike said. "Where you working these days, Rowdy?"

Kitts was a bit taller than I, with straight blond hair slightly darker than mine, slicked back without a part, and sharp features that matched his lean physique. "I'm on the mayor's security detail. Same stuff I was doing for Kerik."

"Talk about landing on your feet, man. Sweet deal," Mike said.

I leaned over to talk to Cyril, biting my tongue so as not to swipe at Kitts's uncanny ability to work his way back into such a plum assignment. I asked the young man if he would tell some of the other passengers we were going to move them to the buses.

"No, no, lady. Nobody gonna leave till ship is empty."

"Who's looking out for you?" Mike asked Kitts.

"I got a good lawyer. Once they cleared me, he fought to get me reinstated to the same kind of position I had when I was dumped," Kitts said. "Scully's not my biggest fan, but I used to get along fine with the mayor, back in the days before he got elected. Still got my street cred, Chapman."

"You here with him?" Mike asked. I looked around to see if Vin Statler—the popular businessman who had succeeded Bloomberg to the mayoralty—had arrived.

"Nope. I'm on my own dime. For years I've had a piece of a small marina just over the border in Nassau County. Sent a couple of my guys around with their boats to assist." Kitts shaded his eyes and tried to make out his craft among the growing flotilla surrounding the old freighter. "They're out there somewhere."

"Good thinking, Rowdy," Mike said.

"Is that Mercer up ahead? Let me see if they need help at the morgue. Later, Mike. Nice to see you again, Ms. Cooper," Kitts said. The sarcasm was thick in his voice. "You really oughtta lose that attitude."

Kitts took off and I could read the words on the back of his jacket, printed under the logo of a small dead bird: PIPING PLOVERS

TASTE LIKE CHICKEN—the recreational boaters' rebuke to the local beach environmentalists.

I was trying to coax Emilia to get to her feet, but whatever direction I gave her was being overridden by Cyril.

"C'mon, pal," Mike said to him. "High and dry. Do it the nice way, okay?"

Cyril shrugged and pretended he didn't understand Mike.

"What's your beef with Rowdy? You see any prosecutors out here volunteering to help? Not like cops and firemen. Suck it up, blondie. The guy hit on you once, is that why you're all pink up to your eyeballs?"

"It's a professional blush, not a personal one," I said, trying to think of a better approach to Emilia. "Remember Jeannie Parcher?"

"The name sounds familiar."

"You know who I mean. That very attractive paralegal who worked for Ryan Blackmer."

"Oh, yeah. She was a sweetheart. Left the office last summer." Mike called to a pair of detectives to move Cyril and Emilia along, then started walking with me across the wide stretch of beach.

"Exactly. A few months earlier than that, when the feds were trying to make their case against Rowdy, Jeannie phoned late one night and asked to see me at my apartment. She'd been working with the assistant DA who had an indictment in the push-in rape that got tossed because Rowdy's testimony was so compromised. He'd made the collar, recovered the knife, and taken a statement from the perp. The guy had a rap sheet a mile long, and his admissions to Rowdy put him close enough to the crime scene to be useful."

"Bet that dismissal ticked you off."

"Of course it did. We had no DNA and a victim who was unable to make an ID 'cause she was yoked from behind, so there was no way to go forward," I said.

"Hey, that perp'll be back."

"Most likely at the expense of another woman."

"What brought Jeannie to your doorstep?" Mike asked. "She confuse your living room with a confessional?"

"I guess so. She had a fling with Rowdy, and the feds found out about it while they were digging into his life. They called her in to question her and she went down to their offices without telling me or anybody else on the staff first. No supervisor, no lawyer."

"Both of them were single," Mike said. "What did she have to give the feds?"

"Hard to reconstruct after the fact. Jeannie was so vague and emotional. I'm sure she gave them more than anyone would want to know about her sexual encounters with Rowdy, and probably way too much about the other internal affairs—and, yes, I do mean affairs—of the DA's office to suit the boss."

"So why the meltdown?"

"Jeannie didn't know who would be more unhappy—Battaglia or Kitts. I couldn't offer any advice about Rowdy, but I calmed her down about the front office. No need to shove it under Battaglia's nose unless the feds made something stick against Kitts."

"You didn't rat her out to the DA? That's my girl, Coop. She must have been grateful."

I stopped to tighten my scarf around my neck and brushed a branch of seaweed out of Mike's hair. "If she was, she forgot to tell me," I said, smiling. "Jeannie quit the next week."

"Over that?"

"I don't know the reason. She seemed spooked about Rowdy. Worried that he'd do something to get back at her."

"Why?" Mike asked. "Did he get rough?"

"Jeannie never said anything like that. I think she was concerned that if he was dirty—if the feds made any charges stick—she'd be toast in our office anyway." I wiped the grit off my mouth with the back of my glove. "Ten days later, I called to buy her lunch to check on her, but she was gone. Gave notice and told her friends she got a great job offer in the fashion biz."

"Sounds like a good career move. Can't expect everyone to be a lifer like you."

"Lifer? I'm thirty-seven years old. I've got endless possibilities for my next—"

"Face it," Mike said, gesturing at the forlorn castaways. "You're beginning to think the world's flotsam and jetsam have been heaven-sent to the Criminal Court Building so you have a purpose on this earth. You gotta move on, Coop. Trying to restore all these broken souls is going to tear the guts out of you before too long."

"Hey, Chapman." Mercer's voice boomed across the open space from the flapped tent door of the morgue. "The medical examiner wants you over here."

"They're human beings, Mike," I called after him as he walked away through the narrow path that led to the parking lot. "It's a sad fact that you have more interest in dead ones than the living."

"I got no problem with the dead." He faced me so that I could hear him speak but continued walking backward toward Mercer. "They can't talk back, they don't bullshit me all day like half your witnesses do, they rarely disappoint me, and they never, ever, ever tell lies."

"Are you looking for victims or a date, Mr. Chapman? You want something with a pulse or no pulse?"

"Chill out, Coop," Mike said, laughing at me as he started to turn. "When I need your help finding a live one, I'll let you know."

Cyril began to speak to Emilia. He was excited about something, quite suddenly, and pulled her to her feet. He seemed to have recognized someone in a small boat that was bobbing close to shore, amid the whitecaps.

There was no point trying to stop the couple as he grabbed her hand and ran to the water's edge, part of the crowd that was growing more difficult for the cops to control.

I watched Stu Carella plunge back into the surf, followed by a scuba team. This time they seemed to be after items they could see floating on the surface, being drawn away from land. I knew there would not be a great concern for personal effects of the travelers at this point, but investigators wanted evidence that linked this human cargo to conspirators in New York, perhaps things jettisoned by a nervous crew.

A uniformed sergeant began barking orders at the victims, and I skirted the restless groups of men to join the officers in the make-shift morgue past the path that bordered the bird sanctuary.

I saw Donovan Baynes exit the tent and headed over to talk to him.

"Can we strike a deal, Donny?" I asked.

"I don't know what you're thinking, Alex. It's not the time." He was dialing a number on his cell phone as he tried to blow me off.

"The women. That's all I want you to give me. No detention centers, no custodial settings after all they've been through. Let me work with Safe Horizon," I said, talking about the city's leading victim advocacy organization. "They've got shelters we can put these young girls in to protect them. If we make them feel safe, they'll cooperate with us. If we don't, we'll never gain their trust. I realize to you feds they're not legal, but I just can't see treating them like prisoners."

Baynes spoke into the phone, asking to be patched through to Commissioner Scully. He answered me while he waited.

"We've got a new set of circumstances, Alex. You don't even know what you're dealing with. Want to give me a minute?"

I ducked my head and stepped into the morgue. There were ten gurneys lined up in a row, with just inches between them. Seven had bodies on them, and six of those were covered with sheets.

Willis Pomeroy, the deputy chief medical examiner, was standing at the head of the fifth body, explaining something to Mercer, Rowdy, and Mike, who were closer to me, at the feet of the deceased.

The sheet was only partially draping the young woman, whose lifeless eyes were fixed on a point above her head. Her auburn hair was snarled and tangled, and the skin of her malnourished body was almost gray in hue. Everything about her looked so youthful, even the nails that had been bitten to the quick. All except the rough surfaces of her hands.

"In water this cold," Pomeroy said, "that wrinkled appearance—that washerwoman look on her fingers—sets in pretty quickly."

"Does it matter whether she was dead or alive when she went in the water?" Mike asked.

Pomeroy shook his head. "No difference. Her palms, the soles of her feet. They get that way no matter whether she went overboard breathing or not."

Was this the changed circumstance Donovan Baynes had mentioned? "What am I missing, Doc? Didn't these people all drown?"

"It looked like that at first, Alex. Only the full autopsy will tell," Pomeroy said, pulling the sheet back a few inches to show me a wound on the left side of her chest. "But this girl was probably dead when she hit the waves. See that bruise?"

Mercer stepped aside and let me edge in near the gurney.

"I see lots of marks."

"All the bodies got tossed around on the ocean floor, Coop," Mike said. "Scrapes from rocks and shells. Bloodless, postmortem wounds."

Pomeroy's gloved hand pointed to the middle of the girl's rib cage.

"That's bloodless too," I said.

"Yes, but that's because immersion in the water probably leached out the blood. The ocean does that to antemortem wounds. I'm pretty sure that's a hole in her chest. It wouldn't surprise me if this girl was stabbed to death—maybe even shot—before someone threw her in the drink."

"C'mon outside, Alex," Rowdy Kitts said to me. "You look like you need some air."

I focused on the young woman's face but I was reeling as I tried to think of the implications of this medical finding.

"I'm okay, thanks, Rowdy. I'm just stunned," I said, turning around to Mercer. "I've been trying to persuade Donovan to let us keep the women in shelters. That's beginning to look unlikely."

"Always a master of understatement, blondie," Mike said. "This whole operation is illegal, and we have no clue who the players are or who's pulling the puppet strings from Stateside. Dead bodies are still washing up, the captain is nowhere to be found, and this broad was probably murdered before she took her swan dive."

"Rowdy's right, Alex," Mercer said. "Let's get some air."

Mike pushed ahead of me to exit the tent. "It's not air Coop needs. It's a tourniquet for her great big bleeding heart. That and a set of directions back to Manhattan."

"I intend to do something about these displaced girls to make their lives a bit easier over the next few weeks," I said. "Then I'm happy to leave you to your lifeguard duties."

"Look them over good, kid, before you go. I always forget you've got magic powers so you can just eyeball people and figure out who the bad guys are. You separate the snakeheads from the snakes for me, 'cause there are likely to be perps standing here in the sand up to their kneecaps, while you're feeling sorry for them," Mike said, gesturing with both hands. "And the murderer, Coop—got any ideas about that? 'Cause till you finger the perp who stabbed that kid lying on this slab, every one of them's a suspect in *my* book."

THREE

"What have we got here, Alexandra? Dress-down Wednesday?"

"I'm sorry, Lem," I said, glancing down at my inappropriate attire. "I apologize for keeping you waiting. I asked Laura to call you to postpone our meeting."

It was two fifteen and I had come straight from the beach in the Rockaways to my office on the eighth floor of the Criminal Courthouse at 100 Centre Street.

"She did indeed, but I had to be down here anyway," he said, helping me off with my jacket and hanging it on the hook behind my closed door. "You had a shipwreck on your hands and I've been tied up with a new client matter."

"And that wreck is exactly why I'm going to be rude and send you on your way, as much as I'd love to chat with you. Laura's got my appointment book. She'll give you a new date."

"Windblown, breathless, and with the slightest bit of sunburn on the tip of your nose," Lem said, smoothing his pale blue silk tie against his chest. "You've already brightened this dreary midwinter's day considerably. I'd say the case of the *People of the State of New York against Karim Griffin* can kick back a few weeks. You haven't seemed inclined to give him much of a break anyway, despite my most eloquent pleadings. Just one thing, my dear Ms. Cooper, before I—"

"Hold that silver tongue, Lem," I said, motioning him to leave, with a smile. "Save it till Karim can hear you purr for his benefit. What is it, five rapes we've got him linked to so far?"

"Tentative, speculative, gossamer-thin shreds of matter that you're trying to spin into some form of evidence. Latents and patents, whorls and swirls, ridges and—help me here, will you?"

"Talk to Laura. You'll have plenty of time to work on that lost image before your opening statement."

Lemuel Howell the Third was one of the finest litigators in the country—and one of my first supervisors in the district attorney's office before he went into private practice—known to the bar as Mr. Triplicate for his habit of using three phrases, often when one would do, to emphasize every point he made. His sleek elegance and smooth moves likened him, in Mike's eyes, to a panther. He had the fine-featured looks and wavy pomaded hair of a 1940s film star, and the eloquence of a Southern black preacher.

"I need your attention, Alex," Lem said, taking hold of my wrist as I pointed at the door.

Lem had always been tactile, using his hands to establish a rapport and intimacy when he spoke to friends and colleagues. With criminals he represented, his touch implied a sense of safety or measure of trust that he expected would transfer to the jurors who watched the pair interact throughout a trial.

"I haven't got time for this. Put together some numbers for Karim if he's talking plea and I promise to think about it. Just don't lowball me."

Lem squared off in front of me. "You and I have a bigger headache on our hands than Karim Griffin."

"Give me two Tylenol and tell me what that might be."

Howell dusted some sand off my eyebrow, touching my face to remind me of the closeness of our friendship. "I'm in the Leighton case, Alexandra. I'm sure you've heard about it by now."

"So, that's the new client matter that got you down here to your old 'hood today? Well, nobody ever accused the congressman of being stupid. You're the perfect choice for him, Lem. One of the best lawyers in town, and—"

"And half his constituency is African American. I may even be able to work it so he keeps his seat." Lem looked at his watch. "He'll be arraigned as soon as I get downstairs."

"I've got nothing to do with Ethan Leighton's case. It's a vehicular."

"And you're specializing in shipwrecks now, my dear, is that right? Well, you and I are going to be working closely for a few weeks, Alexandra. On damage control."

He was whispering now, staring me straight in the eye.

"What kind of damage?"

"There'll be some rumors in the press. They may even go viral before your head hits the pillow tonight."

"More about Ethan?" I asked, pulling my hand away and turning to leave. "Let me guess, Lem. Don't tell me he beats his wife?"

Claire Leighton seemed to be the perfect political partner for Ethan. She'd given up a promising job as an investment banker to support his career and raise their children. There was no other angle for which Howell could need my help in this case.

"It's not Claire, Alexandra. Claire won't do anything to make matters worse."

"Then if there's no domestic violence angle to Leighton's bad behavior, you know I won't be involved."

"Trust me. This will wind up in your unit."

"Think of the magnitude of my trafficking case, Lem. I won't come up for air for months."

"Wasn't I the man who taught you kids how to juggle when you got your feet wet in criminal court? Don't know a time since the Lord created felons and miscreants that the bad guys slowed down for a minute, even though you're sitting on center stage with the biggest, fattest, most hopeless case of your young career. This isn't the movies. Take off your blinders, girl. The crimes just keep on happening."

That was one of the many lessons I'd learned from Lem Howell years ago. My desk was already piled sky-high with detectives' reports when my first high-profile rape investigation was handed to me. And that hot summer season had seen a spike in sexual assaults that threatened to choke me and my colleagues as arrests skyrocketed because of the latest forensic breakthroughs. Keep all the balls in the air but focus on the case at hand.

"So if it's not about Claire Leighton, what is it?"

"Ethan's girlfriend, a woman named Salma. She's unstable, volatile . . . ," Howell said, searching for the third phrase to complete his trilogy.

"I get it, Lem. The girlfriend—Salma, is it? She's a loose cannon. Or you're going to paint her as one. Salma's going to try to make herself the victim in this scheme."

"It's worse than that, Alexandra. She claims that Ethan Leighton tried to kill her."

FOUR

"Too much foie gras?" Nan Toth asked. "Those jeans look like they're glued on."

I rubbed my hand over my stomach. "New Year's Eve at L'Ami Louis. You know it, in the third arrondissement? It's been there forever on this dark little side street, and Luc adores it. I was afraid to get out of the car 'cause it looked like an absolute dive, but it's the most sinfully delicious place in the world. I gained three pounds on this trip."

Marisa Bourgis, Catherine Dashfer, and Kelli Ollsen came into my office right behind Nan. The five of us had been great friends since they started as young prosecutors several years after I did.

"You weren't in court dressed like that today, were you? Didn't you have something on in front of Judge Straub?" Marisa asked. "The poor guy has a problem with his blood pressure as it is."

"Never got there. Besides, if Straub is looking at my derrière, as you ladies obviously are, then blood pressure isn't his biggest problem. Have you been watching the news?"

My secretary, Laura Wilkie, had rounded up my senior staff when I called to tell her I was on my way back to the office. They arrived just minutes after Lem Howell delivered his message to me.

"All day. NY-One has a constant feed and the networks cut in on the half hour with live crews on the scene," Nan said.

"You probably know more than I do at this point."

Marisa looked at her notes. "Nine dead."

"Only seven when I left."

"That channel beneath the Atlantic Beach Bridge was dredged to make it deeper for boats. They say the rip is fierce."

"Were these latest bodies men or women?"

"One of each," Marisa said.

"Any mention of cause of death?"

"Everyone drowned, didn't they? That's what the news jocks are going with."

"Good. That means the only thing leaking so far is the *Golden Voyage*," I said. "Sit down and let's make a plan."

Catherine handed out legal pads from the stack on top of one of the file cabinets. "You're suggesting they didn't drown?"

"Pomeroy thinks one of the girls was dead before she hit the water."

"How?"

"Shot, maybe. Stabbed. We should have answers tonight," I said.

"Well, the reporters seem clueless so far," Nan said. "You can catch a glimpse of Mercer and Mike every now and then, so that's good for us."

"Did you see Rowdy Kitts?" Kelli asked. "That brunette from CNN thinks he's hot. She's following him all over the beach with a mike in his face."

"Face it," Marisa said. "Rowdy's a fox."

"And you're happily married with two kids," I said. "He's back on the mayor's detail, which goes to show you what my judgment counts for. Meanwhile, Donovan Baynes is giving us the female victims in the trafficking case to handle."

"I only know Baynes by reputation," Nan said. "Do you like him?"

"Very much. He's smart and easy to work with."

Since the feds had so little experience investigating sex offenses, and because Battaglia's Sex Crimes Prosecution Unit—which I'd been supervising for almost ten years—had pioneered most innovative practices in that field for more than three decades, Baynes had welcomed me to serve with his crew. He didn't tolerate any of the tension that characterized so many of the NYPD-FBI turf battles.

"Then we just clear the decks," Catherine said.

"Nobody's on trial, right?"

"I've got two weeks before I get sent out. What do we need?"

"I lost the battle to get them housed decently at a shelter. In a sense, for the moment they're all suspects in this homicide and whatever other crimes may have resulted from this last-minute mutiny."

"That's crazy," Nan said.

"What do you expect?" Marisa shrugged her shoulders as she scribbled on her pad. "Feds."

"They'll be separated from each other, detained in a nearby facility, examined by a medical team starting tonight," I said. "We round up some Ukrainian interpreters and a bunch of paralegals and we get to work. What they were promised, how much they paid for this deadly cruise, who their contacts were, what they expected to happen here."

"When do you think we get them?" Kelli asked.

"Not as fast as I'd like. Every one of them will have to be physically examined. Between the shipboard conditions for the last month, the malnourishment, and this morning's unexpected exposure, there'll be health problems to deal with first. Then Baynes will have them spread out in detention centers—God knows where."

"He'll be lucky if he finds room in Westchester or Suffolk County. All those facilities are crammed with illegals and detainees. This is going to move slowly," Nan said.

"I've got plenty to keep you busy in the meantime." I flopped my papers on top of the shortest pile on my desk and sat down. "Get everybody over the holiday slump. You want to handle finding the interpreters?"

"Sure. The four of us will set up teams. We ought to get someone undercover in the Ukrainian bars and clubs, don't you think? Check the network for connections, for word about the anticipated arrival of this new group."

These women, all in their late thirties and early forties, were consummate professionals. They had seen the darkest side of human nature, sharpened their litigation skills against lawyers for murderers, rapists, and child molesters, and restored hope and dignity to the most traumatized victims ever to pass through a precinct door. Yet at the end of their long days they went home to their families and functioned as loving wives and mothers—their humor, compassion, and souls somehow intact, their style never compromised.

"Mercer will take the lead on this, won't he?" Marisa asked. "Did you have much chance to talk?"

"He was one of the last men to arrive at the beach, actually."

"Will you have the lead on the trafficking?"

I shook my head. "Donovan's going to be calling the shots. I'll fight to keep some NYPD in the mix, but the feds want to run this," I said. "The reason Mercer was late is that he's got a piece of Ethan Leighton."

"Sounds like everyone but Claire has a piece of Ethan Leighton," Kelli said. "What's the dish on that?"

"This doesn't leave the room, ladies, okay? There's a girlfriend named Salma, and Ethan's fathered a child with her."

"I knew he had political ambitions," Catherine said. "This puts him well on his way to the top."

"Mercer said there was a big battle last night at Salma's apartment."

"Like a Jewish Selma?" Marisa asked. "Upper West Side? Too creepy, but I'm picturing a blue-rinse old lady who could be Ethan's mother."

"Think again. Like Salma Hayek. This one's from Mexico. Twenty-two years old."

"Only has a couple of years on Ethan's twins, then. Ugly."

"He's apparently installed Salma in a brand-new condo on East End Avenue."

"Condo, of course. No co-op, so no board approval necessary. And his own district, so she gets to vote for him too."

"Stop the commentary, Marisa," Nan said. "Let Alex finish."

"The baby was sick," I said, standing to notch up the numbers on my thermostat, as the draft from the cracked window behind me chilled my neck. "Spiked a really high fever and Salma wanted Ethan to go with her to the emergency room. He refused, a screaming match followed, and two neighbors called nine-one-one. Ethan had been drinking. Must have figured Salma's antics were attracting a little attention, so he made it out of there before the cops arrived. Maybe you have seen the clips. Flipped the car and all that."

"Hungover in handcuffs is not Ethan's best look," Catherine said. "What happened to the baby?"

"She's doing fine, according to Mercer. Probably home with Mama by now."

"I swear if I see Claire Leighton standing by her man for the postarraignment perp walk, I will lose all my sympathy for her," Marisa said. "My guy did that to me I'd hang him out to dry. For this little story you swear us to secrecy?"

"She's got more," Nan said. "So far, all you've given us is what everybody else will read in tomorrow's *Post*."

"It's Lem who told me the rest," I said. "He was dashing down to the arraignment, but gave me a heads-up that the congressman will be painting Salma as a whackjob. Volatile and all that. Lem says she's claimed Ethan's tried to kill her in the past."

"Blame the victim—blah, blah, blah. Lem's just going to use you because you've always been so loyal to him, Alex," Kelli said, pulling on strands of her naturally curly hair. "Unlike your experience learning from him, my first bureau chief was a total bitch. Watch out for Lem. I bet he had his hands all over you. Besides, who'd she claim it to?"

"All Lem had time to tell me was to check the nine-one-one records. That Salma's called for help a couple of times before."

"Don't you think somebody would have put those complaints right under your nose? He's a congressman, for heaven's sake."

"According to Lem, the cops got there each time but Salma refused to cooperate. Never named the perp."

"Want me to ask headquarters to hunt down Salma's phone number and run a check on calls from it?" Catherine asked. "I won't mention what I'm looking for."

I nodded and then smiled at Kelli. "And if you think I can't read Lem Howell and his hand signals after all these years, give me a little more credit than that. Want to check and see who McKinney assigns to handle the Leighton case?"

The head of the trial division, Patrick McKinney, didn't play well with me in the sandbox. He was the most unpleasant individual in a famously collegial office, and resented the fact that I bypassed him and reported directly to the district attorney. His on-again, off-again affair with the head of the Firearms Trafficking Unit had not only broken up his marriage but soured his already difficult personality and exacerbated his penchant for privacy.

"You going to tell Pat what you learned from Lem?"

"Kelli, you're giving me zero points for my judgment today, aren't you? I'll tell Battaglia, of course, and see if he wants me looking over the shoulder of whoever gets the Leighton DWI case. Do we have a plan, ladies? Will you figure out everything there is to know about human trafficking before we meet tomorrow? Do a crash course on Ukraine and where these women were likely to end up living and working? Identify who their runners were to be?"

"Done," Marisa said. "I have no life anyway. You're planning an evening at the morgue?"

"Yes. None of the feds would know how to find the place anyway," I said. There were very few homicides that fell under federal jurisdiction. Our senior prosecutors knew the morgue as well as the courtroom. "Gives me the jump on learning what happened to the young woman who was apparently murdered on the boat."

"Well, be sure to ask Mike what his New Year's resolution is when you see him later," Catherine said as she gathered her papers and stood up to leave.

"Sorry?"

"He hasn't told you yet?"

"What?"

"Roger Hayes had a party on the thirty-first," she said, referring to the popular jurist who had run the trial division in the DA's Office before ascending to the bench. "Lots of Supremes, prosecutors, court personnel, detectives who worked his cases when he was here. Unfortunately, none of us made the cut."

"What about it?"

"My sources tell me that Chapman left the party with Fanny Levit."

"You know who she is?" Marisa asked.

"No. Should I?"

"Perfect name for Chapman," Catherine said, checking the polish on her nails. "He'd be the first guy to make a joke about dating a woman named Fanny. Really."

"The mayor just appointed her to the civil court. She was in private practice at one of the big firms," Marisa said. "Judge Levit now. Very fine-looking brunette with a big brain. Heard she had herself wrapped around our Mikey like a python on a mongoose by the time they left Roger's party."

The phone rang. The plastic button that illuminated told me it was Paul Battaglia himself, dialing me directly on what he liked to call his hotline.

"And—?" I placed my hand on the receiver but waited for Catherine to make her point.

"That's all," she said as they filed out. "Just wondered whether he's told you anything about it—his new romance with a judge."

The phone rang for the third time and I picked it up as I tried to figure out why I was distracted by a knot that tightened in my stomach while my pals fed me the rumor about Mike.

"Alexandra?"

"Yes, Paul."

"I've left dozens of messages for you all day."

For each of the four I received, he must have repeatedly hectored his longtime executive assistant, Rose Malone, to try to find me.

"I apologize, Boss." Battaglia hated to be the last to know anything—on the record or off—that related to any case pending in the office. "I can come in now to tell you what's been going on."

"No, actually, you can't."

I recoiled at the sound of his sharp voice barking at me on the phone.

"Meet me in front of the building in two minutes, Alexandra. No powdering your nose, no spiffing up. I'll be waiting for you in twenty-two hundred."

The courthouse had been built as a WPA project in the 1930s, with a private elevator shared by the district attorney and the judges. The 2200 New York State license plate number had been assigned to the DA for half a century, made anew every two years by prisoners we had sent up the river for every crime in the book. Battaglia kept his SUV in the only parking spot at the entrance to our office on Hogan Place.

"Don't you want—?"

"Yes, I want everything. But the mayor is demanding to see you, too, Alexandra. You can brief me on the way to City Hall."

FIVE

"You don't say anything at all, Alexandra. Understand that?"

I was in the backseat of the SUV with Tim Spindlis, the long-time chief assistant district attorney. Tim was more like a jellyfish to Pat McKinney's pit bull, the yes-man that Battaglia seemed to need as his second-in-command. To the troops he was known as lazy and spineless, the latter an easy play on his name. The detective from the DA's Squad who served as Battaglia's bodyguard was driving, and the district attorney had a cigar clamped in the right side of his mouth as he talked to me out of the left.

"He's going to ask me questions, Paul."

The five-minute walk to City Hall was quicker than any car could make it through the narrow one-way streets of Lower Manhattan, but Battaglia preferred the statement of passing through the mayor's tight security detail in his own vehicle with his own bodyguard. During the short ride, I told him everything that had happened since the moment I got to the site of the beached *Golden Voyage*.

"I'll answer them. Give him nothing about Leighton, Alex. Am I right, Tim?"

"Absoutely, Boss."

I turned my head away from Spindlis. His constant toadying to Battaglia was embarrassing.

"Vin Statler has a real hard-on for Leighton's old man. Failed business dealings from ages ago," Battaglia said. "You hate to see a smart young comer like Ethan fail, and fail so publicly, but I'll bet Statler's only too delighted with this news. You know Mayor Statler?"

"Not really. I've seen him at a few press conferences and shaken hands at meetings, but I've never spoken with him apart from that, or met him socially." Statler, a fifty-two-year-old divorcé, had been in office for one year, and although I'd been at many functions with him, I had no personal connection to him.

"Well, he's no Bloomberg. Made a lot of money in business but can't seem to translate his talent to the public sector."

The police detail at the tiny City Hall parking lot, at the very hub of the Civic Center, recognized the district attorney and let his driver pull in close to the gated entrance.

We had come to this building together more times than I could count, usually providing facts and details for Battaglia's legislative proposals or budget arguments he made before City Council members who met within.

Battaglia was out the door and trotting up the front steps before I could unbuckle my seat belt, with Spindlis at his heels. He turned at the top of the staircase, under the portico, and yelled to me. "Hurry up, Alex. It's getting late."

City Hall, one of the finest architectural achievements of the early nineteenth century, looked like a miniature palace—a mix of Federal form and the detail of French Renaissance architecture, with a copper statue of Justice sitting as its crown. I knew, from meetings that Mike and I had attended together, that it was the oldest City Hall in the country that still housed its original government function.

I followed the two men through the front door, where we were ushered in around the side of the metal detector that filled half of the foyer.

"Good afternoon, Mr. Battaglia," a mayoral assistant said, rushing toward us from the direction of Statler's office, in the northwest corner of the first floor. "Thanks for coming over. He'd like to see you alone first, sir, if you don't mind."

"My chief assistant, Tim Spindlis, will be with me. It's fine for Ms. Cooper to wait."

"Would you mind following me upstairs? The council's in session and the mayor is waiting for an important vote. He's in the Governor's Room."

The aide led Battaglia, Spindlis, and me up one of the twin spiral staircases—all marble—to the Corinthian-columned rotunda that served as the staging area for both the City Council Chamber and the old Board of Estimate Chamber. Overhead, in sharp contrast to the public works décor of our own building, the stunning coffered dome soared above us, recalling the Roman Pantheon.

"Before you go in, your cigar, sir."

"Can't you see it's not lit?" Battaglia said, walking past the young man and opening the door to the ceremonial room that fronted the building, between the two chambers. Still chewing on the Cohiba, he called out to me, "Stay put, Alex."

Spindlis followed the district attorney in, looking back once to give me his best shit-eating grin.

I had stuffed the list of phone messages in the pocket of my ski jacket and took them out to triage the order in which I'd return them. I flipped open my cell and before I could dial, one of the uniform guards with his back to the door of the council room signaled to me. "Take it upstairs, miss. The noise carries."

The cantilevered staircase led up to the third floor, directly beneath the cupola. I positioned myself against the banister beneath the beautifully restored ornamental swag so that I could keep an eye on the door to the Governor's Room, and managed to reach an adversary in a child abuse case, a doc from the Bellevue emergency room, and an anxious victim inquiring about her case status. An incoming call finally interrupted me.

"Hey, Mercer," I said, as his number appeared on my cell screen. "Where are you?"

"Still out at the wreck. Two more bodies. Males, apparent drownings."

"Coming in soon?" It was after five o'clock and darkness had enveloped the city.

"I hope so. Real drop in temperature. We've been moving folks off the beach all day. I think we're almost done."

"You must be running on fumes. Are you still planning to be at the ME's office?"

"Yeah. Something weird happened, I thought you ought to know."

"What?" It was usually this way in complex cases. Rarely was there a linear unfolding of events, with cops taking one clear turn after another.

"Salma Zunega. Know who I mean?"

"Yes, Mercer. Lem's handling Ethan Leighton's case. He's already made his first hands-on appeal. This is the girlfriend, right?"

"Exactly. Well, she called nine-one-one an hour ago."

"What for? Something happen to the baby?" That was my worst nightmare in a heated domestic.

"Not the baby. She was treated and released. You know how kids run high temps," Mercer said. His son, Logan, was almost three years old. "I haven't heard the tape yet but Salma was screaming that Leighton was going to kill her. Talking in Spanish, mostly."

"Lem knew Ethan was going to be ROR'd today, after he left my office at two fifteen," I said. A public official with no criminal history would be released on his own recognizance for anything short of murder. "But it's not possible he got out of the courtroom, past the paparazzi, and all the way up to Ninety-first Street to get to Salma by an hour ago."

"His behavior in the middle of the night wasn't exactly what you'd have predicted either."

"I'm not saying that after this performance he couldn't be that stupid, but Lem would have corralled him for a sit-down the minute they left the building. You know how rigid he is about client control."

"Did Howell talk to you about the woman at all?"

"Exactly this way. Says she's high-strung and hysterical. Kelli thought Lem was just setting me up for Ethan's defense. What happened when the cops got there?"

"Nineteenth precinct uniform responded."

"She let them in?"

"Yeah, Alex. But she denied making the call. Said she didn't do it. Two detectives took a ride over just to double-check that she was okay. Looked like she'd been napping, still wiped out from the night's activity."

"But the call came in from her phone number?"

"Definitely. Salma's landline. That's what shows up on the sprint report."

"So, you're suggesting she's nuts too? Lem's already laying that groundwork."

I saw the door below open, and the aide poked his head out, probably looking for me. The guard who had shooed me away earlier pointed, and I held up a finger to ask for another minute.

"I'm only the messenger, Alex. I haven't met her yet," Mercer said. "I just think we're going to have a handful with Salma. Maybe you ought to plan to meet with her pretty soon—nip this in the bud. Reach out to her before the problem officially lands in your lap. Just keeping you up to speed."

"I'm at City Hall with Battaglia. About to meet Statler. Call you later."

I went downstairs and the aide stepped aside so that I could enter the room.

Paul Battaglia had his back to one of the five large arched windows that overlooked City Hall Park. Tim Spindlis had tucked himself into a corner of the room, positioned to catch everything that went on. The DA lifted a hand to gesture to me, formally introducing me to Mayor Statler, who came forward to greet me.

"Want to close that?" he said, his deep voice resonating like a friendly growl as he gestured to someone behind me.

I turned to see that he was talking to Rowdy Kitts, standing behind the door, beneath the portrait of some long-forgotten politician. Not only was Rowdy back on the mayoral detail, but he was clearly welcome and trusted in the inner sanctum.

"Thanks for coming over, Alex. I know you've had a long, difficult day. Roland, here, told me you were out at the scene of the disaster quite early. He's told me even more about you than your boss. You've done some fine work for the city, young lady. I can't think of anything more despicable than men who abuse women and children."

Kitts came around to stand beside the mayor, and I smiled to acknowledge him and his effort to make up with me, before I thanked Statler.

"You've been here before, I know," he said, watching me take in the elegant appointments of the reception area. "It's my favorite place in City Hall."

The Governor's Room, I had learned from many long waits through council testimony, had been named that because it was used almost two hundred years ago whenever New York's governors were visiting the city from Albany. It boasted a brilliant collection of American portraiture, and had played host to everyone from the Marquis de Lafayette to Albert Einstein. It was the backdrop for both Abraham Lincoln and Ulysses Grant when they lay in state in the adjacent rotunda, and the desk that Statler sat at had belonged to George Washington, in the days when New York was the nation's capital.

"Easy to understand why it is."

"I'm going to have to give a press conference tonight, Alex. There's been an enormous amount of pressure on my staff about both of these breaking cases, and for a change, it's national media that's wanting to know details. It's not just a matter of the *Post* making up ridiculous headlines over nothing at all."

"I think I've told you everything Alex knows, Vin," Battaglia said, walking to the center of the room. "You're not going to have her standing next to you for this media circus. It's simply not appropriate."

Battaglia didn't like his assistants talking to the press. He was a genius at manipulating reporters himself—even entire editorial boards—on issues of great significance or on petty personal gripes, but he was right to expect us to try our cases in the courtroom, and not on the steps of the courthouse or City Hall.

Statler stared at me, not responding to the district attorney. "Roland has given me a pretty good idea of what went on with all the detainees this morning. And the poor victims who died. It would be very helpful if you were available to answer questions about trafficking and, well, sort of how these women are duped and used by the perpetrators."

"I'm not going to expose her to that kind of publicity before the investigation is even under way, Vin."

The mayor continued to stare at me. I felt stupid not being able to answer for myself, but those had been Battaglia's orders.

"Roland says you're the only person who has the experience and credibility on this issue to speak for me," Statler said.

"He's exaggerating, of course." I didn't think Battaglia would mind if I politely demurred.

"Use Donny Baynes," Battaglia said. "It's his goddamn task force."

"What do you think happened to that one young woman on the boat, Alex?" the mayor asked, ignoring Battaglia. "The one who might have been killed on board ship."

"Go on, tell him what you told me," Battaglia said, removing the cigar from his mouth and pointing it at me with eyes as sharp as a cattle prod.

"I'll know more by tomorrow. I think it would be premature for you to say anything about that victim's specifics until there's been an autopsy. I'm sure Detective Kitts has explained that the

ME's preliminary observation suggests some causality other than drowning."

"I think they're going to want more specifics than that, Alex. This isn't going to be covered just by local kids on the crime beat. I'm talking Brian Williams and Katie Couric and Larry King. This is a major disaster on our beach, in our city. It's an international story."

"Use Donny Baynes," Battaglia said again.

Tim Spindlis nodded his support across the room. I wondered if he knew how foolish he appeared to be to the rest of us. I wondered why Battaglia had felt it necessary to cart Tim along to this meeting.

The mayor turned toward the district attorney and took his hands out of his pants pockets. "I can't very well use Baynes and you know it, Paul."

"Why not?"

"Because Donovan is one of Ethan Leighton's closest friends. Weren't you aware of that?"

I had forgotten to tell Battaglia about Baynes's relationship with Leighton. It hadn't seemed important as we rode to City Hall. The district attorney looked at me and scowled. Tim Spindlis mimicked his expression.

"I put Baynes next to me on the podium and when these reporters move on to story number two, the congressman who mistook his penis for a brain—excuse me, Alex—they'll jump all over Donny. 'Did you know about the love nest? Ever meet Leighton's girlfriend? Donny, did he tell you about the baby?'" Statler was shaking his head. "Baynes is a good guy. I can't hang him out that way."

"That's why you want Alex? Hang her out for press potshots? It's not happening, Vin," Battaglia said. "Sit down. Alex'll tell you everything you ever wanted to know about human trafficking right now. Then we'll get out of your hair."

"Give me the basics, will you? Tell me the relevant laws while you're at it."

I knew how smart Statler was, and spent the next fifteen minutes trying to educate him about this difficult subject. The questions that would most interest the media—who the snakeheads were, where the Ukrainians would have been sent if they'd landed, and what would become of them now—were things that no one could answer tonight.

Battaglia folded his arms and listened as I told the mayor what information I thought he'd need for the press conference. Watching over us—hanging on the walls of the stately room—were all the major politicians from the time of the Revolution, heroes of the War of 1812, and luminaries from every walk of the city's history.

When I paused to think of what other legislative issues might be raised, the mayor took another direction.

"What do you know about Leighton and his lady friend?" the mayor asked. "There must be some details you can tell me."

"Not her case," Battaglia snapped.

"But I understand one of the detectives who's involved in the investigation also met with Alex on the beach. Someone from the task force."

"Don't let the press go there," Battaglia said. I'd filled him in on what Mercer had told me. "They'll have all they need from the criminal court arraignment. That's been finished by now. Public hearing. More facts than we've got to give you."

"Ethan's a sick kid, don't you think, Paul? Terrific wife and family, throws it all away for some little—who, who is she? What do you know about the girlfriend?"

"We don't know anything yet," the district attorney said. "Do we, Alex?"

I didn't want to lie to the mayor, but I didn't want to lose my job either.

"Don't put Alex on the spot, Mr. Mayor," Rowdy said. "We can have all that from the department. I'll get a call into DCPI for those facts."

The NYPD's deputy commissioner of public information, Guido Lentini, would give the mayor's aides anything they needed.

"The girl's Hispanic, isn't that right, Alex?" Battaglia said, realizing there was no need to stonewall Statler completely. He didn't want to look like he didn't have as much info as DCPI.

"She's from Mexico," I said. "Her name is Salma Zunega."

"And there's really a kid?"

"Yes, a baby girl."

"This Ms. Zunega, is she here legally?"

"I don't know yet," I said.

"Where was Ethan coming from when he had the accident. Spanish Harlem?"

Battaglia laughed. "Don't let your constituents hear you, Vin. Bad ethnic profiling. She lives across the street from you."

"From *me*?"

Like Bloomberg and Koch before him, Statler kept his own apartment, a lavish co-op on Fifth Avenue, rather than live in the mayor's official residence, Gracie Mansion.

"Well, spitting distance from the mansion. That fancy new condo on East End, just below Eighty-ninth Street."

"Moses Leighton always thought his kid was going to be the first Jewish president," Statler said. "Poured his heart, the last fifteen years of his life, and about thirty million dollars into trying to make that happen. For what? For this?"

"Are you looking for facts about Ethan's case," Battaglia asked, "or just ways to shove it down his father's throat? Lots of politicians have had second acts after a sexual indiscretion or two."

The door opened and Statler's assistant stuck his head in. "The speaker would like a word with you, sir."

"Hold her off a minute, okay?" Statler said. He was standing practically nose to nose with Battaglia now. "Anything else I ought to know?"

"Tell me who you want Alex to keep in contact with. You'll get whatever we get."

"Very good, Paul. I'll have my office set up a liaison. In the meantime, Alex," the mayor said as he put his arm around my shoulder to escort us out of the Governor's Room, "let me know what you find out about the nine-one-one call this Zunega woman made earlier this afternoon, will you?"

Battaglia snapped his head to look at me. "What call?"

"What did you tell me, Roland?" the mayor said, turning to Rowdy Kitts, whose pipeline to case information was proving far better than mine. "Something about Ethan Leighton threatening to kill his paramour."

"Today? He threatened her today?" Battaglia said, talking to Statler but looking me in the eye, skewering me as though I'd neglected to tell him another important fact.

"I just got word from the nineteenth squad myself, Mr. Battaglia. Right before you walked in here," Kitts said. "Wasn't any way Alex could have known about it. They're probably trying to reach out for some advice from her right now."

SIX

"Get everything you can on that nine-one-one call before I see you in the morning," Battaglia said. He was in the front seat of his official car, and I was trying not to choke on the cigar smoke that wafted back into my face. "Keep Tim in the loop on this. All of it."

"Will do." I hated it when Battaglia inserted Spindlis as an intermediary. I was never sure what he filtered out of conversation with the boss when I passed facts along through him.

"We're going to the West Side for a community council meeting. Can we drop you off?"

"The office is good. I need to pick up some work to take home with me."

When the driver stopped for the light at the corner of Centre and Worth, a block south of the courthouse, I took the opportunity to say good-night and hop out.

I was going against the flow. Lawyers and secretaries waved at me as they rushed downtown toward the large subway hub at the City Hall station. I envied the few who weren't carrying briefcases or litigation bags full of work, and would be home in time to enjoy dinner with family or friends.

"Alexandra!" A car door slammed and as I turned into Hogan

Place, I saw Lem Howell step out of a black limousine. "Time to call it a day, Ms. Cooper. Let me deliver you home on the way uptown."

I blew him a kiss, shook my head, and continued walking toward my office.

"I promise I won't say a word about Karim Griffin."

"Going home isn't in my immediate future. Remember those all-nighters at the morgue?" I turned to say good-night to Lem, and he waved me on again.

"Get your case folder. My chariot awaits."

"The cameramen all gone?"

"Would I be talking to you, young lady, if I had the slimmest of chances, the shortest of moments, the briefest of sound bites to make my case to a tristate viewing audience of millions? Check out the eleven o'clock news. I gave them my best stuff. Be quick."

It was a combination of the cold evening, my long friendship with Lem, and the thought that he might reveal something to me about Leighton—whose personal problems seemed more intriguing to the higher-ups than the mass disaster in Queens—that moved me to accept his ride up to Thirtieth Street and the Office of the Chief Medical Examiner.

I pushed through the revolving door, went up to my office to grab the last batch of messages Laura had stacked on my desk, and took a new Redweld with colored folders—blue for the autopsy notes, red for witness interviews, green for the first day's pile of DD5s—the Detective Division reports of the shipwreck that would grow to overwhelm us within a week's time.

When I got back downstairs, Lem was leaning against the limo, talking into his cell, the collar of his trim black overcoat turned up against the wind. I walked toward him and he opened the door so that I could slide across the backseat.

He got in beside me and before he slammed the door and the driver stepped on the gas, despite the dark tinted windows and the dim lighting in the overhead panel, I could see there was someone sitting across from me.

"I think you two have met before," Lem said.

Ethan Leighton leaned forward out of the shadowy corner. "Hello, Alex."

"You taught me well, Lem. But never dirty tricks," I snapped, trying to keep my temper under control. "Be honorable, you used to say. All you've got to trade on is your reputation."

"I asked him to do this," Ethan said. "It wasn't Lem's idea."

Leighton's face was lined, his eyes were bloodshot, and his voice quavered. It was completely inappropriate for us to be meeting in secret, given the circumstances, yet I couldn't help but feel a pang of sympathy for him. I had met him years before when I was cross-designated on a sexual assault investigation that the feds were conducting at a Veterans Administration hospital. He was handsome in a nontraditional way—a prominent, slightly crooked nose, wavy brown hair that was thinning on top, and green eyes set a bit too close, but when he smiled the whole package presented attractively. He wasn't smiling tonight.

"I don't care whose idea it was. It's lousy."

"Look, I used to be a prosecutor. I understand how you feel." Tonight, in the dim lighting of the limo, Leighton's eyes resembled the beady stare of an animal in the sights of a predator. The long, bony fingers of his hands twisted and then untangled from each other, knuckles cracking as he tried to find the words to calm me.

"My least favorite introduction. 'I used to be . . .'" Every new defense attorney opened with the lame attempt at bonding by claiming former prosecutorial understanding.

"Don't throw a scene and storm out of the car," Lem said.

"I'm actually too tired to do that. Too tired and too disappointed in you."

"Sit back, Ethan. Listen to me, Alex." Lem eased himself forward to try to get me to look at him while he talked. "Ethan was in the holding pens while I was in your office. He wasn't arraigned for another hour after that. Then I did my little dog-and-pony show on the courthouse steps. Already one of the detectives has called to accuse us of threatening Salma. I swear to you, Ethan hasn't left my sight."

There was no point arguing with Lem. Mercer hadn't yet heard a translation of Salma's 911 call. The threat she reported could just have easily been phoned in from 100 Centre Street.

I leaned my head against the padded headrest. "What are you guys setting me up for?"

"It's nothing like that, Alex. Please don't take this the wrong way. I have nothing but respect for you, professionally. Donny Baynes says you're reasonable and measured. He suggested—"

Lem held his hand up to stop Ethan's sudden flow of information. The congressman dug his front teeth into his lower lip, almost deep enough to draw blood, as though it was the only way to stop himself from spilling his guts.

"When did you talk to Donny?" I asked.

Had Baynes been playing dumb when Mercer told him about the car crash this morning? Or if Ethan had reached his best friend from the jailhouse, maybe he had managed to place a call to Salma too.

"Let's slow this train down," Lem said. "You will always be my go-to person in that office, Alexandra. I'm the one who called Donovan Baynes. Then Ethan reminded me you'd once worked together. I'd like to lay a foundation here before certain aspects of this case snowball out of control."

"I swear to you I never called Donny," Leighton said, lurching forward at me, almost as though unable to control his movements. Instinctively, I pressed back against the cushioned leather seat.

Lem Howell reached out an arm to push Leighton back. "What'd I tell you, son?"

"What's your suggestion? I tell Battaglia the three of us cruised around town to celebrate Ethan's release? I'm missing the point where I describe to him how honorable this meeting has been. Sort of the minute after he tells me I've lost my judgment."

"Let's say you don't tell Paul Battaglia anything, Alex. This is just you and me together for a short ride. Ethan's not talking to you. It's only me, my idea. I just want you to see there's a human being behind these tabloid headlines that his enemies will try to use to bring him down. Flesh and blood. There but for the grace of God go you and I."

The space between the streetlights played games through the tinted windows of the car. There were seconds when I couldn't see Leighton at all, and then he darted forward and his close-set eyes bored into me with a frightening intensity.

Lem saw me clutching the door handle. "Well, then, Alex. Maybe not *you*. Maybe you're above that. Surely we all make mistakes, we all—"

"I've made my share of mistakes, too, Lem. I try not to drag down people I love when I do."

"I never meant to hurt anyone, Alex." Leighton held his arm out as though to stop my response. "You've got to believe I never meant to do anything to bring my wife into this."

"Ethan—"

"Don't muzzle me, Lem." Ethan was on the edge of the seat now, demanding to speak for himself. "None of this was supposed to happen, Alex. I'm a public servant—just like you. I've given every ounce of my wisdom, my soul, my energy, my good works—all for the people of this city and for building a better government."

I opened my mouth to speak but he was directly in my face, punctuating his remarks with his bony fingers. He may have thought he was pitching to help his case, but he was scaring me instead. Leighton was leaning too close to me, jabbing at my shoulder, boring into me with those icy eyes.

"I can't be drummed out of office by rumors and innuendo, by things that don't matter in the grander scheme. You've got to make Paul Battaglia keep his perspective on all this."

The driver braked to a stop and Leighton lost his balance, tipping forward so that his hand landed on my thigh. He gripped it for just a moment to regain his seating. I brushed him away.

"Get off me," I said. The thought of his touch was revolting. "Save the laying on of hands for Mr. Howell. He does it so much more deftly."

There was a gas station at Houston Street that all the cab fleets used to fill up. As we approached it and the driver paused for the light, I reached over Ethan's shoulder and knocked on the glass panel dividing the rear compartment from the driver.

He pulled it back and I asked him to stop on the left, so that I could get out.

"You call me when your cops get snarled up in all the lies they're going to hear, Alexandra," Lem said, following me out of the limo to put me in a yellow cab. "I wanted you to look Ethan Leighton in the eye for yourself. He's got a bright future ahead of him, if he isn't sidetracked for some inappropriate horseplay. Let him speak the truth, is all I wanted."

"Creative thinking, Lem. But he'll have to tell it to the judge."

SEVEN

"Battaglia'll be over it by morning," Mike said. He was sitting in Dr. Pomeroy's chair, his feet on the desk, throwing back a mouthful of M&M's while he riffled through autopsy photos of a young man who'd been shot in the head and chest. "No need to go downstairs and lay down on a slab in the fridge, blondie."

"He totally jammed me up. Even had that sycophant Spindlis along for the ride, just to humiliate me even more. Battaglia didn't want me giving anything to the mayor without his permission, but then Mercer called before I could get him alone to tell him about the conversation."

"Don't get yourself in a swivet. We got work to do."

"I'm telling you, something's got the boss in a horrible mood. Something bigger than today's news. He tried to control me like a puppet. Didn't do anything when we walked out of City Hall but berate me for holding out on him. The world is upside down when Paul Battaglia is nipping at my tail and Rowdy Kitts is trying to save face for me."

"Tell me you took the subway. Good for you to mingle with the people every now and then."

"That's not my favorite station," I said. I hardly needed to remind Mike about our trip together around the loop that snakes under City Hall, an incident neither of us would ever forget. "Beside that, I was totally sandbagged. Lem was waiting for me in front of the office."

"You ride up here in his pimp-buggy?"

"The first ten blocks. It's worse than that. Ethan Leighton was in the car."

"Talk about burying the lead. What was that about?"

I told Mike exactly what happened. "It was creepier than I can possibly describe. So if Battaglia's already set off at me, imagine when I tell him I actually got in the car."

"You take that little factoid to the grave with you. I know. We'll tell Mercer. Sit on that piece of information for now, okay?"

"Maybe Kelli's right. Maybe Lem's trying to use me for something I'd rather not be in the middle of. Where's Dr. Pomeroy?"

"Scrubbing down. Give him ten."

"And Mercer?"

"I thought he'd beat you here. He must be close. You mind turning on the telly?"

Pomeroy kept a small set on a high shelf in a corner of the room that he used to monitor stories of fatalities that would involve his staff.

I reached up and pressed the power button. The TV was set to the local all-news station. The reporter was describing the still-unfolding scene on the beach in Queens, the hood of a parka pulled over his head, muffling his voice.

Mike searched the desktop, then opened drawers till he found the remote clicker. "Almost time. Get your twenty bucks ready."

For as long as I had known him, Mike had a habit of tuning in to the last five minutes of *Jeopardy!* to bet on the final question. Although the son of a decorated police officer with a legendary reputation in the department, Mike had set out on a different track, majoring in history at Fordham College. When his father dropped dead of a heart attack just two days after retiring from the job, Mike decided to honor that legacy by following in his footsteps.

"Any autopsy results yet?"

"Waiting on Pomeroy. He wanted to get two done today—one of the supposed drowning victims, and the girl with the mysterious injuries. Compare and contrast the findings." Mike switched channels and muted the commercial. "What did the mayor have to say?"

"Nothing to me. Keenly interested in Ethan's situation."

Mike saw Alex Trebek on the screen above my head and clicked on the sound. "That's right," Trebek said, "the category of tonight's question is THE COLOR PURPLE. THE COLOR PURPLE, folks."

"I spoke too fast. Literary stuff."

"Double or nothing." I had majored in English literature at Wellesley before deciding that my interest was a career in public service, and went on to study at the University of Virginia School of Law.

"That's taking candy from a baby, Coop," Mike said, offering me the small brown bag of chocolates. "Wipe the grin off your face. All I've got is my M and M's and twenty-four bucks. It's almost payday."

"Spent too much on the holidays?" I bit my tongue to prevent myself from making a crack about New Year's Eve.

"Back to purple. Spielberg movie," Mike said. "Eleven Oscar nominations."

"Walker novel. Pulitzer Prize." I could take him on a handful of topics like literature, but Mike knew more about military history than anyone I'd ever met. Mercer's father had serviced planes for Delta and he'd grown up with maps of the world's airline routes papering his bedroom walls, so he took the kitty whenever the subject was related to geography.

One of the attendants came to the doorway. "Dr. Pomeroy would like to see you downstairs."

Mike put one foot on the floor. "Be right there."

At the morgue or in fashionable mansions, at crack dens or social clubs, very little interfered with Mike's evening ritual of watching the final question, even if it delayed for a few minutes the crews bagging bodies and recovering evidence.

"Here's your answer, gentlemen," Trebek said, as the board pulled back to reveal the phrase. "The answer is 'City from which this purple hue, worn for centuries by royalty, derives its name.'"

Trebek repeated the answer while his three bespectacled contestants studied the words before starting to write on their video tablets.

"I can see it in your face, Coop. Not on your reading list, as you'd expected, right?"

I was walking to the door. "Let's go."

"Wait a minute. You doubled me down, didn't you? Check it out."

Trebek approached the first young man, who hadn't been able to come up with a good guess. "What is—?"

"Sorry. Oooh, and you wagered seven thousand five hundred on that one. Very sorry."

"And you, sir? You've written 'What is Maroon?'"

"Like where in the world would that city be?" Mike said, balling a piece of paper and throwing it at the screen. "Maroon, Italy? The guy's a jerk. Won the last three nights on sheer luck."

He had drowned out Trebek, who moved on to the third player. "You're shaking your head already, Scott. And your question is, 'What is Indigo?' Wrong again."

Mike had both feet on the floor. "What is Tyre? I'm telling you, get me on that show and I'll make enough money to quit this job tomorrow."

"What is Tyre? That's what we were looking for," Trebek said. "The color Tyrian purple. That's the name we wanted. Also called imperial purple, first produced by the ancient Phoenicians in the city of Tyre, and royal figures everywhere used it almost exclusively to flaunt their stature."

"And you know that because . . . ?" I asked, as we headed down the quiet corridor to go to the basement where the grim work of the medical examiners was performed.

"Alexander the Great crushed the Tyrians. Three thirty-two B.C. Tyre was one of the great early seaports of the world. The people dissed Alex—wouldn't let him enter the city when his troops arrived—so he practically wiped them out. All the great ancient emperors wore Tyrian purple robes, Coop. Very expensive stuff. And you know what it was made from? Mucus. A mucus secretion from the gland of a predatory sea snail in the Mediterranean."

Mike opened the door to the basement and I could smell a strong antiseptic odor, as though someone had just cleaned up the autopsy rooms and overwhelmed the familiar chemical smells with even harsher fluids.

"Don't turn up your nose at me. Too much reading about female empowerment with those weepy women's novels and not enough cold, hard facts."

"I wasn't sniffing at you, Mike. It was the idea of the colorful dye coming from mucus."

He took a package of mints out of his pocket and offered them to me. Every detective had different ways of dealing with the strong scent of death, and Mike had something ready for almost every occasion.

Gurneys lined the wall of the long, narrow staging area, which led from the bay in which the bodies were received from morgue vans and hearses into the autopsy theaters.

The first room, where Pomeroy usually worked, was empty. Someone had just mopped the tiled floor and wiped down the stainless steel table, ready to receive the next unfortunate voyager.

"Good evening, Alex. Hey, Mike," the doctor said as he came out of the locker room, wiping his hands on a towel before extending one of them to us.

"How'd you do today?" Mike asked.

"We've actually finished three autopsies. Not too much competition on the homicide front."

"What's the news?"

"We started with the two young women. Jerry also had time to help me with one of the men, so I could make the necessary comparisons," Pomeroy said, leading us into the second theater, where a sheet appeared to be covering one of the bodies. "Two of them are most certainly accidental drownings."

"Most certainly?" I asked.

"I've told you before, Alex, that drowning deaths can be difficult to call."

"What's the mechanism?"

"Well, submersion in water is usually followed by a struggle to reach the surface. Most often, it's a panicky process."

Panic kills. Exactly what the guys had told me on the beach.

"The energy reserves get exhausted," Pomeroy continued. "People try to hold their breath, till the carbon dioxide accumulation builds up. Then they open their mouths and end up inhaling large amounts of water. Once they swallow the water—it's pretty gruesome, Alex. You really want to understand this?"

"I need to, of course."

"Then the gagging starts. Coughing, sometimes throwing up. The air escapes from the lungs and it's replaced by water."

"So, it's an asphyxial death?" I asked.

"Rarely. Less than twelve percent of the time. Though more so in salt water, like these cases, than in fresh. The salt moves into the bloodstream to establish an osmotic balance, which makes it appear more like an asphyxial death."

I listened to Pomeroy but looked at the still form covered by sheeting.

"Me and science weren't a natural match, Doc," Mike said. "What does that mean for these guys?"

"The victims become unconscious. Often suffer convulsions.

It's anoxia that causes death—low oxygen as a result of the inhalation of large amounts of water."

"So the tests you do to say they drowned, those are all done?"

"There are no reliable tests."

"Water in the lungs?" Mike asked. "Water in the stomach?"

"No real significance to those facts. The water can easily reach those organs after death. In a situation like this with rough ocean movement," Pomeroy said, "water, sand, seaweed, all get forced into the body."

"So what do you need?"

"The key question is whether or not we have facts that establish whether the person was alive when he—or she—entered the water. All the background observers give to you, what the scene was actually like, what the condition of the deceased's clothing is when we recover the body."

"I got a shipwreck in the middle of the night with a boatload of hysterical Ukrainians. So far nobody can tell us anything I understand. What next, Doc?"

"For the moment, Mike, while you put the pieces together, I'm quite confident that the first two bodies autopsied—one male, one female—are accidental drowning," Pomeroy said, stepping to the table and lifting the sheet to fold it down to the waist of the young woman we had seen earlier, at the temporary morgue. "This is Jane Doe Number One."

Her eyes were closed now. The auburn hair had been brushed neatly off her face in the postautopsy washing, revealing an uneven line of scrapes and cuts across her forehead.

Pomeroy pointed his finger to the small bruise on her left chest. "That's it."

"That's what?" Mike asked.

"This girl was stabbed to death."

"The mark is so small it looks like a bullet wound."

"That's what I thought, too, at first. But it's a single thrust, right into the heart. Someone knew what he was doing, or got very lucky."

"A knife did that?" I asked.

"Not likely. Something pointed and very sharp. Something with a fine, thin tip."

Homicidal stab wounds usually involved some cutting as well as thrusting, the knife pulled down or up, twisted during its insertion or removal. The injury was usually longer than the widest part of the blade.

"What then?"

"A sharp pair of scissors, maybe. A pick of some sort."

"Crime Scene take any weapons off the ship?" I asked Mike.

"Control your control freak instincts, Coop. That sloop crossed the ocean. There's a galley with kitchen equipment to prepare food for hundreds of people and a boiler room with enough tools to keep the damn thing afloat. That's not to mention that half the men on board had homemade shivs and all kinds of metal to protect themselves. And don't ask me to start dragging the ocean bottom tonight, okay?"

"We will need to see every sharp object you find," Pomeroy said.

"Yeah, Doc," Mike said. "What kind of public statement will you make about her death?"

"That's up to the chief. To my view, Jane here was stabbed to death and disposed of to simulate drowning. Something we don't see very often."

"Why not?"

"Because, Alex, it would be fairly easy to discover the bullet hole or track the internal hemorrhaging of a stab wound at autopsy. Your killer must have counted on this body not being found for days, if at all."

"The vicious riptide," Mike said. "We're not done waiting for bodies to wash up."

"Far likelier for this girl to have been dragged out in the ocean. If and when she came ashore, the odds are pretty good that she would have been skeletonized. All those marine creatures would have gotten to work on her. You'll see, if there are more deaths in the next few days."

"So almost the perfect crime, Doc, right? One well-placed thrust between the ribs and overboard with the mutineers. Jane just surfed the wrong way."

"Possibly."

"So I'm looking for someone who heard her squealing like a stuck pig just before the other desperate souls decided to jump."

"Those bruises," I said, pointing to the marks on the young woman's forehead, "are those—and her hands—signs of a struggle?"

Pomeroy lifted the girl's left hand to point out the abrasions on the wrinkled skin of her knuckles. "They're not defensive wounds, Alex. Nothing to suggest that she struggled. She was dragged by the tide along the shallow bottom of the ocean, drifting below the water's surface. Those scrapes here, on her forehead, and her knees are all postmortem, all superficial."

"I'm just thinking about Mike's comment about her squealing. Someone certainly took advantage of all the commotion if she was killed after the ship beached itself on the reef. That should help us once we get to talk to these people."

"I'll bet half the boatload was wailing and screaming," Mike said. "You know how long she was dead before she was tossed in?"

"The waterlogging makes it hard to determine lividity," Pomeroy said. "There's a loss of translucency of the upper layers of the skin, can you see? The internal organs display lividity normally, though. I'd say she wasn't dead many hours before she was found."

"We're not talking about Jane being on ice since she left home?"

"No, we're not."

"How about her clothing?" I asked. "There must have been blood all over it."

On a workbench in a far corner of the room, Jane Doe's clothes had been laid out to dry. "I'm afraid they won't be all that much help. Yes, exsanguination was the cause of death, Alex, but most of the bleeding went into the body cavities."

I knew that was common in stabbings that didn't involve the head or neck. Often, the track of the wound closed up after the weapon that pierced the flesh was withdrawn.

"This was on Jane's upper body, more or less," Pomeroy said, pointing at a black fleece jacket with a zippered front and a hood. "Those tears in it may well have been caused by the ocean floor. They're too ragged, too uneven, to have been cut."

Mike pulled a pair of latex gloves from his rear pants pocket and lifted the jacket to examine it. "Still damp. Looks pretty chewed up."

"That hole in the chest area is a spot we cut out for the lab. I assume it's blood, but it's a pretty discreet little stain. Easy to miss in light of all the action."

"Any labels?" I asked. I wanted to know where the clothing had been manufactured and, if very lucky, where in the Ukraine it had been sold.

"*Nada*," Mike said. "Your generic sweat jacket."

"And the pants?"

"Kinda look like pajama bottoms, don't they?" he said, holding up a pair of thin cotton pants with a drawstring waist. They had also been shredded, presumably, while being tossed around in the sea. "Brrrrrrrrrr. Guess she didn't mind the cold very much."

Mike looked in the waistband and along the interior seam of each leg but shook his head to indicate he had found no markings.

"Underwear?" I asked.

"It's a sports bra, right?" Mike said. He hoisted it up with his fingertip. It appeared to be some sort of Lycra stretch material, again with no label.

"No panties," Pomeroy said. "Probably set to bunk down for the night."

"That's odd. I'd have thought they'd all be warmly dressed and ready to be unloaded for their arrival in America," I said.

"Maybe she was offed while she was suiting up," Mike said. "It doesn't take every broad in the world as long to get herself presentable as it does you."

Pomeroy looked at me for a response or change of expression. People who had worked with Mike and me for years tried to guess at whether his personal jabs reflected an intimacy that meant we had crossed professional lines. I sometimes wondered the same, but had put up with them for so long that now they rarely distracted me.

"How about the two drowning victims?" I asked.

"The young man was wearing a sweatshirt and jeans. Very American style," Pomeroy said. "I think my assistant said they were made in China."

"And Jane Doe Number Two?"

"Her things are spread out across the hall, if you'd like to see them. A coarse sweater that looks homemade."

"Intact?" I asked.

"Practically unraveled," Pomeroy said, screwing up his face as he searched for words to describe the items. "Her underwear was in tatters. Sort of dingy-looking stuff. And both girls had tattoos."

"Did you know that?" Mike asked me.

"No. Are they the same?"

Pomeroy covered the victim's head—as though he didn't want her watching while he exposed her lower torso to us—and folded back the sheet from her feet up to her waist. "The other girl has a small flag."

"Blue on top, yellow below?"

"Yes, Mike."

"The Ukrainian flag—they were all over the ship too."

"Where? I mean, on what part of her body?"

"On her shoulder blade, Alex. The right one."

"But this girl—Jane Doe Number One—where is hers?"

Pomeroy moved his gloved hand along Jane Doe #1's thigh. "It's a flower of some sort. Looks to me like a—I don't know. I'm not into gardening."

The small tattoo—bloodred ink within a black outline—sat almost at the crease in the skin where her inner thigh joined her body.

I bent over to study the image.

"Do you recognize the design?" Pomeroy asked.

"No, Doctor. It's the placement of the tattoo that's significant to me."

Mike cocked his head and stepped in closer. "Talk, Coop."

"When victims are trafficked into this country, they're often tattooed by someone who works for the snakehead. Stakes her out as his property. The girls being sold for prostitution—the better ones, the younger ones—are often marked right here, close to the opening of the vaginal vault. It's a symbol of their pimp's control."

"So we know what kind of work she was destined for," Mike said. "Now we've just got to identify the bastard who set her up."

"Jane Doe Number One," I said. "Personal property of . . . the rose."

EIGHT

It was almost nine P.M. when Mercer walked into Dr. Pomeroy's office, where Mike and I were waiting for two of the shipmates who'd been treated and released from the hospital to be brought into the viewing room to try to identify the deceased.

"Got anything for a headache, Alex?" he asked.

"My tote's on the floor in the corner. Open the cosmetics bag."

"Don't take the ones that make Coop hallucinate that she's going to solve this mother anytime soon," Mike said. "You know any bad guys use the nickname 'The Rose'?"

I handed Mercer my bottle of water and he downed the tablets, shaking his head.

"I hate to ask what took you so long," Mike said, "but what took you so long? I thought you were coming through the tunnel when you called."

"Detour to East End Avenue," Mercer said, turning to me. "Salma's goin' all crazy on us. Or on Leighton."

"What now?" I asked.

"Another nine-one-one call. Screaming for help."

I leaned back in Pomeroy's desk chair and rested my head.

"About what? That Leighton was threatening her, while he was sitting in the courthouse with Lem?"

"Worse than that. She said that the congressman was actually in the apartment, trying to take the baby away from her."

"You're sure that's what she said? There goes her credibility."

"Wait a minute. Exactly what time?" Mike asked. "Tell Mercer about tonight."

"I'm too embarrassed. You tell him."

Mike and Mercer tried to construct a time line, based on my estimate of when I left the office. "Entirely possible," Mike said.

"The nine-one-one operator who got the call speaks Spanish. That's what Salma said."

"They responded, right?"

"And so did I."

"Well?"

"No sign of Leighton. The doorman said nobody except Salma's sister showed up for her today. Left with the baby around six o'clock."

"You talk to her yourself?"

"Salma wouldn't let the uniformed guys in at first. She thought *they* were just harassing *her* again. "

"How's her English?" Mike asked.

"Good. Perfectly good. The doorman confirmed that when she gets excited or upset, she's pretty shrill in both languages, but Spanish first."

"So she understood why you were there?"

"You bet she did. Denies making the calls, denies having heard anything from Leighton since he left the apartment early this morning. Says one of his aides called her several times to tell her what happened to him and that she should avoid the reporters. Lem phoned too."

I grimaced. "Thank goodness he hasn't had time to meet with her yet."

"First thing tomorrow morning," Mercer said. "I'll tell you, Salma makes no effort to keep her temper in check. She started chewing out the cops for disturbing her. Told them they better not come back 'cause she'd been up all night and wanted to get some sleep. She doesn't care how many nine-one-one calls they claim to get, she's not the one making them."

"You checked to see if there's anyone else in the apartment? A nanny, another relative with a screw loose who could be calling nine-one-one while Salma doesn't even know?"

"All clear, Mike."

"And the basement? No one tinkering with the phone lines there?"

"I went down myself to double-check the techs who came over. Nothing touched."

"The baby was well enough to send to her sister?" I asked. "When you checked the place out, did anything look amiss?"

"Now, you know how I am about kids, Alex. I got the sister's info and called over to her. She confirmed that Salma told her she needed to get herself some sleep and the baby is fine. Has two of her own, so she seems to know what she's doing."

"And the apartment?"

"Leighton set her up nice. Neat and clean, everything in place. Great river view, by the way. It overlooks Gracie Mansion—maybe Leighton has her keeping an eye on the mayor," Mercer said with a smile. "You can practically see out to the Montauk lighthouse."

"Did she let you poke around?" I asked.

"Salma got into such a spitting match with the cops, I just helped myself into her bedroom and the nursery. No signs of a struggle, nothing out of place anywhere."

"Tell me about her," Mike said. "What makes a guy with such promise throw it all out the window? Salma must be really hot—some kind of fox. What does she look like?"

"Could we stay on point here? Why was she fighting with the cops?"

"I told you, Alex. She was yelling at the rookie in Spanish, telling him—like he told me—that if they came back and bothered her again, she'd get Leighton to have them fired. That kind of thing. Seems pretty clear she's used to throwing his name around."

"Might have had some value until a few hours ago. Ethan Leighton's name will get her squat now," Mike said.

"Officer Guerrero tried to make that clear," Mercer said, chuckling about the encounter. "I didn't get the exact translation, but she blasted him after that. He told her she could call nine-one-one as often as she wanted, but nobody was going to show up again. Told her they'd had enough craziness for one day."

"The fox who cried wolf," Mike said. "Not to worry. I'm assuming the congressman's wife will have him securely tied to the mattress tonight. By his balls. And in their spare bedroom, I'm sure."

"I'd really like to talk to Salma before Lem sits her down," I said. "We'll never get the true story once he starts spinning her."

"And I'm gonna pass out if I don't put some dinner in my stomach soon."

"I'm right behind you," Mercer said.

Pomeroy's assistant reappeared in the doorway. "Dr. P is ready for you, Mike. The men are here."

I followed Mike and Mercer down the corridor to the family reception room. I wasn't usually involved in this painful stage of the process, but I had been to the morgue often enough to observe the anxious loved ones of homicide victims waiting among strangers to confirm the news that no one wanted to get.

"I'll stay outside the viewing room. Let's not overwhelm them," I said.

"Neither one of these guys is missing a relative or close friend,

Coop. They're just shipmates. They volunteered to try to give us names, if they recognize these first three victims."

Mercer and I listened as Mike introduced himself, explained the process to the Ukrainian interpreter the cops had found during the day, and then separated the two men so that neither could hear what the other one told us.

He led the first guy—Pavlo—who appeared to be in his twenties, into the cubicle adjacent to the reception area with the interpreter. When Mike had positioned him in front of the glass partition, he pulled back the short blue curtains that covered the space. In the old days, when I first came on the job, the viewers were in the same room as the deceased. Now there was the small extra comfort of being on the far side of a piece of glass—unable to smell death, not tempted to touch the corpse one last time.

I could see the side of Pavlo's face when he looked at the body of the young man the city had named John Doe #1. His expression didn't change, but he swallowed hard and the lump of his Adam's apple protruded farther before resting back in his neck as he pursed his lips and gulped in a breath of air.

He spoke in a whisper to the interpreter. "The boy is from his hometown," the interpreter said. "Doesn't know his name, but he has a brother on the ship, who made it off safely. Is maybe seventeen, eighteen years old, this one. Brother is Viktor. You will find him, please?"

Pavlo put his head down and stepped back.

"How do you say 'I'm sorry'?" Mike asked the interpreter, who repeated the sentiment to the young man. "Tell him we've got to do it again, understand?"

The young man nodded his head.

"Jane Doe Number One," Mike turned and said to me, since I couldn't see the body that had been placed on the elevated lift for display.

Pavlo looked at the murdered girl on the gurney and seemed to be studying her face.

The interpreter gave us the English version of the phrases he had heard. "Says the girl looks familiar to him, but he doesn't know anything about her. Doesn't remember seeing her, speaking to her, on the crossing. But most of the girls kept to themselves, unless they were married or they had brothers and cousins on board."

"Would you ask him," I said, speaking softly, "if there is even a single thing about her that he remembers?"

The interpreter put his head closer to Pavlo, then turned back to us.

"Is pretty girl, no?"

"That's what he said?"

"No, no. Is what I am saying. Pavlo says nothing. Tells me there were three hundred people on this ship, maybe more. Can't remember meeting this girl. Me, I think you wouldn't forget her. Is very pretty."

"If I wanted to solicit the opinions of the Little Odessa Senior Citizens Lonely Hearts Club, I wouldn't have started with an evening outing at the morgue," Mike said to me under his breath as he closed the curtains.

When they opened again three minutes later, Jane Doe #2, one of the drowning victims, was displayed to Pavlo. I couldn't see her, but knew that she had been cleaned up—her skin washed, all the grit from the beach gone, and her gnarled hair untangled by Pomeroy's assistants after he had finished his meticulous dissection of her body.

The young man picked his head up and again, there was very little reaction. He talked to the interpreter, who turned to Mike to fill him in.

"This one he doesn't know either. He and a friend tried to talk to her once, because she was very sick—how you say stomach sick?"

"Nauseous?" Mike said. "Seasick?"

"Yes, is that. Was very sick one day when sea is rough and being thrown up. But she seemed very shy and didn't want their help."

"But does he know even her first name? What city she's from?"

The interpreter asked but drew a blank. "Pavlo says the young women slept in different part of boat, ate apart from guys, hardly no mix at all. Doesn't know."

Pavlo was sent back to reception and Mike guided in a second youth named Taras. Like Pavlo, he had been dressed in ill-fitting clothes that the NYPD must have picked up at the nearest thrift shop in Queens. This one was nervous and appeared to be frightened.

"What's going to happen to him?" the interpreter asked Mike. "Is all he wants to know. What you going to do with *him*?"

"Coop, how do we tell the kid it's going to get worse before it gets better?" Mike scratched his head.

"You tell him," Mercer said, "that the first thing he has to do is help with this. Then I'll take Pavlo and him inside and explain where they're going tonight. There's a facility in Nassau County that's got beds. It's actually not too bad."

"C'mon, Taras," Mike said. "Pick up your head."

At the sound of the curtains rustling, Taras looked up at his ship-mate. Immediately, startled and shaken, he stepped back, bumping into the interpreter and crying as he blurted out what he knew.

"The boy's name is Gregor, he is telling me. They went to school together. Yes, he is Viktor's brother and, yes, is he seventeen. They were very good friends."

Mercer stepped over and encircled the young man's slim shoulders in his strong embrace. "Thank him for us. Thank him for doing this. We know how hard it is."

The interpreter conveyed the message, which was merely Mercer's introduction to a further probe.

"Were they together last night? Did he see Gregor jump? Does he know why?" Mercer asked the questions slowly, hoping to get answers that would lead us firmly in a particular direction.

"No, is telling me. No. They got separated when the excitement—how you call it? When the hysteria started. Viktor, the older brother, was one of the guys who got upset when they saw the government boats, like a police boat, coming at them. Viktor is one of the ones who attacked the captain."

The interpreter paused and raised his finger, getting more information from Taras while we waited. "Gregor followed Viktor, he is telling. Of course he followed his brother. That's the last I seen of him, he says. He wants to stop now, okay, Mr. Mike? He's had enough."

"We're almost done. Tell him," Mike said, closing the curtain and signaling for the body of Jane Doe #1 to be raised again, "we just need him a few more minutes."

When Mike was ready for Taras, Mercer had to nudge his body a few steps forward.

"Why are you crying?" Mike asked. "You know this girl?"

The interpreter said something to Taras, then turned back to Mike. "Is crying for himself. Doesn't know girl. Me, I think he isn't even looking. Is very upset, Mr. Mike."

"And she's very dead, okay? Pick up your head, Taras," Mike said in as stern a voice as he could muster in the quiet of the morgue. "Look at her."

Taras grudgingly raised his chin and spoke a few words.

"Doesn't know her. Never saw before."

Minutes later, his response to Jane Doe #2 was exactly the same.

"I can't tell if he's just shutting us down," Mike said, "or he doesn't recognize either of the women."

"Let him get some sleep," Mercer said. "We'll have fresher recruits by morning. There have got to be people who were on that ship who'll have something to give us, who'll want something in exchange for information and help. He's a kid, Mike. It's not going to help us tonight to keep Taras here."

It was like Mike to get on a case and set a relentless schedule for himself and everyone working with him. He lived alone in a tiny walk-up apartment not far from my high-rise, so small that he had nicknamed it "the coffin." Since the death of his fiancée more than a year ago, he had driven himself even harder, trying to bury his grief by seeking those who had taken human lives without reason.

"Mercer's right. Think long range. Let's grab a bite," I said, "and make a plan so that we can pick the aspects of this investigation that we want to concentrate on. We can't do it all, Mike. There are scores of potential witnesses, and Donovan will welcome our suggestions. We've really got to pace ourselves. This could take weeks to sort out."

Mike walked away from us, telling the interpreter that he would be free to leave as soon as the officers who were going to escort Pavlo and Taras to the Nassau County detention center arrived.

He came back, rubbing his stomach, and obviously too wired to call it a night. "Feed me, blondie. Nothing like a day at the beach to work up my appetite."

"Want to shoot up to Primola?" I asked. The three of us spent a lot of time at my favorite Italian restaurant on Second Avenue and Sixty-fifth Street. The staff knew us and treated us like family, no matter when we dropped in, nor how casually we were dressed.

"Sounds good," Mercer said. "Then I can drop Alex at her place and slip onto the drive. Vickee might even be talking to me if I get home before midnight."

Mercer's wife was also a police officer and the daughter of a well-respected detective. She had a little more tolerance for the terrible hours he kept, even with the addition to the family of their young son, Logan.

I gathered my things, said good-night to Willis Pomeroy, and walked out onto First Avenue with Mercer and Mike, refreshed by the blast of cold air.

Mercer's cell phone rang and he lifted it to his ear. "I'm sorry, sir. Who is this?"

"Can't be too important if he doesn't even know the guy," Mike said as he kept walking while Mercer stopped to take the call. "You riding with him or me, kid?"

"Whoever is parked closer," I said, pulling up the collar of my jacket.

"Did you get his name?" I heard Mercer ask.

"Call Fenton," Mike said, referring to the bartender at Primola. "I want a vodka martini straight up. An olive and three onions. And I want it waiting on the table when we walk in."

"You did the right thing, Fitz," Mercer told his caller. "Just call the precinct if he shows up again."

"I'm thinking maybe that lasagnetta with a *veal ragù*," Mike said.

The morgue always depressed my appetite, but never seemed to have an effect on Mike at all. I'd be happy with a shot of Dewar's and a bowl of soup.

Mercer seemed in no hurry to catch up with us. I turned to wave him on. "Something wrong?"

"That was the doorman at Salma's apartment. Harry Fitzpatrick. I gave him my card when we left there tonight and told him to call me if anything unusual happened."

"So what happened? The congressman tried to convene a special session?" Mike asked.

Mercer walked toward us slowly. "A guy just showed up fifteen minutes ago. Not Leighton, Alex. Don't worry about that. Made Fitz call upstairs to Salma, but she'd already told him not to bother her under any circumstances. And not to let the police in either. Fitz knew she wasn't going to answer, but he says he rang her anyway."

"Why?" I asked.

"Says he didn't want to create another scene in the lobby," Mercer said. "It might also have something to do with the hundred-dollar bill he says the guy slipped him."

"Who's the visitor?"

"Fitz says the guy wouldn't give a name. He said he was there to pick up his baby."

"*His* baby?"

"Yeah, Fitz claims the man said that he was the father of Salma's child."

NINE

"Get in the car, Coop."

"It's fine for you to disagree with me, Mike. I can just head home."

"What's your point?"

"Look, maybe Salma's unhinged at the moment. How could she not be with what's going on around her?"

"I'm getting unhinged myself. The combination of cold and hungry kills all my good instincts. It's twenty-six degrees out here with a wind chill that makes it feel like minus five. It's right behind that gray SUV. Get in."

"Since when did you become Doppler Mike, the weather maven? The woman is scared enough to phone the police repeatedly—"

"Salma denied making the calls," Mike said, stuffing his hands in his jacket pockets.

"They came from her landline. There's no question about that," I said. "The cops respond a few times, and when they get fed up, they tell her they're not coming back under any circumstances."

"That's what she wants. She threatened to make a civilian complaint for harassing her."

"Well, I'm not comfortable with it, okay? Salma has absolutely no lifeline to the police right now. You two go on to the restaurant. I'd like to go up to her apartment and have a talk with her. I can't figure what Lem and Ethan were up to, but it stinks."

"It's almost ten thirty, Alex. What makes you think she'll let you in?" Mercer asked.

I stepped off the curb to try to hail a cab.

"That stubborn streak is going to get her hurt someday," Mike said, reaching for my hand to pull me back. "Coop thinks the sensitive-broad-to-sensitive-broad approach is always going to work for her. Thinks it's better for crazy people than twenty-four hours in Central Booking. Meanwhile, all she really wants to do is get up close and personal with Salma before Lem Howell shuts her down."

"You guys go have a drink and start eating. I don't like the idea that this woman is all alone tonight, her life coming apart on national television, her baby sent off with a relative—"

"Her choice," Mike said.

"She probably has no idea what she wants right now. Another man shows up at her door staking out rights to the kid, and bottom line? In case anything really does go wrong tonight—like Ethan Leighton deciding to try his hand at calming her down—the police have already told her they're off-limits to her. Can you imagine? Who's she going to call if there really is a problem?"

"I'll take you back there, Alex," Mercer said, stepping between Mike and me. "Ride up with me."

"Sweet Jesus. Now you're walking down Coop's path? Drinking her Kool-Aid? Tell you what. I got no piece of your action, guys, okay? I'm assigned to the Ukrainian flotilla 'cause I handle real cases like murder. You got a drunken congressman who's a John Edwards wannabe, go stroke the broad for an hour. Where's the crime?"

Mike was parked at the corner. He walked over and got in, gunning the gas as he took off up First Avenue before we reached Mercer's car halfway up the block on Thirtieth Street.

There was no traffic. We cruised up First, catching most of the lights to reach Salma's building in twelve minutes.

Mercer parked his car across the street, in front of the tall wrought-iron gates that surrounded Gracie Mansion. Christmas decorations and lights still covered the outside of the building and the park around it, but the interior of the old house was dark.

The glass tower high-rise sparkled against the sky, a glitzy new addition to the classic prewar apartments that lined this quiet street that bordered the East River. Harry Fitzpatrick recognized Mercer as we approached and opened the door to admit us to the lobby of Salma's building.

"Evening, sir. I didn't mean to get you up here again, Mr. Wallace. All's quiet now. The man hasn't come back," Fitz said, swinging his arms across each other like an umpire announcing a player safe on base. "Haven't heard from Miss Salma. It's good."

"I'd like you to ring up to her for me."

The doorman, built like a linebacker, tried to refuse politely. "Can't do that, sir. She's a tough cookie."

"I'm Alexandra Cooper, Mr. Fitzpatrick. I'm an assistant district attorney in Manhattan. We need to talk to Salma Zunega. Now."

"I—uh—I can't do it, ma'am. It's after ten thirty. I'm sure she's resting."

"Is it the hundred dollars the last guy gave you, Mr. Fitzpatrick? 'Cause you're not going to get that from me, and I don't think she'd like to hear you got it from him."

"I just can't. I don't want to lose my job."

I walked past Fitzpatrick and down the three marble steps that led into the opulent lobby. "Which elevator bank, Mercer?"

"To the right. Ten-A."

I held open the door for Mercer, then pressed the button. Fitzpatrick didn't seem to know whether to leave his post and follow us or break his word and call upstairs.

We got out on the tenth floor and I followed Mercer into the corridor. There were only three apartment doors, one on each end of the hallway and one right opposite the elevator. We walked the long hall on thick beige carpeting that muffled the sound of our steps.

There was a brass knocker on the door and a peephole below it, but no name in the small plate that identified most residents.

Mercer struck three times with the knocker.

"You hear anything?" I asked after several seconds.

He shook his head, then knocked again.

"Maybe she can't hear it if she's in the bedroom with her door closed."

"This thing is big enough to make noise in the Bronx," Mercer said, rapping with the knuckles of his huge hand.

The door at the other end of the corridor opened and a man emerged, pulling the leash of a black Lab that came out slowly behind him. "What's all the banging about at this hour?"

"Sorry if we've disturbed you," I said.

"Take your business inside, why don't you?" he said, yanking on the leash again as he and his charge disappeared into the elevator.

"Call her phone, Mercer. Maybe she took something to help her sleep."

He dialed her landline—we could hear it ringing—but she didn't pick up after six rings, so he hung up.

"You want to try the door?"

"What are you thinking, Alex?"

"I don't like this whole thing. I don't want to leave her stranded from everyone who could help her. Just try it."

People in New York's toniest buildings, coddled by doormen and valets and concierges, often left their doors unlocked. There was a false sense of security that the high cost of rent or maintenance and the abundance of uniformed staff guaranteed in many of the city's finest addresses.

Mercer put his hand on the shiny brass doorknob and turned it to the right. I heard it click and saw the look of surprise on his face as he pushed it open.

"Salma? Salma, it's Mercer Wallace. I'm one of the detectives who was here today. You okay?"

The lights in the hallway were on and the living room beyond it was brightly lit.

There was no sound from anywhere in the apartment. Mercer took a couple of steps in and I followed him. He called her name out again, then extended his arm to stop me from going farther.

"Let's back it up, Alex. You're right. Maybe she knocked herself out with some pills and needs a good night's sleep."

"See the coffee table?"

The living room facing the river was glass windows from floor to ceiling on two sides. There was a striking vista of the river, with the lights of the bridges and highways glittering in the distance.

"Yeah. A bottle of red wine."

"And two glasses. Not exactly the plan she announced to you."

Mercer motioned to me to stay in place as he walked to the table, then returned.

"The bottle's unopened."

"Which way is the master bedroom?"

"Alex—"

"What if she tried to hurt herself?"

"You're playing with dynamite here. Be ready to duck if she throws something," Mercer said, pointing to the archway behind me. "Over there."

I started down the narrow corridor, passing the child's bed-room first. I peeked in and could see from the moonlight pour-ing through the window that the crib was empty and the room was neatly arranged.

I kept walking to the end of the hall, with Mercer on my heels.

The door was ajar and even without lamplight the tall windows fronting on the open panorama of the bright city sky revealed the emptiness of the room.

"Salma's not here, Mercer." My heart was racing as I tried to guess at where she might have gone and what prompted her to flee. "I'd better call Battaglia right now. Looks like Salma Zunega's on the run."

TEN

"The woman vanishes and you call that excellent circumstances?"
Mike said. "You take Mercer on a break-in into this broad's love
nest?"

"That's not what I said. Exigent circumstances. That's why
Mercer and I went into her apartment. Perfectly legal." I reached
over and wiped the pasta sauce off the corner of Mike's mouth with
my napkin. "Can you possibly put your fork down for a minute and
get serious?"

"Giuliano," Mike called out to Primola's owner. "Mercer's sticking to sparkling water but we might need to go intravenous Dewar's
on the princess here. *Rapido.*"

"I called the precinct and they've got a man stationed at both
doors to the apartment," Mercer said. "We went in the front one
and there's also a service entrance off the kitchen."

Another feature of upscale apartments was the rear service door,
so that garbage and deliveries—and the servants who managed those
duties—were kept out of the carpeted common hallways.

"Kitchen? Bathrooms?"

"Not there. I didn't go into her closets, Mike," Mercer said.
"She's not in the apartment."

"So what's the plan?"

"That's why we came back to get you," I said, smiling at him. "CSU responds more quickly when you call."

"Crime Scene wouldn't come out for you?" he asked, mopping the dish with a piece of garlic bread. "I'm supposed to be perplexed by that? You still got nothing, kid."

Adolfo, the head captain, placed a steaming hot bowl of *stracciatella* in front of me, serving Mercer the same hearty pasta that Mike had eaten.

"I've made the mistake of thinking that way before." Just months earlier, I had delayed my follow-up on a woman who had been reluctant to report a rape. Her decision to pull away from the police investigation was a deadly one. "I called Battaglia and Commissioner Scully on the way back here. We've got the same dilemma. No missing persons report for forty-eight hours."

Most police departments had a firm policy on adults who disappeared without evidence of foul play. They were presumed to have removed themselves from their homes or businesses, and no professional wild goose chases would be launched in the absence of evidence of related criminal conduct.

"You check with her sister?"

"She's fine," Mercer said. "Just a little surprised that Salma isn't home. The baby's okay too."

"Chow down, Coop," Mike said, clicking his martini glass against my scotch. "What did the wide-awake doorman have to say?"

"He never saw Salma leave. Swears it. One of the porters covered him for his dinner break and didn't see her either."

"How many doors?"

"Front and rear. And the garage. But that's attended day and night, and nobody there saw any sign of her. Rear door gets locked at six o'clock."

"There must have been deliveries after six," Mike said.

I spooned the hot soup while Mercer answered all of Mike's questions.

"Yeah. Guys come to the front door. Fitz sends them around to the rear entrance and buzzes them in."

"Has he got a list of tonight's action?"

"Nothing written down, but he says it was the usual. Supermarkets, florists, liquor. They were still coming till close to ten o'clock." That was routine in a city where stores stayed open throughout the night and people were willing to pay for—and tip for—every kind of convenience to suit their busy lives.

"Fancy building like that must have a security system. They video the entrances or elevators?"

"Nothing recorded. Fitz has four monitors of the door, the basement corridors, and the laundry room. But that's only when he remembers to watch them."

"You think he could have missed her if she walked out the front door?"

"It's possible," I said. "If she had a coat on with a hood up against the cold or a scarf bundled around her I guess he could have mistaken her for someone else. Even if his back was turned for a minute. I can't say that she didn't walk out. It just doesn't feel right."

"Don't go getting all spooky on me, Coop," Mike said, reaching out and clasping my hand. "That last one wasn't your fault. Just work with the facts."

"That's what I'm trying to do. The facts suggest Salma should be home in her bed, sound asleep. She can't go to Leighton's place—"

"Look, it's still early and she's still erratic. Who's the man that showed up? Maybe she went to hook up with him. Maybe she'll get to her sister's before the night is over."

"Please? Just do this for me tonight? I'll owe you, Mike. Anything you want. Scully will put a team on this instead of waiting forty-eight hours if we can just give him a scintilla of evidence. Anything, Mike."

"You heard her, Mercer. Now, how do I collect on this one? Do what, blondie?"

"Call Hal Sherman. Ask him to bring a crew to process the apartment."

Mike stood up and downed his martini, then sucked the olive into his mouth and chewed on it. "Tell you what, let's go over and poke around. If I find anything of interest, I'll call CSU. But if Salma walks in on the middle of it, I'm going with your excellent circumstances legal argument. And I'm already drawing up a monster list of what you owe me."

I pushed away from the table. "Mercer's parked right across the street."

When we reached East End Avenue, Mercer left the car near Gracie Mansion and threw his police identification placard on the dashboard.

"Pretty swell digs," Mike said, looking up at the sleek residential tower. "Maybe there is something to being kept after all. You check out the rear entrance?"

"Nope," Mercer said. "It's a good place to start."

We crossed the avenue and followed the sidewalk past the garage entrance and around to the rear of the building. The pavement was bordered by the building on one side, and the solid dark brick wall of an older apartment on the other.

The walk was well-maintained and lighted. The security camera was visible above the door, but appeared to be raised too high to capture visitors in its lens. Several grocery shopping carts were stacked inside each other, like luggage carts at an airport awaiting the arrival of the incoming flights.

Mercer pulled on the door but it didn't give. Next to it was a bell marked RING FOR ENTRY. When he pressed the buzzer, several seconds elapsed before we heard the crackle of the intercom.

"Yeah? Who's that?"

"Fitz?"

"Who wants to know?"

"Mercer Wallace here. I'm at the back door, Fitz. Can you see me?"

"Where?"

"At the back door of the building. Check the monitor."

"I'll buzz you in."

"But can you see me, Fitz?"

"I recognize your voice, Wallace. When you hear the buzzer, come on in."

Mercer, standing on his toes to extend his six-foot-six-inch height, reached up and pulled the neck of the camera back into proper aim.

"High-tech security," Mike said. "The Fitzpatrick try-not-to-bother-me-while-I'm-on-duty voice-identification system. Follow me."

Small signs with arrows pointing east and west indicated the service elevator, the laundry room, the passenger elevator to the lobby and apartments, and the staircase.

Mercer had given me latex gloves while we were in the car. We each put on a pair and I watched as Mike lifted the lids of the four supersize trash containers on wheels that were lined up adjacent to the service elevator.

He led us up the stairwell to the lobby, and Mercer introduced him to Harry Fitzpatrick.

"Ten-C has already complained to the super," Fitz said, taking off his hat and mopping his bald head. "I'm going off at midnight. You back to make more trouble?"

"We're going up to Ms. Zunega's apartment," Mercer said. "She comes along—or anyone else asking for her—you buzz up immediately."

Each of us had our hands in our jacket or pants pockets. The latex gloves would have puzzled most of the residents.

The uniformed cop sitting on a folding chair outside Salma's apartment door stood up when he saw us get off the elevator. He assured Mercer that nothing had occurred in the forty-five or so minutes we were gone.

Mike turned the doorknob and followed us into the apartment. He adjusted the dimmer to brighten the hallway, then walked to one of the windows to take in the view.

"I'd say Salma landed on her feet, all right."

"This place is too sterile, too impersonal, for my taste," I said.

There was so much glass that there was little wall space in the living room to hang any art. But there were also no photographs—not even baby pictures—displayed on any of the tabletops or surfaces.

Mike looked at the wine bottle and two empty glasses.

"Can't we take those for prints?" I asked.

"You're always harping on me about getting a search warrant. You want to wake up some judge in the middle of the night and make your case, go for it. I don't happen to have one in my back pocket."

"A search warrant or a judge?"

"Neither, Coop."

Mercer led him down to the bedroom and nursery, and I watched as they used their gloved fingers to open closet doors, look under the dust ruffle of the undisturbed king-size bed, and pull the handles of dresser drawers.

The master bathroom was perfectly neat. I could see that Salma used the same makeup that I did. The distinctive black-and-gold packaging with the *C* logo stamped in white was everywhere on the countertop and bath shelf.

"Tomorrow I'll need to get a court order to get the baby's DNA—and Ethan Leighton's," I said, making my checklist out loud while the guys looked for any minor sign of trouble. "I'd love to know who else claims to be the father."

"You're so far ahead of yourself with court orders and search warrants. Somebody has to report a crime."

"Leighton's up to his eyeballs in trouble, Mike."

We retraced our steps through the living room to the kitchen.

"You beginning to feel any better?" Mercer asked.

"I've got no choice. We're coming up empty."

"Nothing out of place," Mike said. "Plenty of milk in the refrigerator for the kid and food on the shelves for both of them. Not a dish in the sink. She gets triple points for being a neat freak."

A long corkscrew wine-bottle opener with a carved wooden handle was resting on its side on the counter next to the sink.

Mercer pointed to it. "Maybe she was expecting someone who never showed, Alex. That could explain the wineglasses and the setup."

The edge of a shiny black object was protruding from beneath the front of the toaster oven. Mercer saw it, too, but couldn't slide his large fingers under to reach it.

I stuck my forefinger in and pushed out a razor-thin cell phone, small enough to fit in the palm of my hand and slimmer than a compact.

"Now, I don't know anybody who would leave home at night with all this turmoil going on and not take her cell," I said, fumbling with my latex gloves to pick up the lid.

"Hers?" Mike asked.

I pressed the button to light up the small screen, which showed the evening's time and date. "I'll figure that out next. Right now, all I can tell you is that whoever had it last got as far as punching in three digits, Mike. Nine-one-one. But they're still in the display box, so it doesn't look like the caller ever got to hit Send."

"You may be sneaking up on some probable cause, kid."

Mercer took the phone from my hand while Mike picked up the corkscrew opener.

"And I don't think you're going to like the vintage of the stain on the tip of this lethal weapon," Mike said. "Here's your scintilla, Coop. I'm guessing it'll likely come up human blood."

ELEVEN

"You're late, Alexandra," the mayor said on Thursday morning. "You asked for this seven-thirty meeting and here we are."

"I'm very sorry, of course."

"It's the hair thing with Coop," Mike said, getting up from his seat to close the door behind me. "She doesn't leave home until it's perfect. Busy times like this, you never know when you're going to get caught in a perp walk."

I knew he was covering for me. Battaglia had refused to come back to City Hall for the emergency meeting I suggested to Tim Spindlis—he didn't want to take direction from the mayor—but insisted on being briefed before I filled Vin Statler and Keith Scully in on last night's events. I had lost ten minutes talking to him.

"Sit down, please," Statler said, pointing to the chair next to Mercer. We were in the Blue Room—the mayor's public receiving suite on the ground floor, resplendent with its ceiling medallions, rope molding, and wainscoting.

"It was actually my suggestion that we bring you in on this, Vin," Scully said. The commissioner had been appointed by Bloomberg, but had done such an extraordinary job reducing the city's violent crime statistics and improving the quality of the police force that

Statler had kept him on. "You wanted to know more about Ethan Leighton's lady friend."

"Well, in the sense that there have been so many political scandals lately that this kind of nonsense is likely to trump the more important news, like the human trafficking story."

"Why don't you tell the mayor what happened after you left here," Scully said to me.

It was just the five of us in the room, and I told the mayor everything from the autopsy results to our efforts to talk with—and then to locate—Salma Zunega.

Mike had the morning's additional fact. The substance on the tip of the wine opener was indeed human blood. He'd had one of the precinct cops drop it off at the lab when we left East End Avenue shortly after midnight, and had stopped there to get that report on his way to City Hall.

"I'm struggling with whether to go public with this," Scully said. "It's going to bring more heat on Leighton and—"

"What's wrong with that?" the mayor asked, tossing his head back so that we might not see his smirk.

"I don't need an all-out manhunt if this woman just slipped away for a few days to catch her breath, but like Alex says, it's unusual to leave home without a cell phone these days."

"And it's unlikely she was giving herself a manicure with the corkscrew," Mike added.

"I've got Crime Scene going over her apartment now, Vin. I'd like to be ready to ramp up full bore on this if we get a break on where she is and what her condition is."

"That's fine with me."

"What I'd like, actually, is to borrow the mansion," the commissioner said.

"What? Gracie Mansion?" Statler raised himself out of the chair, striking a pose almost identical to the Charles Jarvis portrait of Thomas Jefferson behind him. "Impossible."

"I just need it for a couple of days, Vin. Think about it. The girl's apartment is right across the street. Once word gets out, the press will be camped on your doorstep anyway."

Statler was angry now. "It's not my doorstep. I don't live there."

"That's my point. Let us use it to get started. Except for your occasional breakfasts or teas, the house sits empty most of the time. And I've got an entire police detail already in place there." That was routine, since the mansion was the mayor's ceremonial home. "What's the harm? This whole thing may blow over if the woman just went back to Mexico for a week."

"I don't want any part of this run from the mayor's office or Gracie Mansion. Do you understand that? It'll just look like I'm out to get Leighton. And you—you, young lady. Haven't you got your hands full with all those women from the ship?"

"I do, Mr. Mayor. I certainly do. But it will be days until most of them are settled in and physically examined and ready to be interrogated. I'm truly concerned about the disappearance of Salma Zunega."

"This isn't about Alex or the district attorney, Vin. I want a handful of my men operating out of the mansion. Are you saying no to that?"

"This woman will turn up soon enough. Thank you, Ms. Cooper. Why don't the rest of you step out while the commissioner and I finish this conversation?"

"Thanks for your hospitality, Mr. Mayor," Mike said, pulling back my chair as the three of us accepted the abrupt end to the meeting. "Till next time."

We were leaving as many of the City Hall employees were coming in through the metal detectors in the lobby of the building.

"Pittsburgh Paint. Bohemian blue," Mike said.

"What?"

"In case you wanted to know the color of the paint on the wall. It's historic, Coop."

"I didn't give it any thought."

"It used to be green. Back in the day, I mean. But it had to be made more telegenic, so now it's Bohemian blue," Mike said. "I've spent so much time in that room waiting for press conferences on homicide cases, I can tell you every detail of the décor. It was a real pleasure to be in and evicted so fast today."

"Well, I'll go on up to my office and get to work organizing my unit for our interviews. Hizzoner was a bit testy with Scully, don't you think?"

"Guess it's his mansion whether he's there or not," Mike said.

"Will you be at your desk all day?" Mercer asked.

"I expect to."

I walked out the front door and was buffeted by the fierce wind.

"Hold on to that railing," Mercer said. "The steps look icy."

There had been a light dusting of snow during the night that covered over patches of ice from the most recent storm.

"I was stupid not to wear boots today. I was running late and just hopped in a cab."

There was construction on the east side of City Hall Park between the front steps and Centre Street, the wide thoroughfare that started right there, at the foot of the Brooklyn Bridge. One of the guards asked us to stay on the walkway that led toward Chambers Street, behind the building in the direction of my office.

"I'll peel off here," Mike said. "I'm back at the morgue for the autopsies of more of the bodies from the ship. You good?"

"My car's up by the courthouse," Mercer said. "I need to spend some time with Alex."

"Talk later." Mike waved good-bye to us and turned south to exit the park.

The badly rutted concrete path hugged the side of City Hall, then wound through the northeast corner of the park under the brittle arms of the bare trees that dotted the landscape. Tall mesh fences stood to the right, protecting dark green tarps that were spread over large sections of the ground.

"You missed the commissioner's news, Alex," Mercer said.

"What?" I asked, turning my head to better hear him. We were walking single file on the narrow strip of pavement.

"Careful," he said, as he watched me balance on the slippery surface. "Two more bodies came ashore this morning. A couple of miles farther out in Nassau County."

"Oh my God. Do you know anything about them?"

"Both young men. Both seem to have drowned."

"How many people from the ship are still unaccounted for?" I asked.

"What's that?"

"Doesn't anyone have a manifest for the damn thing?"

"It's a slave ship, Alex. When we find our Simon Legree, I expect we'll find the documentation too."

There was definitely black ice underfoot on the unshoveled walk. I paused and grabbed on to the mesh fence so that I could take Mercer's arm when he caught up with me.

As I swiveled to face him, my shoulder hit the mesh and ripped the two stakes closest to me out of the ground. I fell onto my side, taking the fence with me as I landed on the tarp. I heard it rip open as my back slammed against the ground through the hole I had made in the old, weather-beaten material. My bag flew from my shoulder and emptied onto the dirt around me.

"Alex!" Mercer shouted as he bent over to reach for me. "Are you okay?"

My neck ached and the cold, damp earth was caked against both my legs and head. I was in a ditch, flat on my back.

"Shaken, Mercer. Not stirred. And I don't think anything's broken. Just badly shaken. If you want to talk omens, I think I'm on a killer course."

"What is it, girl?"

My head rested on a pile of dirt and I was staring at the jawbone of a human skull.

TWELVE

"What do you mean it's been here a couple of hundred years?" I asked, standing a few feet back from the large hole in the ground. "Where'd you get that idea?"

Nan Toth had gone to my office and retrieved the gym clothes and sneakers I kept there for the occasional times we were able to get away at lunchtime to work out. The officers had let me back into the restroom at City Hall to change clothes, and I had thrown out the black pencil skirt that had been torn almost in half along a sharp rock, just like my pantyhose.

Alton Brady, the park supervisor, was on his knees next to Mercer, while his men had already started the task of reinforcing the structure surrounding the twenty-foot-square site where someone had been digging.

"It's the anthropologists says how old the stuff is," Brady said. "Besides, you wasn't supposed to be in here, miss."

"Nothing I planned. I can promise you that."

"What's that museum in Washington? The Smithsonian?" Brady asked. "That's where they're sending the bones. Supposed to be all hush-hush."

Mercer stepped down into the ditch. The ancient roots of rotting trees dangled on the edges, and protruding from the dirt were pieces of bone that looked like fragments of skulls and other skeletal remains.

"Is this part of the African Burial Ground?" Nan asked.

Mercer knew the answer to that. "No, that's two blocks north of here. I wasn't even a detective yet when we handled those protests."

Digging to build a parking garage for an office complex on Lower Broadway in 1991, construction workers unearthed the remains of almost five hundred bodies.

"Who protested?" Nan asked.

Mercer scratched at the soil just six inches below the street level and the remains of a human hand—long, thin ivory fingers—stretched out toward his own.

"My people," Mercer said, winking at Nan. "Bones and bureaucrats don't mix too well, as you may already know. Politicians don't like to remind folks that their cities were built on the backs of the disenfranchised. African American New Yorkers—those who didn't already know it—learned that outside of Charleston, South Carolina, we had the greatest slave population in the colonies. So the city fathers weren't any too anxious to deal with the remains."

Alton Brady reached out to pick up a fragment of bone.

"Don't touch that, please," Mercer said, as he flipped open his phone and hit a number. "Mike? You at the morgue yet? We're still in City Hall Park—I'll explain later. Well, as soon as you're done with breakfast, tell the ME to send his bone doc down here to the park, behind the building. I'll meet him at the gate. Alex stumbled onto something."

The ME's office had a forensic anthropologist, Andy Dorfman, who helped in the difficult analysis of old skeletal discoveries.

"Look here, Wallace," Brady said. "This is my property. We're getting this done without your help, okay?"

"Why don't you think it's connected to the African Burial Ground?" I asked.

"Not a chance," Mercer said. "I'd like to claim credit for knowing this, but you understand I got all the history from Mike."

"That figures. How is it different?"

"African slaves were brought here to New Amsterdam in 1626. But they weren't allowed to be buried in any of the church cemeteries within the city proper. And in those days, when Manhattan started at the Battery and covered only the southern tip of this island," Mercer said, "the northernmost part of the city ended right over there, a block away. There were palisades built—fences with stakes on top—to defend the settlers. The slaves were given five desolate acres north of that, outside the original city, to bury their dead."

"Five acres?" Nan said. "Then there must have been more than five hundred bodies."

"Something like twenty thousand. Many of them infants and children stacked on top of each other."

I was still reeling from the fact of all the women and men being trafficked to the States, and how common modern-day slavery actually is. I'd never thought much about slavery in the North, in a place like colonial New York. "What became of all those other graves?"

"Dust and detritus, Alex," Mercer said. "When the city moved past here, beyond its colonial walls, it just appropriated the cemetery and paved over it."

I scanned the skyline. It appeared that the entire Civic Center that was adjacent to the north side of City Hall Park had been built on top of the remains of thousands of African slaves. "I'm embarrassed to say I don't even know when slavery was abolished in New York."

"Eighteen twenty-seven. Shockingly late, isn't it?"

"Yes, it is." I said. "So who are we looking at here, Mr. Brady?"

"This just for your information?" Brady was checking Mercer for an answer as he straightened up.

"Yeah, I'm a curious guy."

"The mayor knows all about this, if that's what you're thinking. Been going on for years. It's a historical project."

"Pretty sloppy one," Mercer whispered to me.

"This here City Hall was built in 1803. You can read that right on the sign over at the front gate. Before that, all this land was an almshouse. A homeless shelter, a poorhouse, and a jail, all balled into one part of town. Had its own cemetery next to it. For whites, of course. No blacks."

Mercer nodded at me. "Of course."

"I was working here when Giuliani was mayor. That's the first time some bits and pieces of bone came up, all jumbled together. We was making over the park for the new millennium celebration—taking out the dead trees, fixing the pavement, putting in new lights. Holy cow," Brady says, "one of the guys calls me over to show me this cluster of bones—like a whole human leg. Spooky as all hell."

"What did Giuliani do?" Nan asked.

"Sure didn't like anybody talking about it. Guess he was afraid all those people would come back and protest again. Though it ain't like slaves. Don't know anybody who'd claim an old relative from the poorhouse or jail. Sent what was found to the Smithsonian. Can't say I know what ever come of it. Now, whenever we come upon an area of the park that needs renovation, we have to put up this here fencing and tarp it over."

"The city morgue has its own anthropologist, Mr. Brady," Mercer said. "Gonna have him take a look too."

"Kinda unnecessary if you ask me," Brady said. "We got this here hole and the one just southeast of the front steps. Nobody pays 'em no mind."

"Every now and again maybe somebody should," Mercer said. "What else you find in these digs?"

"Dead animals get in. Sometimes you come across old buttons or shards of glass. Even some shroud pins."

"And modern-day things?" I asked.

Brady studied me for a few seconds. "You police too?"

"Nope," I said with a smile.

"You'd never believe she studies ballet," Nan said, drawing a laugh from the wizened Parks Department worker. "Clumsy as she is to fall in your ditch."

"All kinds of stuff gets tossed in by people heading into the building. Scraps of paper, tennis balls, empty cans. Sometimes we find a pocket knife or something out in front that wouldn't make it through the metal detector. Then there's your food and garbage. That's what attracts the rats, what start draggin' the pieces of bone around."

"How sad is that?" I said aloud to no one in particular.

"You know what they say about cross-examining," Nan said. "Never ask a question to which you don't already know the answer. Or don't want to know the answer. Let's head back. We've got so much to do."

"You two go on ahead. I'll wait to show this stuff to Andy when he gets here."

"Not because it has anything to do with what we're working on?" I asked. I didn't see any connection.

"Course not," Mercer said. "I just can't imagine letting anybody's folks spill out of the ground like this and not be treated properly. Shoo, ladies. I'll be along soon."

Nan and I walked back to my office, going over our checklist of things to do. I pressed the elevator to take us to the eighth floor.

"What'll you give me for not telling anyone about your giant flop?"

"I'm running out of IOUs. I had to promise my life away to get Mike to take me to Salma's apartment last night."

"I'm much easier," Nan said. "I'll take lunch at Forlini's when you come up for air. I want to hear how things are going with Luc."

"Luc, Paris, and all the romance that went with the week seem light-years behind me," I said as we approached Laura's desk.

"Ah, Paris. Only the extra pounds remain. I have a feeling you'll work it off in the next month."

"You're later than I expected, Alex," Laura said. "And another casually chic outfit, I see?"

"Don't ask."

"Not even about the dirt that's clinging to the back of your hair?" she said, following us into my office so that she could straighten me out before handing me my messages. "And don't bother to look at these yet. Go see the district attorney. Rose said it's ugly in there. He's chewing her head off waiting for you."

"See what I mean, Nan? The boss is gunning for someone. I hate to be in the crossfire until I figure out who the target is."

"You're all set with the conference room, Nan," Laura said. I'd be lost without her self-starting efficiency and ease of operating in a maelstrom. "I've reserved it for the next couple of weeks, and there are actually two official Ukrainian interpreters able to start working with you today."

"Great. All we need is a way to get our victims back to us. Go ahead, Alex. I'll call Donny Baynes and get us on the same page."

"Am I supposed to be knocking out subpoenas for the phone company?" Laura asked. "Mike left a message with some numbers for a Salma someone. Landline and cell, right?"

"Not until Nan opens a grand jury investigation," I said, putting my hands together as if praying to my colleague. "Jump the line, Nan. Make it dinner, and all the gossip I know."

"Last thing for the moment," Laura said. "Lem called. Wants to know what you did with the congressman's package. Something about what he was expecting this morning."

"Package? Is that a new euphemism for piece of ass? Don't call him back, Laura. Resist Lem's charm and his persistent calls. Tell him nothing."

"You know he'll show up here if you ignore him."

"I'll take my chances," I said, heading off to see Battaglia. "Lem would be comic relief by the time the boss gets through with me."

THIRTEEN

The security guard buzzed me into the executive suite. The handful of lawyers who held administrative positions had offices in Battaglia's inner sanctum, and I passed by them as I walked toward Rose Malone, his longtime loyal assistant. Her expression often mirrored the district attorney's mood, and today it was unusually cold.

"Good to see you, Alex. Go right in." We didn't even bother to exchange our usual pleasantries.

I made the turn into Paul Battaglia's large office. He was sitting at the conference table at the far end—not his desk—and he wasn't alone.

"I told you she wouldn't keep you waiting very long, Boss," Pat McKinney said. "Look at that, Alex probably ran all the way down here. Sweats must be the new power suit, no?"

The chief of the Trial Division was a perennial thorn in my professional side. McKinney was a few years my senior, and although he was reputed to have capable investigative skills, his rigid and humorless manner made him an unpopular choice to lead the hundreds of smart young lawyers who staffed the division that was the heart of every good prosecutor's office.

"Good morning, Paul," I said, closing the door behind me. "It's so rare for you to compliment my outfit, Pat. I'm flattered."

"How'd it go at City Hall?" the DA asked.

"I left the mayor and Scully bickering over staging the next phase of things."

"Really? Bickering about what?"

"The commissioner wants to use Gracie Mansion because it's so convenient to Salma Zunega's apartment. Statler said no and asked us to leave."

"Why won't he let Keith use the mansion?" Battaglia asked, sitting up straight and making eye contact with McKinney.

"He wouldn't talk in front of Mike or Mercer or me. I don't know."

"You don't usually defer to authority so meekly, Alex," McKinney said. He saw Battaglia reaching for a new cigar and stood up to strike a match for him.

"She barely said a word yesterday," the DA spoke out of the corner of his mouth, as he dragged on the Cohiba to get it lighted.

I didn't realize Battaglia had lifted the gag order he had imposed for my meeting with Mayor Statler. "Just depends on whether I respect the person giving orders, Pat."

"There's something very serious I've got to tell you, Alexandra. I'm going to take you into my confidence on this, because it may impact what's going on with Ethan Leighton and, well, even with his mistress. Obviously, Pat knows about it too. Can I trust you with this?"

I stood up to leave. "Maybe that's a leakier boat than I want to get in, Paul."

"Sit down. Sit right down."

McKinney's affair with Ellen Gunsher, who ran the office GRIP unit—Gun Recovery Information Program—had not only broken up his marriage, but it had also made him the laughingstock of many of the lawyers and cops. Gunsher's mother was a former newswoman whose career had washed up due to her own carelessness and unprofessional behavior. But McKinney was always trying to stay in her good graces by feeding her exclusives on crime investigations that should never have been discussed.

"Did the mayor bring any other politicians into the conversation today?"

"No. No, he didn't."

"The reason I wanted you to go over there this morning without me—and without Tim—was that I thought Statler might have let down his guard and mentioned names in response to what you told him."

"That didn't happen. Of course, he and the commissioner were still together when I left."

"How about Lem Howell, Alexandra? I'm sure he's tried to speak to you since yesterday."

"Actually, yes, Paul. Laura says he called me this morning. I expect he's peeved because Salma Zunega didn't show up for his first meeting with her today."

"That's the way to go, Boss," McKinney said. "Lem Howell. Lem thinks he taught Alex everything she knows. Maybe she can get something out of him?"

I watched carefully as they talked between themselves. McKinney's sharp, pointed nose and pinched mouth morphed into a rodentlike face when he schemed, especially in regard to someone he disliked.

"That's an idea."

"What's an idea?" I asked.

Paul Battaglia stowed his cigar on the edge of an ashtray, a sign that he was ready for a serious talk. "Have you met the lieutenant governor yet?"

"No, Boss."

Eliot Spitzer, the New York governor who resigned after the scandal caused by his involvement with the ultra-high-priced prostitutes of the Emperors Club VIP ring, had also been a prosecutor in Battaglia's office in his first years out of law school. When he stepped down, Lieutenant Governor David Paterson was sworn in as his replacement.

A year later, in a special statewide election, a powerful former state senator from the Albany region named Rod Ralevic succeeded Paterson as the new lieutenant governor.

"Ralevic. You know the name?"

"Of course I do."

"Do you know that the feds have had him under investigation for months?"

McKinney was like the cat that swallowed a canary and then washed it down with a bald eagle. He loved being in the know while I looked dumbfounded.

"No, sir."

"Don't you want to know why?" McKinney said.

"I assume Paul's about to tell me. Don't forget to wipe your mouth, Pat. I think there are some bird droppings on your lip."

McKinney lowered his beak and actually tried to see if something was wrong.

"Ralevic's been trying to sell patronage in Albany for years now. Probably has. He's already starting bragging that for the right price, he can control the party's pick in the special election to replace Ethan Leighton's congressional seat."

"It's only been a little over twenty-four hours since Leighton went belly-up on the FDR Drive," I said.

"And every couple of hours that go by represents a two-year ticket to Congress or some other vacant post, Alex."

Paul Battaglia had won reelection term after term using the slogan "You can't play politics with people's lives."

"It's not Ralevic's position to give, is it?"

"Not exactly, but it's Ralevic's style to claim he can influence the party endorsement," Battaglia said. "It's not like a vacant Senate seat, where the governor can choose someone to finish out the term. For the House of Representatives, Paterson has to set an election date—usually one hundred twenty days out—then each party nominates a candidate. Theoretically, the district leaders here in the city would try to control the apparatus that does that, but Ralevic's trying to flex his muscle—and his pocketbook."

"Not with the governor's approval?" I asked.

"Certainly not, Alex. Paterson's a thoroughly straight shooter, but that doesn't mean that there aren't people who would pay dearly to show on his radar screen, to try for an advantage, whether it gets them there or not."

"So you think Leighton is in on this scheme?"

"Leighton or his old man. The father would sell his grandkids if they brought the right price. Don't shudder, Alex. That's why they call it hardball. Leighton's father has always been his fixer. I'm sure he'd like a say in who succeeds Ethan. Someone who may be willing to step aside when all this is over, if his son's name is eventually cleared."

"If the feds have been all over Ralevic about this, Paul, what do you need from me?"

"Lem Howell would follow you if you jumped off the Brooklyn Bridge," McKinney added.

"Oh, please, Pat. Don't be ridiculous," I said. "And Pat? Don't hold your breath too long, because I'm not jumping."

"I need you in this, Alex, because I have to come out of this clean as a hound's tooth," Paul Battaglia said.

There had never been a whisper of a scandal surrounding the district attorney. "But you are that, Paul. I don't understand."

"It's about Tim Spindlis, Alex."

Something happened between Battaglia and Spindlis after I got out of the DA's car last evening. There must have been a reason the chief assistant hadn't piggybacked with me to City Hall this morning. There must have been something he told Battaglia that meant he couldn't be in the room with us right now.

"What about Tim?" I asked.

Spindlis was in his sixties, with little to show for a thirty-eight-year career in law enforcement except an endless series of lesser decisions that Battaglia had sloughed off in his direction.

"I'd like to see him on the bench this year. I'd like to get him named to the Court of Claims. And I don't want that designation snarled up in any monkey business or pay-for-play talk that sleaze-ball Ralevic brings into the picture."

That gubernatorial appointment to the Court of Claims was an absolute plum for a lawyer under any circumstances, but for Spindlis it would cap his lackluster career and ensure that he would have job security until he reached the mandatory retirement age, as well as top-tier pension benefits.

Battaglia had been close enough to Spitzer when he was governor to make the kind of behind-the-scene deals that placed many protégés—most of whom were well-qualified—in important jobs. Scores of former prosecutors were staff for the attorney general and the governor, dozens more wore judicial robes or ran administrative agencies. There were no bribes or illegal payments ever at issue, just the traditional political back-scratching, and the all-important blessing of Paul Battaglia.

But Battaglia didn't have that relationship with the new governor, couldn't call in the chits that a mentor might request of the kind of protégé Eliot Spitzer had been.

"You think Ralevic and Ethan Leighton have some kind of relationship?" I asked.

I could see now why Battaglia had been in such a foul mood yesterday. He didn't want these events to queer the deal he had made for Spindlis. And of course Pat McKinney was in on this political positioning, because he would be the likely successor to the role of chief assistant that Spindlis now held—the consigliere to Battaglia.

Something in it for almost everybody.

"The less detail you know the better, Alex."

"I take it someone's been wearing a wire." I wondered if either one of them noticed that I was beginning to squirm.

"Like I said, the feds have been after Ralevic for quite a while."

"So you're worried where Tim comes out in all this?" I said that, although I was well aware that Battaglia never actually worried that much where anyone else came out except himself. But Tim Spindlis was too connected to him not to expect fallout close to home.

Battaglia crushed the cigar in the ashtray, like he was stomping the life out of a venomous bug. "Someone is going to try to hurt Tim in all this. Maybe Leighton himself, maybe Ralevic, or maybe even a smart mouthpiece like Lem Howell."

I was thankful that Mike had told me to keep my limo ride with Lem and Ethan to myself. I was trying to sort out all the players and their positions.

"You listen to me on this, Alex. There'll be no letting Chapman off the leash during your investigation—none of his antics, no one going rogue on me here. You get a whisper of anyone trying to trash my name—or Tim's—you're on my doorstep before you blink your eyes."

"I understand, Paul," I said, ignoring the smirk on McKinney's face. "Am I off-base asking why you think Tim's at risk in all this maneuvering?"

"Rumors. Only that. No substance to them, but he's apt to get bitten in the ass by an ugly rumor."

"I'd like to be prepared. Don't you think it makes sense to tell me what it's about? I understand it's just garbage."

Battaglia got up from the table and walked to the window. The gargoyles that crested the building across Hogan Place stared back at him, some with fierce expressions of defiance, others mocking him with their tongues sticking out in derision.

"Tim was Eliot Spitzer's supervisor when Eliot was a young prosecutor here. Both Harvard Law, both bright young men interested in public service. God knows Eliot couldn't keep up with Tim's drinking habits, but who the hell can figure what else they did together when they bonded here?" Battaglia said.

"Both were very loyal to you, Boss," McKinney added, trying to get his pointy nose as close to the DA's rear end as possible.

"I'd rather not be reminded of Eliot's connection to me at all,

Pat," Battaglia said, turning around to look at me. "Client Number Nine, Alex. You know what I mean?"

When Governor Spitzer had been identified by the feds as one of the regular customers patronizing high-priced prostitutes, he'd been cited as Client 9 in the criminal complaint.

"There aren't many of us who missed that, Paul."

"Whatever it is those girls were giving away at five thousand bucks an hour," Battaglia said, pounding his forefinger into a pile of briefs that sat on his desktop, "I didn't need every reporter in town trying to make a name for himself asking whether Tim and I knew anything about Eliot's—well, *proclivities* is the nicest word I can come up with."

"Nobody believes Eliot was involved in that mess at the time he was working here. That all came much later."

"You and I know that. But it won't stop the media from noting their professional relationship when Tim's name comes up for consideration."

"What's the rumor about Tim, Paul?" I asked again.

The district attorney knew that despite my disrespect for Spindlis, he'd have to trust me to be on the lookout to run interference for him in case things got ugly. Reluctantly, he repeated the malicious story.

"There's someone out to get him. Someone who claims Tim's the one who introduced Eliot to the Emperors Club, to all his high-priced whores."

I caught my breath before assuring Battaglia that the story couldn't possibly be true. It wasn't that I thought better of Spindlis than that, I just knew he didn't have the money to cavort with the former governor at five thousand dollars a shot.

"No one will believe that about Tim. Those rumors simply won't fly."

"Of course Tim wasn't in that game, Alex. You understand that, don't you? Of course none of it's true."

FOURTEEN

Laura left me alone in the conference room with Nan Toth and two hot cups of coffee. I had given her orders not to disturb us for anything until Mercer arrived.

"Have you heard any gossip about Tim?" I asked Nan.

"Not a peep. He's on the way to the bench, isn't he? A done deal?"

"Would you figure him for a sex scandal?"

"Socks or no socks?" Nan burst into a laugh. Eliot Spitzer was alleged to have kept his footwear on during all his sexual engagements. "It's frightening to even think of Tim engaged in any kind of intimate act."

"That's the party line. Battaglia's one hundred percent in his corner, so that's my position too. Personally, I think it would humanize the stiff if he'd been right at Eliot's side as Client Number Ten. But it's only wishful thinking on my part."

"Can you imagine anything worse?"

"Yeah. A ménage with him and McKinney."

"You need to see a good doctor, Alex. That's a sick thought."

"Well, I'm betting Ellen Gunsher has been there," I said. "Humor me, Nan. It's been a withering twenty-four hours."

"So Battaglia's worried about the rumor?"

"Of course he is. But not about the substance behind it. He says he and McKinney have done their own internal investigation of Spindlis. The boss read him the riot act and said he'd be put out to pasture without his pension if there was any truth to it."

"But the damage is it's the kind of rumor that stays in the brain, right? Once people hear that Tim was Spitzer's mentor in the office—"

"That's the harm. It's obviously making Battaglia crazy. He hates to spend his time proving the negative. And McKinney's in there panting like a dog in heat, anxious to get Tim on his way so he can be promoted."

"I know how the boss hates this kind of thing. He's got you on such a tightrope."

"Tell me something good might actually happen soon."

"Okay. We've got our first couple of professional interpreters signed on. I've just spent twenty minutes with them and they'll be easy to work with. They've been qualified before the grand jury on other cases. Did some good work with the robbery squad."

"That's a start."

"I called Donovan to see when we can get going with the interviews." Nan flipped the pages of her legal pad. She was a striking brunette, about my height, with dark good looks and a gift for cross-examination that made her a great case partner. "I think he'd turn the whole thing over to us if he could. He sounds completely overwhelmed."

"So where are the girls and when do we get them?"

Nan had already sorted out which of the young women were at area hospitals, held overnight for observation or awaiting treatment, and which had been sent to detention camps. "You willing to start with two?"

"It worked for Noah."

"I followed up on your idea. Put a call in to Safe Horizon to see what their shelter situation is in Manhattan."

The nonprofit organization had been around for more than thirty years, and had done groundbreaking work in advocating for victims of violence in a criminal justice system that decades ago was hostile to many of their needs. Providing decent living conditions for women in battered relationships was one of the few means of offering them an alternative to life-threatening situations, and Safe Horizon had created havens in each borough of the city for just that purpose.

"Great. Baynes told me he wouldn't allow it."

"He's rethinking everything today, Alex. Have you ever been to the Manhattan shelter?"

"Yes. It's in Washington Heights. It's called Parrish House. One of the generous board members donated a small fortune to create a very livable space," I said.

Most animal shelters were in better shape than facilities for domestic survivor victims.

"Baynes wants to know the address. Is that a deal breaker?" Nan asked.

"It is for me."

In order to protect its residents from their offenders, Safe Horizon never released the location of its shelters. Victims were taken to the nearest police station house and waited there until staff was notified to pick them up to escort them to their new homes.

"Try and be flexible," Nan said, tapping her pen on the table. "They can clear two beds for us at Parrish House for four months. That's a clean, safe apartment with its own kitchen, some clothing, counseling on-site. It would be a wonderful way to transition these young women to a new life, and gain their trust at the same time."

"You're right. I have no issue with Donny, of course. I just don't think we put the street address in any reports, okay? There are twenty-five families living there who need to be safe. I don't want the feds, the mayor, and the media circulating the address. We can even take Donny there for a site visit if that satisfies him."

"I'll get moving on that. The first two that he's willing to give us are nineteen and seventeen years old. Both checked out fine medically. A bit undernourished and terribly skittish, I'm told, but we can begin our interviews tomorrow. He insists on a fed sitting in on each meeting."

"Will we have medical records by then?"

"Catherine's dealing with that right now."

"Do they have tattoos?"

"I realize you wanted this all solved yesterday, Alex. Just slow it down. No, we won't know that until we meet the women or see the medical records later today, if they're even that specific."

"Does anyone have a handle on how many people were actually on board, and how many have been accounted for?"

Nan was twisting her engagement ring as she talked. "Baynes said there's one guy—about thirty years old—who's the most cooperative. He wasn't part of the mutiny and he actually speaks some English. He's got relatives who immigrated to Texas and all he wants to do is get there."

"What's he given them?" I asked.

"They're going to set up with him today for the first time," Nan said. "Close as he can tell there were three hundred and ten people on board, less than thirty of them women."

"And three of the women are dead."

"At least three. Six people are still missing, by this guy's count."

"So what's next?" I asked. "Somebody out looking for snitches?"

Turning in a snakehead in a case of this magnitude would be a deep reservoir of insurance for someone in the criminal underground who was hoping to buy points with federal prosecutors.

"The task force is flooding the Ukrainian community looking for information, and Kelli's going to be working that piece of it for us. Marisa's got the lead on women from Eastern Europe who've been busted for prostitution in the five boroughs in the last few years."

"We do have the best team, don't you think? We get to add Sarah, who'll be back from maternity leave in another three weeks," I said, referring to the unit's deputy. "She'll keep all the daily perverts under control. Can't wait for that."

"What's Chapman up to?"

"Back at the morgue for more autopsies. They're starting with the third woman—the one who jumped in after her brother. They're going to see if he can ID the two Jane Does from last night as well. It would be good to know who they are, be able to find their families back home."

The heavy door creaked open as I was crumpling my second coffee cup. I threw it in the trash can before glancing over my shoulder.

"Oh, no. What is it they do to keep vampires away?" I said to Nan, groaning as I saw Lem Howell in the doorway.

"Time for me to get back to my office," Nan said.

"Not yet." I hoped she could see the desperation in my look. "Sit right down, please."

I didn't want to be alone with Lem.

"Good morning, ladies," he said, slicking back his pomaded hair and unbuttoning his overcoat.

"I'm about to get all the blood I've got left sucked out of me, Nan. Mr. Triplicate doesn't seem to understand that he is unwelcome, unwanted, and unwise to disturb us at this particular moment."

"Would you mind very much stepping out for a few minutes, Nan? Ms. Cooper seems to have forgotten her manners in dealing with an old friend."

"Nan's not going anywhere, Lem. C'mon. You have something to say, let's get it done."

Lem walked over behind my chair and put his hands on my shoulders, kneading them gently. "You shouldn't start the New Year all stressed out, Alexandra. I just need to chat with you for a few minutes."

Nan stood her ground and kept her poker face.

"What have I told you, Nan?" I asked. "Talented, tactile, and, oh, so transparent. That's what you are, Lem."

I swept his hands off my shoulders and stood up, walking to the end of the table.

"Maybe I taught you too well."

"Anything you want to say, you say in front of Nan. We're working together on this."

"And by *this*, which case do you mean, Alexandra? Is Nan helping you out on Karim Griffin?" He knew full well we weren't holed up together working on a cold-case serial rapist this morning.

"Well, if Karim's time is what you want to discuss, I'm happy to talk deal."

Lem had one hand in the pocket of his coat and the other across his chest inside his jacket, Napoleonic style. The Griffin case had taken a back burner in both our professional priorities.

"Don't you wish real life was like a television show? The big case comes along and everything else stands still for the detective and prosecutor? Yesterday's perps are suspended in time, the victims stop calling to ask for updates and orders of protection, new crimes don't happen every day, and the piles on your desk simply disappear?" I was talking to Nan, mocking Lem's advice in light of our second encounter last evening. "She and I are partners on everything, Lem. Tell us what you want."

He took a few steps in my direction, then pulled out a chair and sat down. He had put Nan out of range of his eye contact, isolating me at the end of the room.

"What have you done with Salma Zunega, Alexandra?"

"What have *I* done with her?"

"Where is she?"

I didn't answer.

"I told you yesterday that I was meeting with her this morning. Now, it would be just like you to have spirited her out of her home before I had that opportunity."

"I don't know where Salma is, Lem. Truly, I don't."

He was focused on me like a laser beam. "Nobody else knew about our appointment. I trusted you, Alex."

"With good reason. I'm sure your client knew about it. And I'm sure his father knew you were meeting with her too."

Lem leaned in at me with one elbow on the table. "You had no business interfering with Salma."

"She kept calling the cops yesterday. I was worried about her. Worried for her life. That used to be a good reason, Lem, when you were breaking me in to be a compassionate prosecutor."

"She didn't make those calls to nine-one-one."

"Now, how would you know that? Your client wasn't supposed to be in contact with her."

"Ethan wasn't in contact with her. I was. She talked to me."

"You're the one who told me she was crazy, Lem. Now, why would you believe her story if the nine-one-one tapes show in a black-and-white printout that the calls were made from her telephone? You can't have it both ways. Is Salma crazy or is she credible?"

"When she didn't show up at my office at nine A.M., I sent my investigator to her building, Alexandra. The cops are crawling all over it. Now, why is that?"

I took a deep breath and glanced at Nan.

"Don't be looking around for help. Where's Salma?"

"One would have to think the congressman has more to gain by her disappearance than I do, Lem. He and some other guy who showed up last night claiming to be the father of her child. Ethan's child, I thought she was. So you tell me what *you* know about it. You tell me what you and Salma discussed."

Lem chuckled. "I'll give you points for trying. You move the baby for safekeeping too?"

"What time was it you had your conversation with Salma?" I asked.

"Why is that important?"

"I just assumed you knew that her sister picked up the baby."

"You're playing with fire, Ms. Cooper," Lem said, wagging a finger at me as he stood up. "Scorching, red-hot, blistering—"

"Temper, temper, Mr. Howell. There's no jury here. What's your problem?"

"Not my problem, Alex. It's yours. Salma Zunega doesn't have a sister."

FIFTEEN

Mercer had just arrived at my office as Nan and I were moving our papers back in after Lem stormed out of the conference room.

"You opened the grand jury investigation, right?" I asked Nan, double-checking what she had told me she would do when I left her earlier to go to Battaglia's office.

"We're legal." It was the grand jury—not prosecutors—that had the power to issue subpoenas for the production of evidence.

"Laura's getting records from the phone company for Salma's landline and cell," I said to Mercer. "Better add the number of that woman you spoke with who claimed to be her sister. Lem Howell just hit us with the bombshell that she doesn't have one."

Mercer didn't rattle easily, but the thought that he had been misled about the possible endangerment of a child's life clearly upset him.

He checked his cell for the number he called yesterday to confirm what Salma had told him, then directed Laura to ready another subpoena to the phone company. "I'll get my man over there to expedite these records. You're going to fax the requests to him right away, okay? We'll have what we need before the end of the day."

Then he dialed the number and waited through ten rings that went unanswered.

"It's ringing dead. I'll call the lieutenant and put him onto Scully, Alex. You'd better tell Battaglia. We'll have to do an AMBER Alert on the kid. There's no luxury of waiting for Crime Scene to finish the search of her apartment."

The rules were different for infants and children than for adults. The news bulletins and neon highway signs would broadcast the description and images of the child the minute we reported that we didn't know her whereabouts. Whatever Ethan Leighton and Salma Zunega thought they had left of their private lives when they fought less than forty-eight hours ago would now be blasted all over the media.

"I don't even know the baby's name. There were no photos of her in the apartment last night," I said. "Call the guys who are processing the place and get me the details before I go see Battaglia."

Mercer reached Hal Sherman, who was supervising the Crime Scene Unit in 10A.

He told Hal what he needed and we waited for the callback.

"What did you do with the cell phone we recovered last night in her kitchen?" I asked.

"It's at the lab."

"Maybe she took photos of the kid," I said.

"I'll check that," Nan said, stepping around to my phone.

Hal was back to Mercer in less than three minutes. He listened to the information and then passed it along to me. "Ana. She goes by Ana Zunega. Nineteen months old. So far, not a photograph in the apartment."

"How can that be?"

"Hal got a scrip from the doorman. Baby's Caucasian, like her mother. Hispanic, very white skin. Wavy dark brown hair. Brown eyes. Says she left yesterday with a woman who resembles Salma and seemed perfectly happy."

"Brown hair, brown eyes, and no photograph. You can't send out an AMBER Alert like that."

"Start with Battaglia."

"Would you please tell Rose I'm on the way over?" I said to Laura.

I walked across the hall slowly, sliding past Tim Spindlis's office. It was just after noon and I would be lucky to catch him before he left for lunch. Rose motioned me right in, and I was pleased that he was alone.

"What now?"

"There's been a terrible development in the Zunega matter, Paul. Lem Howell did one of his drop-ins this morning. He's blaming me for making Salma vanish. I didn't want to tell him what we discovered at her apartment last night before Scully's ready to go public with something, but he—"

"Did he mention Tim?"

"Actually, no. Tim's name never came up in the conversation."

Battaglia looked up from whatever memo he was reading and squinted at me. "You're sure? How about mine?"

"Nothing, Boss. It's about the child. We've got a bigger problem than Tim's appointment."

His nose was back in the memo. "Bigger than my reputation, Alex? Keep your eye on that ball."

"Ethan Leighton's girlfriend doesn't have a sister, according to Lem. We don't know who the woman is who took the child from her apartment yesterday. Scully's going to have to issue an AMBER Alert before anyone's ready to answer all the questions about the case that the press will ask."

He picked his head up again. "Find the damn woman, then, will you? Get them cracking on getting the kid back."

I walked the quiet corridor that led away from Battaglia's office. It was lined with photographs of the grave and distinguished elected district attorneys—all men—who had held the position throughout the last two centuries. Until the 1970s, only six women had served on the staff of several hundred lawyers who labored for the political powerhouse. There were days like this when I wondered what was so desirable about butting up against the glass ceiling that tradition-ally capped the criminal court.

Laura was standing at the door to her cubicle as I crossed the hallway. "You've got Mike on line one."

"Give him to Mercer," I said. "I'm whipped."

"Mercer ducked out to pick up sandwiches for you, and Nan's back at her desk."

I took the receiver from Laura's hand. "I've had a miserable morning, Mike. I think I'd rather be at the morgue."

"I haven't exactly been picnicking, either, Coop. Listen, I've got—"

"Battaglia's all over me. He wants to know why you can't find Salma."

"Be careful what you wish for, kid. She's not missing anymore," Mike said. "And she's very dead."

I sat in Laura's chair and rubbed my eyes with my free hand. "Where is she?"

"At the bottom of a well, twelve feet down. Headfirst."

"And the baby?"

"No, no, Coop. No sign of the little girl."

"Thank God," I said, beginning to process what he had just told me about Salma. "Hey, Mike? How far out of town did they find her? I mean, where's the well?"

"Right here. Right close to home."

"We've got wells in Manhattan?"

"It's the first one I've seen. All dried up now, but it's a well."

My mind was racing visually up the streets and avenues of the city, lined cheek-to-jowl with brownstones, tenements, high-rise buildings, and housing projects.

"You've lost me, Mike. What kind of house had a well?"

"I guess if you owned a mansion, you had a well, Ms. Cooper. This one just happens to be at the mayor's house," Mike said. "I'd like to see Battaglia's face when you tell him the body was found at Gracie Mansion."

SIXTEEN

"Nice diversionary tactic you worked for us," Mike said, as he opened the passenger door of Mercer's car to help me out. "Keep your head down and walk as fast as you can on the paved path around the side of the house."

"What tactic? What's all the action on East End Avenue?"

East End was one of the shortest avenues in Manhattan, a mix of small, elegant town houses, two of the city's finest private schools for girls, a quiet park, and some fancy apartments. It started at Seventy-ninth Street and ran just twelve blocks north. Mercer had driven as close as he could to the entrance—the rear door, actually—of Gracie Mansion, past the small guardhouse on Eighty-eighth Street that was a fixed post for an NYPD cop. It was just after three in the afternoon.

"Your pal Lem Howell let out the news that Salma went missing from her apartment last night and how worried the congressman is about her. The press hounds have staked out her building, which required Scully to send a few uniformed teams for crowd control."

"Nobody's noticed yet that right across the street we're in the process of recovering her body."

"You mean—?"

"She's still in the well."

There were dark clouds overhead and a raw chill in the air.

"But you're sure it's Salma?"

"Yeah."

"How?"

I was trying to keep up with Mike as he walked off the path to the north of the handsome old building on the lawn that sloped away toward a long wrought-iron fence.

"We lowered Katie Cion down to take some photos. That's one tough broad," Mike said. "Good thing the department bought out all the Polaroid film on the market when they stopped producing it. I don't know what CSU will do when they run out of it. The super across the street made the ID from one of those."

Katie Cion was one of the few women assigned to the Homicide Squad. She had earned the gold shield with some clever and courageous detective work on a gang initiation slaying in the Bronx a year ago. Petite and agile—maybe five three when she drew herself full up to salute Scully at her promotion—she was as fearless as she was smart.

I stepped between a stand of trees and around some neatly trimmed hedges. I was just ten feet from the wide esplanade that formed a sinuous border along the water's edge, staring at the churning gray river.

"Welcome to Hell Gate," Mike said.

I had been to the mansion before, for receptions and ceremonies, but had never been out on the lawn to see the dramatic vista.

"Seems like the right name for it today."

Mike pointed straight out across the river. "It's been the right name for it for four centuries. That's what the Dutch called this narrow strait in the sixteen hundreds. Treacherous tides and a watery grave for more ships than we'll ever know."

He pulled aside more branches and I could see the setup for the recovery operation. Most of the blue–and–white police vehicles had been left on East End Avenue, where they would be presumed to be part of the security detail. Four green Parks Department vans ringed a small area of the drive, and one NYPD Emergency Services truck was wedged against the fence on top of a flower bed that had been put to sleep for the winter.

Mike led me between the vans, into the circle of police officers and park employees who were gathered around the gaping hole in the ground. The chief medical examiner himself—Chet Kirschner—was overseeing the procedure.

"Hello, Alex," he said, greeting me with a handshake and an explanation. He was a quiet man, well-respected for his medical brilliance and his dignity with the dead. "We're about to bring the woman up now. I want to do this without causing any more post-mortem artifacts than are inevitable in this kind of situation."

Kirschner would need to establish a cause of death, complicated by the disposal of the body in such an unusual location and the injuries that might have been sustained in the dumping.

"Who found her?" I asked.

"Three kids from the projects. Taft Houses over on a Hundred and twelfth Street. Lieutenant Peterson has them up in the squad right now," Mike said. "They weren't supposed to be playing around here, of course, so when the Parks Department cleanup crew came to get them out, they were already screaming about the lady upside down in the hole."

"Was the well covered?"

"Apparently it's been covered for as long as anyone can remember. There's the lid."

A four-foot-square plank of plywood pieces stood against the side of one of the vans. Some of the boards were warped and appeared to have rotted on the sides.

"How old are the kids you're talking about?"

"Fourteen, fifteen."

"By any chance, are they Mexican? Could they have known Salma through the immigrant community?"

"Not that easy, Coop. African American."

Three of the powerfully built men from the NYPD's Emergency Services Unit were maneuvering around the opening of the well. They had an empty gurney standing ready, and they were talking to someone who was out of my sight within their truck.

"Anybody think they had something to do with Salma's death?"

Mike shook his head. "Too early to know what we've got. They were probably just hanging out on their way home from the playground."

Fifteen-acre Carl Schurz Park, directly adjacent to the mansion, was one of the most family-friendly places in the city. A beautifully landscaped oasis, its playground, dog run, and hockey court were a Mecca for children. Although I had grown up in the suburbs and attended a public high school in Harrison, I had visited often with friends who'd gone to elite schools like Brearley and Chapin, right next door to the park.

"What are they saying?"

"The ringleader—Jalil—he says they were just fooling around, trying to go down by the fence to see whether they could climb over it to get on the esplanade. Got curious because the ground was covered with snow, but the board on top of the well wasn't. They didn't know it was a well, of course. Just wanted to see what was there."

"You mean in all these years, the cover wasn't—I don't know how you'd keep it on—but it wasn't nailed down?"

"That's the thing. Sure it was. There were large nails in each corner," Mike said, pointing to the areas of deterioration. "But it looks like you just had to pull on them to lift them up."

I walked over and touched one end with the leather glove on my hand.

"Watch the nails. You could get a mean case of tetanus scratching up against one of them."

"Ready for me?" I recognized Katie Cion's voice and turned to the rear of the EMS truck. She was inside, trying to keep warm. "Hey, Alex. Not exactly the job description I got with the shield, is it?"

Katie's jacket was off—probably to make it easy for her to get in and out of the well. She was dressed in loose-fitting jeans and a thermal sweater, no shoes and thick socks on her feet, wearing latex gloves with a mask over her nose and mouth.

The hefty sergeant in charge had helped his men jerry-rig a series of ropes, attached on one end to the bumper of the EMS truck. Katie climbed down and let him fit her into a harness that the trio would lower into the well. It would be her responsibility to hold on to and guide Salma Zunega's body while the team hoisting the ropes brought them both to the surface.

Dr. Kirschner was giving her instructions, explaining how best to grab the dead woman around the waist, if at all possible, and attach a similar harness to her corpse. She would position Salma's back to herself, and try to do a reverse rappel with her feet braced against the old well walls.

"Why are they sending Katie down?" I asked.

"A few too many donuts in the bellies of those boys, Coop. Katie's the only one who fits. She's been in twice to scope it out and take photos. Came up with this blanket—we're thinking it was covering Salma's body when she was brought out of her apartment. Katie'll do fine."

Mercer tried to steer me away. "We can wait on the porch."

"No, thanks." I was looking at the pulls in the yarn on the lush off-white blanket that had been Salma's body bag. "What about rigor? How can Katie move her?"

We knew that Mercer had seen Salma alive at eight o'clock last evening. By eleven, she was missing from her home and, if the blood on the corkscrew opener was hers, may have already suffered a mortal wound.

"Kirschner doesn't think it will be a problem," Mike said. "Dropping the body in here last night was like putting her in a freezer. Unlikely there was any onset of rigor mortis yet because of that. And they've dropped some Styrofoam panels in to line the walls, to lessen the chance of any postmortem bruising."

Katie checked her harness, stood on the lip of the well, and gave the men the signal to begin. They first had to lift her several inches above the ground so that she didn't drop off the side, and I watched with great admiration as she slipped down out of view, where she got to work strapping the body to her own.

Within minutes, Katie called to the men to pull her out. The sergeant and another man dropped to the ground beside the opening and the two larger detectives steadily worked the ropes, hand-over-hand.

The bare feet of the dead woman came into view before the top of Katie's head, as she twisted herself to stay centered.

"Got it!" the sergeant shouted. "Hang on, Katie. Great job."

Chet Kirschner stepped forward to put his gloved hands on the legs of Salma Zunega. "Gently, men."

The crumpled and broken body of the woman came into full view. Her mouth was wide-open and it appeared her skull had split practically in half. Stones and small rocks were embedded in her face and on her shoulders, and when her head swung around in my direction, I could see a hole in the front of her neck that was caked with dried blood.

She was clad only in a teddy—a pale yellow piece of lingerie that was encrusted with snow. Her upper back and places on her legs and arms were imprinted with even lines that formed rectangles on her skin, as though she had been pressed against the bars of a cage.

I didn't move. I was fixated on the face of the young mother who had died so violently. Why had she denied her earlier calls to 911, and then failed to make the last one in time to save her life? And after the odd back-and-forth about those calls, would anyone have responded if she had managed to press Send?

The ESU men followed Kirschner's directions, while Mike and Mercer held on to Katie Cion until the body was removed from her grasp and lowered onto the gurney.

"It looks like she was tortured," I said softly. It would be Kirschner's job to sort out which of the injuries had been fatal. "Why is her skin so pink?"

"It's the lividity, Alex," Kirschner said.

I knew that the blood settled into the skin's capillaries as they dilated after circulation ceased—usually causing a purple discoloration in the dependent parts of the body.

"It's often this light pink," he went on, "when a body has been recovered in icy conditions."

"Let's get her out of here before the vultures across the street smell blood," Mike said. "Can we transport her in the EMS vehicle so we don't have to bring a marked morgue bus in here?"

"That's fine," Kirschner said.

Two of the ESU guys raised the gurney up from the ground and I heard it lock into place. Katie Cion had already gotten into the rear of the truck to put on her jacket and boots. The men draped a sheet over the twisted form of Salma Zunega.

The four ESU men surrounded the gurney and started to wheel it down the slight incline. The ground was uneven, and as they moved ahead Salma's body shifted on its temporary bed and her leg dropped over the side of the gurney.

"Hold it a minute," I said, from a step or two behind the group. "Could you just stop while I take a quick look? I think I saw something on her leg."

The sergeant who was trying to bring this difficult operation to a successful close rolled his eyes at Mike as I moved in next to the body.

Chet Kirschner was there before me. With his latex glove, he moved the left leg of the mangled corpse a bit farther apart from the right and brushed some dirt away from the exposed skin. On the upper left thigh was a familiar marking.

"It's a rose, Alex. There's a tattoo here of a small rose."

SEVENTEEN

"Salma Zunega must have been trafficked into this country," I said.

Visions of what that meant for her, what her first years in New York must have been like, flashed through my head. Like the Ukrainians who had just survived their journey, I knew only too well what that life was like, I had met scores of women like Salma throughout my career. And far too many of them had shared her ultimate fate.

"It would have been years ago, no doubt. Property of the same scumbag snakehead who was running the *Golden Voyage*," Mercer said. "Property of the rose."

We were standing on the front steps of Gracie Mansion, facing the river from a higher vantage point than the slope on which the well sat.

"Good to know the American dream still works, Coop. Somebody in the family spends his life savings to smuggle his kid over the border, and she winds up being the best-looking one so she makes a living on her back instead of picking grapes."

"Can we at least wait inside, Mike? It's freezing."

The mayor had directed us to stay at the scene until he could get here. He didn't want any news released until he had a clear understanding of how this discovery had unfolded.

The door had been opened for us by the housekeeper, a short dark-skinned woman with a generous smile who had worked there, she said, since the earliest days of the Koch administration.

I followed her inside, through the large reception space with its distinctive black-and-white diamond-shaped flooring. "I think you'll be most comfortable here in the library," she said, depositing us in the handsome room with floor-to-ceiling windows, denticulated cornices, and furniture that looked original to the building.

"I don't believe in coincidence," Mike said. "Not on this scale."

"Neither do I."

"So go back to the night before last. You've got a shipload of immigrants desperate to get ashore, who panic when they can see the land, smell it, practically touch it, but nobody shows up to take them ashore."

"Except what looks like a government boat coming to intercept them," Mercer said.

"And right up the street from the mayor's house, a congressman goes nuts about something. Was it a baby who wasn't really sick by the time she got to the hospital?"

"And if it wasn't Leighton's baby, why would he care so much?" I asked.

"We know for sure he was drunk and flying downtown on the highway," Mercer said, "which is when he got into an accident."

"One girl with a rose tattoo, probably Ukrainian, washes up in Queens. Her Mexican comadre starts playing phone tag with emergency operators, then someone shows up to visit her last night and sticks a corkscrew in her throat before he takes her out for a stroll," Mike said, fingering one of the old cannonballs that sat on the mantel over the fireplace. "And deposits her here, in a well at Gracie Mansion."

"Where, for some reason, the mayor most definitely did not want Scully to post his men this morning," I said.

"We need to get back to the squad and chart this all out," Mike said. "It's part of one big pie, and we just got to figure out who the baker is. What's holding Hizzoner up?"

Mercer was staring out the window, then abruptly walked out of the library without saying a word.

"Maybe we can get the housekeeper to show us around before Statler gets here," I said. "You think it would help your noncoincidental theory to see any other parts of the house?"

"Better to do it without telling her. Where did Mercer go?"

The elegant building with its custard yellow frame and green trim was one of the only Federal Period wooden houses still standing in Manhattan.

Several years ago when I was dating a reporter who worked at NBC, we were frequently included in cocktail parties and dinners hosted by the former administration. I knew a few things about America's first official mayoral residence and its careful restoration a decade ago, but I couldn't figure how it would play as a site in this widening investigation.

"Give him a minute. He must have seen something going on outside," I said.

The housekeeper appeared in the doorway. "Excuse me, miss. We're expecting fifty people for tea at four o'clock. Will that be fine?"

"No, no, no," Mike said. "Tea?"

"Yes, sir. We have tea tours several times a week."

"Well, there'll be no tea today. You call out to the guardhouse and tell them no one comes in this afternoon until Mayor Statler gets here."

She appeared to be thinking about talking back to Mike, but changed her mind and withdrew.

"Want to look upstairs?" Mike asked me. "That's the private quarters. The master suite and guest bedrooms."

I stepped to the doorway and saw the velvet rope that blocked the staircase off from public access. "I'd rather not be snooping around without Statler's permission."

"Coop, it's 'the people's house.' That's what the mayor always says."

"Wait."

Mercer came back inside, rubbing his hands together for warmth. "I'm not sure I agree with you, Mike. I mean about this whole mess being connected to Gracie Mansion. Look out the window."

We both followed Mercer there.

"See the well? And the fence right behind it? I'll bet whoever did this was on his way to the river with the body. You dump the girl in there, just over the fence, let the currents of Hell Gate do their job, and nobody sees her again till it's spring and she floats to the surface."

"Maybe so," Mike said. "Maybe the river was the final destination. That makes sense. But what, you think the killer just got lucky and found a well? Nope, it's not that coincidental. Too convenient."

"Please don't tell me you're looking to jam up the mayor," I said.

"Course not. I just think we need to spend a little more time getting him to answer questions, before you have to wind up inviting him to the grand jury to do that."

"Battaglia would probably pay admission to see him testify."

Mike was pacing impatiently, rolling the heavy cannon shot in his hands like Captain Queeg nervously playing with steel balls while his crew planned their mutiny. "The city gives you a house like this to live in, with all its history, and most of these guys would rather crib somewhere else. Can't figure it. I'll give him another fifteen minutes and we're out of here. We got work to do."

"You've never been assigned to the mansion, have you?" I asked. Every detail of the house was a perfect reflection of the Federal Period. The antique convex mirror facing the windows was topped with a gilded eagle. Each sofa and chair had been upholstered in fabric copied from old designs and paintings. A block away from Salma Zunega's modern high-rise was this graceful step back in time that looked like it belonged on a movie set.

"Dignitaries and protocol, Coop? Not exactly my bailiwick. But when I was in the Academy and the British prime minister stayed here for a week, they needed extra men for the detail."

"Let me guess. Mr. Gracie was a warrior, right? That's how come you know so much."

"Nope. It really started long before Gracie," Mike said, replacing the cannonball on the mantel and leading me back to the window. "You're standing on one of the most historic sites in the entire city, which has owned the mansion and this point of land since 1896. Back in the 1640s, when New Amsterdam was a little village on the southern tip of Manhattan, this was a farm owned by a Dutchman and called Horn's Hook. An English family took it over a century later, since it was one of the choicest properties in the city."

"Why so?"

"Can't you see for yourself?" Mike said, pulling back the curtain. "Think like a general once in a while, not like a lit major."

"I'll try," I said, shrugging while Mercer tugged at a strand of my hair.

"First you've got this high promontory of land, looking out on the turbulent body of water. From the roof of this building, you can actually see all the other boroughs in the city. It was rich soil for farming and there were oysters and fish of all kinds teeming right down on the shore. Sort of like your place on the Vineyard, kid."

"I get that."

"The family that owned the land was named Walton, and they picked the wrong side during the Revolution."

"Loyalists?" Mercer asked.

"Exactly. When Washington sent his men to New York in 1776 to prepare the defense against the British, American troops seized this home and built two forts—one here at Horn's Hook and one across the way at Hallett's Point in Queens—to block the passage by boat through Hell Gate."

"So the front lawn right out here was a major battleground in the Revolutionary War?" Mercer asked.

"Yeah. The king's army attacked from Long Island, and from all these little islands in the river, bombing the life out of our rebels. The Walton house, tucked inside the fort right here, was set on fire by a shell and burned to the ground. Cannonballs just like this one brought the place down. This point remained occupied by the British until 1783."

I never tired of learning of the city's past through Mike's boundless enthusiasm for history.

"Gracie didn't come along until later?" I said.

"Archibald Gracie. Born in Scotland, but sailed to New York right after the British evacuated to start a commercial enterprise. He recognized the importance of the tobacco industry, so he moved to Virginia for a few years to make contacts there, until he married and returned here. Took a big house in the heart of the city—lower Broadway—where he both lived and conducted all his business."

"What was the business?" Mercer asked.

"Importing European goods in exchange for tobacco. The man got rich, Mercer. Very, very rich. Began buying his own ships. Came time for him to own a country house. Just like Coop."

Mike and I had come to our strong friendship from such different backgrounds that he was always poking fun at my privileged roots. My father, Benjamin Cooper, was a cardiologist whose invention of a half-inch piece of plastic tubing when I was twelve years old had changed the way heart surgery was performed all over the world. The Cooper-Hoffman valve had afforded me a great education and a financial cushion—even in the difficult days of our recent recession—that made public service a far easier lifestyle for me than for most of my colleagues.

"I thought you'd forgotten about the Vineyard. You haven't been there in way too long."

"My French isn't good enough, I guess."

"We still speak English in Chilmark," I said, pinching his cheek. "Bring a date. You weren't alone on New Year's Eve, were you?"

"Seems so far back I can hardly remember," Mike said. "Now,

in 1799, at the same time City Hall was going up—right where Manhattan ended—Archibald Gracie started to build his country estate."

"Man, it's hard to imagine East Eighty-eighth Street as the country," Mercer said.

"But it was. In fact, there was so much cholera in the city that wealthy New Yorkers built this colony of summer places up along the river, trying to escape to clean fresh air. It's more than five miles north of the original city walls, and the easiest way to get here at that time was by boat. It was a world apart from Manhattan."

"So throughout the last three centuries," I said, thinking of all the modern construction that recycled precious space on an island that had experienced such radical development since it was colonized, "there have only been two houses built on this site. That's really remarkable for New York."

"C'mon, let me show you the second floor. It's like a museum."

"Statler will be here any minute," I said.

"Suit yourself. You must have been the kind of kid who never got caught with your hand in the cookie jar. Take a chance every now and then, why don't you?" Mike started out of the library across the reception area to the staircase. He moved the stanchion holding the velvet rope and headed up the steps with Mercer.

I could hear a commotion coming from the hallway that led to the rear of the house, and then Vin Statler's voice. "Where are they? In the library or out by the well?"

He charged toward me from the dining room at the head of a group of three men. One was Rowdy Kitts and the other was a second detective I recognized who was also assigned to bodyguard him. "Never mind. Here they—"

Statler raised an arm and shouted when he saw Mike and Mercer on their way upstairs to the private quarters. "Where the hell do you think you're going?"

"It's okay, Mr. Mayor, they're the good guys, remember?"

Rowdy said, shaking Mike's hand as he came back down the steps and replacing the stanchion.

Statler charged past me into the library and introduced me to his other bodyguard.

"Sit down, Alex. Gentlemen? Have a seat in here. What is it you're trying to make of these events exactly?"

Mercer joined me on the burgundy velvet sofa but Mike wouldn't sit. He knew the mayor was trying to stake out a superior position and refused to let him have it. It was imposing enough that he was flanked by two NYPD detectives.

"I'd like to figure out why somebody thought your house was the appropriate dumping place for the congressman's dead girlfriend."

"The poor young woman lived across the street, Chapman. I certainly didn't know that until yesterday's briefing."

"See, sir, I just don't believe in coincidence."

"You don't have to. This mansion happens to be in the middle of a beautiful park. It's an attractive nuisance. There are teenagers and hooligans running around the park late at night all year. The house sits dark and empty most evenings anyway."

"Not always empty, sir. Tea and crumpets, I understand."

The mayor was fuming. "There are tourists several days a week. There are occasional dinners and celebrations. In the summer there's always a tent out on the lawn so we can entertain. But the grounds, including the park, cover a great deal of acreage."

"And there's a police guard at the gatehouse twenty-four/seven," Mike said.

"Well, I guess he was working twenty-three/seven last night, wouldn't you say? We've had muggings in the park before. We've had women assaulted there over the years. Wouldn't be the first cop to fall asleep on the job, would he?"

"Afraid not, Your Honor. So you're thinking this just happened to be the closest well in town?"

Statler took a step toward Mike. "Or perhaps, Chapman, someone decided to try to embarrass me. Has that thought occurred to you?"

"It had, actually. Maybe you'd like to sit down with us and talk about it. Give us some ideas about who you think would have a reason to do that."

"It's your job to come up with ideas, Detective. And with suspects. It's my job to run this city."

"I'm just wondering why you put up such a stink this morning when the commissioner asked if we could use the mansion here to stage his operation. Of course, that's when those of us looking for Salma Zunega had no idea where she'd been dumped."

"One had nothing to do with the other, Chapman. Are you suggesting I intended to keep you away from here because I knew where this—this whore—was disposed of? That's a shocking suggestion."

I was pained at his choice of words for the dead woman.

"Maybe you ought to rethink your language, Mr. Mayor," I said.

Statler put his hands in his pockets and looked at me. "Do you really think that Paul Battaglia wants you to ambush me? I've got nothing to say about this matter. I came up here to get answers from *you*."

I stood up, practically face-to-face with Vin Statler. "We haven't got any answers to give you, Mr. Mayor. This wasn't the direction we were hoping the case would take."

"How did the girl die?"

"Too early to know."

"And here? Was she killed on this property?" Statler was agitated, and clearly not used to being the last to know.

"That's unlikely."

"Congressman Leighton, what does he have to say about this?" Statler looked from me to Mike to Mercer. "I see, I see. You're not giving me anything. You're treating me like I'm irrelevant."

"We haven't spoken with Leighton yet. I'll call his lawyer when we leave here."

"I've got a lawyer, too, Alex. I've got the best. You call Justin Feldman from now on if you have any questions for me."

"Good choice, sir," I said, venturing a smile at the mayor. "Smart man. I may need to come back and see the grounds again. Check the access to the property from every angle. May I call him for that? Or would you prefer I stay in touch with Detective Kitts?"

"My assistant will make all those arrangements, as you need them. Roland, will you give her Nancy's number?"

Mike had walked to the window and pulled back the curtain, watching as the CSU men worked at processing the scene before dusk.

"And you, Chapman, you like your assignment? Homicide's a big deal in the department, isn't it?"

"I like it fine, sir."

"Then show me the proper respect, Detective. Do I look like a common criminal to you?" The mayor smoothed his tie and tried to joke with Mike.

"You see that water out there, Your Honor?"

"The East River? Are you talking about the river?"

"I'm talking about what people call a river."

Vin Statler smirked. "But you're going to prove to me you're smarter than I am, Chapman, aren't you? I guess I was supposed to say it's an estuary. It's the place where the river and the ocean mix, is that where you're going?"

"Sorry, sir. But it's not an estuary either."

Statler's expression changed, and the men standing beside him stiffened. "What are you doing here, Chapman?"

"See, it's a tidal strait, Your Honor. It's a water passage between Manhattan and Long Island. It's not an actual river because rivers flow from freshwater sources like springs and mountain runoffs. This? This connects on both ends to the Atlantic Ocean. So it's a strait, really, but because of the tides, it seems to flow just like a river."

"What's your point?" The three words came out sharply, like bullets at a target.

"Congressmen, governors, prosecutors, mayors, police commissioners. They don't necessarily look like common criminals, to answer your question. But just like this river, sir, things aren't always what they appear to be."

EIGHTEEN

"You went way too far, Mike."

"He pressed the wrong buttons with me."

"Your buttons are so loosely attached that anybody pressing them might get tangled in the threads," I said. "I'm only surprised Battaglia hasn't beeped me yet to try to rein you in."

We were just leaving the back steps of Gracie Mansion.

"Relax. Statler will never admit to being humiliated by the likes of us. You want to see how Hal's doing with Salma's apartment?"

"Sure."

"Here, Alex," Mercer said, reaching into the pocket of his overcoat. "This should get you past the photographers without a problem."

He handed me a black knit watch cap, and I stood at the curb, twisting my hair into a knot and pulling the hat down to cover half of my face.

"Perfect. You look like an ordinary mook," Mike said. "Nobody'd ever make you."

Cops had set up wooden horses to keep the paparazzi back from the entrance of the building. "Why don't we back-door it?"

No one seemed to notice as we trekked around to the rear. Mike buzzed, and this time, with a uniformed cop at his side and the camera focused on the badge Mike held up next to his face, we were let in immediately.

When we stepped off the elevator on the tenth floor, the apartment door was ajar and Hal waved us in from the foyer. "Hey, guys. Alex. You here to get in my way?"

"Nah. Just trying to make sense of all this," Mike said. "ESU did a great job getting the body out."

"So I heard. My second team's over there."

"You alone?"

"No. Jack Egan's beginning to work the back rooms."

"What's taking you so long, Hal? You've been here half the day."

"Interruptions like you, pal. Explaining things to all the bigwigs."

"Like who?"

"Like Scully. Like the mayor's office. Like Leighton's old man, who thinks he had a right to come in here 'cause his son paid for the pad. I'm trying to get it done, Mikey. You want to help? Gloves and booties, please."

"Have you found anything of interest yet?" I asked as Mike passed us each another pair of latex gloves.

"Sarge called from ESU. Took a white wool blanket covered with blood out of the bottom of the well," Hal said. "Jack found white fibers in one of the trash bins they use to take recyclables down in the service elevator."

"We saw some of those out in back."

"That must be how whoever did it got her out of here."

"But she had these awful gridlike marks on her shoulders," I said. "What do you think could have caused those? Is there any surface like that in the apartment?"

We were following Hal through the living room toward the kitchen.

"I'm not sure exactly what you mean. Nothing in here that I've seen."

"I can do a sketch of it for you," I said.

"Coop's not content unless she's butting into everybody's job," Mike said, throwing up his hands. "The ME will tell you what did that to her skin."

Two people rarely saw the same things when they looked at a dead body. The medical examiner searched for signs of the fatal injury, cops for any clues that might offer a solution to the killer's identity, and often I was hoping—quite unrealistically—that the corpse would tell me how its final moments were spent.

"Any word yet on your corkscrew?" Hal asked.

"Human blood. Now they'll have what they need to compare," Mike said.

"Isn't it odd that the place would be in such good order but the killer would leave that behind?" I asked.

"You wanna know what I think?"

"Yes."

Hal planted himself in the middle of the living room floor. "First of all, Salma wasn't entertaining a stranger, right?"

"She may have started life here as a hooker," Mike said, explaining the tattoo to Hal. "Can't rule that out entirely."

"This guy knows the building well enough to get himself in, and there's nothing in the apartment to suggest a struggle."

"So it was a blitz attack," Mercer said.

"She's in her nightie," Hal went on. "Gets rid of her kid for the evening—no word on that front?"

"Nothing."

"Sets out the vino and the glasses, and when she goes into the kitchen, *bam!* Her buddy gets her into a chokehold and jabs the tip of the screw right into her neck."

"Good thinking, Hal," Mike said. "He's either a surgeon or a damn good wine steward, right?"

"I'd expect blood to be everywhere," I said, holding my hand to my throat as Hal spoke.

"And it was, Counselor. And it was."

"No, Hal, there was nothing when we got here last night except the wine opener."

"Bleach, Alex. He bleached the kitchen floor and sink. Just took a couple of minutes to sponge it down. Might have been more blood on him than on the tile. But we picked up some spatter in there. Probably thought he'd gotten the corkscrew too. Then he sprayed air freshener to mask the smell."

"The princess wouldn't know from cleaning the kitchen floor. The only bleach she cares about is the kind that keeps her hair blond."

"What does that tell you about him?" I asked. "Chance he's an ex-con?"

We had seen lots of cases recently in which men sent to jail by DNA evidence continued their criminal ways when released, but came to crime scenes armed with condoms when they raped or prepared to destroy evidence as they departed.

"Or he watches too much TV," Hal said. "Everybody's an expert on TV, you know? Every lazy slob thinks he could do my job. Find this guy soon and get a warrant for his laundry bag. He's gonna have blood all over his shirtsleeves, if I'm right about how he was holding her. And blood on his shoes. It had to drip on his shoes."

"I should be that lucky I find him soon," Mike said. "Or her."

"Her?" I asked.

"Why, you think it couldn't be a broad? You don't figure Claire Leighton had a grudge to settle? Maybe while Salma was waiting for her date, Claire knocked on the door and the girls had a catfight."

My stomach churned a bit. I'd never thought about Leighton's wife as a possible suspect, but there was good reason to consider her.

I was scanning the clean white walls and stainless steel appliances, looking for any signs of blood, but there were none. "Too clean for a catfight."

"Just like a dame to straighten up the mess."

"Hey, Hal!" His partner was shouting for him from the other end of the apartment. "Bring your equipment and get your ass down here quick."

Mike stepped aside so Hal could go first, stopping to pick up his camera from the living room sofa.

"Whatcha got, Jack? You find a skeleton in the closet?" Hal made his way quickly down the hall to the master bedroom.

Jack Egan was standing on a stepladder. At his feet were half a dozen cardboard shoe boxes—all designer labels—with their lids removed, and another two dozen stacked on shelves in the closet.

"Better than that," Jack said, opening the cover of the box he was holding. "I found a gold mine."

Like the one in Jack Egan's hands, the boxes on the floor were filled with money. Mike crouched beside them and scooped out a fistful of bills.

"Hundred-dollar bills—Ben Franklins all," he said, playing the edges of them as he counted the wads. "Each one of these little wrappers holds ten thousand dollars. I know Coop would just as soon have the shoes, but we're probably looking at a million or more in cash."

"What the hell was this broad doing with all that money?" Hal asked. "Where'd it come from, do you think?"

"You'll be the first to know, Hal. Meanwhile, you better tell your other team to check the bottom of the well for loose change."

NINETEEN

"You don't want to be where the money is, Coop," Mike said. We had taken the elevator down to the rear entrance, making our way out past the lineup of shopping carts left behind the building, no doubt, by lazy deliverymen who'd been relieved of their bags.

"Why not?"

"By the time it's sorted and accounted for, some muckety-muck will demand that Internal Affairs empties the pockets of all of us who were up there. Big money scares me."

"Why don't we go back down to my office? We can spend the evening putting this whole thing together. It's so much more quiet than the squad."

"She's right, Mike," Mercer said.

"You take her with you. I'll stop by the morgue and then meet you there."

The damp cold and darkness didn't seem to bother the press corps. They were still staked out on East End Avenue, hoping for a sighting of someone related to the scandal of the disgraced congressman or news of the missing woman.

I got in Mercer's car and as he made a U-turn to get on the

Seventy-ninth Street entrance to the drive, I called Nan to tell her everything that had happened. I also asked if she could round up at least one of the other women in our group so that we could reboot our investigation over takeout and triple doses of caffeine.

My next call was to Donovan Baynes. I hesitated before dialing, wondering whether he was passing information to his old friend Ethan Leighton, but his position in charge of the task force left me no choice but to tell him. He was as intrigued by the news of Salma Zunega's abduction and murder, and the rose tattoo, as we were. Baynes agreed to participate in our evening meeting.

Traffic slowed us as we inched downtown on the FDR Drive. I put the phone in my pocket, my head on the headrest, and closed my eyes.

"Things okay with you, Alex?" Mercer asked.

"Everything's been good till this series of disasters."

"Your folks?"

"Happy to spend some downtime with me," I said, shaking off my exhaustion to talk about something more personal than the investigation. Mercer knew that my parents, who retired to a small island in the Caribbean, had spent the week leading up to Christmas with me in the city, before going out West to visit with my brothers and their kids in Colorado.

"And Luc?"

I had flown to Paris the day after Christmas. Luc Rouget, the divorced restaurateur I'd been dating, lived in a small village in the south of France. But we had planned a romantic interlude in the glamorous city of lights.

"We had a wonderful time together. He'll be here next month," I said. He was making progress in his business plans to open here in Manhattan, where decades ago his father had created one of the world's classic French restaurants, Lutèce. "You and Vickee will have to have dinner with us."

"Happy to do that. You know how I feel about this."

Mercer had become so grounded and pleased with his newfound

family life that he had taken to urging me to ease up on my professional duties and put my relationship with Luc in full gear.

"It scares me a bit, Mercer. I've told you that."

We were slowed to a standstill in the underpass next to the United Nations. "It wouldn't mean anything if it didn't do that."

"It's different," I said, looking at him. "I know these decisions aren't easy for anyone, but Luc doesn't live here. Even if he gets the restaurant going, he's in this country six months a year at best. I'd have to give up all of this—"

"Give up what? Chasing these animals around town? Righting all the wrongs of the world? You've proven you can do some of that. Time to turn a page, maybe."

"I'm afraid I like it too much." I knew it seemed strange to my friends outside the criminal justice system when we described our jobs in such upbeat terms. But the satisfaction in doing justice—convicting the guilty, exonerating the innocent, and trying to restore some measure of relief to those victimized—was a constant source of pride. "I can't see myself sitting on a stool behind the cash register in Mougins, asking people if they enjoyed the special of the day."

Mercer laughed. "The man's too smart to have you doing that, Alex."

"That's why his first wife split."

"Is that what makes you leery, my friend, or is it the intimacy? The fear that if you give in to happiness something will come along to destroy your center again?"

I had been engaged to marry a medical student I'd fallen in love with while I was at law school in Virginia. Together Adam Nyman and I had bought our dream house on Martha's Vineyard, and I'd allowed myself to plot out all the fantasies of a long life together. On the drive from Charlottesville to Chilmark for the wedding weekend, Adam died when his car plunged from a bridge on the interstate to the riverbed below.

I bit my lip. "Maybe that, Mercer."

"Why is it you fall in love with guys who are impossible to fit into your life? First Jed, then Jake, now Luc. You've got to work at it some yourself, Alex. This guy is mad for you, isn't he?"

"Who set you up for this chat?" I said, reaching to turn on the car radio. "Nina? Joan?"

My two closest friends had teamed up, from Los Angeles and Washington, D.C., to hector me about my love life and raise the volume of the ticker on my biological clock.

"Vickee's been talking about you a lot."

"That's bad for me. I can tell."

Vickee Eaton was a second-grade detective herself, with a great desk job in headquarters, and had married Mercer many years earlier. But as the daughter of a cop who'd been killed on the job when she was fifteen, she had broken up their relationship, unable to cope with the dangers that he was constantly exposed to in the field. We had all celebrated with them when they remarried several years ago.

"It's been good for her, Alex. She wants it for you too."

"But she didn't give up the work she loves, *and* she got you in the deal. How do I make that kind of thing happen?" I said, reflecting for a few seconds before I spoke again. "Want to do a movie tomorrow night? Get our heads out of this mess for a few hours? Let Vickee tell me herself?"

"Wish we could," Mercer said. "Her cousin's engagement party is tomorrow. I got the whole mother lode of Eatons to contend with."

"Who's minding Logan?"

Mercer's son was almost three years old. Vickee worked her schedule so that she could be with him every evening and weekend, while her younger sister was the main babysitter at other times.

"Vickee's on the hunt. One of her pals will turn up."

"Forget that. The boy is mine for the night." I was delighted to be able to offer the comfort of a close friend to stay with Logan while they celebrated with family. Mercer twisted his head and smiled at me. "I hear you right?"

"I've done it before. I haven't even given him his Christmas presents yet. You tell Vickee that I'll drive out and take care of everything."

"It may get late. Those Eatons can party."

"If it gets too late, I'll sleep over. Let's see if this domestic tranquillity is all it's cracked up to be."

"Deal."

It was almost six o'clock when Mercer parked in front of the entrance to the DA's office on Hogan Place. The space for Battaglia's car was empty, and the security officer greeted us and let us pull in.

Laura was still at her desk when we walked down the quiet corridor to my office.

"You are the most loyal human being in the world," I said to her, hanging my jacket and scarf. "Why didn't you go?"

"Nan told me it would be a late one. I ordered in a vat of coffee for all of you and some sandwiches. Your phone's been going off the hook."

"Anybody I want to hear from?"

"Not a one. I'm happy to stay if I can be useful," Laura said. "Mercer, that guy from Verizon wants you to call him. Some kind of problem with the information I faxed over to him. And nobody touch the chocolate chip cookies—they're for Mike."

Laura had an unabashed crush on Mike and did everything she could to provide his creature comforts in our sterile bureaucratic environment.

Mercer helped Laura on with her coat while I flipped through the messages. "How'd I get lucky enough to miss the district attorney tonight?"

"Rose called to ask if you were back yet. Said he was on his way to City Hall."

"Again?"

"No, no. Nothing to do with you."

"Really?"

"You trust anyone more than Rose? She told me that it has

something to do with either a fraud case, or a judicial appointment. Maybe both."

"Good." If it was about Tim Spindlis, I didn't need to take the heat.

Mercer went inside my office, sat at the desk, and made his call to the phone company. I was saying good-night to Laura when Howard Browner appeared in the doorway.

"I'd say Happy New Year to you, Alex, but it doesn't seem to be starting off like a good one."

"Thanks, Howard. You must be swamped with everything that's come into the lab in the last forty-eight hours."

Browner was one of my closest friends at the forensic biology lab. With every cutting-edge advance in this scientific field that continued to evolve, Browner and his colleagues educated us and prepared us for the challenges of the courtroom.

"Can I talk to you about Karim Griffin for a minute?"

I stepped into the hallway with Howard so Mercer could finish his conversation. "I don't ever mean to blow you off. I just can't concentrate on anything but today's events, Howard. Let me get back to you in a couple of weeks, when things calm down."

We were an incongruous pair. Howard was much shorter than I and a lot rounder, with a head of dark, untamed hair and a full beard. But he had helped me through some of the most difficult issues I had ever faced with patience and a wisdom that he was pleased to impart to others.

"I was here to testify on that murder case in Times Square. I ran into Catherine and she said you'd been meaning to call me about Griffin," he said. "That's the only reason I dropped by. I have an idea on the push-in with your eighty-two-year-old victim, but it'll wait."

"Here's hoping she has time to wait. I shouldn't have put you off, Howard. What is it?"

"I'm going to try to get some touch evidence for you. I know it's the weakest case in the pattern."

I was trying to look at Mercer to see what was taking so long yet still pay attention to Howard.

"Sorry. I thought you'd reviewed everything. I thought all the swabs were negative for seminal fluid," I said. "There was nothing to analyze for DNA."

"That's the old-fashioned way. I can try for touch DNA now. It's different—we're looking for skin cells, for things the perp put his hands on. Instead of swabbing with distilled water, I can actually scrape the items he had to touch to attack her. The cotton undergarments she was wearing, the housecoat he ripped off. You and Mr. Howell were supposed to have a meeting this week. I just wanted to know if I had time to give this a try."

I put both hands on his shoulders and kissed him on the cheek. "Go for it. You can't imagine how happy Wilma would be to get a chance to be on the witness stand."

"I'll let you get back to what you're doing. We'll probably have lots to talk about in the next few days anyway."

"For sure. Thanks for sticking your head in."

Howard left and Mercer motioned me back to my office as he finished the conversation and hung up.

"It's not good news, Alex."

"Won't they give you the phone records?"

"I can pick them up in the morning," Mercer said. "Problem is, it turns out that flurry of calls to nine-one-one yesterday that we thought were from Salma Zunega's landline?"

"Yeah?"

"She was telling the truth. She never made those calls."

"I don't understand. I thought everyone was so certain they originated from her apartment."

"That's what showed up as the incoming line on the caller ID," he said. "That's what it looked like till they did the actual computer search today. She was spoofed."

"What?"

"Spoofed. Somebody wanted us to think she was crazy. Somebody wanted to make sure that cops wouldn't respond if she called again."

Phone "phreaks," as they were known in the trade, had mastered dozens of ways to alter the caller ID information on the telephones of individuals whose numbers they knew. Web sites had developed as commercial enterprises to sell the software to anyone interesting in spoofing, either as a prank or as a criminal enterprise, and law enforcement agencies had been slow to shut the programs down.

"Can't we get the real number?" I asked. "Can't we get to the number of the person who made the calls?"

"It's laborious, Alex. These guys use Internet services with all kinds of blind lines and different providers that link to the real number." Mercer rarely displayed any sign of a temper, but he was angry now. "They even come with scramblers to disguise the voice of the caller. Damn it, it's going to take days to find the real person behind all this."

"No wonder Salma was so hostile to all of you last night."

"Shame on me for not even thinking she was telling the truth."

"There's nothing different you could have done, Mercer," I said. "Why would any of us think it was a death spoof?"

TWENTY

"Did you call the commissioner yet?" Mike asked.

He was the last one to arrive in the conference room, where Mercer and I had taken our place with Nan and Catherine, and a large chalkboard to map out the links between the various crime scenes.

"Scully, Battaglia, the mayor," Mercer said. "They're all tied up at City Hall. Coop's been assured by Rose Malone that it doesn't involve us."

"He's going to be ripped that his department got spoofed," Mike said. "He'll be loaded for bear."

"It's not a first," Nan said. "There was a major incident in a Carolina town last year. Someone spoof-called a hostage situation and the entire SWAT team responded. The lady inside had a heart attack."

"Bet that lawsuit set the department up for a pretty settlement. Remind me not to tell that one to Scully."

"I'll get you some better examples."

Mike reached up and turned on the television set that was mounted over the long conference table. "Might as well see what's got their blood boiling at City Hall."

He was flipping to the local all-news channel when he stopped on the *Jeopardy!* game board.

"I know better than to say it's inappropriate, don't I?" Nan asked.

"I've already got a mother. Two, if you count Coop's more-than-occasional nagging," Mike said, reaching for half of a ham-and-cheese sandwich. "A few minutes too early for the big prize. Let's check the Blue Room."

There were a handful of reporters standing on the steps at City Hall. They were the young men and women assigned to the local political beat, not the raucous tabloid crowd that I presumed was still keeping vigil outside the Zunega apartment.

We picked up the sound as the NY1 correspondent was talking. ". . . don't know why this flurry of activity escalated inside the mayor's office, but he was joined this evening by District Attorney Paul Battaglia and Commissioner Keith Scully. Those names put crime on everyone's mind, as we wait out these unexpected appearances."

"I think it's all a ruse so the mayor doesn't have to show up at Gracie Mansion and face that music," Mike said.

"Ssssh," I said. "You want to know what's happening or not?"

I was at the board, drawing a map of the location of the shipwreck in Queens and the various sites in Manhattan that seemed to be in play.

"And over my left shoulder," the reporter continued, "you can see that the lights are still on in the City Council, where some kind of special session seems to be in progress.

"In the meantime, at the bottom of the steps here, the security detail made an interesting discovery this morning."

"Coop made one too," Mike said. "That her formerly skinny ass was taking on so much *fromage*—am I right? How's that for a cheesy Frenchman?—that she crashed right through the tarp and went jawbone-to-jawbone with a colonial corpse."

"That's not where I fell, Inspector Clouseau."

"No, Alex," Mercer said, moving closer to the screen. "But this guy's talking about the other burial pit right below the front steps. See?"

The reporter was standing with a Parks Department employee who had removed a section of fence to expose another piece of green tarp like the one I had fallen through behind the building.

"A minor accident here today refocused attention on the abandoned project that involved determining the occupants of these centuries-old graves that predated the construction of City Hall. Budget cuts put a halt to the excavations years ago, and a previous mayor's protocol mandated that intact remains were not to be excavated.

"Uncovering the tarp today, which is riddled with large tears and damage from foul weather, we learned that these burial grounds have become a resting place for a wide assortment of objects that probably wouldn't make it past the metal detectors at the top of the staircase, in the lobby of City Hall."

"Nice take," Mike said, swigging his soda.

"Mixed among the human remains, park crews found four switchblade knives, two box cutters, a whole bunch of sharp tools and instruments that were made long after the *Half Moon* sailed through these waters. You'd be surprised at the number of papers and identification cards that were just discarded like junk, here at the very entrance to the controls of our city government."

"No different than the courthouse," I said.

Every morning, perps and their entourages approached our building, often forgetting until they walked in the doorway that the metal detectors would reveal any weapons they were carrying. The first shift of court officers searched the two-foot-wide dirt perimeter daily, looking for discarded weapons.

"This is creepier than doing it in front of our building," Nan said. "Imagine tossing all this stuff into someone's grave? They really need to solve that problem."

Mike had turned back to Alex Trebek, just as he announced the Final *Jeopardy!* category. "That's right, I said DEATH VALLEY

LIFE. You've got sixty seconds to figure out how much you'd like to wager."

"Mercer and I have this one. He's big on wildlife. We'll take on you three girls. Twenty bucks."

"Fine, guys." I was drawing the links between Salma's apartment and the well on the Gracie Mansion lawn that overlooked Hell Gate, and the place on the FDR Drive where Ethan Leighton crashed his car. I circled the Leighton home and wrote Claire's name, with a big question mark beside it. "Then we get to work."

Each of us was nibbling on halves of the large sandwiches that Laura had ordered when Trebek revealed the answer and repeated it twice. "Devil's Hole denizen facing extinction."

The three contestants each seemed to be struggling to write a question.

"You think California condors live in a hole, or the hole name is just to throw us off?" Mike said to Mercer as he started on his second bag of chips. "Gotta be some kind of prairie dog or burrowing owl. You call it, Mercer. You give it the what-is that's about to become a what-was."

The theme music was playing in the background. I started to chalk a list of local political figures recently tainted by possible links to scandal. Congressman Ethan Leighton, former governor Eliot Spitzer, Lieutenant Governor Rod Ralevic, former police commissioner Bernard Kerik.

"What's the Devil's Hole pupfish?" Catherine said, surprising me as she took the chalk from my hand. "Humor me, Alex. Let's just put Tim Spindlis here to round out the list."

"He didn't do anything bad," I said. "And he's not a politician."

"But I so enjoy seeing him in such lousy company, even if you erase him later. Exonerate him whenever you'd like."

"Now, how'd you know that about pupfish?" Mike asked, offering her some chips as Trebek consoled the three men who had guessed wrong.

"Studied the case in law school. It's a little blue minnow that's lived only in that hole, in a spring-fed pool in that hellishly hot desert, for tens of thousands of years," Catherine said. "One of the original fish protected in a landmark water rights case before the Supreme Court."

Nan and I looked at each other and laughed.

"You two girls must have been too busy partying to do your homework, I guess. Used to be five hundred of those fish. Probably aren't even fifty today. The court curtailed groundwater pumping meant to develop irrigation in the Mojave to save these guys. They had to put up a chain-link fence to keep all the law students from peering down into the little pupfish pool."

"Probably wouldn't let Coop anywhere near the hole for fear she'd crash through that fence too," Mike said. "Crush all those little minnows to death."

"Okay, kids, recess is over," I said, sitting down at the table. "Somebody want to take a stab at suggestions about Salma and where all this leads?"

Mike muted the volume but turned the set back to NY1 so that we could keep an eye on developing events at City Hall.

"First we got to figure out who she was," Mercer said. "I'm assuming you're right, because of the tattoo, that she was trafficked in. When did she get to the States? Did the snakehead pick her out to breed her for high-end customers, and bring her to New York?"

"Who introduced her to Ethan Leighton and how often were they together?" Nan asked. "Was there any paper in her apartment? Passports, bank records."

"Not that Hal and Jack had come up with by the time we'd left."

"That's really unusual. Most of the time, if these women make the transition and become legal, they cling to that documentation like a life jacket."

"Maybe Salma thought she had a better form of protection," I said. "Maybe her local congressman offered all the coverage she needed."

"I'll call Hal in the morning. If he took any paper out of there, I'll let him bring it here to voucher and I'll go through every piece of it," Catherine said.

"So we've got to talk to Ethan Leighton," Mercer said. "That's clear."

"Which means I have to offer Lem Howell everything under the sun to bring his man in to sit down with us." Maybe I shouldn't have hustled out of the limo so quickly.

"Look," Mike said, leaning on the table, "Battaglia'll toss the drunk-driving case to get a leg up on the murder investigation, don't you think?"

"He tosses that, and what's to prevent Leighton from keeping his seat in Congress?" I asked. "Not so fast. Battaglia may have a horse in that race. I have no control over offering to drop the charges."

"Who's handling the vehicular?" Catherine asked.

"Ryan Blackmer. But he's cool with it. The front office has told him it gets folded into whatever direction we take with Salma," I said.

"So we probably have to work with Ethan's father too," Mercer said.

"Moses Leighton? He's tougher than nails. And not above trying to bribe his kid's way out of any situation."

Catherine walked to the board and added Moses Leighton's name. "Let him give it his best shot. I've always wanted to wear a wire."

"Well, then, how about Claire?"

"I don't think I could look Claire Leighton in the eye," Nan said. "She must be crushed."

"Not half as crushed as she's going to be unless she comes up with a decent alibi," Mike said.

"Let me try to get Claire in," I said. "We've got a number of mutual friends."

"Don't go there unless you've got Mercer or me with you. She's got a shitload of proverbial beans she might be looking to spill, Coop."

"Yes, but I think the source of all our trouble—all of Salma's trouble—comes back to the spoofing. Who would have done that to her—and why?"

"Five days, at best, is how much time the phone company is telling me it's going to take to see if they can source the calls," Mercer said. "The software to do the scam and even the voice scrambler is available all over the Internet. Really tough to trace."

Catherine hadn't left the blackboard. Off to the left of the main list, she drew an arrow from Claire's name and made a subgroup, including Moses Leighton and Lem Howell.

"Oh, Catherine," I said. "That's really a stretch. Lem's all talk but he'd never do anything that unethical."

Days ago, I would have said those words sincerely. Now I questioned everything that had been going on.

"He's in this deep, Alex. I'm not saying he's the player, but he's capable of being the puppeteer pulling the strings. Don't let your affection for him blind you."

"Shit, Catherine. Coop never lets affection get in the way of anything. You know that," Mike said. "Used to be I was her favorite guy on the planet. Now that X-ray vision of hers just slices through me like a laser."

"You'll always be my favorite, Mike," I said, walking over beside him to hand him one of Laura's chocolate chip cookies. "Would I take your kind of abuse from anyone else?"

"What's in it for Lem?" Mercer asked.

"Get the congressman off the hook. Paid dearly to do that by Moses Leighton," Catherine said. "After all, in Lem's very first conversation with you in court yesterday, he was hell-bent on convincing you that Salma was wacky. He set you up for that from the minute you talked, didn't he?"

I paused for a moment. She made a fine point. It would never have occurred to me that Ethan's girlfriend was emotionally unstable had Lem not planted that seed.

"Good thinking, Catherine," Mike said. "Now we need a common denominator between a dinghy full of Ukrainians and a bus-load of Mexicans."

"Snakeheads aren't partial to any ethnic groups, Mike. People are trafficked from every corner of the globe, wherever there's poverty and hunger and a strong desire to get to a better place," Mercer said. "The day laborers can work anywhere in this country they can get to, and there's always a market for pretty girls, whether they're twelve or twenty-five."

"It's a sick world we live in," Mike said.

"Will you be able to focus tomorrow?" Nan asked me. "Do an interview here with one of the Ukrainian girls? I'll do the other."

"Sure. Mike will stay out of my hair and we'll get the first few done."

"I thought you said Donny Baynes was coming over tonight," Mercer said.

"He should be here any minute. I don't know what's holding him up," I said. "There's Battaglia on the City Hall steps. Turn it up, Mike."

On the television screen, I could see the phalanx of cameramen turning on their high beams as Battaglia joined Mayor Statler and Commissioner Scully at the top of the staircase.

"Good evening, folks. It's cold out here, so we're going to make this announcement mercifully short. You all know the district attorney," Statler said, stepping back so that Battaglia could move to the microphone. "Paul, it's yours."

As they shifted positions I could see Tim Spindlis over Battaglia's shoulder.

I nodded to Catherine. "Put Tim on your list. What if the rumor about him and Spitzer and the prostitutes has a basis in fact?"

Mike smiled. "So Battaglia tries to hide him in plain sight. I like that idea, Coop."

"This afternoon, we unsealed the indictment of two aides to members of the City Council," Battaglia said. He looked at the paper in his hand and read the names aloud, explaining that the charges were conspiracy, money laundering, and witness tampering.

"No wonder the lights are burning so bright in the council chamber," Mike said, whistling before he spoke. "The DA trots Spindlis out, I guess, to keep his whipping boy's credibility rating high. Tim rubs against the pure prosecutorial patina of Battaglia's shoulder in front of all the reporters. What's this about?"

"For months, my chief assistant has been overseeing the investigation looking into the council's finances, which involves more than twenty million dollars in discretionary funds that were earmarked to entirely fictitious—I said fictitious—organizations. Tim, I'd like you to explain how this scheme worked."

Spindlis's opening line was inaudible—delivered with his usual lack of enthusiasm—and one of the reporters yelled to him to speak up.

"Last year, in addition to all of the city's carefully budgeted monies, each council member received almost half a million dollars in discretionary funds—some allocated to youth programs, some for senior initiatives, some to be used as chosen by the individual council member."

"Pork barrel spending, Coop. Isn't that what it's called?" Mike asked. "Which little piggy is it?"

"Much of the funding reached legitimate groups—neighborhood sports programs for kids and soup kitchens for the homeless—but it turns out that a good number of the designated charities were fake. They simply didn't exist. For example, Informed Citizens for a Clean Water Supply is a bogus operation," Spindlis droned on, naming several other phony setups.

"How would anybody know?" Mercer asked. "Sounds like a decent cause."

"Save the Aqueduct Bridge," Spindlis said into the bank of microphones. "The Alexander Hamilton Memorial Restoration Fund is a nonexistent organization that was supposed to provide money to aid the city's Historic House Trust in preserving the Grange

Mansion, which was Hamilton's home. There simply are no such funds."

I looked at Mike when I heard the word *mansion*. There weren't that many of them on the island of Manhattan.

"And instead," Spindlis said, "that fund primarily served as a conduit to provide cash and other personal benefits to the aide involved. Stolen city funds walked out of here by council employees."

"What's the timing on this?" Mercer asked. "What's the rush to judgment, do you think, that made the district attorney unseal this thing today?"

Paul Battaglia took control of the microphone from Spindlis. "Kendall Reid is charged with skimming almost two hundred thousand dollars cash, so that you're clear on this, designated for an agency he selected that doesn't even exist. So far as we can tell, this is a practice that has been going on for more than twenty years, a result of the charter revision of 1989."

"There's part of your answer, Mercer," I said, as Battaglia identified the other City Council aide involved. "Kendall Reid was Ethan Leighton's aide before he gave up his council seat to run for Congress. The DA's decided to turn the screws on Leighton as well as on the City Council members."

"Depends on which way Battaglia spins it," Nan said, aware of how well the boss liked to control leaks to the press. "That's the way we'll know whether he's trying to tie this to Leighton, or take the heat off the congressman."

"The tabloids will have a field day. That's what I'm going to do in my next life. Write headlines for the *Post*. The bad guys make it so easy. CITY HAUL, that's what I'd dub this scandal. SLUSH PUPPIES," Mike said, boxing the banner headlines with his hands. "Meanwhile, someone walks out the door with all that slush."

"Or it's cash stashed away in shoe boxes in someone's closet," Mercer said. He was thinking of the find at Salma Zunega's apartment today.

"Sounds like Battaglia's firing a salvo over the bow of Leighton's ship," Mike said. "Wipes out all his political enemies in one fell swoop."

There was a knock on the door and Donovan Baynes let himself in before I could get over to open it. "Sorry to be late. I got held up on another matter," Baynes said. "What's the matter, Alex? You all look shell-shocked."

"If all politics is local like they say, it just never occurred to me how filthy it is right around here, in government offices." Mike was chewing on his second chocolate chip cookie.

Donny Baynes looked up at the television screen and recognized the press conference participants. "What's got your boss all fired up tonight?"

"Phantom funds, Donny," I said. "Just a few million city dollars missing from these phantom funds."

TWENTY-ONE

Catherine was at the blackboard again, adding Kendall Reid's name and linking it to Ethan Leighton's, with a series of dollar signs beside it. She drew a question mark above Salma Zunega's apartment, and enclosed it in a chalk-outlined shoe box with more dollar signs propping open the lid.

"This political corruption graph is just for starters," Catherine said. "We're missing a few sleazeballs, but you can help me fill in the blanks. Sort of feel we should have a guy in the men's room at City Hall, taking a wide stance."

"Don't go trolling in those bathrooms, Catherine," Mike said. "I'd hate to lose you."

"There are some days that private practice seems so appealing," Nan said.

Mike narrated the day's events to Donny Baynes, who was taking copious note in a small book. "Autopsy on Zunega?"

"I'll be there," Mike said. "Tomorrow at eight A.M."

"Any word on tattoos on the other women who've been examined?"

"I made the calls on that today," Nan said. "A lot of them have tattoos, but none in that same spot on the thigh that Alex has told you about. And no roses."

"Anybody else view the bodies—the two Jane Does?"

"Three more young men were taken to the morgue today. Can't get a make on our Jane Does either. It's like they spent their time in the hold being sick," Mike said, "or they were just smart enough to keep their distance from the men for the entire ride."

"We've got hundreds more people to talk to," Baynes said. "We'll find out who they are. I'm sure of it."

"Spoken with all the confidence of your first big trafficking case," Mercer said. "You'll be fortunate if even half your population on that boat wind up with real identities. There's nothing in it for them to help you while they're in detention. They'll just be looking to bust out of whatever facility you send them to and start life over."

"No backpedaling on women you're giving us tomorrow?" Nan asked.

"They'll be delivered here by ten," Baynes said. "You have my word."

Each of us took up a position around the long table. Nan, with Laura's assistance, had stacked several piles of DD5s that had been prepared since the grounding of the *Golden Voyager* and the events following Ethan Leighton's drunken crash on the highway.

"Let's skim through what we've got here," I said, "to see if we've missed anything obvious."

There had been so many cops who responded to both scenes that it would be impossible to talk with all of them in the days to come. This was a way of marshaling the evidence for clues or connections we might have overlooked.

I opened another can of soda and read accounts of the highway patrol officers who had come upon Ethan Leighton's accident. That was less familiar to me than the awful image of the foundering ship and its weeping passengers that was embedded in my mind's eye.

"Anybody know what kind of mansion the Grange is?" I asked.

"What page are you looking at?" Nan asked.

"No, I'm thinking of what Spindlis said at the press conference. All that slush fund cash, and some of it going to restore a mansion. That's two mansion mentions in the same day. It's unusual for Manhattan."

"Now, you ladies need to spend some time in Harlem," Mercer said. "I can help you with this one."

"Please."

"You probably know as much about Alexander Hamilton's career as I do."

"Revolutionary War hero, a New York delegate to the Constitutional Convention of 1787, wrote the Federalist Papers with James Madison and John Jay, became the first secretary of the treasury," Nan said, ticking off the major accomplishments, "and then had a lucrative law practice here in the city."

"So he built himself a country estate too," Mercer said. "A bit farther uptown, in Harlem."

"Before the Jeffersons moved on up, right?" Mike said. "The television Jeffersons?"

"Yessir, my paragon of political correctness. Hamilton built the Grange around the same time Mr. Gracie was staking out his mansion. Named it for the old family property in Scotland."

"Then he didn't get to live in it very long," Mike said. "'Cause Aaron Burr killed him in a duel in 1804."

"Well, the house still stands, Mr. Chapman. In fact, in 2008 the whole thing was moved from Convent Avenue down the street to St. Nicholas Park."

"They moved an entire mansion?" Nan asked.

"They sure did. I went up there with my cousin to watch, 'cause I knew the Grange. It's a beautiful old building, and it used to abut Cousin Eugene's church."

"St. Luke's up on Convent by a Hundred and forty-first Street?" Mike said. "Now I get the picture. That place was huge. How'd they move it?"

"Lord, it was quite a fantastic operation. They put steel beams between the foundation and the first floor, to support the weight of the place. Held those up by cribbings, and then hydraulic jacks inside the cribbings lifted the house eight inches a shot," Mercer said. "Then they installed roller beams to create rails along Convent Avenue, with rams pushing the steel beams horizontally."

Mercer was telling the story with his hands, taking the Grange along the avenue with its nine dollies and its own braking system bolted to the steel beams. Both Mike and Donovan Baynes were riveted by the description.

"Must be a guy thing," Nan said.

"Sorry I started it," I said. "I just wondered if there could be any connection between Gracie Mansion and the Grange. You know, two Federal Period houses—both mansions, both country estates. Both renovated at great cost, apparently, and both connected to historical figures. That's all I was getting at."

"Not very likely, Alex. Gracie's a New York City landmark, patrolled by the NYPD and used for whatever functions the mayor wants," Mercer said. "The Grange is a national memorial. It's a cultural resource in Harlem, I guess, for the handful of people who even know it's there."

"It wasn't likely that a Ukrainian refugee and a Mexican—well, I don't know what to call Salma anymore—would have the same tattoo. It wasn't likely that half the legislators in this city would have phantom funds or that our congressman would have a phantom family," I said. "This case is all about things that aren't likely."

"Amen," Mercer said.

"A rose is a rose is a rose," Mike said. "What's so unlikely about that? It's a very common flower."

"There are probably twenty thousand varieties of roses in the world. Those two images are identical—in their shape, in their size, in their design, in their coloration, and in the exact same spot on each woman's body. You saw them, Mike. Do we have Polaroids for everyone to look at?"

"Yeah, in the middle of the table."

Catherine reached for the small pile of photographs, studied them, and then passed them on. "I'm with Alex on this."

First Nan and then Donny Baynes agreed with me.

"Okay, okay. The Hogan Place Horticultural Club rules with the princess. Okay, I'm reading," Mike said. "I'm concentrating on the reports."

"Who tried to take the weight for Ethan Leighton at the scene of the accident?" Nan asked. "That's somebody to look at."

"It's in the first fistful of DD-fives," Mercer said. "I wasn't there myself. It was his wife, Claire, who told me it was one of his aides. I didn't work the accident. I was just brought in because of the possible domestic."

We were all shuffling papers, literally trying to get on the same page.

"Now, this has a familiar ring to it, guys. DD-five, number eight," Mike said. "How about that it was his former aide who tried to intercede with the highway patrol after Ethan fleet-footed himself away? How about that it was Mr. Moneybags himself, who was Ethan's best bud before he got the congressional seat?"

Donovan Baynes read the name aloud. "Kendall Reid. So tell me why Battaglia—and the spineless wonder at his side—chose today of all days to unseal Reid's indictment? Why'd they choose this moment to charge him, and make it impossible for you to interrogate him?"

TWENTY-TWO

The two young women from Ukraine were brought to the waiting room outside my office by federal marshals shortly before ten o'clock Friday morning. Laura tried to make them comfortable until the interpreters arrived, but their fear was palpable.

"You take the conference room, Nan. I'll work in here."

"Did you get any sleep last night?"

We had broken up around eleven P.M., and Mercer dropped me off at my apartment. I soaked all the day's tension out of me with a steaming hot bath, and a double shot of Dewar's as my nightcap.

"Actually, I slept pretty well."

"No nightmares about Salma?" Nan asked.

"She was crowded out by my visions of the bodies from the ship, if you know what I mean." It was only my friends in the office and the NYPD who themselves experienced and could understand the emotional toll the job took many days.

"Did Luc call?"

"The time zones don't help this relationship," I said. "He left three messages, but it was crazy for me to wake him up in the middle of the night."

"Have you seen Battaglia?"

"I haven't talked to anyone this morning. If he didn't come looking for me, I figure I'm already ahead of the game. Mike's at the autopsy, Mercer's leading the canvass of Salma's apartment, and I'm with you. No McKinney, no Spindlis, no bad karma, no new bodies on land or sea. So far, so good."

"I'm cooking dinner at home tonight. We have a few neighbors coming in. Want to join us?" Nan asked.

"I've had a better offer. I'm going to babysit for Logan while Mercer and Vickee go to a family party. I'll skip out early if everything stays calm."

"Good for you. The little guy has to eat something, you know? That's pretty hard when the sitter can't cook."

"All planned," I said, standing to greet the pair of interpreters who were presenting themselves at Laura's desk.

The Simchuk sisters appeared to be in their midthirties. They introduced themselves in lightly accented English, detailed their academic backgrounds and experience, and listened carefully as I explained why it was necessary for Nan and me to separate each of the witnesses—victims, despite whatever Donny Baynes and Mike Chapman thought of their possible involvement in criminal affairs—as we started the process of questioning them.

"I'll take the younger girl," I said to Nan. "Let's see how we do."

Ms. Simchuk invited the teenager to come into my office. The two girls looked at each other but neither one moved. Simchuk tried to coax them gently but they refused to stand up.

I knelt beside her and put my hand on her arm, but she recoiled as though I'd been about to slap her. "Tell them they'll be safe with us," I said. "Tell them that's our job—to help women who've been hurt."

The older one spoke softly, in Ukrainian. "If she goes with you, do I see her again?"

They had been separated from all of the others on the ship. How could they possibly know what would come next in this strange new land?

"They will be together in a very nice house tonight," I said. "A safe house. Nan and I will take them there ourselves. They'll be very well taken care of by the staff."

The third time the pair of interpreters worked on their subjects, the girls released each other's hands, embraced, and followed us as we took them in different directions. I brought the tall, slender woman into my office and drew three chairs into a small circle. The desk would impose too much formality between us.

I asked the marshal to sit behind the girl—a slip of paper told me her name was Olena—out of her range of sight, simply to be an observer, as Donny Baynes had insisted.

"My name is Alexandra. Alex to my friends. What's your name?"

Everything took twice as long to do through an interpreter. It would take half an hour before the two of them became more or less comfortable with each other—if at all—and as long as that for me to get a sense of whether Ms. Simchuk was editing the translation, intentionally or not. Sometimes a feeling of empathy for what the subject had undergone seeped into what I hoped would be a word-for-word retelling of the facts.

"She is Olena," Simchuk said, trying to warm the girl up with a smile. "In our language it means the light of the sun."

I was getting the edit already. Olena had answered with only one word. The interpreter gave me more. There was no need to correct her yet, until the substance of the responses became more critical.

"Are you warm enough?"

The girl nodded but didn't speak.

"Are you hungry?"

She looked at Simchuk out of the corner of her eye.

"Would you like a good breakfast, Olena? Some eggs and some fresh juice?"

Again she shook her head up and down. She didn't look any happier for the suggestion that we feed her, but she clearly wanted to eat.

I stepped to the door and asked Laura to order in from the coffee shop for both of the girls. Neither one looked like she'd been fed well in a long time.

"How old are you, Olena?"

The answer was too long to have been her age.

"What will become of her, she wants to know," Simchuk said. "She says she won't answer questions until you tell her that."

I had no idea what would become of her. She seemed to sense that in my hesitation.

"What would you like to do, Olena? Of all the things you could choose, what would you like to happen to you now that you're here?"

Simchuk translated and the girl shrugged her shoulders.

"Do you want to go home? Do you want to go back to Ukraine?"

Her eyes widened and the vehemence with which she responded was a universal no.

I asked questions and still I got nowhere. "Why did you want to come to America, Olena? Did you know anyone else on the boat? Was someone you know supposed to meet you here?"

They were all met by a stony silence and a scowl more serious than the teenage pouts that regularly confronted me in my office.

"Tell her this, Ms. Simchuk, if you would." I explained what the district attorney's office is and how it functions. I told her about the creation of our unique unit, and the pioneering work we had done since the 1970s, to address the terrible epidemic in our own country of violence against women and children. Olena wouldn't make eye contact with me at first, but began to pay attention when I told her specifics of some of the cases that I had handled involving girls who were roughly her age.

The food was delivered and we left her alone for fifteen minutes, as Nan left her shipmate, so that they could see that we hoped they would relax, that we would continue to respond to their needs, and that we wanted them to be comfortable in our offices.

"How far have you gotten?" I asked Nan.

She held up her thumb and forefinger in a circle. "Goose egg. She's not talking until I tell her what we're going to do with them," Nan said. "And I don't mean this weekend, I mean next week and the week after."

"They must have made a pact not to talk."

"Well, we certainly can't lie. They've had enough of that to last a few lifetimes."

Laura signaled to me that Olena had come out to discard her garbage.

"Round two. I'm trying to tell her about other girls who've been saved from this awful trafficking life. I'll let you know if it works."

I told a few more stories about teens who'd been forced into prostitution, which seemed to impact Ms. Simchuk more than it did Olena.

"Where these girls live now?" Simchuk asked me.

"That's you speaking, or Olena?"

"Olena."

The conversation picked up and within the next half hour, the interpreting became far smoother as I tried to answer questions that the girl wanted to know. She was beginning to open up a bit.

"Where they live and what they are doing now depends on their age in some cases. Depends on how willing they were to cooperate," I said. "Young ones have been adopted here by families from their own countries. Others have gone to school to study, to learn a trade."

"Tell me about detention centers."

I looked at Olena while I spoke, letting Simchuk describe the impossible dilemma the government often faced when dealing with large groups of illegals who'd been smuggled into the country.

"We can try to get you asylum," I said. "There are organizations, good people who will fight for you."

Olena picked up her head. "Will you fight for me? I want to know if you will fight for me."

"Of course I will. I'll do everything I can to make you safe."

Her head dropped to her chest again and she spoke to Ms. Simchuk, who gave me the answers. "Sixteen. She wants you to know she is sixteen years old."

I was poker-faced. Olena was getting ready to disgorge to me the ugly facts of her young life. Any sign of shock that I displayed might be off-putting to her, so I prepared to listen to her story while she was in the mood to tell it.

"Be precise, please," I said to Ms. Simchuk. "Speak exactly the words she tells you. Nothing more, nothing less."

"Certainly."

It was well over an hour after we started, and now I would be hearing Olena's story through the voice of another woman.

"I was fourteen when I ran away from home. My father was an alcoholic who had a girlfriend and my mother beat me. He was never home, and she was cruel. Not to my brothers, but to me."

Olena described life in her small town and her dreams of escaping it. The fall of the Soviet Union caused many of the small satellites formerly in its grasp to suffer economic collapse. I knew that its borders had become porous, and that human rights activists estimated that as much as 10 percent of the female population of countries like Ukraine had been sold into prostitution.

Ms. Simchuk continued to narrate. "A neighbor in the village— this is very poor village, you understand—told my mother she could have money, maybe five hundred dollars—from guy who was coming to find wife for a man in Italy. I heard them talking. My mother agreed this is good idea."

Olena paused and took a long drink of water. "Next day, instead of going to school, I ran away and I hid in the forest."

"By yourself?"

"Yes, alone."

"For how long?"

"Three days. Till I was so hungry I couldn't stand it. Went back to my town. Me and my friend decided to leave Kotovs'k. She knew guy who would take us to new life. Would pay us the money, not my mother."

"To get married?"

"No. I'm too young to get married," Olena said to Simchuk, with the hint of a wistful smile. "Pay us seven hundred dollars each to work in *kafane*. To be a waitress there. Sometimes to dance with the boys who come in."

"*Kafane?* What's that?" I asked. "A place?"

"No, no. Is word. It means a café sort of bar," Simchuk said. "They often operate as brothels in many towns. That's why I was surprised. Forgot to make translation."

"Try not to show your own feelings to Olena," I said. "She'll shut down if you make judgments about what she did."

"I understand. It just happened, is all."

"This place was in your town? In Kotovs'k?"

"No, no. Is far away."

"Who made the promise to you?"

Olena looked up and fixed on my eyes. "Why?"

"Do you know the man who made the promise to you? To give you that money?"

"I didn't see him till we get there. My friend Karyn tell me. She come too."

"Did you learn his name?"

"You want name?" There was a defiance in Olena's voice as she said that to Simchuk.

"Yes, please."

"Name is Zmey," and as Simchuk said that to me she giggled nervously.

"You're laughing now?" I said to the interpreter. Olena didn't seem any more pleased about that than was I.

"Sorry. I wasn't expecting that. She says his name is Dragon. In Ukraine, Zmey is a dragon who is green, with three heads, and spitting fire all the time."

"You said you met Zmey when you got 'there,' Olena. Where, exactly?"

"Why is important this, she wants to know? Was two years ago."

"I think it will help explain to me why you are here today. It lets me know the kind of care we need to give you." It might also let me understand the level of desperation that had fueled this tragic voyage she undertook at such a tender age.

Olena's back hunched over as she went on with her story. "They took us to Macedonia. To a town called Velesta."

My heart sank. Trafficking was the only industry in that small town, which international police agencies had long considered one of the most dangerous places for young women introduced to the sex trades.

"I know Velesta," I told her. "I know what goes on there. Did you have papers of any kind? A passport?"

Olena looked at me as though I was stupid to ask the question. "What for would need papers? Karyn and me, we traveled in the trunk of a car, of a boy from Kotovs'k. Don't need papers in car trunk."

From Ukraine, she had been smuggled through Moldova, Romania, Bulgaria—across the Danube at some point—stopping occasionally at night at the homes of men friendly to smugglers. Border guards were bribed to look the other way, I knew from my experience with other cases.

"What happened when you reached Velesta?"

It was a long, slow process to get the story from Olena. I couldn't push her, for fear she would stop altogether.

"What do you think happened? The Dragon put me to work in the *kafane*."

I needed to hear her words, her description, though I knew what it would be.

"As a waitress?"

Simchuk translated my words and Olena just glared at me.

"What kind of work?"

"You know what kind of work. You stupid if you don't," Simchuk said. "I'm sorry, Ms. Alex. Is her word—*stupid*—not mine."

"That's fine. Tell her I know the questions seem silly to her, but I have to ask them. Otherwise I'd just be guessing. I'd be thinking of someone else's story that I heard another time."

Olena listened to my reason, took a drink of water, and slumped down in her chair to continue.

"You and Karyn, where did you live?"

"No Karyn. Karyn didn't stay with me. Dragon said she wasn't pretty enough. Was lucky thing for Karyn."

"And you?"

"In the basement of the *kafane*. Three other girls and me. For days I just cried. The door was locked and someone threw in the food and bottles of water. But the Dragon said I couldn't come out until I stopped crying. Till I put on the lingerie like the other girls and didn't show no tears."

And so Olena was welcomed to her new life, her fantasies of freedom and opportunity shattered before she had been driven very far from her home in Kotovs'k—shattered in the trunk of a smuggler's car and the dingy basement of a demon pimp.

She told us the story of how she started to work for the Dragon's men, who owned the bar and the brothel. She told us how her youth and beauty—masked now by her abuse and the long confinement—had made her so popular among the clientele. She told us that she believed that being forced to sell her body for sexual favors was enabling her to pay off her debt to her captors, and that after a period of time they would keep their promise to let her go.

"How long were you held there, Olena?"

"I know exactly how long. Fourteen months and five days. I could tell you almost to the minute."

The next question was one of the hardest to ask. It would imply that I expected the action I asked about. "Did you—did the other girls—ever try to escape? To run away, the way you tried to run away from your home?"

Olena swallowed hard and looked up at the light fixture on the ceiling.

"Would you like to take a break, Olena?"

"No, Ms. Alex. Not if I have to come back and you ask me again. I thought you knew this story from other girls. What is it you don't understand?" Simchuk was trying to translate as rapidly as Olena was now talking, looking everywhere in the room except at me. "I was living in a basement with no windows, no light. I was kept there under lock and key, by men who are monsters. If I disobeyed orders—small orders to do things, when I sick or when I was exhausted—I was made to be on my hands and knees and to clean the floor with my tongue."

Olena's voice was flat. She made her case without any emotion built into it, a form of self-protection that had probably allowed her to survive the experience.

"I was raped over and over again. I was beaten for nothing, for no reasons at all. Passport, you ask. I'm in Macedonia then. Where can I run without papers?"

"Please, Ms. Alex," Simchuk said after Olena stopped for a few seconds. "Is too hard on her to do this more. Please stop."

"She's asking you that, is she?"

"No, no. Is me who is unhappy," Simchuk said.

"Ask her how *she* feels, okay? That will decide when we stop."

Olena started to talk again. "I thought you know so much about this."

I sat back and waited for her to look at me. "I thought I did too. Each one of you is different, Olena. I'll never understand how you endured so much pain."

"You want to know how I got out, yes?"

"Please."

"I got pregnant, Ms. Alex. Was near the end of one year. Pregnant and sick all the time with it," Olena said, tilting her head as if it would help her remember. "Was nothing sick compared to the boat ride, but was bad. When my belly got big, I was no use to the Dragon anymore. He didn't want me. No men wanted me. Lots of younger girls to take my place."

"Then they let you go?"

"Someone pay again," Simchuk said, leaning in to hear the soft voice of Olena. "Everybody make money excepting me. A man whose wife and two children died in car accident, he bought me. Lived on a farm outside town."

"Was he—?"

"Kind? You will want to know if he was kind, of course. He was good to me until I lost the baby. Miscarried, how you call it? The baby came very early. I was by myself at the house. Was already dead."

Olena had delivered a stillborn child at the age of fifteen, without any medical care, alone at the home of a stranger in the cruel countryside of Macedonia.

"So I left. Hitchhiking to home. Hundreds and hundreds of miles."

I must have looked incredulous. I could tell immediately that I had spooked her.

"You don't believe possible, right? You're thinking passport," Simchuk picked up speed again and Olena's staccato dialogue poured out. "My best customers, Ms. Alex, is border guards. My best customers is police who actually—first time—give money to *me*. Fed me and let me sleep."

"At least you got home safe. You got home in one piece."

"What home? My mother dead from alcohol. And my brothers don't let me in house. I was not family anymore. It was like throwing a dog out on the street. Only some people in my town would have taken in a dog, been good to a dog."

I didn't have to ask why she was discarded.

"No more their sister. Now I was a whore, which everyone would tell."

"How would anyone else know what had become of you?"

"Girls run away in Ukraine, in Moldova, in Macedonia, is the work that they are forced to do. I was naive. I believe the guys who talked to me. I get home, couldn't be with the boys from my town, Ms. Alex."

"You're smart, Olena, and so pretty. You could have been with boys again, if that's what you wanted."

"I'm marked too many ways boys don't want. Scars on my breast where I was burned with cigarette, bite marks on my arms that got infected. Tattoo from the Dragon where is everybody knows what it means."

"Where is the tattoo, Olena?"

"You want to see?" she said, standing up.

"No, no. Just tell me where."

She pointed to the same spot on her inner thigh as the tattoos I had seen on Salma Zunega and our unidentified Jane Doe #1.

I couldn't think fast enough about what it would mean if she had the same image as they did burned onto her body almost two years ago in a small town in western Macedonia.

"What is it, Olena?"

"It's Zmey, Ms. Alex. A green monster with three heads and fire that came from his mouth," she said. "I was property of the Dragon. No one would touch me if they knew that."

It had been too much to hope that Olena could lead us to the snakehead whose tattooed rose had linked Salma Zunega to one of the victims of the *Golden Voyager*.

"I'm going to let you rest now, Olena. It's almost time for you to have lunch," I said, trying to disguise my disappointment, which was meaningless in light of the odyssey she had just recounted.

"You want to know why I come on this boat, Ms. Alex?"

"Yes, Olena, I'd like to know that."

"There is an orphanage in Kotovs'k. The nuns who run it, they took me in, let me go to school. I read about America in their books," she said, finally offering me a smile that showed off her best features.

"I'm glad they did."

"You had a great war once," she said to Simchuk, and even the translator seemed happier now. I heard Olena say the name Abraham Lincoln. "Abraham Lincoln freed all the slaves in America. You have black man even who is president."

"Yes, we do." I thought of the hundreds of slaves who sailed to New York centuries ago and the African burial ground, just a few blocks from where we sat.

"I was a slave, too, Ms. Alex. I came to America, even though very scared still, because that can't happen to me here."

The wreck of the *Golden Voyager* may have been the only break in Olena's young life. This wasn't the moment for me to tell her that the American traffic in sex slaves—local and international— still flourished and thrived, and that this disastrous accident may have been the thing that saved her from another round of forced prostitution.

"No, Olena," I said, taking her hands in mine and squeezing them. "That can't happen to you now."

TWENTY-THREE

My SUV was parked on First Avenue, across the street from the medical examiner's office. Nan and I had just taken the two young women, Olena and Lydia, to view the bodies of the victims at the morgue. One of the Simchuk sisters remained with us to translate, both at the ME's office and as they settled in to the shelter.

"So far, everybody's accounted for except Jane Doe Number One," I said, herding the group across the avenue when the light changed.

"I've got an idea about that," Nan said.

"Let's hear it."

"What became of the captain and crew of the ship?"

"They're in federal lockup. Donny Baynes has them."

"Are they American?"

"No. Eastern European. I'm not sure if Baynes said they're Ukrainian, but the captain was pulling the no-speak-English bit on Wednesday. They're in on trafficking charges and illegal entry, and they've all got lawyers by now. The captain had the proper papers to be in command of a ship, just not with the cargo he was carrying."

"What if that woman—the one no one has positively ID'd yet—was part of the captain's reward for his safe passage?" Nan asked.

"Suppose she spent most of the trip in his cabin, forced to service him."

"Interesting thought," I said, as we opened the doors for our charges.

"It helps explain why nobody on board had any contact with her. It also figures she could have been caught up in the physical battle when the guys mutinied. Maybe she was injured accidentally."

"That's the most well-placed accidental stabbing I've seen in a while," I said.

"But I'm thinking maybe the captain threw her in the way to protect himself, or maybe one of her countrymen thought she had betrayed the others by becoming the captain's woman."

"You need to call Donny so he can get one of his guys working on that," I said. "It's a really good idea."

"I hardly know him. Why don't you call?"

"'Cause it's your idea, and I'm driving."

Olena and Lydia seemed overwhelmed by the sights and smells of New York. They were craning their necks from each side of the backseat as Ms. Simchuk described the buildings we passed on our long afternoon drive up to the northern end of Manhattan.

"I'll go across Thirty-fourth Street so they can see the Empire State Building," I told her, "and then through the theater district. Let's get the business out of the way so they can enjoy the ride."

"Very good," Simchuk said.

"The shelter has very tight security. All of the women and children—about twenty-five families—are being protected because they are trying to get out of abusive relationships."

Simchuk translated and the girls listened.

"That means their access is controlled. There is a nine o'clock curfew for all the other residents, and the police precinct is one block away, so it's quite secure," I said. "They will share a small apartment—"

"Excuse me, you mean a room, yes?"

"No, I mean a small apartment. There is one bedroom with twin beds, a separate bathroom, and their own kitchen."

Olena and Lydia were talking between themselves, excited by the description.

"They each receive a welcome package with some clothing, kitchen utensils, and food."

"But, Ms. Alex," Simchuk said, "they are afraid to believe this."

"It's true."

They didn't need to know how I had fought every point out with Donny Baynes last night in the conference room. He had wanted them each to wear an ankle bracelet to monitor their whereabouts. While they had clearly risked flight before, I couldn't imagine subjecting them to such humiliation after what they had endured to get here.

Nan took over. "They will not be able to leave the building without an escort, though. A federal marshal will come for them every morning at nine, and will return them here at the end of the day. Even on weekends. We're trying to get translators to be assigned around the clock, but for tonight, you'll stay as late as you can, and after that it will be sign language to communicate their needs."

We were losing our witnesses to the great spectacle of the New York City streets. I took the slow, scenic route, circling Rockefeller Center so they could ogle the enormous Christmas tree and the ice skaters out in full force, despite the cold.

I went up Sixth Avenue and into Central Park, passing the horse-drawn carriages at the Fifty-ninth Street entrance and taking the drive north, behind the Metropolitan Museum of Art and the glass-enclosed Temple of Dendur, which didn't interest the duo a fraction as much as the endless assortment of bikers and joggers, dog walkers and performance artists, and the carefree attitude so many of them seemed to radiate to the two tired hostages inside my SUV.

"You have to stop at the station house first?" Nan asked as we reached the Heights.

"That's the way it's done," I said, pulling in front of the building on Broadway that housed the Thirty-fourth Precinct.

I double-parked and we all got out, although Olena and Lydia were not pleased about the stop. "Don't worry," I instructed Ms. Simchuk to reassure them, "it's just to let them know where you're going to be."

The desk sergeant called up to the squad, and one of the detectives came down to meet us. I told him who the women were and that Safe Horizon agreed to put them up at Parrish House.

"You need us to sit on the place, Counselor? They expecting any trouble from anybody?"

"Neither one of them knows a soul in this country except the people who sailed over with them."

"And the newspapers say those poor folks aren't exactly footloose and fancy free. Legal limbo, I guess."

"It's a horrible situation," Nan said. "We're hoping the task force can clear them in a reasonable amount of time."

"Our only worry is making sure these two don't decide to run away. I'm kind of on the hook with the feds for that," I said. "I'm afraid you'll get the first call if they take it on themselves to disappear."

"Trust me. They won't get very far in this neighborhood," the detective said, "unless their Spanish is really good."

I didn't think that language barriers were an issue for these desperate young women.

"I'm betting on you, 'cause it's my head that's going to go on the chopping block if they do," I said. "I'm going to call the shelter's manager now."

"Yeah, we got a good relationship with them over there. They'll send an escort to show you to the house. That's their rules, even if you know where it is. Sorta lets us know what's going on."

He and Nan chatted while I spoke with the social worker who was in charge of Parrish House. She said it would only take her a couple of minutes to walk the block and a half to the station house.

"Don't worry, Ms. Cooper," the detective said, stopping at the front desk, "we'll give the place a little extra attention. I'll ask the sarge here to tell the guys at every roll call we got some foreign dignitaries we gotta look out for, okay?"

I thanked him and we stayed inside the lobby until the advocate from the shelter arrived and introduced herself.

"Why don't I walk back with you?" Nan asked. "Alex can follow with the others."

Simchuk, Olena, and Lydia got into the SUV and I pulled away, stopping at the traffic light. I had to square the block because of the one-way streets that crossed Broadway, and by the time I pulled over in front of the fire hydrant just past the entrance to the large redbrick building, Nan and her guide were waiting on the steps.

It was a quiet residential block, with a small old church across the street and a bodega on the corner. The girls got out and looked around at their new environs, stepping back to let a young black woman with a little boy at her side pass between them as she left the shelter.

"Welcome to Parrish House," the advocate said to Ms. Simchuk, ringing the buzzer for admission and holding the door open to invite us in. "Please tell them we're happy to have them here."

Before the four of us could mount the steps, I saw a dark minivan approaching down the narrow street. It caught my attention because it was so much newer and cleaner than the other beat-up cars nearby.

Ms. Simchuk went first and the girls followed. I watched out of the corner of my eye as the shiny vehicle seemed to be braking near the curb in front of the building, but its windows were so darkly tinted that I couldn't see inside.

"Let's go, Alex," Nan said. "Stop looking for trouble."

Olena and Lydia turned their heads to look at me when they heard Nan call out my name.

I put my first foot on the step just as lights seemed to burst from within the minivan. Someone was shooting photographs of our arrival.

TWENTY-FOUR

"Call nine-one-one!" I screamed to the advocate who was inside the hallway.

"Why?"

I dug in my tote for my cell phone and dialed as the door closed behind us.

"What did I miss?" Nan asked.

"Yes, Operator. I'm an assistant district attorney. I need someone from the Three-four to come to Parrish House," I said, giving her the address. "What? No one's hurt, no."

I signaled to Nan to move Olena and Lydia into the small office at the end of the hall.

"What's the crime?" I repeated the operator's question. "Well, I'm at a shelter for crime victims and some guy— No, I didn't see who but I assume it was a guy, was taking photographs of us, or maybe of the house— Excuse me? I know that's not a crime, miss. But I just need some officers over here as soon as possible."

I opened the front door again but there was no black minivan anywhere on the street.

"Did you see a guy, really?" Nan asked me. "Ms. Simchuk, why don't you take the girls into the office and let them get started.

They'll need to give some background information about themselves, and then we'll show them around and introduce them to the
team that works here."

I waited until the interpreter led Olena and Lydia away before I
spoke. "I'm not sure what I saw. Did you get the make of the car?"

"Get what about it? It was a station wagon, I think."

"I could swear it was a minivan. Did you see a plate?"

"Alex, I wasn't even aware of the thing. Why are you so freaked
out?"

"In the first place, no one's supposed to know that we're here."

"True. But nobody was following you."

"How do you know?"

"Because they'd be dizzy from the ride you took to get here.
C'mon, you would have noticed. Whoever it is would have rear-
ended you each time you stopped to point out a famous site. What
do you think, they wanted some snaps of us for *Cosmo for Prosecutors*
'cause we look so hot at the end of a long week like this?"

I laughed. "Imagine, I almost had an entire day without a Chapman dose of reality, and here you are, doing it for him. So it wasn't
a glamour shot?"

"Lights and sirens coming your way. Pull yourself together, my
dear friend."

"Seriously, Nan. The bigger issue is whether some other lowlife is looking for his ex and figured out this is the spot. The cops
just need to know about it. So does the executive director of the
agency."

The buzzer rang and I looked through the peephole to see a
young uniformed cop standing outside before I opened the door.

"Hi, I'm Alex Cooper. This is Nan Toth. We're with the DA's
Office."

"Nice. I'm DeCicco," he said, pointing to the name tag on his
chest. "What's up?"

"Nan and I are just bringing two of the victims from the shipwreck—you know the boat that was grounded in Queens early Wednesday morning?"

"Victims? Victims of what? They're all illegals, right? Somebody on board killed somebody else, right?"

I was looking for a guy with some concern and empathy, but clearly drew the short straw.

"Two of these young ladies who I'm willing to vouch for aren't murderers, okay? Can we start with that? And they're not going to take your job away from you anytime soon. Commissioner Scully thinks they'll be safe here."

"Guess he knows. Somebody bothering them?"

"Not exactly. Nan and I drove them up here, and of course, no one's supposed to know the address of this safe house, and as we were coming up the steps this car stopped and—"

"What car?"

"A black minivan, I think it was."

The cop was looking at the expression on Nan's face. "Not what you think, is it?"

"I mean, Alex really saw it. Might have been dark gray or green. I didn't actually—"

"But you don't think it was a minivan, do you?" DeCicco asked.

"Look, I don't want to disagree with Alex because she's the one—"

"What is she, the boss of you or something?" He looked at me again. "Where did it stop?"

"It didn't exactly stop. I think the driver kind of braked and slowed down."

"You're beginning to sound like one of your own witnesses," Nan said. "You would be coming down on the poor thing so hard right now."

"Was he taking pictures or not, Nan?" I asked.

"He. You're sure it's a guy, right?" DeCicco asked.

"I didn't see him. I'm assuming it was a guy, okay? The windows were very darkly tinted."

"He—maybe she—was photographing you or the Russian broads?"

No point stopping for a geography lesson.

"I don't know. It seemed like the flash went off four or five times."

"You sure he wasn't photographing the church across the street? People come here all the time to take pictures of it. Must be one of the oldest churches in the city."

I looked across the street at the building, which had no remarkable architectural features.

"Understand me? I mean, can you say the camera was pointed at all of you and not across the street?" DeCicco asked.

"The windows were so dark I can't honestly say where the camera was pointed. I just saw flashes of light."

"Passenger window open facing you?"

I shook my head from side to side.

"So you couldn't see if the driver's window was open?"

"No."

"Sort of makes more sense he'd be shooting at the church through an open window on his side and not through the tint at you, right? Don't make sense."

"Can you just take a report of this—this—?"

"It's not a crime."

"Okay, the incident, then. Just a record of the time and a description—well, a sort of description of the car."

"Sure, miss. Sure, I'll do that," DeCicco said.

I'd been blown off more diplomatically in my life. "Thanks."

"It wasn't a department car, was it?" he asked.

"You've got minivans out here—unmarked vans?"

"We've got some wagons," he said, nodding to Nan.

"Not all shiny—?"

"Sometimes we even wash 'em, you know?" DeCicco said, on

his way down the steps. "Not to worry. They call us if there's even the smell of trouble here. You take care, girls. See you in court."

"Don't say it, Nan. I lost that round."

"Now, there's a guy who could give Lem Howell a run for his money. Let me see—a cross that was rapier sharp—"

"Risible and rude. There's your triplicate."

We waited until Olena and Lydia had toured the facility, seen their first large-screen high-def television mounted in the lounge, greeted some of the other residents, and cried with joy when they were taken into their own little apartment.

At four thirty, Nan and I said good-bye to them and walked out to my SUV.

"Perfect timing," I said, checking my watch. "I promised Vickee I'd be at the house before six."

"I'll hop on the train."

"Don't be silly. I'll drop you at Fifty-ninth Street and get on the bridge there."

Mercer and Vickee lived in a gracious house in Douglaston, one of the most attractive neighborhoods in Queens. It borders on Nassau County and has a suburban feel. Blessed with excellent public schools, it's a great neighborhood in which to raise kids.

"Still seeing ghosts around here?" Nan asked as I got in the car.

"All clear. Thanks for your trust," I said. "You stood your ground with DeCicco. Remind me, am I the boss of you or what? It's so refreshing to be humiliated every now and then."

"I'm really much more worried about what you're going to cook for Logan's dinner. You know Vickee doesn't let him have junk food."

"Her sister saved me. Made some meat loaf today and all I have to do is warm it up and nuke the veggies."

We talked all the way downtown, jumping back and forth between the case facts and our personal lives. I dropped Nan off at the subway on Lexington Avenue. "Speak to you tomorrow, I'm sure. Thanks for everything."

I beat the rush-hour traffic over the bridge and coasted out on the parkway with Smokey Robinson singing to me.

When I reached the house, I parked in front and before I could get across the sidewalk with my shopping bags, Vickee opened the door and Logan dashed down the walk to greet me. I dropped the packages and picked him up, spinning around with him in my arms.

"Are you staying with me, Lexi?" That was as close as the almost-three-year-old could get to my name. "What's in the bags? Is it for me?"

"Logan, that's a terrible thing to say," Vickee called out from the open doorway. "You haven't seen Auntie Alex in over a month."

"That's all right. We've got lots of time to play tonight," I said. "Wow! Look at you, Detective Eaton. Don't you look fine."

"Cousin Velma's into sequins, can you tell? And I'm cohosting, so I went all out."

Vickee stepped back and twirled for me, a striking image in a sparkling silver gown and three-inch heels that had her towering over me.

"Doesn't Mommy look beautiful?" I asked Logan.

"She looks silly," he said, laughing as he foraged through the wrapped boxes I had brought.

"Hey, little guy," Mercer's voice boomed from the top of the staircase, "did Aunt Alex say anything about those being for you?"

He was still adjusting his tie as he came down from the master bedroom, dressed to the nines in a handsome suit and cobalt blue tie. He kissed me on both cheeks. "There's still time to change your mind, Alex. You can borrow something from Vickee's closet and go in my place."

"Don't go breaking Velma's heart," Vickee said. "You're her favorite outlaw."

"Open, Lexi? Can I open?" Logan asked.

"You bet."

He sat on the floor and began to tear at the Christmas wrapping.

"You got the drill?" Mercer said. "Listen up, Logan. You get to play with Aunt Alex for a while. Then you've got to eat all your dinner. You get a bath, three stories, and then to sleep. That good? Lights out the minute Alex tells you so."

The child would have said yes to anything as he ripped at the paper.

"Look, Mommy, look! Legos!"

Vickee had given me part of Logan's wish list for Santa. The Legos Airport was my first order and got the desired response. He knew his grandfather had worked at LaGuardia, and he, too, was fascinated with everything that flew. He wrapped himself around my leg and said thank you over and over.

"Come into the kitchen," Vickee said. "I'll show you where everything is."

The prepared food was laid out on the counter. I reassured Vickee of my ability to heat, plate, and serve it, while Logan shouted about the two Bionicles he had opened.

"Over the top, Alex."

"I'm allowed to spoil him. That's what aunties are all about," I said. "Any special instructions?"

"There's a nice bottle of white wine on ice. It'll go well—"

"No drinking on duty, ma'am. My charge is too important."

"Well, if this doesn't rock on too late, we'll have a nightcap together later."

Logan walked into the kitchen, dragging a large Paddington Bear in one hand and clutching a small leather-bound book in the other. "Will you read me?" he asked, holding it out to me.

"Aunt Alex can read after we've gone, babe," Vickee said. "Come into the den and play with your new toys while I talk to her. And give me the book."

Reluctantly, he handed the slim volume to his mother. It was my tradition to give the children in my family and among my close friends books with which they could start and grow a collection. I had always found great joy in the stories that were read to me as a child, and my love of literature remained a stabilizing force in my life.

"*Aesop's Fables,*" I said.

"I'll put this high on the shelf with his others. No sticky fingers, no danger it will get used as a projectile," Vickee said, as we followed Logan into the den.

We talked until Vickee and Mercer were ready to leave. Logan was so engrossed in his new bounty that he had to be reminded to get up and give them good-night hugs.

Getting down on the rug to help Logan put together the tiny pieces to build the airport was the perfect tonic to the end of a long, crazy week. We played for almost an hour and when I told him it was time for dinner, he merrily came to the kitchen with me, explaining everything there was to know about Gresh, one of his new Bionicles.

I put him in his booster seat, warmed up the meat loaf in the preheated oven, and microwaved the rest of the meal. He cleaned his plate, drank two glasses of milk, introduced me to the imaginary buddies who were seated around the table with us, and made the whole process of caring for him seem like a cakewalk.

"Time for your bath, Mr. Logan," I said.

"Gresh come too?"

"Why not?"

The child headed for the staircase and climbed as fast as he could, talking to the odd-looking creature all the way up.

I rolled up my sleeves and ran the water in the tub, checking the temperature to make sure it would be comfortable. "Okay, sweetie, let's get in."

He undressed and I lifted him into the bathtub. "Bubbles, Lexi. Where are the bubbles?"

"Whoops! I forgot them. I don't know why, 'cause I love bubbles when I take my bath too," I said, adding them till they completely covered his plastic toy and the surface of the tub.

"You take baths, Lexi? My mom likes showers better," Logan said. "How come you don't have a little boy like me to play with?"

I was washing his neck and sat back on my heels as he stared at me and asked again. "How come?"

"I expect I might someday, Logan." I couldn't even catch a break from a toddler. "It would be nice to have a boy or girl who could come hang out with you, right?"

"Daddy says he doesn't think you ever will. How come, Lexi?"

"Maybe I'll surprise your daddy. Would you like that?"

The boy splashed the water with both hands, delighted by the prospect of pulling off a surprise for his father. "Yes, Logan like that."

"How about I tell you a story about the first time I met your daddy?"

"Yeah," he said.

"It was a very long time ago, long before you were born—"

I was plotting the narrative when the doorbell rang. I was startled by the loud, jarring sound and the prospect of an unexpected visitor.

"Who's that?" Logan asked.

"Might be the wrong house, sweetie. Let's rinse off the soap and get you dry and warm before we go downstairs."

Again the shrill ring of the bell.

I lifted Logan out of the tub and wrapped a large bath sheet around him, carrying him in my arms and rubbing him as I walked through the hall to the master bedroom, to see if there was any other car parked in front of the house.

Now there was a pounding on the door—an impatient, insistent knock that seemed to get louder.

"Who's that?" I never ceased to be amazed at how often kids could be repetitious.

"I don't know yet, Logan. Why don't you get into bed so I can go see," I said, crossing down the hall to his room. I thought it would be smarter to leave him there while I explored the situation at the door.

"I don't want to get in bed," he said, kicking before I could set him down and start to get his pajamas on.

"Logan, you've got to get ready—"

The brass striker hit the door again just as my cell phone rang. I stood Logan on his bed and pulled the cell out of my rear pants pocket.

"Yes," I said brusquely into the mouthpiece.

"Jeez, I was afraid you took my godson and ran out the back door when I rang the bell," Mike said. "That's me freezing my ass here on the front steps, waiting for you to open up. All you see is the bogeyman, waiting for you everywhere you go. You better get a life for yourself, Coop."

TWENTY-FIVE

There was no corralling Logan Wallace. He idolized Mike and was ecstatic about the surprise visit, squealing and laughing like he'd never stop.

"Lo-lo-lo-Logan," Mike said, stopping for a high-five before he marched a shopping bag into the kitchen while the kid tried to keep up with him. "What are you doing still awake, m'man? It's eight o'clock. I'm gonna fire your babysitter."

"No, you can't," he said as Mike put the bag down, grabbed the boy's pajamas by the waistband, and began tickling him. "It's Lexi."

"I thought Lexi was your date."

Logan buried his face in Mike's thigh, still laughing. "Logan have no date."

"You had your stories yet, little guy?"

"No."

"I was just about to start reading to him."

"Go on upstairs with Lexi," Mike said. "Get in bed and I'll tell you a good one."

"Three good ones, Mikey. I can have three." The child grabbed my hand and started pulling me away.

The moment Logan turned his back, Mike removed his gun

from its holster and stowed it on top of the tall refrigerator. It was the first thing most cops did when they spent time in a house with kids, but that particular hiding place would only work until Logan got a little older, when he'd be able to climb up on the counters to explore all the hidden surfaces.

"Let's gather your animals and go on upstairs," I said, stopping in the den to retrieve the stuffed brontosaurus and ragged teddy bear he slept with every night.

"Wait just a minute," Mike said, coming in behind us, scooping the boy up and hoisting him onto his shoulders. "Lexi, put on the TV, will you?"

Logan was clapping his hands from his new perch.

Mike's timing was impeccable.

"When we come back from the commercial break," Alex Trebek said, "we'll see which of our contestants has the right question. Who'll become our champion tonight? Remember, the Final *Jeopardy*! category is MYTH OR MADNESS."

"Who's the champion, Logan?" Mike asked, letting the child ride him like a bronco.

"Logan! Logan is!"

"What do you give me, Coop?"

"Whatever it takes to encourage you to put my guy to bed."

Myths, especially the classics, were among Mike's specialties, full of warriors and heroes whose legends and exploits captivated him. I was the resident expert on madness, a popular theme of literature and art.

"We'll hold at twenty, right, Logan? You my partner, pal?"

"Yeah."

"We gonna beat Lexi?" Mike asked. "Dudes rule?"

Logan's clapping and laughing were almost at a fever pitch.

"And the answer is, Contraband in America—for almost a hundred years, this liquid was reputed to drive men mad," Trebek read from the board. "MYTH OR MADNESS."

"Was there a liquid opium?" Mike asked.

"If that's your question, then you lose," I said. "What is absinthe?"

"How did I miss that? The bartender in me should have known. But what's the myth?"

"Supposedly it's what Van Gogh was drinking the night he cut off his ear and gave it to a prostitute. Poe, Baudelaire, Wilde—a lot of far-fetched stories about how dangerous a liquor it is."

In Le Zinc, the chic bar in Luc's restaurant in the charming village of Mougins, he had a vintage poster of a madman drinking the green spirit, with the warning: *L'Absinthe Rend Fou*—absinthe makes you crazy. It had been banned in this country in 1912, and only legalized again in 2007.

"Lexi wins, Logan. Got to brush your teeth and get ready for story time."

Mike flipped the child over his head and sent him running back to me. We went upstairs and after cleaning up, Logan went directly to the shelf in his room to grab a fistful of books and threw himself onto his bed.

"Which one do you want me to start with?" I asked, sitting beside him as he put his head on the pillow and snuggled against me.

"You've probably read that one a gazillion times," Mike said, walking into the room. "Don't you want me to tell you about the time your daddy and I had to battle the dinosaurs in Central Park?"

Logan was clapping his hands, so wired that I doubted he would ever sleep. "Yeah, tell that one."

He was at the age when everything about the prehistoric creatures fascinated him. He could recognize the shapes of each species and knew their names, but couldn't quite get the timeline that made Mike's tales so outrageously fanciful.

Mike pulled up the rocking chair and placed it directly in front of Logan so the child could see every expression and gesture. There was no better storyteller I'd ever seen than Mike, as he primed the background for Logan—the "good guys," Mike and Mercer—who were rookies in the Police Academy, setting out to protect the city from the invasion of the dinosaurs who had been hiding for centuries in the Rocky Mountains.

The story was complex and colorful. In addition to the wide variety of predators Logan knew, Mike made up dozens of others, colored them with stripes and polka dots, and crafted them to graze on favorite foods—the detectosaurus on police officers, the toddlersaurus on kids who didn't go to sleep on time, and the Lexisaurus on babysitters who weren't any fun to have around.

Fifteen minutes in, I was squished into the corner where the bed met the wall. Logan had laughed at the funny parts and practically crawled over my head when he was scared by the final confrontation near the zoo inside the park.

"Let's not set up any night-m-a-r-e-s, Uncle Mike," I said, spelling out the second half of the word. "There's enough adrenaline going here to keep my guy up till dawn. I'll really lose my job."

"We always close happy," Mike said. "Don't we, Lo-lo-lo-Logan?"

The story ended with the dinosaurs agreeing to help Mercer patrol and keep the bad guys in line, with the swat of a long tail or the threat of a velociraptor claw.

"'Nother one, Mikey. 'Nother one."

Logan was exhausted but fighting the end of his happy evening.

"No way, my friend. That was a two-book extravaganza. Lexi has to read you something about bunnies or balloons," he said, leaving me to calm the child. "I'll be right downstairs, making sure your mom and daddy don't come home while you're still all wild and wooly."

"And whose fault would that be?" I asked.

Mike leaned over for a hug and Logan locked his arms around Mike's neck. When he straightened up, Logan came along with him. They kissed good-night as I scrambled out of the bed and smoothed it for the little boy to get ready for sleep.

I picked a brightly decorated book with a cheerful title that I thought would help soothe Logan, and read the short story to him. When that was done, I closed the light and lay down next to him for ten minutes, stroking his baby soft skin and feeling his warmth against me.

When he dropped off to sleep, I turned on the night-light and went downstairs. I could hear Mike in the kitchen.

"Did you eat?" he asked. It was almost eight thirty.

"Not yet, but there's some meat loaf," I said. "This is a really pleasant surprise. To what do I owe the pleasure of your company tonight?"

"Nan called me. She thought the babysitter needed a babysitter. Or maybe a straitjacket. She told me about your reaction and the nine-one-one call this afternoon."

"I don't need anything, actually, but I haven't seen you—I mean, to talk to or anything like that—in far too long."

Mike was taking things out of the shopping bag and stacking them next to the stove. "Forget the meat loaf. I stopped at Patroon. Ken loaded me up with a feast. Light a fire in the den and we'll eat in there."

I was thoroughly taken with Mike's thoughtfulness and confused, as I had been for a very long time, by my feelings about him. I had wonderfully loyal and devoted girlfriends, but he was the man I had become closer to in the last ten years than any of the guys I had dated. I had fallen madly in love with Luc a year ago, but I loved Mike too— although I thought in a way that was not romantic. Every now and then a sweet moment like this presented itself, while I was too tired and emotionally wrought to figure out what was going on inside my head and heart.

"I'm starving. I could eat a bear."

"Hate to disappoint but Ken was fresh out of grizzlies. Fix me a drink, will you?"

"Mercer put some nice white on ice."

"White doesn't go with bear—or with a porterhouse. I guess you haven't spent enough time in France to figure that out."

Ken Aretsky was one of New York's great restaurateurs and a dear friend of mine. I had introduced Luc to him, because his upscale eatery on East Forty-sixth Street was a model of fine dining—first-class food, a wine list with incredible depth, and an elegant setting for any good meal—the kind of place Luc was planning to reinvent in his father's style.

"I hope you brought sides. He's got the best onion rings in the world—and garlic mashed potatoes. And sautéed spinach," I said. "Can you tell I skipped lunch? You want vodka or red wine?"

Patroon was anything but a take-out place, yet Ken had frequently arranged deliveries to my apartment when he heard I was under the weather or hunkered down in preparation for a trial.

"You get the fire going, find the red wine, and I'll set out the dinner. I know how much you go for guys who can cook," Mike said.

I walked into the den. There were logs in the fireplace and matches on the mantel, so I poked around until the sparks seemed to take on the dry wood.

I went into the powder room and freshened up. I hadn't put on lipstick or blush the entire day, and now I found myself borrowing Vickee's things to apply a bit of makeup, brush my hair, and dab on perfume. I stared at myself in the mirror, barely recognizing the tense and exhausted face that stared back at me.

Then I checked the fire, which was going full force. The wine rack and bar were across the room, and I selected a nice California red to avoid any more conversation about France. When I picked up the corkscrew bottle opener, my stomach churned at the thought of Salma Zunega's neck.

"You want to get the silverware and some napkins?" Mike asked. He had come into the room carrying a platter with a black-and-blue porterhouse for two that he had sliced for us. "Give me the wine opener. Bad territory for you to revisit."

I passed it off to him and went into the kitchen. When I returned with the place settings, Mike had uncorked the bottle and set out the glasses on the table in front of the sofa. We both made another trip back to bring in the little plates with the veggies and potatoes that Ken had included, knowing my favorites.

"Sit down and help yourself," Mike said.

"Let me just run up and make sure Logan's out."

I climbed to the top of the stairs and peeked into his room. He had curled up under his quilt, surrounded by his favorite stuffed animals, and was sound asleep.

I came back down as Mike was pouring the wine. He lifted his glass and clinked it against mine. "Cheers—here's to everything you want in the New Year."

"You make a resolution to be nice to me? That's top of my list."

"How could I be nicer than this? The best grub in town, a really fine house, a cute kid. You look great with him, Coop. You look like a natural with that little guy snuggled up tight against you."

"Here we go again."

"You have a good time in Paris?"

I didn't answer.

"No, really. I'm being sincere now. Can't you tell me if you had a good time?"

"I had a very nice time, Mike. Luc's an easy guy," I said, putting down my fork and reaching for the wineglass. Luc adored me and seemed to understand my commitment to the erratic lifestyle of a big-city prosecutor. "His life is so different from ours. There's no urgency to anything he does, people's lives don't hang in the balance. A crisis is whether someone in the biz gets two stars or three."

"I hear the great chefs kill themselves over that, Coop. I wouldn't make fun."

"I'm not. It's just like living in a fairy tale to fly away from home, leave all my cases for a week, and suspend time in a kind of fantasy life in the middle of the most beautiful village in the world." I stopped for a minute and put my head back on the thick chenille pillow. "I just don't know where this is all going."

"Mind if I take this other end piece?" Mike asked without waiting for the answer. He was eating through all the conversation, as he always did. He handed me one of the enormous onion rings and I munched on it while I watched the flames dance in the fireplace.

"What about you?" I said.

"I'm chewing. You know how you always tell me not to talk with my mouth full?"

I leaned forward and cut a few more bites of steak for myself. Mike had been in love with an architect named Valerie who had survived a bout with breast cancer, only to die in a freak skiing accident more than a year ago.

"I know what Val's death did to you," I said. I thought I knew its impact as well as anyone, because of my own immeasurable loss. "She wouldn't want you—"

"Here's what's stupid, Coop. Number two on my list of stupid things people say, okay?"

Mike's number-one peeve was the word *closure*. He hated that families of murder victims thought the arrest or conviction of a killer would bring closure to their painful journeys. Instead, while it offered some sort of resolution, he knew that nothing could ever provide what people really wanted—to see their loved ones again, to undo the crimes themselves and the irreplaceable loss of a human life.

"Sorry, Mike. I didn't mean—"

"Number two, Coop. How does anyone know what Val would want? She's dead. Why are folks always so sure what the dead would want? People use that expression all the time and I happen to think it's stupid. Maybe she'd want me to go to a monastery and meditate. Maybe she'd want me to try out at first base for the Yankees. I didn't know she was gonna die so I really never asked her what she'd want."

I could see that I'd touched a raw nerve.

"Objection sustained," I said, and Mike smiled at the legalese.

"Let me rephrase that, Detective Chapman. Does what I want count for anything?"

"Depends on what it is," he said, stabbing another piece of steak and holding it out like an exhibit before putting it in his mouth. "If it was this particular piece of meat, I'd have to say it doesn't matter what you want."

"I take it you're dating again."

"Spinach is good for you, blondie. Put some on your plate," Mike said. "I'm trying to get myself out there."

"That's great. I really think it is. It's time, Mike."

"You know me. Most of the broads I meet are too high maintenance."

"Rumor has it you met a judge at Roger's Christmas party."

"I—I met a lot of people at the party. Saw a lot of old friends."

"And left with a very attractive judge. Want to tell me about her?" I pushed my plate away, kicked off my shoes, and curled up on the sofa.

"You crack me up, Coop. You got me tailed? Which of your girls has the big mouth?" Mike said, reaching over and taking the steak from my plate.

"What's to say the judge isn't talking?"

"I'm here, aren't I? Not with her."

"Judge Levit," I said. "Fanny Levit. Just appointed, Civil Supreme. Age?"

"Thirty-nine."

"Hmmmm. An older woman." Mike had turned thirty-eight in the fall, six months ahead of me.

"By a year."

"Lighten up, Detective," I said, sticking my toe in his side. "How many times have you seen her?"

"I met her at Roger's. Took her to dinner the other night," he said, getting to his feet and carrying our dinner dishes into the kitchen.

"So why *are* you here?" I called after him. It wasn't the few sips of wine I'd had that was making me feel frisky.

Maybe Mike was stuck with the same dilemma I was, wondering how our superb professional partnership would be affected by a change in personal direction. At the same time it both interested and frightened me. Once we crossed the line of intimacy, we'd never be able to work cases together again.

He returned from the kitchen carrying a bowl stacked high with profiteroles—Patroon's best dessert and one of my sweet-tooth weaknesses—covered with chocolate sauce.

"I'm here 'cause of you," he said, handing me a spoon and offering first dibs on dessert.

"Sometimes you come out of nowhere at me, Michael Patrick Chapman, and I am so pleasantly surprised," I said, reaching over to brush the crumbs off his sweater.

"I'm here because you never even bothered to call me today about the autopsy on Salma, and you got to help me figure something out."

We'd had mixed messages before, but this one caught me totally off guard.

"You drove out to talk to me about the case?" I asked. I sat up and folded my legs beneath me, feeling like a fool for having put any kind of personal spin on his Friday-night drop-in. "You could have just called, you know?"

"Yeah, but then I wouldn't have seen Logan, and I didn't want to bother Mercer before the big family prom."

I was embarrassed by my ridiculous assumption that Mike had driven out to see me for some reason other than the case. Of course this hadn't been a social visit, or at least it was no more personal than two friends and colleagues catching up before inevitably turning the conversation back to our work.

"What's the news on the autopsy?" I asked. I tried to focus again.

Mike stood up with his glass in one hand and leaned against the mantel. "Cause of death was obvious. The wine opener pierced Salma's trachea. Asphyxia due to blood inhalation."

I'd had cases like that before. Death was usually quite rapid, the victim often convulsing as blood obstructed the air passages. It was as ugly a picture as I had imagined.

"You expected that."

"Yeah, well, what do you know about pregnancy?"

"Precious little."

"Dr. Kirschner says he's willing to bet that Salma never gave birth."

I put my glass down to try to clear my head and rethink things. Claire Leighton had told Mercer that Ethan admitted fathering Salma's little girl. The baby had been in the apartment shortly before Mercer's visit. The doorman described the woman who had taken her.

"What do you mean, Mike?"

"You know MEs, Coop. They'll never say never. But it's something about the cervix that has Dr. Kirschner convinced."

"Like my Riverside Park homicide victim two years ago. When a woman has given birth to a full-term baby," I said, "there are changes in the cervix. The opening gapes a bit—the medical term is *patulous*."

"That's the word. He said she wasn't patulous. There's nothing in Salma's body to reflect any signs she gave birth. No scars on the abdomen to suggest a C-section. He took one look at the uterus and said there was no way anything that small had ever held a baby."

Now, there was an entirely new set of concerns to deal with. Whose baby was it and what had become of the child? Who was the man who had shown up on Wednesday night, claiming to be the baby's actual father?

"So Ethan Leighton probably bit the bullet on a phony DNA

test," I said. It wouldn't take much for a forger to fake a genetic test result to convince the congressman that he had indeed impregnated his lover.

"And you can add a touch of extortion to the list of motives that's growing deadlier by the hour."

TWENTY-SIX

I got up from the sofa a bit later to check on Logan, who had barely shifted positions since I tucked him in and turned out the light. When I returned to the den, I put another log on the fire and settled into a comfortable armchair.

Mike found a college football game on ESPN and stretched out on the sofa. I pretended to watch while I wondered whether he would always be as much of an enigma to me as he had proved to be tonight.

Vickee and Mercer got home shortly after one o'clock in the morning. They had seen Mike's car down the street and figured we had planned to spend the evening together. They were as mistaken as I.

"How was the party?" I asked.

"We had a good time," Vickee said. "The relatives behaved and the bride-to-be is happy as anything. All fine with Logan?"

"If he wakes up fighting with people-eating dinosaurs, I'm not the perp," I said, pointing a finger at Mike. "He's good as gold and I loved the chance to be with him for a few hours."

Vickee stepped out of her shoes while Mercer took off his jacket and undid his tie.

When she went upstairs to look in on the baby, Mike told Mercer about Salma's autopsy and I started to relate the details of my interview with Olena.

"What can I fix for you, Alex?"

"I'm good. I'm going to drive back into the city."

"Why don't you stay? Guest room's all made up."

"I need a decent night's sleep, Mercer. It won't even take half an hour for me to get home."

Mercer poured himself a drink from the bar and Mike helped himself to another glass of wine. "This is taking the courthouse rent-a-baby scheme to a new low."

It was commonplace for felons—especially those facing a sentence date—to show up with a woman who'd been nowhere in sight throughout the trial. The plea for sympathy worked best if she carried an infant in her arms, not likely to be any relation to the defendant, but something to tug at the heartstrings of judge or jury.

"It also explains how sterile it was in Salma's apartment," I said. "Sure, she had a crib and a high chair and enough toys in the bedroom when she needed to convince the congressman that she'd had his kid. But no photographs, none of the out-of-place disorder you'd expect with a nineteen-month-old—well, it was a setup, in all likelihood."

"Probably worked for as little time as he had to spend with her," Mike said, "between being in Washington and his own home here in the city."

"I would so love to corner Ethan Leighton and just confront him with all this," I said, picking up my jacket and tote. "Too bad Lem's in the way of that."

"You blew the chance."

"I'll walk you out to your car," Mercer said.

"G'night, Mike. Thanks for bringing dinner."

"I put it on your tab, Coop. The least I could do was make the delivery."

"Watch it on the steps," Mercer said, opening the door and steering my elbow. "There are a few icy patches."

I didn't say anything as we walked to my SUV. I was thinking that Mike was staying on behind to drink with Mercer because he didn't want to deal with following me back into Manhattan—his usual style if we were in separate cars—and saying good-bye at my door.

"You okay, Alex?" Mercer asked. "You're so quiet."

"Yes, of course. I'm just tired," I said, reaching up to kiss him. "Tell Vickee I'll call her tomorrow. What an absolute joy to get to spend time with Logan."

He opened the car door and I got in, letting the engine warm up before I pulled away from the curb.

The CD picked up where Smokey had left off when I arrived. *"Ooh, baby, baby . . ."* I wasn't up for brokenhearted love songs at that moment, so I shut off the music for a quiet ride home.

I turned left at the end of the long street, retracing my route to the expressway through the dark, quiet neighborhood. I was driving slowly, concerned about the ice on the streets of the outer borough, always among the last to be plowed.

There was a right turn after a stop sign, and as I eased the heavy SUV around the corner I noticed a car approaching behind me.

I tried to pull over so that the driver, who seemed to be in more of a hurry than I was, could pass me, but there wasn't room for any-one to get by on the one-way residential street, lined on both sides with parked cars.

I sped up and my car fishtailed on the icy road. I glanced in the rearview mirror and was grateful that the driver in back got the point. He—or she—had slowed considerably and seemed to have accepted my pace.

Another three or four blocks and I knew I would see the large green sign that marked the entrance to the highway. I took my time, looking in the mirror at every turn to see if the car was still there. I wasn't really concerned because the route I was taking was the one to the main artery leading both into the city and out to Long Island. I'd expect other drivers to use it.

I crossed a large intersection and the driver stayed on the same path. The car was a larger SUV than mine, a light silver color— nothing like the minivan that had alarmed me at the shelter in the afternoon. But its windshield had the same kind of dark tint.

The street I was on narrowed and doglegged to the left, so I braked again going into the curve, careful to avoid the piles of slush bordering the pavement.

Suddenly, the driver behind stepped on the gas and plowed into me, ramming my SUV and aiming it at the large utility pole straight ahead.

I swung the steering wheel as hard as I could, sharply left, and the powerful machine responded like a small sports car. I veered into the driveway of the last large house on the block and leaned on the horn for a full minute as I came to a stop inches from the garage door.

The SUV that hit me sped off as my horn blared and lights went on in all the houses on the street.

TWENTY-SEVEN

The two uniformed cops who answered to the flurry of 911 calls in the still Douglaston neighborhood asked for my license and registration.

I apologized to the man whose driveway I'd entered in such a wild fashion, before I backed out and waited for the police. I'm not sure he believed my story about being followed and forced off the road, but he seemed to want me out of his hair so that he could go back to bed.

"Where were you coming from, Miss Cooper?"

I decided not to pull out my badge and tell them I was an assistant district attorney. I didn't need to wind up in a tabloid gossip column or be the butt of any more of Mike's jokes. Maybe I really was seeing too much of the bogeyman.

"A friend's house," I said. I gave them Mercer's name and address.

"You have anything to drink?"

Officer Tarranta was talking to me as he eyeballed the damage to my car. His partner was sitting in the RMP, using the laptop now in each radio motor patrol car to see whether I had a criminal record or vehicular violations.

"Half a glass of wine about four hours ago. I'll blow for you."

"I tell you," Tarranta said, "these TV shows are too much. They even got the lingo down. All of youse learn your cop talk on *Law and Order*, I guess. Most of the people I stop aren't so willing to blow for me."

"This was ice, I think. Not on the rocks, but on the street."

"I seen you walk fine, your breath don't smell, and you're totally coherent, ma'am. I just have to ask about the liquor. It's routine." He squatted by my rear fender and jiggled it. The right side was badly dented and hanging off the end of the vehicle. "You may not be hammered, but your car took a hit. How's your head?"

"I'm fine."

"You want to go to the ER? Be checked out?" Tarranta asked.

"No. Nothing's wrong with me."

"You got to sign this for me, then," he said.

If I told him I knew it was an RMA form—that I had refused medical attention—he might have figured I had something to do with law enforcement. "Sure. What is it?"

He explained the procedure and then told me to get in the car to stay warm. I watched as he walked down the street, in the direction from which I'd come.

When he got back to me, he was shaking his head. "I don't understand it, ma'am. This roadway is clean as a whistle. Nothing to skid on, unless you were wide to the side of the main lane."

"Maybe I was." I smiled lamely at him.

"I put a call out for a speeding silver SUV. See if anything comes from that. You think it was intentional? Some guy follow you from the party?"

"No, Officer. It wasn't a party. It was just four of us at the house, and no one followed me when I left the street," I said. One of the city's best detectives had packed me into my car and waited as I drove away.

"Did you see him in the rearview mirror?" Tarranta asked. His partner approached and gave a thumbs-up, confirming that I had no record.

"I saw the car about a block after I pulled out from my friend's house. I think I was just going too slow for the guy."

I could tell Mercer about it tomorrow, but no need making a big deal out of it with these officers.

"Anything come back on the radio about the silver SUV?" Tarranta asked his partner.

"Nothing yet."

"I'll give you this number, Miss Cooper. You can call in for the police report tomorrow, for your insurance company."

"But it's okay for me to drive it, don't you think?"

The two cops looked at each other. Tarranta got down on his knees and tugged on the fender, then stuck his head beneath the rear of the SUV, probably to see how firmly it was still attached.

He stood up and talked to the younger, thinner cop. "Give it a feel, will you? I don't want to send this lady out on the highway and have the damn thing dragging behind her."

Officer Richards didn't seem too happy to have to get down on the pavement to examine the underside of my car. He knelt and then flattened out on his back. His head disappeared from sight as he tried to jam the loose fender back up in place.

"I'm so sorry to have caused all this trouble. Please get up. I'll be fine."

"Hey, Anthony," Richards called up to his partner. "It's not the bent metal that I'm worried about."

He was sliding out and sitting up, holding a black object in his hand. "The problem is, she's been tagged."

I didn't have to rely on television cop shows to learn the latest lingo. I knew exactly what that little object was. The young cop was telling Officer Tarranta that a Global Positioning System monitor had been concealed in the undercarriage of my SUV.

"I know what that means too," I said to the startled cops. "This wasn't an accident, guys. Someone's been using a GPS to chase me around all day and night."

TWENTY-EIGHT

"Why didn't you just tell us you were a district attorney when we got to the scene?" Tarranta said, as we pulled into the garage at my apartment.

His boss had given the pair permission to drive me home, and Richards had followed in the RMP.

"It seemed easier not to make the connection at the time," I said, as Tarranta trailed me through the locked door that led up the back stairwell into the lobby. "I had no reason to think anyone was targeting me for trouble."

"You gonna talk to Mr. Battaglia in the morning?" he asked, as Vinny—one of my favorite doormen—greeted us and handed me a bundle of the day's mail.

"Yes, Anthony. I'll do that first thing."

"'Cause, you know, my CO has to fill out an 'unusual' on this."

We were standing near the elevators as Tarranta reminded me that the commanding officer of his precinct would indeed have to file a formal department report about something as potentially threatening as the stalking of a prosecutor.

"I understand, of course."

Tarranta lowered his voice. "I mean, if this is a domestic or anything—if this is a boyfriend out of control—Richards and I will help you out on it."

"You're really kind, Anthony. I promise you it's not that."

"You want us to sit on your place?"

"No, thanks. You've done enough already. Vinny's got my back tonight," I said, winking at the doorman who had seen me through several worse situations. "Then Oscar comes on at eight. I just need some rest. I'm working on a tough case and I'll be talking with the detectives in the morning."

"Okay, then. Stay safe," Tarranta said, as the elevator opened. We shook hands before the doors closed to take me up to the twentieth floor.

I came inside and double-locked myself in, putting the chain across too. I turned on lights—more than I needed at this late hour—and went to the bar to pour myself a Dewar's to carry into the bedroom.

I played back my messages as I undressed to go to sleep.

The first one was from Nina, who was at home in Los Angeles. "Gabe's going to New York in two weeks for business. I'll come along if you can solve that horrible case and clear your calendar. Call me."

She and I had been roommates at Wellesley and best friends ever since. Nina knew as much about me as any human being could know about another. She and Joan Stanton had been through every romance, celebration, and crisis of my adult life, and I communicated with both of them almost every day.

"Darling, it's almost midnight in New York." It was Luc's voice, strong yet sexy—and comforting at a bleak three o'clock in the morning. "Thank goodness I don't have a jealous streak. I would be sad if it's business you're doing still at this hour, and hope you're out with friends. I'll call tomorrow. *Bonne nuit, mon amour.*"

I stripped off my clothes and slipped on a cashmere nightshirt.

The third recording started to play. It had come in only half an hour ago, at two thirty.

There was no spoken message. It was the noise of a car crashing against something—maybe a recording of my own incident—and then the sound of tires screeching as a vehicle sped away.

I took a deep hit of scotch and checked the caller ID on the last message, but the number was blocked.

I relied on the fact that I lived in a very secure building with two doormen on duty for every shift—24/7—and after I washed up and got into bed, I kept my cell in my hand as I settled in to try to sleep. I turned out the light but sat upright for almost an hour, using the alcohol like medicine to steady my nerves and allow me a few hours' sleep.

I remember looking at the clock every fifteen minutes until five A.M. I must have drifted off around then, and slept fairly well.

The phone rang and awakened me at nine thirty on Saturday morning.

"I'm at your door again."

"What?"

"I'm sure you've got the dead bolt turned and eight chairs stacked against it, but I'm right outside your apartment door," Mike said. "I thought it would be more polite if I called first this time instead of just banging."

The doormen liked Mike and Mercer. It would never have occurred to them to stop him from coming up to see me.

"I'm not in the mood this morning. I'm barely awake."

"You were in the mood last night, blondie. I can bet you that."

"Look, why don't you give me a break and call me this afternoon?"

"'Cause you're late."

"Late? For what?" I knew we hadn't made any appointments for interviews today.

"Class. Ballet class."

"Can you get the fact that I am totally out of sorts, Mike?"

I had studied ballet since earliest childhood. It was my favorite form of exercise, and I spent an hour at a studio on the West Side almost every Saturday morning.

"You've missed class for two weeks in a row 'cause of the holidays and your trip. You're going to lose that fine shape, Ms. Cooper. Then I'll have a wallflower on my hands for the rest of my life."

"I'm going to hang up on you, Mike."

"Just open up, Coop. There's something important I have to tell you."

The timbre of his voice had changed. He was dead serious.

"Are you all right?"

"I don't know. Just open the door."

I threw the phone on the bed and got up, wrapping a robe around me. I ran to the door and slid off the chain, unlatched the dead bolt, and pulled the handle.

Mike was on his knees in the hallway, his head bent over so that I couldn't see his face.

"What's wrong?" I asked, putting both my hands on his shoulders.

"I'm such a jerk, Coop." He looked up and smiled at me. "There are some things a guy just has to say face-to-face and this apology is one of them."

"You don't have to—"

"Sure I do. There *was* a bogeyman after all, and I let you walk out into the night without a second thought. I'm sorry. I'm really sorry I made fun of you for being so yellow-bellied. I was wrong. Now, can I come in, Coop? I got to put these in water."

Mike bent over to pick up the newspapers and to the side of the door was a pile of lilies, huge white ones—maybe six dozen in all. He scooped them up in his arms and brought them inside.

"How's the whiplash, kid?"

"Who told you about the accident?"

"The CO was a lot smarter than the two cops who took the report. He knew exactly who they were dealing with and called Lieutenant Peterson," Mike said, referring to his boss at the homicide squad. "The loo woke me up this morning, and I was just worried about you going out before I got here. Move along. Point me to the vases, jump in the shower, and let's get this beautiful day up and running."

"Vases are in the cabinet below the window in the dining room. Don't tell me I'm on the hook for all the flowers?"

"Nope. Bodega lilies. They might be dead by tomorrow, but they make quite a statement, don't they? You can tell I'm sincere."

It was hard to pass many street corners in commercial areas of Manhattan that didn't have small grocery stores with outdoor flower markets. You could buy an extraordinary array of flowers for very low prices, even if they didn't live too long.

"I'm going to skip class. William will understand."

"You'll skip nothing. You're always telling me how your ballet lessons relax you, help you focus, take you to another zone."

That was true. It was hard to think about anything else while I stood at the barre engaged in the disciplined physicality of the dance, concentrating on positions for the pliés and relevés that warmed us up at the beginning of each class.

"Let me get ready," I said. "I'll be quick."

I ran a steaming hot shower, toweled myself dry, pulled my hair up into a ponytail, and dressed in a black leotard and tights. I threw an oversize sweater and leg warmers on top of the outfit, and grabbed the bag with my ballet slippers.

When I got to the living room, I could smell something cooking. I kept little in my refrigerator except English muffins and an assortment of strong cheeses to serve with cocktails, the only serious entertaining I did in the city.

"What did you possibly find to cook?" I asked.

"Brought my own eggs. Knew it would be slim pickings."

Mike whipped up scrambled eggs with onions and fried some bacon while I showered. He had poured us each a glass of orange juice and was ready to serve the food and coffee.

"Talk about a full-on apology—on your knees, armloads of flowers, and a hot meal. Keep this up and I can think of a whole lot of things you should be sorry about," I said.

"Start with last night."

"After you made light of the car taking pictures in front of Parrish House, I didn't want to get myself all jacked up again. I never thought GPS."

"Why would you?" Mike asked.

"I've had enough cases now to know it's a problem."

The brilliant navigational system formed by twenty-four satellites orbiting the earth, transmitting time and location to receivers on the ground, was one of the most dangerous tools in the hands of offenders. It had become especially popular in domestic violence cases, in which estranged spouses and stalkers could know the whereabouts of their victims as soon as they got into the family car, often with deadly results.

"You think it's connected to what we're working on?" Mike asked, chewing on a strip of bacon.

"How could I know when the device was stuck in there? Wednesday, when I drove out to the shipwreck, was the first time I used my car since the holidays. And then I took it to work with me yesterday."

"Where were you parked?"

"On the street near the office."

"And the garage in this building is public, too, isn't it?"

"Yes."

"It wouldn't take two minutes for someone to slip a GPS under the fender. Pretend he was checking out a tire. Anybody could do it."

"It's that easy?"

"Coop, they've tagged snow leopards in the mountains of Pakistan and Yunnan snub-nosed monkeys in China. Maybe they can't get a GPS on Bin Laden, but your car would be an easy target at home or at work."

"But why do it?"

"That's what Mercer and I gotta figure out. You think you were followed to the shelter with Olena and Lydia, right?" Mike asked. "No one doing that would need a photograph of you. They could pull one off the Internet. So it's more likely that the snapshots were something to do with the Ukrainian girls."

"I'll buy that. But last night, following me from Mercer's?"

"Put a good scare into you like it was supposed to."

"You had to see the curve, Mike. It could have put me into a coma, not just a scare, if I'd taken a header with the SUV into the utility pole."

"So somebody owes you an even bigger apology than I do."

I carried the dishes and put them in the sink, pouring us each a second cup of coffee.

"When you find out who, I expect more than bacon and eggs."

"Get a move on, kid. You need a good workout," Mike said.

I picked up my bag and reached into the closet for my ski jacket.

"Better bring a suit."

"A suit? I'll shower and change when you drop me off after class. I promise I'll stay here all day. I've got bills to pay and calls to make. I need some down time."

"Get it another day, Coop. I suggest you clean up at William's studio. That nice gray flannel pinstriped suit with one of your fancy scarves will do fine, and take your blow-dryer so you get your hair out of that ridiculous topknot."

"You have plans for me?" I asked.

"The mayor wants to see us this afternoon. He wants us to meet him at Gracie Mansion."

TWENTY-NINE

The guard in the small booth at the East Eighty-eighth Street walk-way that led to the Gracie Mansion grounds was expecting us when we arrived at one o'clock. I had gotten to William's studio in time to do my stretches for the eleven A.M. class, while Mike ran errands and came back for me after I showered and dressed in my professional clothes.

"Front or back?" Mike asked.

The elegant formal entrance was the original front of the house, facing the river, since most guests arrived by water those hundreds of years ago. A newer access had been designed for the rear of the building, closest to the street, the way most people came to the residence now.

"Right here," the man said, pointing to the back steps.

Mike led me up and the door was opened by the detective from the mayor's detail—the same one who had been with him and Rowdy Kitts when Statler stormed into the mansion on Thursday afternoon, after Salma's body had been recovered from the well.

Mike shook his hand and said hello. "You know Coop?"

"Only by sight," he said. "I'm Dan Hardin. Pleased to meet you."

If he was pleased about anything, it wasn't reflected in his expression.

"Alex Cooper. Thanks."

"The mayor's waiting for you in the dining room. He's just finishing lunch."

We followed Hardin up a short interior staircase, lined with a rich bright-blue-and-gold runner, which spilled into an enormous ballroom.

"This is the Wagner Wing, isn't it, Dan?" Mike asked.

"Yeah."

"What do you mean?" I asked.

"It's named for Susan Wagner, the wife of Robert Wagner Jr.," Mike said, "who was elected in 1953. She hated everybody tromping through the mansion, putting out cigarettes on her carpet and parking cocktails on her furniture. All this big reception space was built for public functions in the 1960s. It's not original to the mansion."

Dan took us down a hallway that opened on the dining room.

The mayor was alone at the head of the antique mahogany table, surrounded by several piles of paper. He had a thick report of some kind in his left hand.

I had been there with Jake for dinner and knew that the room could accommodate dozens of people. The furnishings were exactly as I remembered them—exquisite period pieces like the paw-footed sidebar, a dazzling brass chandelier, green moiré curtains, and the exquisite panorama of Paris on wallpaper that covered the four sides of the room.

"Here they are, Mr. Mayor."

"Oh," he said looking up from his work. "Come in, Alex. Mike. I'm just finishing up here. Would you like the chef to fix something for you?"

"No, thanks, sir," I answered.

"Don't be shy. We keep these going all day." Vin Statler was pointing at a stack of tea sandwiches. "English cucumbers, Mike. Give them a try. Chef Estevez makes the world's best chocolate chip cookies. Even Mother Teresa thought so. Four thousand a week we make for guests and tours. You know in the summer we grow a lot of things in our own garden—right down past the well. Romaine lettuce, eggplant, Brussels sprouts, chives."

"I didn't think you called us here for an Iron Chef throw-down, Mr. Mayor," Mike said.

"I understand you're interested in the mansion, Mike." Statler's plastic smile changed to a momentary scowl. "I've got all the information you might want to know, and you may have something for me."

"No free rides, sir. I'm aware of that. I was hoping we could look around." Mike was still determined to find a reason that Salma's body had wound up on the grounds of this unusual home.

"We'll show you the place. I expect that will put your mind at ease, convince you the mansion has nothing to do with anything so sordid," Mayor Statler said. "Roland tells me you're quite the history buff, Detective. And you, Alex, you've been spending time in France I understand. You know Zuber?"

Mike's brow furrowed at the mention of a name he didn't know. He hated to be left out of the loop.

"Yes, sir. I've seen this room before, but never without a crowd in it," I said.

"Take a good look. It's remarkable, isn't it?"

"I'll bite," Mike said. "What's a Zuber?"

"Jean Zuber ran a company in Alsace, Detective, that was set up in the early nineteenth century. The crème de la crème of French artistry."

Mike was running his hand over the smooth surface of an antique pier table. "What'd he make?"

"Wallpaper."

"You could get rich from wallpaper?"

"This is the grandest quality in the world, Mike," I said. "These panoramic scenes were printed on hand-carved pear-wood blocks. *Les Jardins Français*, isn't it?

"Yes, Alex. Made in 1830." The stunning painting of French gardens covered the room, like a colorful montage of trees and flowers and fountains. "That was the height of the craze for French wallpaper of this quality. It was before photography, so people would pay to have these foreign scenes created in their homes."

"Flocking. My mother was more partial to flocking," Mike said.

"This would have cost a fortune to re-create today. Beyond our means," Statler said, ignoring Mike completely. "But the decorators just happened upon it in the attic of a grand Hudson Valley house, unused and in its original wrapping. Did you know Jackie Kennedy found two Zuber panoramas to place in the White House?"

The mayor was finishing his coffee. Mike poured us each a cup and helped himself to the cookies.

"No," I said, "I didn't."

"We got very lucky. We'd never have afforded this one."

"Ninety percent of police work is getting lucky," Mike said. "Glad it happens under your roof too."

"But there was a fortune spent on restoring this house, wasn't there?" I asked.

"Indeed," the mayor said to me, then turned to Dan Harkin. "Want to ask someone in the kitchen for hot coffee?"

Statler pushed back from the table and stood up. "Parts of the house were falling down by the time Ed Koch moved in. Almost uninhabitable. By 1983, he'd raised private money—millions—to establish a conservancy for Gracie Mansion, to get down to the foundation and rebuild the entire structure."

"That must have been quite a process," I said. Statler clearly wanted to be stroked, to show us he was in charge of the "people's house," before he turned it over to us for examination.

"You can't imagine what they did. Everything from infrared scanning to determine the posts and beams of the original wooden framing, biopsies—really, biopsies—of old paint chips to try to match the original colors."

"It was renovated again in 2000, wasn't it?" Mike said.

"It's very hard to maintain something as old as this building. Despite the earlier work, the deck on the front porch almost collapsed. At the time, there was an anonymous gift to the conservancy here for five million dollars."

Mike whistled. "That could buy a lot of Zuber."

"There was a great effort that went into finding some of the original pieces the Gracie family owned, furniture made for the house when the Gracies lived here."

"Nice job. Bloomberg, huh?"

Statler bristled at the sound of his predecessor's name. "Anonymous, I said."

"We all know what that guy did for the city," Mike said. "Every decent charity and every great cause got an anonymous handful from his deep pocket. The guy is aces."

Statler clearly didn't like Mike's admiration of the popular politician who had preceded him in the post.

"When did Gracie Mansion become the official mayoral residence?" I asked.

"The country's first official mayoral residence, Alex," Statler said. "At the insistence of Robert Moses, who was the very powerful parks commissioner, Fiorello LaGuardia reluctantly gave up his own comfortable apartment and moved in here, to the farm, as he liked to call it. Nineteen forty-two was the year."

Mike was getting antsy. "How come so many of you guys don't want to live here?"

"Each mayor, each family, has its own reaction to the house. You know we had a district attorney who became mayor, Alex, do you?"

"No, I didn't know that."

"Nineteen forty-six, Bill O'Dwyer," Statler said. "He'd been the Brooklyn DA."

"Prosecuted the Murder, Inc., guys," Mike said. The media had given the thriving organized crime group known as Brownsville

Boys, who'd been responsible for scores of murders from the 1920s to the 1940s, their more vibrant name.

"Yes, he did. But his wife hated it here. She thought the proximity to the river made it a lonely place—foghorns, the noise of the buoy bells keeping her awake," Statler said. "Ed Koch used it more than he ever thought he would, though he still escaped downtown most weekends to his own apartment after too much pomp and ceremony."

"Then Rudy ditched the place when he walked out on his bride," Mike said.

The moment that Giuliani held a press conference to announce he was leaving his wife—before telling her himself—had deservedly been one of his lowest points of popularity in the months before September 11, 2001.

"And Mayor Bloomberg?" I asked.

"When he was elected in 2002, he made the decision to live in his own home, all the time," Vin Statler said. "Bloomberg has a magnificent town house. He preferred to use Gracie Mansion for daytime functions and to house the most eminent overnight guests. Quite frankly, I made the same choice. The mansion is a public place, and I'm a rather private man."

"How public is it?" Mike asked.

"Walk with me, please," the mayor said. "Once the Wagner Wing opened, they had to construct this little hallway to connect the two pieces of the house. See? Brilliant, isn't it? We call it 'the hyphen.'"

That's exactly what it was—a narrow, hyphen-shaped passageway between the original parts of the Gracie home and the rooms that had been added hundreds of years later for much larger, public events.

Statler was walking us through, showing us everything from the enormous ballroom, painted the same mediagenic color as the Blue Room in City Hall, to the dainty parlor, to a smaller dining room, and another reception area with huge glass-fronted bookcases and tall shelves that housed a collection of Chinese export porcelain. In each, the dark mahogany furniture gleamed against the deep true colors that had been reclaimed and restored.

As we moved along, Statler described the range of events held weekly in the mansion. "It's not like this glorious place sits empty, Mike. There are seminars of all kinds held here, retreats and meetings of different city agencies. I'm divorced so there isn't a first lady, but Mrs. Dinkins used to read to schoolchildren right in this ballroom every Tuesday afternoon," he said, steering us back to the rear entrance of the house. "What haven't you seen?"

"What haven't you shown us?" Mike said.

The mayor was exasperated. "What the hell is it with you? Do you understand who you're talking to?"

"Yes, sir. Despite my vote, you're the mayor of my favorite city," Mike said. "I'm trying to make an intelligent connection between the young lady who's dead and why she was found in your very own backyard. Is that so hard to understand?"

"If your implication is that I had anything to do with this woman, you might want to start measuring yourself for a new uniform. I'll wave if I see you along a parade route, while you're doing crowd control," Statler said, thrusting his hands in his pockets and stomping on the floor. "You want to see the basement? You think I have skeletons in the closet?"

"Last closet I saw this week was a veritable gold mine," Mike said. "Sure, I'll take the basement. I was here on a detail ages ago. It was built as a bomb shelter in the 1950s when this wing was added."

"That's right, Detective. And now it's a police command center if there are problems in the city or on the river. Dan"—the mayor gestured to his bodyguard—"take Chapman down if he wants to see it."

Statler turned and started charging back to the dining room. "Where's Roland?"

"Upstairs," Dan said, leading Mike to the staircase.

"Fine. Follow me, Alex. We'll show you the private quarters. When you've satisfied your curiosity in the basement, Mike, come right along."

I was trying to elevate the spirit of the conversation with Mayor Statler. "This house has such wonderful bones."

"Indeed. A great classic center-hall layout, wonderful symmetry, and it's completely flooded with light."

"I can see that, even on a gray day."

When we reached the foyer, I could hear the staircase creaking. Rowdy Kitts was descending from the rooms above. He greeted both of us and removed the burgundy rope that normally blocked access as the mayor and I approached.

"All in order, Roland?"

"Yes, sir."

"Did we have any guests this week?" The mayor was climbing ahead of me.

"Not since before Christmas, Your Honor. It's been very quiet."

"Let's show Alex what we've got up here," the mayor said to Kitts. "Living history, young lady."

He led me to the northwest corner of the house, an enormous room with sweeping views of rivers and bridges. "The mayor's bedroom. I suppose this intrigues you."

There was a wood-framed canopy bed that anchored the space, a pair of inlaid chests under the windows, a large bathroom with modern fixtures to provide the most up-to-date comforts.

"It does, actually. It's quite beautiful."

"Remind me, Roland. Whose portrait is that?"

Rowdy Kitts rubbed the scar under his left eye, as though that would help him think of the answer.

The mayor was growing more impatient. "The artist is Thomas Sully. The woman is—well, some nice Quaker girl with rich folks is who she was."

I stepped in the sun-filled room to look around and paused at the painting.

"Nelson Mandela slept here, can you imagine? All the Gracies and their fancy Federalist friends, and still we're adding historical importance to this home," Statler said. "It's great that we can let the city use this for special occasions."

I was thinking of the Lincoln Bedroom in the White House, and the bundles of cash that swirled around the players in this investigation. "Since you're not here at night, do you rent it out to contributors?"

"Nonsense. The fact that neither Bloomberg nor I lived here makes it easy to simply offer it to dignitaries and important guests."

Statler never set foot in the room. He watched me explore it and then guided me across the wide hallway. I stopped to admire a graceful sofa, upholstered in a bright red fabric. "Someone found that at City Hall, just crying out to be here."

Mike was coming up the stairs.

"Satisfied, Detective?" the mayor asked. "We call this the mayor's study. A little office that guests can use. That's its primary purpose, isn't it, Roland?"

"What are you, Rowdy?" Mike asked. "The concierge?"

"I'm whatever the mayor tells me to be."

Dan Harkin, who had come up behind Mike, nodded in agreement.

"Then we have the State Sitting Room," Statler said, leading us down the hallway. "It used to be the family room, when some of the mayors lived here with their children. We've changed all that."

Mike was opening closets and pulling on desk and dresser drawers.

"You looking for some official stationery?" Rowdy joked. "Or Gideon's Bible?"

"Your staff has lists of people who've stayed here, do they?" Mike ignored him.

"Pretty impressive DNA the mansion's guests have, Detective," the mayor said. "How far back would you like to go? Washington Irving spent the better part of a summer here one year. And of course if you're keen on history, then you would have enjoyed sitting at that grand dinner table when Mr. Gracie was entertaining some of the regulars. History—that's your territory, Mike, isn't it?"

"Yeah."

"You know the name Gouverneur Morris?" Statler asked.

"Widely credited for writing the Preamble to the Constitution," Mike said. "He's the 'We the people' guy."

"I should have learned my lesson Thursday not to trifle with you," he said, taking us down the stairs and back to the foyer. "Morris, John Jay, Alexander Hamilton. They were all part of Archibald Gracie's circle of friends."

I reached the bottom step and could tell from the mayor's body language—a slight grimace, his feet planted firmly in place, and his arms crossed on his chest—that he was ready for us to be out of his hair.

"So Hamilton Grange," I said, "was that designed with this mansion in mind?"

"Exactly, Alex. Hamilton was quite close to Archibald Gracie. He admired this house tremendously. He even hired the same architect to design his. You should visit the Grange sometime. There aren't many of these original Federal masterpieces still standing in Manhattan. How many would you say, Roland?"

Rowdy Kitts shrugged and held up his hands. "Not my thing, sir. I don't have any idea."

"Why don't you and Dan show them out?" Statler said. "We've got to be on our way. There's an event at Madison Square Garden before we get to City Hall."

"Mind if we leave by the front door?" Mike asked. "I never get tired of looking. It's got to be one of the most spectacular views in Manhattan."

"Help yourself," Statler said, stepping aside so one of his aides could open the door.

"Gracie didn't have the same political prominence as his friends, did he?" Mike asked, backing away from the mayor.

"He never held office like the others. Gracie was a merchant, first and foremost," Statler said. "Built up his great shipping enterprise but then everything collapsed—first his businesses, then giving up this home he loved so dearly—as a result of the War of 1812. Many of his fleet were captured or burned or lost at sea."

"Interesting that he was so involved with all the great political figures of the day," Mike said, turning to walk with me.

"By virtue of a gentlemen's social group, Detective, Gracie dined with Hamilton and the others regularly. Turtle soup and oysters and pomegranates, all from his own lush property, right here."

"What is it you want to know from us, Mr. Mayor?" Mike asked.

"How fast are you moving on this case?"

"Do you mean Salma's murder, or the *Golden Voyage* investigation? They're all part of one big picture, and even as pieces fall into place, none of it will be so quick to resolve," Mike said. "Why?"

"The rumors flying around are outrageous," Statler said. It was obvious he was trying to keep his temper from flaring. He was used to being the man in control and seemed helpless without his hand on the helm.

"Which ones are you referring to exactly, sir?"

"If they've reached City Hall I'm sure they've filtered down to the homicide squad. Scandal smells, Detective. It's got a disgusting, rancid odor that compromises everything around it."

"Especially when you've got your sniffer aimed on higher office, I guess."

"It's not just rumors about *me*. Those are hogwash."

"Rumors about you?"

"I understand that Commissioner Scully let it leak that I refused to let your team work up here on Thursday, like he asked me to."

"Right in the same breath when you assured us that Salma was bound to turn up," Mike said. "My crystal ball wasn't so optimistic about that as you were."

Rowdy Kitts took a step in Mike's direction. "C'mon, Chapman. Take it outside."

"What would you like to know, Your Honor?" I asked, as Rowdy guided Mike onto the porch.

"These cases—the shipwreck and the mess with Leighton's girlfriend—exactly how are they related?"

"I don't mean to be difficult, Your Honor, but we don't know the answer to that yet. It's possible that Salma Zunega was originally trafficked into this country from Mexico, like the women on the boat from the Ukraine."

Vin Statler lowered his head and paced across the patterned floorboards. "Scully and your boss are both treating me like I've got leprosy. I'm the goddamn mayor of this city. The whole place seems to be up for sale and I can't get the attention of the police commissioner or the district attorney."

"What is it you want to tell them?"

"Nothing you can help with." The noise Statler made sounded like a snicker. "I didn't see you getting too far with them the other day."

"I can usually tweak Battaglia's ear." If case law didn't open that passageway, dicey gossip from high-placed sources often did.

"It's the rumors about pay-for-play that are so pernicious," the mayor said. "Ethan Leighton's father—Moses—and the lieutenant governor—Rod Ralevic—are determined to have an influence on the congressional candidate who'll run to replace Ethan."

"So I've heard," I said. "But Ethan hasn't stepped down yet."

"He may try to ride this one out a few days like Eliot Spitzer did, but it won't fly. Even that congressman from Staten Island tried to do that a few years back—you know who I mean?"

"Vito Fossella." Fossella had shattered a promising political career when his late-night drunk-driving arrest led to his admission about a second family he had sired in D.C.

"Yeah. Fossella. Well, Ethan's affair, the accident, the drinking, maybe his strong streak of ambition has him believing it will blow over in a week. I don't think he realizes that Moses Leighton himself has somebody lined up to keep the congressional seat warm. A dead girlfriend? Murdered? People won't let Ethan Leighton get away with that."

"Get away with it?" I asked. "You have the facts to convince me that it's Ethan who killed her?"

Vin Statler squared off and faced me. "What I'm suggesting, Alexandra, is that you focus on why somebody is dragging this crap to *my* doorstep. I don't know how deep Ethan's problems run. He set the girl up, he knocked her up—"

The mayor paused for a breath. I didn't want to tell him yet that Salma, in all likelihood, had not actually given birth to a child. "What else, sir?"

"Moses Leighton was his son's power broker. He's been living to see that kid fulfill all his own unrealized dreams. Heaven help the person who threatened to undermine that, and if it was the girlfriend, don't put anything beyond what Moses would be willing to do to get rid of her."

"You're just speculating."

"You don't know the man. He's hired thugs to break voting machines on Election Day, he's paid off the opposition with millions of dollars when they've been hungry enough to take it, and he wouldn't hesitate for a moment to have one of his goons slit this girl's throat."

"So that's what you'd like me to tell the district attorney?"

"Your boss isn't known for doing stupid things, Alex," Statler said. "But Thursday night was an exception. Charged in on me with—what's that guy's name?"

"Spindlis. Tim Spindlis."

"Charged in to tell me they absolutely had to announce the City Council indictments then. That moment, that night. The damn grand jury's been sitting on the case for four months. Why'd he do that?"

"Again, sir, I don't know." This wasn't the time to reveal my own suspicions about Spindlis.

"I'll tell you why. Kendall Reid is nose-deep in whatever the Leightons are cooking up. He's dirty, Alex, and for some reason, Battaglia didn't want to wait to see where that road led him. If there are more bodies, Kendall Reid knows where they're buried."

Statler was flailing about. "Your colleague—Mr. Spindlis. You trust him?"

"I do. Of course I do. I've worked with him for years."

"Tell Battaglia to watch his back," Statler said, getting to his point. "Rod Ralevic is going down, you know. People won't stand for that pay-to-play approach. He's out on a limb and I think it's about to get cut off by the feds. And the story I hear is that your man Spindlis goes down with him."

THIRTY

"Hold your mouth till we get down the steps," Mike said.

"Why'd we have to come out this way? The wind is blowing off the river and it's freezing." I pulled on my gloves and stiffened the collar of my jacket.

"Just hang out here for a few minutes," Mike said, walking past the yellow crime-scene tape that enclosed the area of the well and folding his arms as he leaned on the wrought-iron fence. "Don't tell me the Seine looks any better than this."

He turned around to talk to me, but I knew he was really checking to see if the mayor or his men were watching us.

"You like the sculpture?" he asked.

Bloomberg had encouraged the Museum of Modern Art to loan the mansion some of its finest pieces. The wide expanse of lawn that rolled down to the river was dotted with impressive works by notable artists—Frank Stella, Isamu Noguchi, Louise Bourgeois.

"I like it all," I said. "I'd move in tomorrow."

"He's nervous."

"Statler is a no-nonsense guy. He's pretty miserable with all this stuff swirling around him. It's killing him that Salma's body was found here at Gracie Mansion, so he's taking shots at everyone else."

"What did you talk about?"

"He's pointing fingers everywhere. Obviously, tracks this whole thing back to Ethan Leighton. Says what we all know—that Moses Leighton is ruthless and has the money to carry out whatever plans he wants."

"Who else?"

"Kendall Reid," I said, while Mike stared back at the tall windows of the library. "Anybody looking?"

"Walk with me, Coop," he said, leading me to the yellow crime-scene tape that was crisscrossed over the wooden cover of the well. "What does he say about Reid?"

"That he's the Leightons' lackey. That he'd pretty much do their bidding. The mayor's really unhappy with the way Battaglia crashed that indictment Thursday night," I said.

Mike pushed up the sleeve of his jacket and glanced at his watch.

"Statler thinks Ethan's going to try to tough this out and hang on to his congressional seat."

"Lots of luck."

"Set up a political battle between the Leightons and Ralevic, who's already put a price tag on the congressional seat."

"Stoop down for a minute, Coop. Pretend you see something significant in the dirt."

"Who's watching?"

"Either Statler or his boys. Very interested in what you're looking at."

I bent over, picked up a stone, and handed it to Mike, so that he could continue the charade.

"I can almost hear the curtains rustling," he said, examining and pocketing the ordinary piece of rock. "I just like toying with their brains."

Mike looked back at the house and waved, then started to lead me around to the rear. When we reached the driveway, he steered me left, instead of right out to the street.

"Where are you going now?"

"Stay with me, kid."

"It's cold, Mike, and I've got things to do."

The wide path ran behind the redbrick wall that separated the mansion from the acres of beautiful park that ran along the river.

"I bet you've never seen Negro Point."

"Mike—"

"I'm not being politically incorrect," he said.

Several joggers and dog walkers passed us from both directions, but the cold seemed to have kept most of the babies whose mothers and nannies favored this popular children's park off the stroll.

He was walking toward the wide promenade that bordered the river, below the wrought-iron fence of Gracie Mansion.

"That southern tip of Ward's Island, see it? For hundreds of years, on every official map ever made, that used to be called Negro Point. Right there."

I followed him past the benches to the river's edge. The swift swirling current looked as unwelcoming as the cold slabs at the morgue. "No more?"

"Just a few years ago the parks commissioner complained. Renamed it Scylla Point, and there's a playground in Astoria called Charybdis. You go through that dangerous passage in a boat? It's like managing the Straits of Messina. So now it's named for the monsters of Greek mythology that guard Messina."

"Okay, Mike. You're right. I should know these things. Let's come back in the spring."

"One more you gotta know about. The *General Slocum*. Eighteen ninety-one. A passenger boat, a steamship that caught fire during a Sunday church excursion. The waters were so rough, more than one thousand people died right within reach of where we're standing. Some burned to death, the rest drowned."

"I know that story. The city's greatest loss of life in a single day—until September eleventh," I said. "I get your point, Detective. This—this death zone is aptly named."

I was listening to Mike, staring at the rough water in the distance, and was so distracted that I didn't hear the footsteps behind me until I felt a strong hand on my shoulder. I turned to see Lem Howell.

"Somehow, my dear Counselor, I always thought we'd meet at Hell Gate," Lem said.

"Tricky of you, Detective Chapman," I said, barely able to hide my anger at Mike for arranging this meeting. "Tricky, transparent, and probably more treacherous than this current."

THIRTY-ONE

"What's the last thing you said to me last night?" Mike asked me in mock surprise. "You'd give your right leg to corner Ethan Leighton to talk to him, but Lem would never allow it now."

"Stop right there," I said. "Enough about what I said."

Lem walked back and sat on one of the long wooden benches. "C'mon, Alex. Mike was right to call me. What reason would I have to stand in your way?"

"Your client. And your client's father."

"Holy Moses," Mike said, trying to make light of this encounter he'd set up. "Now, there's a guy I wouldn't want to meet in a dark alley."

"Moses isn't driving this train, Alex. I promise you that."

"I don't want to be rude to either of you, but I've got work to do," I said, taking a few steps away from the river.

Mike grabbed my arm and swung me around to face him. "I tried to arrange something to please you, Coop. To help the case. Now, sit down and listen to Lem."

"When was the last time you were sucker-punched like I was by Lem when I stepped into his limo? Either one of you? I've got an office and working phone lines and still prefer doing business during regular hours. What's the part of that you two don't seem to understand? What's this about?"

Lem patted the spot on the bench next to him and I sat down.

"The developments in this case are moving as fast as these waters. Slow it down with me and smooth it out, okay?"

I fidgeted with my gloves while he talked.

"Ethan Leighton may have acted like a fool on a personal level, but he's an extremely smart, exceptionally talented young man. You knew that once, didn't you? You partnered with him on a big case."

I didn't speak.

"Keep your perspective. That's what I'm asking you to do."

I could see Scylla Point in the distance and was trying to find Charybdis. I had the feeling I was destined to be crushed on the rocks in between.

"What's Ethan charged with right now?" Lem went on. "Driving while intoxed. Leaving the scene. Hell, first offender with a strong record of public service, I'll get these charges reduced and dismissed. A third-year law student could get the same result."

"Salma Zunega's dead," I said. "Remember her?"

"It seems to me you'd never heard of her until I mentioned her name."

"Till you told me she was crazy. You seemed to be the first to know that, too, Lem. Well, maybe you've heard she wasn't quite as crazy as you wanted me to believe. Salma was murdered. That's good to keep in mind."

"Ah, murder," Lem said. He got to his feet, raising a finger in the air. "Now it becomes clear, Alex. That's your plan? To use the *m* word every time Ethan Leighton's name comes up?"

"I don't have a plan, Lem. It's up to Mike, to Mercer, to the NYPD, to solve this."

"This? By *this* you mean Salma's death as well as the shipwreck? You think they're connected?"

I glared at Mike.

"You don't want to tell me how. I get it," Lem said. "You can't do this to Ethan. You can't tar him with this crime while he tries to get his good name back."

Now I was following a tugboat's progress downstream. "How well I remember standing next to you during one of my first arraignments on a felony case, Lem. AR-three, night court. The judge was Irving Lang. The defendant had drugged and raped a woman and I was requesting substantial bail. His lawyer started screaming at me—how could I do this to his client?"

Lem cocked his head and squinted, like he was trying to remember the event.

"Don't you hate screamers in the courtroom? Well, that guy was really wailing at me about how I was hurting his client. I remember the sharp tone of his voice as clearly as I can still see the perp's monogrammed shirt and his rep tie, stained with blood."

Mike and Lem were walking back and forth in front of me, both trying to get me to make eye contact. But there was enough going on in the river to keep me engaged while I talked.

"I must have been at a loss for words that night, Lem. Never your problem, is it? You were supervising me and you stepped in and gently pushed me aside. Made this wonderful record for me, about how the prosecution didn't 'do this' to that jackass standing before the court. You described how the defendant himself plotted the evening, selected his victim, bought the drugs, sprang for an expensive bottle of wine, and then spiked the drink," I said. "Well, *I* haven't done anything to Ethan Leighton. He seems to have created his problems all by himself. His greed, his infidelity—"

"People don't go to jail for infidelity, Alex. Half your colleagues in the office would be behind bars."

"Just let me slap the cuffs on Pat McKinney myself when that day comes," Mike said. "Don't give me that look every three minutes, Coop. Stop rolling your eyes."

"We're talking a car accident, Alex," Lem said. "Have you lost your focus? Keep that separate and apart from the murder case."

"I guess this is about the Ethan Leighton press conference that you're undoubtedly scheduling, isn't it?"

"I've got to get him in front of a microphone before the weekend's over. He needs to speak to his constituents and assure them that he's ready to apologize and put this all behind him."

"So, you responded to Mike 'cause you're hoping I'll tell you that when the reporters run from your office to Battaglia's, the DA doesn't say that the newly repentant congressman is the prime suspect in our murder case."

Lem smiled. "That would be helpful."

"We've got an office pool, Lem. I hate to cheat, but I can be the big winner if I bet them all that Claire Leighton will actually stand by his side through this, sunglasses covering her tear-filled eyes. Do the forgiving wife thing," I said facetiously. "We're just dying to know."

"I was working with Claire this morning when Mike called. I'm trying to get her there, but don't bet all you've got on it."

"Go me one better. Tell me she was in on the plot, Lem." I said. "And her father-in-law? How much has Moses offered her to hang tight?"

Lem slapped Mike on the back. "You're spending too much time with Chapman. I've never heard you be so cynical, my dear."

I buried my hands in my jacket pockets. Mike's hair was blowing wildly in the strong wind, catching the occasional spray as water splashed against the seawall. Lem was ramrod straight and serious, his coat belted tightly around him against the chill.

"What do you know about the baby?" I asked.

"I understand you, Alex. You're not giving me anything without a 'get.'"

"Did Ethan believe that he had fathered a child with Salma?"

"He wasn't happy about it. He denied it at first. Salma actually left New York for almost five months. That's when she gave birth, somewhere in Texas. He made her do DNA testing, of course, at some lab near Brownsville. When that proved he was the father, he flew her back to the city and bought her this apartment."

"Did it ever occur to him that the whole baby thing was a scam?" Mike asked.

"What do you know that I don't?" Lem asked.

Neither Mike nor I answered.

"I see. Not my turn to ask questions today, is it? Ethan's quite distraught about the child's disappearance. I assume you know the Leightons have posted a huge reward for information about the little girl."

I was glad that Mike apparently had not told Lem about Salma's autopsy findings.

"You must know something about Salma's background," I said. "Was she trafficked into the country? Who brought her here?"

"Don't know, Alex. I don't know."

"Come back when you do," I said, getting up from the bench. "I'll see you guys next week. I'd like some answers, Lem."

"I can do better than that, Alex. If you come with me into the park right now, I can give you a second chance. You can get them from Ethan Leighton."

THIRTY-TWO

"She does stubborn better than anyone," Mike said to Lem. "Relax, will you, Coop?"

"There's a proper way to do this."

"And that would put more pressure on both you and Leighton than either of you needs, Alex," Lem said. "I've always had your trust. Queen for a day—right here, right now."

"No, Lem."

"I can't walk Ethan into the District Attorney's Office. The press would be all over him—and all over you. 'What did he say, who did he implicate, why'd they make a deal?' You have my word—whatever you want. Talk to him, Alex. Get a sense of the man."

"I heard him snap at you in the car the other night. I felt his eyes cutting through me like lasers. And I saw Salma Zunega's body. I have a damn good sense of Ethan Leighton."

"Bad attitude, blondie. We got nothing to lose."

"Queen for a day" was the name for a process in the criminal justice system that had been developed over the years. Defense attorneys would agree to present their clients—suspects, targets, or mere witnesses in a criminal investigation—to a prosecutor for a proffer of evidence, a sneak preview of what they might say under oath in a court of law.

"Mike's right, Alex. It's Ethan who's got the exposure here."

The proffer would lead to a written agreement, in which I'd assure the congressman that anything he told me couldn't be used against him at a later time. It wouldn't prevent me from getting derivative evidence, developing leads from any information he might give to us.

"I'm not the front man on this, Lem. Donovan Baynes has to call the shots."

"Look at me, Alex. Donny Baynes is one of Ethan's closest friends. If you don't think I placed a call to him before coming over here, you're forgetting how I work."

The feds had far more formal rules for accepting proffers in cases than we did. And Baynes's relationship with Leighton would have disqualified him from handling the matter.

"You're telling me Baynes wants me to take this meeting?"

"Baby steps, Alex. You've got to start somewhere. Donny's hands are tied but, yes, he wants you to do this."

"Has he been talking to Leighton?" I didn't know who was next in line to betray whom.

"No, no, no. Just to me. I was aware of their long friendship."

"Where's your client?"

"This way. He's waiting in that garden beneath the rock wall."

Mike tried to take my arm to guide me down the wide winding staircase but I wanted no part of him. The steps led to a round garden that, in summer, was one of the prettiest spots in the city, surrounded by lush greenery and beautiful plantings. Now, the trees were bare and the bushes looked scraggly, but the stunning rock formations provided a natural shield from the wind.

At the base of the steps, sitting alone on a stone wall, was Congressman Ethan Leighton. He was dressed in jogging clothes, with a hooded sweatshirt pulled up over his head and a short windbreaker on top of that.

When he heard us approach, he stood up and took off his gloves. He didn't look much better than he had the other night, forcing a smile as he greeted me again. Ethan was a bit taller than I, and his normally slim frame seemed even lighter than I recalled.

He held out a hand to me and I nodded at him. His lower lip was raw and red from where he'd been biting down on it. He had a ghostly pallor, a hollowness around his eyes that made them look even beadier than before.

"Sit down, Ethan," Lem said.

I sat a few feet away from him. Both Mike and Lem stood as Lem explained what he had told me. I muttered my agreement to this unorthodox arrangement.

"Why don't you tell Ms. Cooper about yourself, Ethan? What you've been doing since you left the U.S. Attorney's Office."

"Where should I start?" he asked, looking around to each of us.

"We can read the official bio," Mike said. "Tell us something about Salma Zunega."

"I'm just so sick that she's been hurt. It's haunting me."

"Not hurt, Congressman. We call it dead."

I wanted to find out how he'd met her before we got into the subject of the missing baby and whose child it might be.

"How long have you been married?" I asked. I counted on the fact that it would rattle him to talk about his wife and his inamorata in the same breath.

"Twenty-two years." Ethan Leighton had been on the hustings too long. His ability to flash an artificial smile in the middle of this was uncanny. "Claire and I tied the knot when I was in law school. She has a degree in business. She's wonderful—she's, um, really wonderful."

"And children?"

"Two. Two children. One's away at college and the other's in boarding school."

"You forgetting one?" I asked.

"Oh, sorry. Ana, of course. Ana Zunega," Leighton said. "I want you to know we're terribly concerned about the child. We're moving heaven and earth, with private resources, to help find her."

The more emotionally wound up he became, the more the tic in his left eye became pronounced. I'd never noticed it before. He stroked it with his forefinger, which was as long and almost as skinny as the finger bones of that skeleton in the City Hall grave.

"Who's 'we'?" Mike asked.

"My father, Moses Leighton. He's a very wealthy man, Detective. He's got the money to do this kind of thing."

"And Claire," I said, "—how does she feel about this?"

He took a deep breath and answered. "Under the circumstances, she's—she's—well, she understands completely and will raise the child with me as our own."

Mike asked exactly what it was that Claire understood, but Leighton didn't answer. He was listening to me as I spoke to Lem.

"I guess you made your point this morning, Mr. Howell. I guess Claire will be doing her Tammy Wynette 'Stand by Your Man' best on the podium for your press conference. Congratulations." I turned back to Leighton. "Of course, she hasn't yet accounted for her version of where she was the night Salma was killed, by any chance?"

His eye twitched wildly. "You're crazy, Alex. You're f—"

Lem cut him off and told him to control himself. The congressman's front tooth found its groove in his lower lip, drawing droplets of blood as he clamped his mouth shut.

"When did you meet Salma?" Mike asked.

"Three, almost four years ago."

"She was still a teenager then?"

"Twenty, sir. She was twenty."

"Just a tad older than your own kids," Mike said.

"Yes, but could we leave Claire and the kids out of this?" Leighton asked of Lem Howell. "Could we just talk about the accident and Salma's problem?"

"Ms. Cooper, here, is a fan of the big picture, Mr. Leighton,"

Mike said. "She'll tie it all up in a package for you before we're done."

"Mr. Howell told me that you were home with your family the night Salma was killed. You understand that Claire necessarily becomes a witness in all this."

"You're not seriously thinking I had any reason to hurt Salma?" Ethan Leighton pulled himself up into a position, posturing his outrage as though he were making a congressional appearance on C-SPAN. "Or that my wife did?"

"Don't ever try to go where Ms. Cooper's thinking," Lem said. "Just stay calm."

There was nothing a prosecutor liked better than the loving family member as alibi witness. What wife—with everything to lose—wouldn't put her hand on a Bible and swear that her husband had never left her side the night in question?

"Do you have any photographs of your daughter?" I asked. "Of Ana."

"I—uh—I'm afraid I don't. I'm afraid that wouldn't have been very smart, under the circumstances."

"Which part of the circumstances *were* smart?" Mike said.

"How did you meet?" I asked.

"It was at a fund-raiser, here in the city. One of my events."

"Salma was what—a political activist? Rallying the vote?" Mike asked. "Was she here in the States legally?"

Leighton didn't say a word. He looked at Lem but got no help.

"Was she a citizen?"

"I believe she was legal. She had papers, Detective."

"My mother's dog has papers, Leighton," Mike said. "Funny, 'cause cops swept her whole apartment and didn't come up with any documents."

"I don't know why that would be or where she kept them. Maybe at a bank."

"Seems to me Salma's closet *was* the bank," Mike said.

"What do you mean?" the congressman asked. "What are you talking about?"

Was it possible he didn't know about the shoe boxes full of cash?

"So what brought her to your fund-raiser that night?" Mike asked. "Your position on abortion rights? Gun control? Illegal immigrants?"

Ethan Leighton was keeping himself even. "She didn't come because of my politics, Mr. Chapman. She was there as someone's date. We got to talking and—"

"Now, that's classy. Not only are you cheating, but you steal her out from under another guy," Mike said. "A supporter? Somebody who bought a ticket to come in?"

"She was nothing to him, Detective. I don't even remember who it was who brought her. I'm sure she wouldn't either. Salma is a vibrant—"

"Salma was."

"Sorry. I still have trouble believing that," Leighton said. "Salma was a vibrant, intelligent, high-spirited young woman. She was mature beyond her years, because she'd been to hell and back, quite frankly."

"How do you mean?" I asked.

"Salma was smuggled into this country, Ms. Cooper. She was fourteen years old when she was brought across the border from Mexico in a cattle truck, along with thirty or forty people from her region."

Lem was watching me to see if Leighton succeeded at melting my armor with another tale of cruelty and abuse. He didn't realize I had not been able to get Olena's fresh story from yesterday out of my mind. Little chance of trumping that.

"Where was she taken?"

"Near Brownsville, in Texas, at first. With the usual promise that she'd get an agricultural job or be placed as a servant in a family household," the congressman said. "But that never happened. She was held captive in a farmhouse by the man her family paid to get her out of Mexico. For two years, she was raped repeatedly by him."

"I hear these tales more often than you can imagine, Mr. Leighton," I said. "I've learned what many of these young women have endured."

"There's an ugly twist to this one, Ms. Cooper. The man who kept her chained to her bed when he went off on these smuggling trips? He was Salma's uncle," the congressman said. "He was her mother's brother."

Now it was my turn to be silent.

Mike waited thirty seconds before pounding on. "Who brought Salma to New York?"

"It's nothing she would ever talk about with me."

"Weren't you the least bit curious?"

"I was much more than curious, Detective. There were entire pockets of her life that were off-limits to me, just as there were areas of mine that were off-limits to her," Leighton said. "Being sold off to her uncle as an adolescent was nothing she was in any position to change. But once he was ready to get rid of her? I don't think she was very proud of the fact that she spent the next few years of her life selling herself."

"So she came to New York as a prostitute, specifically?" Mike asked.

"Yes, she did."

"Someone must have been pretty well steeped in the trafficking business to get her here," Mike said. "A professional, not a two-bit Mexican in a cattle truck."

"I'm sure you're right, Detective. She never told me who. She wouldn't go there, and frankly, I didn't care."

"Didn't care?" Mike asked.

"That's sounds a bit icy. I mean that I had no intention of pushing Salma to talk about it, and I'm ashamed to say, it's not like I was going to get involved in a prosecution of the man. She had put it behind her and I certainly had nothing to gain by the association with her, or her pimp."

"The tattoo on Salma's body," I said to Leighton, "what do you know about that?"

I couldn't tell if he had reddened because of the nature of our conversation or because the cold air was biting his skin.

"Nothing," he said, with a sidelong glance at Lem. "A flower?"

"Do you know what kind of flower?"

Leighton thought the question was ridiculous. "I—I don't. Everybody's got tattoos, Ms. Cooper. My own kids have them."

"Not in the same place on the body as Salma's was," Mike said. "Just a hunch."

"On her leg—her thigh? So what?"

"Doesn't mean anything to you?" I asked. "That placement?"

"I don't know what you're talking about."

"Did Salma have that tattoo when you met her, or get it afterwards?"

"She had that when we met. I don't know when or how she got it."

"Where was Salma living when you first started to see her?" I asked.

"On the West Side. Near a Hundred and tenth Street."

"Not as well as you set her up," Mike said.

Ethan Leighton didn't speak.

"How long after you met did you begin dating her?" I asked.

"Look, Ms. Cooper. I'd actually never been unfaithful to Claire in all the years we'd been married. I didn't set out to get into this mess. Salma started calling me, texting me on my phone, showing up at all my events. She—uh—she was very interested in starting a relationship with me."

"Oh, man," Mike said, throwing up his hands as he began to circle the rock garden. "Where are these broads? How come nobody's ever after my ass? Her fault, was it?"

"Nothing is Salma's fault," Leighton said. "I'm not blaming her. I didn't have to meet with her, make dates, become involved. I responded—okay—I was just as excited about things as she was. You want blood from me? Is that what you want? Take it, Mr. Chapman."

"Calm down, Ethan," Lem said. "Just let them get this done."

"When you began dating Salma, was she seeing other men?" I asked.

"Obviously, Ms. Cooper. She came to my event with another man, didn't she?" Leighton's smooth tone was developing an edge.

"How often did you get to be with her?"

"Truly, not often at all. Maybe you know something about the congressional schedule," he said. "Monday's my day in New York. Pretty much like clockwork I could see her on Monday. But then I fly to D.C. every Tuesday morning, and the weekend, well—that was always saved for Claire and the kids."

"But this week you were with her on Tuesday night?"

"We're not back in session yet, Mr. Chapman. Salma called. She told me Ana was sick and she wanted to see me."

"And two years ago, when she told you she was pregnant, was she still dating other men?"

"Probably so. Well, yes, I know it was so. And we fought about that."

"About that, or about the baby's paternity?"

Ethan Leighton was steaming now. "You're damn right I wasn't happy about the fact that Salma was pregnant. She'd been on the pill for years before I met her. She knew how I felt about the whole idea, about how an out-of-wedlock child would compromise my political viability. I couldn't figure how she had conceived. And I'd spent so much time in Washington the month she became pregnant I just didn't think it was possible."

"So what happened?"

"We fought. She flew down to Texas, where her older brother had finally moved and had a home. And I was going crazy without her," Leighton said, putting his elbows on his knees and burying his face in his hands. "I guess it was like an addiction."

"Did you bring her back to New York?"

"Yes, yes, I did. She didn't want me around for the birth," he said, as Mike looked at me, "because I had been so vehement in my denial. But once we did the DNA test and she gave me the results, I sort of embraced the whole thing."

If his tic was anything like a lie detector, it was speeding off the charts when he spoke about embracing the news of the child's paternity.

"You bought the apartment for her?"

"I did everything I could to set her up comfortably with the baby."

I leaned in and looked at Leighton's face. "This last year, year and a half, was Salma still seeing other men?"

"You're asking me to think about things I don't want to know, Ms. Cooper. I wasn't going to leave Claire—never. I'm sure Salma had her ways of taking that out on me."

"And Ana, did you see Ana often?"

He was shifting positions, trying to get comfortable. "Look, I wasn't good about the baby, okay? No point lying. Sometimes she was asleep when I got there, sometimes Salma had her spend the night at a friend's house. You find that child and I'll make up for all of that. I swear it to you."

"Money, Mr. Leighton," Mike said. "How'd you pay Salma's bills?"

"You'll see when you get my banking records. I keep an office at my father's business. Family money, nothing that Claire ever had any access to or reason to see. There's a corporation I set up, within my father's firm. The checks were all written on the Leighton Entertainment account. He assumed it was for things I needed for my political advancement."

"How about cash?" I asked the congressman. "Did you give Salma large sums of cash?"

"Five hundred dollars when I saw her, sometimes a thousand if she wanted something special for the baby."

He really didn't seem to be aware of, nor try to explain away, the unusual amounts of cash we had found in Salma's closet.

"Who knew about your affair with Salma?" I asked.

"My secretary," Leighton said, taking time to think. "She wrote the checks. I never told anyone else."

"No one at all? No friends, no colleagues?"

"My closest friends are guys like Donny Baynes, Ms. Cooper. I didn't go there."

"And no one at work?"

"Just Kendall. Kendall was around at the beginning. He picked up on it. He's got a nose for trouble. I'm sure he figured it out."

Mike was all over this. "Kendall Reid, the city councilman who was just indicted on the phantom funds scheme?"

"Yes. Kendall actually worked for me before he ran for the council job. He knows Salma."

"Kendall knew about her, or actually met her?"

"They've met. He knew her, that's what I meant."

"How well?" Mike asked.

Ethan Leighton seemed surprised by the direction of the questions. "I guess, just through me. I guess."

"And it was Reid you called after your accident?" I said. "He's the guy who tried to take the weight for you."

"Yeah, yeah, he did. Crazy, I know."

"Have you talked to him since you found out Salma was murdered?" Mike asked.

At the same time that Leighton answered with a single word—"Yes"—Lem Howell spoke. "Ethan hasn't talked to anyone about this except Claire, his father, and me."

Leighton exhaled as Mike stepped between Lem and the congressman.

"When did you talk to Kendall Reid? Exactly when?"

"I'm sorry, Lem. I should have listened to you," Leighton said to his lawyer, before answering Mike's question. "I met him yesterday, just for a few minutes. Just to commiserate about my arrest and the news of his indictment."

It took a lot to get under Lem Howell's skin, but the long fuse had been lit.

"Where? Where did you and Reid meet?" Mike asked.

"At City Hall. I didn't go in. I was dressed like this—with the hood up, nobody makes me," Leighton said. He didn't even seem to be aware of the distinctive twitch. "Kendall just came out, down the steps—we talked for a few minutes out in front. Sorry, Lem. Sorry I didn't tell you."

I knew the lecture Ethan Leighton would get from Lem the moment they were away from Mike and me. He wouldn't tolerate any stray actions from his client. The congressman didn't need to be lockstepped with another allegedly corrupt politician.

"You and Kendall Reid," Mike asked, "what did you guys talk about?"

This encounter between the two scandal-ridden politicians opened a new vista of issues for us. Had they met to discuss the murder of Salma Zunega, the attempts at a cover-up of Leighton's accident, the untimely indictment of the councilman, or the whereabouts of bundles of the city's cash?

"Just commiserating. I needed to see a friend, and he felt the same way."

"It appears I was premature in my anticipation that this could be a useful meeting, Alexandra," Lem said, signaling Ethan Leighton to get up off his seat on the stone wall.

"Don't gag him now," Mike said. "It's just beginning to get interesting."

"We'll talk during the week. I thank you both for extending yourselves in these unorthodox circumstances," Lem said, as he started to climb the staircase, up from the stark winter garden toward the park walkway. "You know the nature of this work, Alexandra. Often the unexpected interrupts a perfectly lovely day. Keeps me on my toes. Constantly changing, challenging—"

"—and chilling, Mr. Howell. Literally and figuratively," I said, "this case is chilling."

THIRTY-THREE

"Oh, Alexandra," Lem called to me from the top of the steps. "There is one more thing. I assume you know about the bad blood between Ethan's father and the mayor?"

He had left his client at the top and was walking down to join up with Mike and me.

"That's part of the buzz we've heard," I said. "Going back to what?"

"Vin Statler has it in his head that a man with his business experience is what's needed to run the country."

"Vin tested the water at the beginning of the last presidential campaign, didn't he?"

"Well, he was getting ready to, but when he saw what happened to Bloomberg's effort, he gave up. I think he's hoping he'll still be viable when Obama's eight are done."

"He'll be in his late sixties then," Mike said.

"And Ethan Leighton won't even be fifty."

"Ethan's dead in the water, Lem."

"Mr. Chapman, I'm not giving you my point of view. Who do you think makes my hourly rate possible?"

"Moses Leighton."

"And if that man believes he can resurrect his son's image in the public eye, let me tell you, he'll move heaven and earth to do that," Lem said. "Mayor Statler would love to bury my client in the middle of this scandal. Don't ever lose sight of that dynamic, okay?"

"You didn't know anything about Ethan's meeting with Kendall Reid yesterday?" I asked Lem.

"I don't want my man anywhere near someone as toxic as Reid is right now."

"Who's representing him?"

"I'll leave you a message. So far, I haven't heard."

Ethan Leighton came jogging down the staircase, calling Lem's name. "I thought of something else Ms. Cooper and Mr. Chapman should know," he said. "Did you tell them about the well?"

Lem tried to restrain Leighton but he was like an eager puppy. "That's a story for another day."

"Actually, I'd like to hear it," I said.

"It simply can't be a coincidence that Salma's body wound up in this well," Leighton said.

"And why is that?"

"Do you know the story of Levi Weeks?" he asked.

"Never heard of him."

"It's quite a famous case. We studied it in law school—at Columbia—because it was the first American murder trial that was ever transcribed."

"Maybe it was a New York thing. Coop was studying too many mint juleps down in Virginia and too few landmark cases," Mike said.

Leighton was sincerely animated for the first time today. "Perhaps you know who Ezra Weeks was? Levi's older sibling?"

Neither Mike nor I had heard of the Weeks brothers.

"John McComb was the architect who designed City Hall. A fellow named Ezra Weeks was the actual builder," Leighton said. "When he saw the plans for that beautiful structure, Archibald Gracie hired Ezra Weeks, who'd become very popular with the mercantile elite in Manhattan, to build this house."

"Gracie Mansion?" Mike asked.

"Yes, the mansion. And inspired by the beauty of this home, Alexander Hamilton hired McComb and Weeks to create a country place for him."

"Hamilton Grange."

"Exactly. Well, Levi Weeks was a carpenter who did most of the work in both of these homes that his brother was building. While Ezra had become quite wealthy, Levi still lived in a boardinghouse downtown on Greenwich Street. A bit edgier than Ezra. He met a young woman who was also boarding there—Gulielma Sands—and had an affair with her. He probably impregnated her, then refused to marry her."

"Why?" Mike was biting his tongue, ready to make some crack, I was sure, about the circumstances so similar to Leighton's.

"She was too far below his social station. Or at least what he aspired to be. One winter night, Levi and Ms. Sands went out together, but she never returned home. Witnesses reported later that they heard a woman's voice call out 'Murder!' and 'Lord help me!' but no one did. The only thing witnesses saw was a fancy one-horse sleigh, just like the one Ezra Weeks owned, carrying two men and a woman, near the site where Gulielma's body was found."

"Where was that?" I asked.

"Near the intersection of Spring Street and Greene," Ethan Leighton said. I could visualize the location, not far from the DA's office, in the heart of what was now the very fashionable SoHo district. "In a well, Ms. Cooper. The girl's body had been dumped in the Manhattan Well."

"But nothing to do with this mansion, right?"

"Everything to do with it," Leighton said, doing his best to filibuster. "The foreman of the grand jury that brought the indictment against Levi Weeks in 1800 was Archibald Gracie."

"Interesting."

"The mayor of the city at the time—Richard Varick—presided at the trial. A future mayor—Cadwallader Colden—was the prosecutor. And Levi Weeks was represented by his own dream team—the defense attorneys were Alexander Hamilton and Aaron Burr."

"Working as partners?" I asked, surprised by their alliance.

"Absolutely so. Four years later, Burr killed Hamilton in their duel. But at Levi's trial, with his famous brother, Ezra, and John McComb testifying on his behalf, the jury took five minutes to acquit Weeks, despite the evidence pointing to his guilt."

"So all politics is indeed local," Lem said.

"Not to mention dirty and occasionally deadly." The story of an old Manhattan murder case caught Mike's attention. "What became of Levi Weeks?"

"He left town. His brother's business was thriving, but his own reputation didn't rebound here. The public wasn't happy with the verdict," Leighton said, thrusting his hands in his pants pockets, perhaps reminded of his own dilemma. "Levi became the toast of Natchez, Mississippi. He married well, and went on to design and build some of the most beautiful antebellum houses in the city."

"You got a point here, Mr. Leighton?" Mike asked.

The congressman's smile vanished. "Well, Lem seems to think you're convinced I had something to do with Salma's disappearance."

"You think you're doing yourself a favor with the dead-lady-in-the-well story?" Mike asked. "Puts you right in the driver's seat, sir. Takes you directly from Salma's apartment to the only well in town. Not a bad place to dispose of a body if you were a longtime fan of Levi Weeks." ˙

"I didn't even know the mansion had a well on the property. It's not my house, Detective."

"So you didn't know about the well at Gracie Mansion," I said, "but there's nothing to say the mayor knows the story of the Weeks murder case."

"Lem says you don't like people telling you you're wrong, Ms. Cooper," Leighton said, wagging a finger in my face. "But you are."

"Go for it, pal," Mike said. "She hasn't had her tail kicked in almost twenty-four hours. I'm all ears."

"The mayor's Christmas party was held here at the mansion on December twenty-second—just three weeks ago," Leighton said. "That's the anniversary of the icy night that Gulielma Sands disappeared. One of the historians working on the mansion conservancy told the story during the cocktail hour."

"You were here?" I asked.

"Yes, I was invited. It was quite a gathering, Ms. Cooper. Ralevic, the lieutenant governor, was here, half the City Council members, at least."

"Kendall Reid?"

"Of course. And your boss, the district attorney, with his trained chimp Tim Spindlis in tow."

Mike looked over at me as he spoke to Leighton. "Donny Baynes?"

"As a matter of fact, yes. Donny was here. He remembered the story from law school too. He hasn't mentioned that coincidence?"

I remembered how incredulous Baynes had been on Wednesday morning, on the beach, when Mercer Wallace showed up with news of Leighton's accident and affair. Maybe he was just subconsciously protecting his old friend.

"And, of course, Mayor Vincent Statler. He loves regaling folks with all the history of the city fathers and their antics," Leighton said sarcastically. "That's why I'm so surprised he didn't take the opportunity to tell you himself."

"Tell us what?" I asked.

"That it was old news to find a woman's body in a well."

THIRTY-FOUR

"What's your impression of Ethan Leighton?" I asked.

We let Lem and his client walk out ahead of us before we started to make our way to Mike's car on East End Avenue. The mayor's sedan was no longer parked at the rear gate of Gracie Mansion, and the pedestrian traffic was still light.

"That's a hinky guy," Mike said. "He's all buttoned up and stiff, but keeps flashing that ridiculous smile, hoping you'll like him. Not the first one I'd think of to be jumping in bed with a hot Latin lover."

"His emotional disconnect between his affair and Salma's death is unbelievable. It kills me that I voted for him."

"You'll get over it with a cup of hot chocolate. C'mon."

We wound our way back along the path, past the guardhouse where the security officer was dozing, out to the quiet street. We turned right and walked north a couple of blocks, across from the entrance to Salma's building.

Just as I opened the car door and got in, I saw a young man who appeared to be in his late teens. He was emerging from the alley behind Salma's condo, wheeling a grocery-store shopping cart, only half filled with its cargo of white plastic bags.

"That's it, Mike," I said, standing again and pointing at the cart.

"That's what?"

"Remember when we went into Salma's building through the back door on Wednesday night? The large wooden garbage pails that were lined up and the row of empty shopping carts left behind by deliverymen?"

"Yeah. There are always a few of them around."

"That's how the killer got her body out of the building and over here to the well at Gracie Mansion."

"Maybe so."

"See the metal grid on the cart?" I asked. "I'll bet it's what formed the marks on Salma."

"What?"

"The parts of her body that weren't covered by the blanket— underneath her back—or when it shifted with the movement of the cart over the curb and potholes," I said. "Get one of those shopping carts down to the ME's office for measurements. I'll bet that's what formed the pattern we saw on her skin."

THIRTY-FIVE

I waited in the car with the heat on high while Mike called the CSU. He wanted the guys to come up, to photograph and measure the metal structure of one of the shopping carts so Dr. Kirschner could compare the markings.

The sleepy cop in the guardhouse at the mansion confirmed that the carts were a frequent sight, both at the house and on the park grounds. Food deliveries arrived in them throughout the day and evening, and as in other parts of the city, teenagers often made off with them for sport, rolling them through the streets and playgrounds.

I called the shelter to make sure that Olena and Lydia had an uneventful evening. I learned they'd eaten dinner in their apartment, come down to the lounge, and stayed up past midnight—mesmerized by the shows on the large cable television screen—and overslept their morning call. They still managed to go off with the federal marshals at ten.

Mike got back in the car and started the engine. "Where to?"

"Hot chocolate?"

"Sure. You called Battaglia yet? Tell him about last night?"

"Don't be a nag. I've got to have something good to give him before I call him to say I was tagged and we don't know who did it yet. He's liable to ground me."

"They sell those GPS gadgets in every electronic store and on-line site. We'll be lucky to trace yours in a month. By then, someone may have shot you in the ass with a dart and tagged you for real. Make life easier for all of us."

"P. J. Bernstein's Deli makes really good hot chocolate. Drop me at home and I'll order up."

"Tell you what. Take a ride with me. Let's stir the pot a bit."

"I guess I'm in your hands. Where to?"

"City Hall."

"It's Saturday afternoon. Who do you expect to find?"

"The city never sleeps. And Statler said he was going there after a stop at Madison Square Garden."

"Waste of time."

"Look, Coop," Mike said. "Battaglia rattled their cages Thursday night with that sudden indictment of Kendall Reid and the other councilman, and the story of phantom funds. You don't think you got people cleaning out desks and computer files and all their other garbage? I'm dying to see my tax dollars at work."

We made a slight detour to pick up a sandwich and hot drink, then Mike got on the drive for the quick ride downtown.

The Civic Center, hub of all the government offices, municipal building, city, state, and federal courthouses, was usually pretty empty on weekends. We parked on Chambers Street and walked in from the west, past the yellow tape that bordered the hole that the reporter had described at the start of the press conference.

"Is that the crater you made?" Mike asked.

"No, mine's around back on the far side. Just more of the same sad relics, though. They blocked this one off, too, when I broke through the other tarp."

We climbed the steps and stopped at the metal detector in the lobby. Mike and I both showed our IDs and the cop on duty let us through the gate.

"Which way to Kendall Reid's office?" Mike asked.

The cop gave us a room number on the second floor. "You have an appointment with Mr. Reid? Want me to call up?"

"No, thanks. Just dropping by to talk about an old friend."

"You don't value my life at all, do you?" I asked, laughing at Mike's apparent plan. "That's Tim Spindlis's case. I can't walk in on Kendall Reid. He's just been indicted."

"Hey, did old Spineless stab you in the back once last year? Or was it twice? I have no interest in Kendall Reid stealing cash from widows and children and the great unwashed. In our case, he's just an ordinary witness. I need to talk to him about Ethan Leighton. And about Salma. Educate me, blondie, how many councilmen we got?"

Mike was charging up the staircase ahead of me.

"There are fifty-one members of the council. The speaker's a woman, so mind your manners. Fifty-one council districts throughout the city. Reid stepped into the seat that Leighton had before he ran for congress."

"What do they do here? I mean the council."

I was trying to catch up to Mike, but he was taking the great worn marble steps two at a time. "It's the lawmaking body of the city of New York. It governs, along with the mayor. The City Council has the sole responsibility for approving the budget."

"What does that run a year?"

"About sixty billion."

"So a few hundred thou in a shoe box would hardly be missed?" Mike asked.

"I guess that's the theory."

He stopped at the top of the landing. "What do you know about Kendall Reid?"

"What was in the *Times* yesterday morning. Your age."

"Our age?"

"I'm not thirty-eight till spring."

"Yeah, well, you better be lights out a little earlier tonight. You got so many circles under your eyes, they'd match the ones that ring a two-hundred-year-old redwood."

"There isn't enough concealer in the world to cover these," I said. "Reid grew up in Harlem. Black mother, white father who abandoned them when Kendall was four or five. Very smart kid. Stuyvesant High School. Full scholarship to NYU. Law school there after that. Worked for Bloomberg, then for Moses Leighton, until he became Ethan Leighton's aide."

"Where does he live?"

"One of those renovated brownstones. Sugar Hill," I said, referring to an area with some of the finest buildings uptown, part of the Harlem Renaissance.

"Sweet. He must have been sucking up to Moses to get enough money for that."

"Yes. Moses Leighton put him in some deals before Reid went to work for Ethan."

"What kind of deals?"

"Leighton's had some export-import companies, and a lot of real estate."

"Is Reid married?"

"Single. He's supposed to be a real player."

"Could be your moment, Coop."

The second floor hall was almost as busy as on a weekday. I didn't recognize most of the people around, but there were dozens of casually dressed men and women who were scurrying about or stopping to talk in small huddles.

The door to Reid's room was ajar. He was on the phone at his desk, and it looked like his office had already been emptied of file cabinets, in all likelihood a result of a search warrant executed after the unsealing of the indictment.

He covered the receiver with his hand. "Who you looking for?"

Mike flashed his badge again and said his name.

Reid didn't even say good-bye to whoever was on the phone.

He hung up, stood, and began shooing us out of the small room. "Nothing left for you guys. Be gone."

"I've got nothing to do with your arrest, Mr. Reid," Mike said. "I'm here about your friend Ethan Leighton."

Kendall Reid looked at us quizzically. "You'd best talk to my lawyer."

He was about five foot nine, muscular and well-built, with short-cropped curly hair and very light brown skin.

"We just left Ethan."

"Left him where?"

I introduced myself to Reid. "Just an informal meeting."

"Lemuel Howell know about it?"

"Lem was a mentor of mine in the DA's Office. He made it happen."

Reid was giving each of us a thorough once-over. "How's Ethan doin'?"

"That's exactly what I was going to ask you," Mike said. "You're his buddy."

"Well, we've both been a little bit busy. I haven't seen him."

"How strange is that? The congressman told me that just yesterday—"

Kendall Reid got the point. "Forgot that I ran into him right outside. Dammit. Right on the front steps. I had no idea he'd be around here. Come in, come in, Detective. Sit yourselves down."

Reid walked behind us and closed the door. Then he parked himself on the edge of the desk, facing us. The monogram on his shirt pocket matched the pale blue lines in his black striped suit, and his gold fountain pen was clipped neatly in place.

Mike told Reid that we were investigating the murder of Salma Zunega, and that so far, Ethan Leighton had been cooperating with us.

"You've known the congressman for quite some time, haven't you?" Mike asked.

"Sure have. Sure have. I actually met him through his father.

It was Moses Leighton who hired me away right out from under Mayor Bloomberg. I was just two years out of law school, working on legislation for the City Planning Commission."

"You and Moses Leighton became close?"

"Yes, we did. Man is like a father to me. Took a chance, liked what he saw, thought he could teach me a few things. I owe a lot to him."

I'd guess he owed at least the monogrammed shirt and the vintage Montblanc, not to mention the well-addressed town house, to the senior Leighton.

"Was it through working at Leighton Enterprises that you got to know Ethan?"

"Yeah. I'm an only kid, Detective. No sibs. So Ethan liked to take me under his wing, show me the ropes."

"Has politics always interested you?" I asked.

"There's two ways out of the ghetto, Ms. Cooper. Politics and business. The gangsta route? You can make money and live just as well that way, though not likely as long. It's still a ghetto lifestyle, no matter how high the rent. And there's always the risk of prison bars. No, I was focused early on. Politics and business."

I didn't want to say that this week's news made prison bars a strong possibility for Councilman Reid.

"I'm guessin' I can read your mind, Ms. Cooper. How can I talk about being better than criminals when your office just came gunnin' for me?" Reid reached behind him and grabbed the weekend edition of *The Wall Street Journal*. He swatted his hand a couple of times with it as he spoke. "I'm just a scapegoat for this practice that's been goin' on in this here city council for more than twenty years."

"I really don't want you talking about that to us, Mr. Reid," I said.

"You read this yet?" he asked, offering the newspaper to me. "I've got nothing to keep from you. Like the *Journal* says, it was a bookkeeping maneuver that dates back to 1988. I don't even know who the speaker was then, but he set up these fictitious groups, just to pool the money till it was distributed to council members. Nobody's takin' a piece of Kendall Reid's hide for this. That money's goin' to the community, just like I promised. Read this editorial."

I took the paper from him and put it on my lap. "We'd just like to ask you some questions about Ethan Leighton," I said, "and about Salma."

"Such a pity, such a tragedy." Reid was shaking his head back and forth.

"You were the first person Ethan called after the accident early Wednesday morning, I understand." I had read that in the police reports.

"I told you, ma'am, he's like my brother."

"You got to the scene before anybody could find the congressman. You were willing to take the weight for him?"

"Now, don't you be puttin' words in my mouth. There was a lot of confusion at that car wreck. I was just doin' my level best to help sort things out. I had no plans to take no weight for anybody, you hear?"

"He's not that heavy," Mike said. "I thought—like—he's your brother."

"Good try, Detective."

"What exactly did you tell the police when you got to the scene of the crash?"

"That paperwork those boys were so busy fillin' out? I bet everything I said is as clear as day. I don't want to be saying different things to you. Won't help Ethan any." Reid winked at me and went on. "Besides, I know how y'all be crisscrossing us up on the witness stand, you prosecutors. Bet you're good at it, ma'am."

Mike and the councilman were squaring off with each other. Reid had the habit of bouncing back and forth between a very crisp accent that matched his educational opportunities, and the g-dropping lingo of the streets. I could tell Mike was getting the sense that Kendall Reid was more flimflam than substance.

"Why don't you tell us when you met Salma Zunega?" I asked.

"Dates and me, we just don't get along too good."

"Roughly, Mr. Reid. About what year?"

"Goodness, I would have been working for Ethan at the time. Three, maybe four years ago."

"Do you remember where?"

"Does Ethan remember?" Reid tilted his head and pointed a finger at me.

"Yes."

"I'm kind of afraid to say. Don't need to mix him up none."

"Take your best shot," Mike said. "A speech, a party, a funeral, a Bar Mitzvah. Some other rubber-chicken dinner where you politicians hang out?"

"I'm quite sure it was a fund-raiser. That would be it."

"That's what Ethan said." Mike was luring the councilman along, opening his steno pad to pretend he was confirming Reid's answers with what Ethan Leighton had just told us an hour ago. "So you remember who brought her too?"

"Oh, Lordy, yes," Reid said, scratching his head. "That could have been ugly."

Mike flipped pages as though he were trying to find the name, even though Leighton had claimed it was no one memorable. "Yeah, the congressman said he dodged a bullet on that one."

"Salma came in with Rod Ralevic," Reid said. "Am I right?"

"You got it."

"He was a state senator at the time, before he became lieutenant governor. It was a big-ticket Democratic fund-raiser. There was Salma, looking so sweet, just getting on her feet after—you know her background, right?"

"We do," I said.

"Well, she was really fragile and vulnerable. And there's that fool Ralevic, so much hair on the guy's head he's looking like he's wearin' a mop instead of a hairpiece."

So Salma Zunega had already graduated to the political scene before she met Ethan Leighton.

"But she couldn't have been too wrapped up in Ralevic," Mike said, "if she made such a play for the congressman?"

"Rod? He was just in town for a few days from the boonies. Goin' hog wild over women and wine and whatever other people's money could buy him," Reid said. "He didn't care about the girl."

"How do you think Ralevic met her?" I was trying to get back to the common thread among the trafficked women.

"I couldn't begin to guess."

"Pay for play?" Mike asked.

Kendall Reid stood up straight and stretched his neck back. "Maybe so. That's before Salma found her way. Fell in love with Ethan."

"Ralevic never got mad when he learned about Ethan and Salma?"

"Learned what, huh? That affair was a better kept secret than my grandmother's recipe for monkey bread."

"No rivalry there? It has nothing to do with Ralevic rushing in to pull the strings on replacing Ethan's congressional seat?"

"Where you think Ethan's goin', dude?" Reid asked. "Sure as hell you don't know Moses Leighton if you think anybody's got a plan to take Ethan's seat away. The lieutenant governor ain't got no chance against Moses. That's for sure."

"What can you tell me about the little girl," I asked, "—about Ana?"

Reid's mouth tightened and he closed his eyes. "No way."

"But, we're terribly worried about what's become of the child."

"And I want to know who's the baby's father," Mike said. "Couldn't be the lieutenant governor, could it?"

"You know what?" He started to walk around to sit at his desk. "Let me get Ethan on the phone. Let me hear from him that he wants me to talk to you about all this, okay?"

"Try Lem Howell's office," Mike said, getting up and closing his pad. He knew Reid was about to end our interview. "My guess is that's where your brother is."

"Don't be goin' all holier-than-thou on me, Chapman. You want to know about Ethan meeting Salma? Ask your friend Baynes."

"Donovan Baynes?" I asked, shocked to hear his name in that context. "The head of the task force?"

Donny had denied from the first moment the news broke that the congressman had been having an affair.

"Yes, ma'am. He's part of the club."

"Club. What club?"

"You're all so high-and-mighty, don't you think? I find it nice myself when there's something you just don't know."

"What club?" I repeated.

"A gentlemen's social club, Ms. Cooper. By invitation only. I don't think you'd really be welcome."

THIRTY-SIX

"The mayor isn't back yet," Mike said. "I just left him a message. Told him he could call me anytime he remembered the story about Levi Weeks and the girl in the well."

I had waited for Mike in the lobby of City Hall, trying to figure out whether Donny Baynes really knew more than he had offered us. It was troubling to think that he was sitting on valuable information that might compromise his own position.

Kendall Reid wasn't able to reach Ethan Leighton, nor was he willing to go forward with our conversation.

"Statler's as likely to call you back as Judge Crater is," I said. "What do we do about Donny Baynes?"

"We take him head-on. Could be just this guy Reid's nonsense. He's not into prosecutorial love at the moment."

"I can tell."

We walked out the door and Mike pointed at the late afternoon sky. There was a gorgeous streak of pink that cut through the gray backdrop, lightening the dull winter landscape.

"See that dame?" He was shoulder-to-shoulder with me, pointing to something in the distance.

"Who?"

"That golden girl, on top of the Municipal Building."

Directly to the southeast of City Hall was the enormous structure, straddling an entire street, that housed scores of government offices. It was capped by the dazzling figure of a woman—several times larger than life size—cast in gilded copper. The famous statue, known as *Civic Fame*, held the city's coat of arms in one hand and a crown with five crenellations—the boroughs of New York—in the other.

"She's really gleaming against that pink sky."

"She reminds me of you, Coop. Not just the tiara and the veneer."

"What, then?" I asked, stepping down as Mike talked.

"See how she's standing? She's on top of a ball, spending her entire life trying to keep a delicate balance."

"That's me?"

"To a T. You're probably feeling sorry for Donny Baynes right now. Why? That's not your problem. If he didn't tell us something he should have, then screw him. That golden girl? She fell once."

"You're kidding, right?"

"Nope. The pose was too much for her. Toppled right over. Her arm broke off. I don't know how many stories down it was, but she crashed right through the skylight in the cafeteria. Nearly killed a couple of locals. Get my point? You're always trying to balance too much. Know who she was?"

"The statue?"

"The statue was a person. I mean a model. Back in the nineteen twenties." Mike stopped again and looked off at the great golden symbol of the city. "Audrey Munson. I'm telling you her name because it'll never be on *Jeopardy!* Otherwise, I'd try to score the dough off you."

"So how come you know it?"

"'Cause she fascinates me, ever since I was a kid. Artists used her for half the famous monuments around town. She's that strong-looking woman, you know, at the foot of the archway of the Manhattan Bridge. She's in marble at the Firemen's Memorial on Riverside Drive. I used to go there with my pop all the time. Fifteen statues in this city, and that one woman inspired them all."

"She must have been magnificent."

"That's not the part that reminded me of you, kid. It didn't stop her from going mad. Couldn't live with it when her career ended. Spent more than sixty years in an insane asylum, till she died at the age of a hundred and five."

"This is my object lesson for the day, Detective?"

"I've been thinking about it since you got tagged last night. Then I looked up and saw my girl Audrey just now. It's a delicate balance you're living, Coop. You need to step down off that ball every now and then. I'd hate for you to take a fall."

I hesitated before moving on, staring up at the gilded figure. "Okay, so I forget all my personal feelings about Donny Baynes."

"He's made his own bed. Let him sleep in it."

"Got it. When do I get to do my lifestyle lessons for the Chapman retort?"

"I'm hopeless. Get that through your thick skull," he said, trotting down the steps. "You'll never change me."

As I descended behind Mike, I heard a voice calling my name. Ahead of us, at the southern end of the park, was the grounds supervisor Alton Brady, who had responded when I fell in the ditch on Thursday morning.

"Ms. Cooper? I thought that was you standing up there," he said, reminding me of his name and introducing the two workers who were trailing behind him.

"We found some things when we cleaned up the site," Brady said. "I've had the men out here all day, after that news story the other night made us look like we couldn't take care of our own place. Thought you might have dropped stuff when you fell."

"I don't think so. But nice of you to ask. What did you find?"

"The police took all the weapons and metal things from us. But we went back to clean everything out and picked up a boxful of odds and ends. It's in a cardboard carton, right by security. You lose any makeup?"

"You gotta ask that question?" Mike said. "Just look at her. She lost it ages ago."

"I don't know, everything dropped out of my bag. I guess I could have left something behind. I definitely had my wallet and keys, but I haven't looked for anything else. Besides, makeup would be too dirty to use after this."

"No femurs or clavicles?"

"Say what?" Brady answered.

"Take a look, Coop. Not every day you get a graveyard lost and found."

Brady trudged up the steps and we went along with him. The cop on duty handed him the box when he asked for it. He untied the string that latched it and opened it up.

"I threw out all the garbage, of course. Food and soda cans and such."

He scrambled around and came out with a small plastic freezer bag. I could see that it held three black plastic pieces—a compact, lipstick, and a mascara applicator.

"It's actually the brand I use," I said, studying the damp baggie. "Do you mind?"

I reached for the corner of the bag. "You found this around the side of the building, where I fell?"

Brady turned to his men. "That where it was?"

"No, not the makeup," the taller man answered. "I got some other things out of that hole. This was right here in the trench at the bottom of the steps."

Mike pulled back the lid of the box and poked around inside.

"Not my shades, but it's all Chanel," I said. "What are you looking for in there?"

"A smoking gun. A straw, so I can grab at it."

"I may have the straw after all," I said. "Look at this, Mike." I held up the bag between my fingertips.

"What?"

"These three makeup cases. It's the same brand Salma used. We can check the colors against others in her bathroom. It's too expensive for most of the women who work in City Hall."

"Long shot but I'm with you."

"It gets better. See those nubby little things that are caught in the zipper of the baggie? Sort of off-white wooly threads."

"Yeah?"

"They look like the same color wool as the blanket that was covering Salma's body when she was thrown in the well."

"I suppose the lab could give us an answer on that for certain," Mike said. "Now just find me the perp. I've always wanted to put lipstick on a pig."

THIRTY-SEVEN

"What do you mean who's been here lately?" I said, tossing a glance back at the burial ground as we walked out of City Hall Park.

"Like Donny Baynes," Mike asked. We were crossing Chambers Street at five o'clock for the short walk to the entrance of the U.S. Attorney's Office, practically on the doorstep of One Police Plaza. "I wonder if he's done any business at City Hall this week."

"We're about to find that out," I said. "Think of it. The mayor goes up those steps every day, along with his bodyguards. Kendall Reid's office is here. Ethan Leighton came by to see him—against Lem's orders yesterday—which is really interesting."

"And you know what, Coop? After the news story about the burial-ground ditches the other night, it would be the perfect place for someone out to nail Statler—like old man Moses—to have evidence planted, if that's what your little baggie actually is. But don't get too bent out of shape yet. Maybe the Avon lady dropped her stash."

We passed through another security post and took the elevators to the task force quarters on the sixth floor. Most of the doors were closed and the corridor was quiet. The federal prosecutors' offices were much newer and cleaner than our distressed old surroundings.

We reached Baynes's room and I knocked before trying the knob, but it was locked.

"Go around the corner," I said to Mike. "He's got a small conference room."

As we made the turn I could hear voices. One man was shouting at another who kept talking over him—it sounded like Ukrainian to me—and again I knocked.

The shouting ceased. Someone called out, "Yeah?"

I waited for the door to be opened. Seconds later, I was rewarded by the sight of one of the federal agents, shirtsleeves rolled up to his elbows, who begrudgingly cracked it a hair.

"Who you looking for?" he asked as he eyed us.

"Donovan Baynes," I said.

Chairs scraped the surface of the floor and I heard Donny's voice calling my name. "Alex? I'll be out."

The agent stepped away and Donny emerged from the room. He, too, had removed his suit jacket and tie, and appeared to be as exhausted as I felt.

"Sorry to interrupt you."

"Everything all right?"

"Yes. We've had an interesting day."

"What are you up to?" Mike asked.

"The agents started with some of the boat crew yesterday, trying to reconstruct all the events. Find out what they know."

"Who you got in there?"

"A couple of my guys, one of the young task-force prosecutors, an interpreter—and that's one of the engineers from the boat."

"He doesn't sound happy."

"If his happiness were my goal, Mike, I would have gone to clown school, you know?"

The shouting had begun again in earnest, voices overlaying each other, punctuated by the sound of a fist banging on the table.

"You waterboarding in there or just surfing?"

Donny smiled. "This is either the dumbest bunch of seamen

who ever crossed the Atlantic, or the crew's been paid a king's ransom to take one for the team."

"Can we talk to you for a couple of minutes?" I asked.

"What's up?"

"In your office." I gestured at the sterile corridor.

"Oh, yeah. Sure."

He took us back, unlocked the door, and invited us in. It was already beginning to look like the war room of a major investigation. New file cabinets were standing catty-corner to old ones, drawers open, and boxes of documents—just the tip of the iceberg of those that would be collected in the coming months—sat waiting to be organized and filed.

"You look so serious, Alex. Everything okay with the two young women you spirited out of my custody?" He was adjusting the blinds as we lost the day's light.

"We made some progress with the first interview. Nan and I are both optimistic that we'll get these girls to open up. And from what we hear they had a great first night in the shelter. Nothing wrong on that front."

"What, then?" Donny asked, checking his answering machine for messages.

"I think we need to spend some time talking about your relationship with Ethan Leighton," I said.

"He's been a friend since law school. A good one. I don't have to tell you how shocked I am by all this." Now he was sorting the markers in the front of his desk drawer.

"You do, actually," Mike said. "That's just what you have to tell me. How shocked are you? I recall sitting with you Thursday night while Coop charted all the connections between people in this case on her blackboard. I just can't remember seeing a line that stretched from Salma Zunega directly over to you."

We had Donny Baynes's complete attention now. He slammed the drawer shut.

"I did not know Salma. That's a fact."

"Never met her?"

"No," Donny said. He wanted no part of being questioned by Mike Chapman. "Alex, I don't know what gives you the idea—you couldn't possibly think I held out on you about something."

"I'm not sure what to think."

"Why? Where did this come from?"

"Did you ever meet Salma Zunega? Not 'know' her, Donny. Just meet her is all I'm asking," I said.

"Look, can we talk one-on-one?"

"I've got no secrets from Mike."

Donny Baynes hesitated before answering. "What do you have, a photo of me on a rope line at a fund-raiser with Ethan's girlfriend?"

"I don't have anything at the moment except a hunch that you are so close to Ethan you must have been in Salma's orbit every now and then. What am I going to find if I dig a little deeper? Are there photographs? You tell me."

Mike was letting me take the lead, seeing that Donny was more comfortable trying to angle his way through this with me.

"I didn't know her, Alex. Can I swear I was never in the same room with the girl? No, I can't do that," Donny said. "Because I didn't have any clue that my good friend Ethan Leighton had gone off the deep end without a life vest. He's been in one political race after another. There are always attractive young women around in campaigns. It never seemed to get to him, and why would it? He had Claire at home. He had a relationship with his wife that we all envied."

"You and I stood on the beach together Wednesday morning, with bodies washing up on shore and hundreds of victims whose lives had just been turned upside down. You were furious when Mercer Wallace arrived to tell us that Ethan had crashed his car—and by the way, had a lover, and a child he'd fathered with her. Did you fake that?"

"I didn't fake anything," Donny said, pulling on the cord of the

venetian blinds. "Ethan kept that side of his life so compartmental-
ized, I would have given everything I had to believe that Mercer
was mistaken. Ethan's got a public persona that's different than his
private one—sure—but this crazy-ass part of him? I didn't know it
existed."

"I'll ask you again, Donny. When you heard about Salma's death
on Thursday—when you sat at my conference table and saw Polaroid photos of the young woman who was hoisted out of the well—
did you recognize her?"

"Now you're asking a different question. Recognize her? Did
she look like someone I'd ever seen before? You're asking that?"

"Sorry if I didn't make myself clear, Donny. I'm asking that."

"She looked familiar. She's a pretty girl."

"You should have seen her before she went bottoms up in the
well, man. She looked a hell of lot better." Mike had focused his attention on a photo on the wall of Baynes shaking hands with Mayor
Statler. "You keeping Hizzoner up to speed on the boat people? He
knows what you're doing over here?"

"Yeah, he does," Donny said, happy to field a question on another issue.

"Today. You see him today?"

"Last night, when I knocked off," he said, laughing a bit as he
straightened out his blotter. "Jeez, Chapman, I've got to answer to
you now? Something's wrong with that picture."

"City Hall?" I asked. "Did you go to City Hall last night?"

Donny was trying to read my expression. "You don't mean to
imply I should have told you I was going there, do you? Statler
called. I walked over and gave him a quick update, Alex. You've got
nothing to do with the pieces of the case that my guys are working
on."

I was determined to get back on course and stop Mike's
interference.

"I'm glad you went," I said, thinking of the plastic bag in Mike's
jacket pocket. "Go back to Salma, Donny. I wasn't done with that."

"Not much more to say."

"She looked familiar to you, have I got that right?"

There had been no photographs of the elusive Salma in the newspapers, and it was impossible to believe the battered face of the woman in the well, represented in crime-scene photos, would be recognized by anyone who had only met her in a crowd.

"Yes. Vaguely familiar."

"Did you ever talk with her?"

"I wish we could sit down with Ethan," he said, throwing up his hands. "I'm sure he'd confirm I didn't know her."

"Next time you have dinner with Ethan," Mike said, stepping all over my words, "maybe he can refresh your recollection."

"I'd say that's a few months down the road, Chapman. I'll be arm's distance from him, just like everyone else in law enforcement. He'll straighten this out. This situation makes him look awfully screwed up, but he's a good man at heart."

"Damn. I was counting on you to nab me an invitation to that fancy private cabal."

"Just what would that be?" Donny asked, bracing his arms on the edge of the desk.

"That gentlemen's social club you boys got going. By invitation only. Seems totally unfair that Coop can't buy herself a seat, but I had high hopes of joining you. Don't you want to tell us a little something about it?"

THIRTY-EIGHT

"I haven't had anything to do with that group in years," Donny Baynes said as he sat down in his high-backed leather desk chair. "So far as I know, it doesn't exist. Who's been feeding you that crap?"

"Kendall Reid," I said.

Donny cradled his forehead in his hands, elbows on his desk. He took a few seconds to collect himself. "Reid's a thief and a liar. I don't know what the hell he's trying to do by dragging me into this."

"He says you know—maybe you were even there—the night Ethan met Salma."

"Look, if she's the girl I think, I never put her together with Ethan. She was probably at fund-raisers. But I always figured she was Kendall Reid's girl. Maybe he was just the beard for Ethan. Maybe that's how stupid and naive I am."

"What about this men's club?" I asked.

"I just told you it's defunct. Can't have anything to do with this."

"You also told her you didn't know who Salma was, when it turns out you might," Mike said. "It's a good time to spill your guts and let us decide."

The task force prosecutor was silent.

"Don't try to filter the facts, Donny," I said. "You're too tight with Ethan to make the judgment calls. Let us help you decide."

"This is harmless, Alex. I promise you it was harmless," Donny said. "The Tontine Association. That's what it was called."

"Tontine. Haven't heard that word in ages. Michael Caine—*The Wrong Box*. Which brother lived longer." Mike was trying to loosen Baynes up by making light of things. "Which one got all the money. Is that the right movie, Coop?"

"Yup. Robert Louis Stevenson story." Mike knew the movies, I knew the books.

"What's a tontine anyway, Donny?"

"They're schemes for raising capital—like a combination of a group annuity and a lottery. A Neapolitan banker named Lorenzo de Tonti invented them in the seventeenth century."

"They legal?" Mike asked.

"Not anymore, 'cause they're basically swindles. But—but—it was just a name we used. There was no tontine involved."

"Financial geniuses, the Italians. They got Tonti, Ponzi—Gotti—all came up with clever ways for guys to make a buck. I'd think as a prosecutor you'd know enough to stay away from that kind of stuff."

"It was Moses Leighton who formed the club. I was in private practice at the time. It was just a well-intentioned way of raising money for the restoration of some old properties in the city."

"Like how?"

"It's a simple concept. In a real tontine, each member invited in pays a sum—say five hundred dollars from twenty members each. The money's invested, and every year—every good year—you get a dividend. When an investor dies, the money is reallocated among the survivors. Last man standing gets the whole pot—a gamble that in the old days could leave someone with a fortune."

"Your tontine wasn't real?" Mike asked. "Is that what you're saying?"

Mike was baiting Donny and it was working. Asking simple, general questions about the concept to get his subject to open up. And Donny Baynes was talking.

"They've been banned in this country for decades. Moses Leighton had this idea to start an organization for private funding to help the city raise money for neglected projects, things that just wouldn't get repaired or restored because of budget restraints."

"And Ethan was a new city councilman at the time," I said.

"Exactly. It was a lot about paving a future for his son, of course."

"With a swindle?" Mike asked.

"Listen to me, will you?" Donny liked being in the superior position to Mike again. "This is why the first tontines were created—for governments to use to raise capital. They were good things. Louis XIV created a tontine in 1689 to fund military operations when he was broke. It was honest. It worked. The last surviving investor lived to the age of ninety-six with that fortune. The British government copied the idea to go to war against France a few years later."

"So why'd they stop working?"

Donny was gesturing with both hands. "Investors caught on. They bought shares for infants and children, instead of for themselves. If the kids lived till old age, they often made pots of money. The governments weren't able to keep up with the costs. That's why you've got a pension today, instead of a tontine—instead of a death gamble."

Mike nodded his head. "Okay, so what did old Moses have in mind?"

"The city owns a good number of properties in the five boroughs that have historic significance. They're run by a nonprofit trust that raises private funds for them, in tandem with the city parks department, since several of them sit in local parks."

"Is Gracie Mansion part of that trust?" I asked.

"It is. And these are great old houses that date back centuries, so they're enormously expensive to maintain. Moses Leighton had a creative idea to help the city do just that."

"With an eye to restoring Gracie in case his son needed a mayoral roof over his head," Mike said.

"Bloomberg was a little more popular than Moses expected. That's why Ethan took the congressional seat."

"So the club?" I asked.

"Moses invited thirty or forty guys to participate as members. I think he wound up with a little more than half that at every dinner. Some of them were politicians, and others were wealthy businessmen, but all approved of his plan."

"What was it?"

"A dinner club. A perfectly respectable dinner club," Donny said, looking Mike in the eye. "Every second month Mr. Leighton arranged to have dinner catered for us at one of these different properties. Most of them are restored, to one degree or another, and run as museums."

"You rented them?"

"Even you can do it, Chapman. It's one of the ways they make money. Most people don't even know these places exist, especially in the other four boroughs."

"Leighton paid for the dinners?" Mike asked.

"He did. He underwrote them. But we each had to make a contribution to his enterprise. Five hundred, a thousand, each according to his means, I guess. If you were in public service, you paid less, and he had some very high rollers from the investment banking world. You gave him your check, which went to the trust to restore the houses, of course."

"Not the tontine?"

"A pretty harmless tontine, Chapman, like I said. At each dinner, every member had to bring a bottle of wine—a really fine wine. The money went to its designated purpose, and the wine got stored in Moses Leighton's cellar. Last man standing gets a damn good selection of wines, to toast those gone before him."

"Who's in the club?"

"I told you, it's been disbanded."

"Why'd that happen?"

"A few of our original members—uh—had some problems."

"Hit the skids?" Mike asked. "Who were they?"

"Moses and Ethan Leighton, of course, were the founders of it. Ethan invited me to join, along with a couple of our other law school friends who were also at big firms. I'll give you their names if you think it matters. One of them was convicted of insider trading, so he was the first to go."

"A classmate of yours?"

"Yes. And a year later, one of the men was a suicide—jumped out the window of a hotel room where he'd been holed up doing drugs. Had a problem with crystal meth and male prostitutes."

"Guess the screening for club standards was a little loose," Mike said. "Was Kendall Reid in the club?"

Donny rubbed his hands together as he answered. "No. But Reid was around the Leightons all the time back then. Working for Moses, I think, before he became Ethan's aide. He wasn't in on these dinners. Probably because he was just considered staff by the Leightons. That may be why he's so resentful about all this, telling you about me, like I'd done something wrong."

"Did Ethan ever bring a woman to any of these meetings?" I asked.

"Not once. Nobody did. Don't get me wrong, Alex. No reason it couldn't have been that way. Nothing improper. It was just a throwback to the old boys' club kind of thing that Moses Leighton thought would be amusing every now and then."

"Which politicians were involved?" Mike asked.

"We had some councilmen from each of the boroughs, a congressman from Queens. And we had the former police commissioner, before he crashed and burned."

"Bernie Kerik?"

"Yes. A real gent," Donny said, sarcasm dripping from his words. "The guy was a misfit in that group from the first time I met him. You got that feeling his big disgrace was just around the corner, if you could only put a finger on it. When the feds arrested Kerik, that was like the third strike for the Leighton tontine."

"Running clean out of gentlemen, huh?"

"Ethan told his father it was time to let it go. We actually raised a good amount of money for these historic trusts."

"Where had you met?"

"The first dinner was at Gracie Mansion, of course. Bloomberg wasn't involved, but he let us use the dining room, since that house is the real star of the trust—the most elegant of the old estates. I think our next dinner was in the Bronx, at the Bartow-Pell Mansion on Pelham Bay."

I knew the fashionable old property, renowned for its Greek Revival details and its extraordinary gardens.

"And others?" Mike asked.

"King Manor."

"The Kings of Queens?"

Donny tried to smile. "Yes, Chapman. Rufus King was a member of the Continental Congress. He was a senator from New York and later ambassador to Great Britain. I hadn't known anything about him."

"Where's the manor?"

"It's not grand, like Gracie. It's an old farmhouse, off Jamaica Avenue. King was an early and outspoken opponent of slavery."

Donny thought he was lulling Mike into a history lesson, and while he was testing the information, Mike was leading his charge exactly where he wanted.

"Was the Hamilton Grange one of your meeting places?"

"Yes. Yes, it was."

"But Kendall Reid had nothing to do with that evening?"

"I don't remember ever seeing him at dinner."

"A little odd that the phantom funds that Reid's alleged to have stolen are for a fictitious Save the Grange organization. Or was that part of a Moses Leighton plan?"

"Odd, how?"

"That your all-boys club was about getting money for this handful of fancy old houses, and Kendall Reid's council scam arose out of the same concept."

"Hey, maybe that's between Reid and the Leightons," Donny said. "Maybe that's exactly where Reid got the idea for his own swindle, from a corruption of the plan that Moses Leighton had. I'm sure Paul Battaglia will figure that out without your help, Chapman."

"I'll just leave it alone, Mr. Baynes. I won't even breathe the word *tontine* to the district attorney."

"You know why it was named that? I'll tell you. It had nothing to do with schemes and swindles," Donny said, standing up and staring out the window, over the seaport of lower Manhattan. "Right down there, at the corner of Water and Wall streets. That's where the old Tontine Coffee House was located. Ever heard of it?"

Neither Mike nor I had.

"I was a securities litigator before I joined the U.S. Attorney's Office, handling stock frauds, among other things. The Tontine Coffee House is where the New York Stock Exchange was organized, two hundred years ago. It was built by the merchants of the Tontine Association—Archibald Gracie was a charter member—as a daily meeting place."

"Legal and aboveboard?" Mike asked.

"Absolutely. Gracie, Rufus King, Alexander Hamilton, Aaron Burr—the prominent leaders of the time met there from twelve to two, almost every day, when they were in town."

"All the guys who owned your fancy houses."

"And more. It's where the merchants and power brokers of New York gathered, the hub of politics and business. It's the part of the city's history Leighton wanted to recapture. That's why he used the name Tontine, because the coffeehouse was the most important gathering of the city's men in its day. That and the fact that these very men whose homes he wanted to preserve were the original members of the association."

"I'll have to start making house calls," Mike said. "History's my thing."

"Gracie owned a large oceangoing fleet, as you probably know. The coffeehouse had a bell system and a spyglass, so the members could watch the great merchant ships arriving in New York Harbor, look for their own men coming back from sea."

There was no stopping Donny Baynes now. He liked being in charge of the information flow.

"As soon as a ship's captain reached the docks, he was required to come in to the Tontine to register his cargo. All the companies that outfitted, insured, and owned the boats had agents waiting here, just like Gracie, to account for their goods."

"Coffee, tea, sugar, cloth," Mike started to list the inventory of imports.

"Fine furniture, cotton, molasses," Donny said.

"Blackbirders too?"

"Sorry?"

"Did they track their black ivory?" Mike asked, looming over Baynes's chair.

"I don't get it, Chapman."

"You should, Donny. Being in charge of human trafficking and all. Those very same merchant ships carried slaves to the port of New York. Men, women, and children. Their human cargo was referred to as black ivory, in case you didn't know it. And the snakeheads of the day were known as blackbirders."

Baynes's jaw slackened.

"The Wall Street Slave Market was at the very same intersection of Water and Wall streets. The Meal Market across the street from your coffeehouse, I guess, was the place where the enslaved Africans were sold."

"I—I had no idea."

"It's helpful to know how your gentlemen's club came to be, Donny. That original Tontine Association? It must have thrived on human trafficking."

THIRTY-NINE

"Now you've got something to give Battaglia," Mike said. "It's the perfect time to call him and tell him you were tagged with a GPS. He'll lose all interest in you once you explain how much ground we've covered."

We had walked out the door of the U.S. Attorney's Office just after six o'clock and made the left turn that put us directly in front of police headquarters.

"Better than that, he'll be putting the knot in his black tie for whatever event his wife's dragging him to tonight. It's a good idea."

I waited until we reached the quiet lobby of One Police Plaza and were waved in by the cop at the security desk.

The call was a quick one. I assured Battaglia that I was fine, that the NYPD had me covered, and that the small device attached to the rear of my car had a tampered ID number, so it would be difficult to trace.

As Mike predicted, he was far more interested in our meeting with Ethan Leighton, furious that we had stepped on Tim Spindlis's toes by talking to Kendall Reid, and intrigued by the conversation with Donny Baynes. I had bought myself lunch with the district attorney at noon on Monday.

The Latent Print Unit was on the fifth floor of One PP. It ran 24/7 with some of the smartest detectives in the city.

I was from the new generation of prosecutors, spoiled by the revolutionary techniques of forensic DNA, which had only been introduced to the criminal justice system two decades before. But like many other young lawyers, I expected it to solve an increasing number of cases as its methods were refined and its variety of applications expanded almost explosively.

Mike's training, and the fact that he had learned from his father since earliest childhood, kept him centered on good old-fashioned policing techniques. He was skilled at detailed interrogations and he used traditional applications, like fingerprinting, that were updated with high-tech computer assists.

He opened the door to the unit where several detectives were at work.

"Yo, Patty," he called out across the room. A tall, thin redhead with a platinum streak in her long hair was standing next to her desk, thumbing through a pile of fingerprint cards.

"Hey, Mike. How lucky can I get on a Saturday night?"

"Patty Baker, meet Alex Cooper. You could get very lucky if you've got the right answers."

"Remind me to wake up my husband and tell him. What's happening? And if you're asking me to jump the line, I've got way too much *Golden Voyage* business going on to help you."

"We're working that case. Nobody told you they think it's connected to the broad who went headers in the Gracie Mansion well?"

"That's the skinny."

"I want you to take a look at these things for me." Mike lifted the plastic bag out of his pocket, holding it by a corner.

"CSU see it yet?"

"Nobody has. It wasn't found at the scene. Coop and I have a feeling it may be connected, but it was dumped somewhere else and a couple of guys have already had their hands on the bag before it got to us."

"You have used up just about every last favor in the bank," Patty said, sitting at her desk. She looked over at me with her intense blue eyes. "We were in the same class at the academy. That's how come he gets special treatment. Mike knows way too many secrets about me."

"I can relate to that."

Patty put on her gloves, slid back the blue plastic zipper, and spread the bag apart. She set out a clean place to work and rolled the three items out onto the desktop.

Normally, the crime scene officers retrieved pieces of evidence like these. They dusted them with powder, as every television viewer seemed to know—white powder on black surfaces and black on white. Then they placed tape over the powdered area, and lifted it, attaching it to a three-by-five-inch index card. It was up to the latent-print examiners to determine if the retrieved image was of sufficient value to be useful.

Patty readied the white powder as she examined the three makeup cases.

"Forget the compact for the moment. Lipstick too," she said. "The mascara wand is my best bet. I can probably get a good thumb-print off that. What do you think, Alex?"

She was holding an imaginary eye makeup case in the air, grasping it with her thumb.

"It never occurred to me, but it looks like you could be right."

Patty did the lifts herself, taping them onto a card. She was a lefty, and it seemed as though she was doing everything backward as she went about her work.

Then she picked up a magnifying glass and examined the marks carefully, studying three cards. "I've got a nice clean one here. A couple of partials but one good print."

On two of the index cards Patty placed a red dot—a notation that they were of no value. NV is how they would be filed.

"I can try for a match with this one," she said about the single lift from the mascara wand that was OV—of value.

"Go for it," Mike said. "Salma Zunega—that's the woman whose body was in the well—is she in the system?"

The techs at the morgue would have rolled all ten fingers of the dead woman onto a card before she was autopsied, to preserve for identification purposes.

"Yep. Her inked prints were loaded yesterday on the day tour."

"You eyeball them?"

"Me? No. But I saw the entry in the case log. Salma's in. I'd do a visual comparison to the inked card myself, but the boss must have it under lock and key. I can't get in his office tonight either. He's squirrely about his evidence."

SAFIS—the Statewide Automated Fingerprint Identification System—was a giant computer databank that went into operation in 1989, the same year that DNA was accepted in American courts as a valid scientific technique. In tandem, the two sophisticated processes were able to resolve an unimaginable number of cases.

"Can you upload this one now?"

"You have a date or something?" Patty asked, continuing on with her meticulous work. "Patience never was your strong suit."

"I want to know whether to wait or not."

"Take a load off. There are fingerprint images of more than three million people in this computer brain. He's pretty fast, so just calm yourself down."

"We're in there, too, aren't we?" I asked.

Every prosecutor, cop, government employee, elected official, and federal agent was in the system. We all had to be fingerprinted as part of our ordinary background check.

"You bet," Patty said. "I'll scan this in. You know where the vending machines are, Mike? Feel like springing for hors d'oeuvres?"

"Sure."

Patty yawned. "Get me two sodas—whatever promises the most caffeine."

Mike left the lab and I stayed riveted at Patty's side, following her from her work space to the giant machine that would perform the search. "Mind if I watch?"

"Not at all. You get this?"

"I hope so. I've had so many of your colleagues on the stand, I've had to relearn it as each technique has been developed to make it clear to the jurors."

Prints usually appeared as a series of dark lines, representing the high peaking portion of the friction ridge skin. The white spaces—the shallow portions—were the valleys in between. The identification and matching is based primarily on what are now called minutiae—the location and direction of ridge endings and bifurcations along the ridge path.

"I'm going to scan this in, Alex, see? Sir Francis takes it from here for a while."

"Sir Francis?"

"The best partner I ever had. And he's not a ball breaker like Mike. Give me a nice, quiet computer any day," Patty said. "Francis Galton was the first guy to define the characteristics for a scientific identification of unique prints. Galton Points—loops, islands, whorls, deltas—they make up the minutiae from which comparisons are made."

Patty finished scanning, hit the Search button, and walked back to her desk.

"What's Francis doing now?" I asked.

Mike walked back in with an armload of soda cans, bags of chips, and candy bars. "Cocktails are served."

We each grabbed a soda and something to eat, while Patty explained. "He's assigning a numerical value to the fingerprint I just submitted. And he's searching the Latent Cognizant database. Give him a few minutes."

"Is he as good at it as you?" Mike asked, tousling her hair.

"Not always," Patty said. "Sir Francis is a genius—don't get me wrong. But we do things differently. He assigns values to things that I sometimes disagree with. Hey, you—keep your crumbs off my desk, Mike."

Those of us in law enforcement talked about fingerprint identification as a science, but it was much more accurate to call it an art. The skill of the examiner, the ability to distinguish between blindingly similar ridge endings and bifurcations, was something far too complex to take for granted.

"There are a lot of holes in the net," she went on. "Garbage in, garbage out. Had a case last month—a homicide in Staten Island. The perp's been in the system for a lot of years, but his inked prints were done so badly back in 2003 that Sir Francis here missed him. Couldn't get a read at all."

"But you did?" I asked.

"It wasn't easy. We just don't always see things the same, Francis and me."

Mike was on his second candy bar. "How about the plastic bag, Patty? You think you could get any lifts off that?"

"Not my job, sweetheart."

"By the time I find Crime Scene on a busy Saturday night and get them over here to dust it, I might as well go to a double feature, take a nap, come back all fresh in the morning. Like that."

She reached for the corner of the bag with her gloved hand. "You fall for his bullshit, too, Alex? I'm telling you, he wheedled everything out of me except my virginity."

"That was so long gone by the time you got to the academy, Detective Baker, not even Sherlock Holmes could have found a trace of it."

"Then why'd you spend so much time looking?" Patty was bent over again, moving her hand over the bag with her magnifying glass. "Plastic's great for prints. What are you hoping to get?"

"I guess you're going to tell me pretty soon whether Sir Francis can put the mascara case together with Salma."

"Yeah."

"Well, she's not the one who dropped it at City Hall, 'cause she was already dead. I'd like to think the guy who handled the bag might have left his prints on that."

"You got a load of partials on here. But they're mostly smudged. Overlaid on each other. You might have multiple handlers."

"Two tickets to the Super Bowl?"

"You got 'em?"

"Find me a killer and I'll put you on the fifty-yard line."

"See what I mean, Alex? And still I go for the bait."

Patty took the bag over to a larger workbench against the wall and turned on a brighter lamp. "Here's my advice. I'll break the rules for you, Mike. Again. If I get anything of value, I'll give you a call immediately. My guess is that I'm going to get an endless bunch of overlays."

She was already at work, dusting the first side of the bag and taking her lifts.

"We know at least one guy in the Parks Department picked it up out of a ditch," Mike said. "No telling how many hands have been on it."

Patty handed Mike the first of the index cards she was making after marking it with a red dot. "No value."

"You gotta find me one," Mike said. He was throwing back M&M's now, washing them down with soda. "Just one that great big brain can read."

"I'm giving you something better, okay? When you leave here, you going uptown?"

"Yeah."

"Stop at the DNA lab. Give 'em this. See if your blarney works on those dames."

"It's no value, you said."

"Fingerprints, sweetheart, are a mixture of sweat and oils and skin cells. You figured that out yet, Mike? There are tiny little repositories of DNA in all that minutiae," Patty said. "That smudge is of no value to me, but I can give you a whole bunch of lifts that may just have the genetic fingerprint—the DNA—you're looking for."

"Touch DNA," I said. "That's what they're working on for me on that old case I have against Lem Howell. We'll have them rush it. Howard Browner will do it."

"Let me get the four or five best partials for you."

We waited another fifteen minutes for Patty Baker to finish her work. She straightened up, packaged together the lift cards, and handed them to Mike.

"I think Sir Francis has spoken," she said.

"How'd you know?" I asked.

"Just used to his whirring sound. I heard something coming into the printer."

"I'll get it," Mike said.

"Mitts off, sweetheart. Keep that leash on him for a few minutes, will you, Alex? The computer may kick out a handful of close possibilities. I do the final comparison, and I do it without a bloodhound breathing sour-cream-and-garlic-chip odors over my shoulder."

Patty walked to the machine and scooped up a sheaf of papers. She returned to the desk, picked up the magnifier, and got back to work. "You heard me, didn't you, Mike? Back off."

Mike turned away from Patty and began to pace. Another twenty minutes went by before she raised her head to speak to us.

"I hope you weren't too wedded to that match," she said. "The computer didn't kick out Salma Zunega for you."

"Maybe Sir Francis is wrong again, Patty. Can't you call the lieutenant and dig her card out of his office?"

"I think the old boy knows exactly what he's doing, sweetheart. He and I are ready to declare the same match."

"The thumbprint on the mascara wand actually comes up a hit against someone in your database?" I asked. "Someone other than Salma Zunega?"

"I'll walk you through the ridges and minutiae if you like. You got more than enough points of comparison to stand up in court."

My head was spinning. The expensive makeup was sold in up-scale department stores and boutiques, but I had thought if the fingerprint on it matched anyone in the statewide identification system, it would have been Salma.

Patty Baker held out the computer result and the lift card she created an hour earlier. "Looks like the girl with the midnight black mascara washed up on the beach the other day. It's the *Golden Voyage* case, all right. She's still got no name in my database, but the woman who used this makeup is your other murder victim. She's your Jane Doe Number One."

FORTY

"You want to come up?" I asked Mike. "I can order in a Peking duck from Shun Lee."

We were parked in the driveway in front of my apartment. It was almost nine P.M.

"No, thanks. I overdosed on junk food. And you need to get some rest."

"You going home?"

"Making a stop first."

He had blown up his date with Fanny Levit last night to hang out with me at Vickee and Mercer's. I had it in my head that he would stop by her place tonight. It was none of my business and I tried to push my curiosity out of mind.

"You have any thoughts on how Jane Doe got her hands on such expensive makeup?" I asked.

"Your guess is as good as mine. Who knows what the snake-heads did to lure those girls to make this trip? Ask Olena when you see her on Monday."

"I will, but she didn't seem to have anything more than the shirt on her back."

"I'll talk to the guys who searched the ship. Find out what was left on board. Maybe the baggie was in Jane Doe's pocket when she washed up."

"I'll give you that one. She had on a sweat jacket, right?"

"Yeah," Mike said.

"Now, how did it get from the beach to the front doorstep of City Hall?"

We were both stumped by that one. Mike started ticking off the names of people who'd been at both the beach and the mayor's office.

"The mayor choppered in after we left, and both his bodyguards—Rowdy Kitts and Dan Harkin—were there. Commissioner Scully. Donovan Baynes and most of the JTTF crew. You and Mercer and me. And Lord knows how many cops and rescue workers who've been in contact with Ethan Leighton and Kendall Reid. Lots of people coming and going from City Hall."

"I feel bad making Patty and the DNA techs go through so many hoops for us," I said. "Could be an innocent explanation."

"Like somebody picked up some flotsam and jetsam at the scene of the wreck, and didn't think it was connected to the case? Just tossed it out in a ditch at City Hall?"

I smiled at Mike. "You've been looking for the cross-dresser in this case from day one. Maybe that's all it was—debris on the beach, so far as anyone knew. Somebody grabbed it and forgot to throw it away. Whoever had it in his pocket didn't want to be embarrassed getting caught with makeup going through the metal detector."

"Good for you, Coop. At least you're not seeing the bogeyman everywhere. Maybe we just wasted the last few hours. Show me Donny Baynes in lingerie and makeup and I'll be satisfied."

"All worth the time just to meet Patty," I said. "Maybe the puzzles will unravel in my dreams."

"Do me a favor?" Mike asked as I opened the car door.

"Sure."

"Double down on that Dewar's tonight. I want you to sleep like a baby."

"I'll talk to you tomorrow."

"Thanks for pushing them on that touch DNA rush," Mike said.

"Sure."

We had dropped the plastic bag off at the lab on our way here, causing no small annoyance to the terrifically overworked staff.

"You got plans or you staying home tomorrow?"

"The Sunday morning newspaper, a pile of bills, Christmas correspondence that stacked up while I was away, and a long afternoon nap. I promise not to cause any trouble."

One of the doormen came to help me out of the car and escort me inside.

I went upstairs and let myself into the apartment. The quiet of my own space was comforting after the day's unexpected encounters.

I undressed and pulled back the comforter just far enough for me to slide into bed. I didn't even feel like a drink. I pressed the button and listened to messages from friends. Joan and Jim had flown in from D.C. and tried to find me for dinner, and the office team was eager for updates. My parents were urging me to join them for a warm weekend in the Caribbean sun later in the month, and I hoped they were blissfully unaware, at that very long distance, of the turmoil that had enveloped my professional life.

Luc's voice was warm and loving. I put my head on the pillow and replayed his message several times. His day had started at dawn, at the market in Cannes; then he took his kids to the museum in St. Paul de Vence for the afternoon; and described in detail the feast he enjoyed with two other couples I knew at his restaurant in Mougins. A little too much champagne, it sounded, infused his words with a slight slurring of affection, but it was a calming way to end the evening.

I couldn't remember the last time I'd turned my lights out this early.

Sleep washed over me and I gave in to it without resistance.

The phone rang shortly before four A.M. I sat up, pleased I hadn't anesthetized myself with alcohol.

"Hello?"

"Hey, Alex." There was no mistaking Mercer's voice. "I'm just through the tunnel on my way uptown. I think you might want to tag-team me."

"On what?"

"The Three-three just broke up what they thought was a domestic. Not quite the usual thing. A guy in a Jaguar arguing with a woman."

"A Jag in the Three-three? The jerk might as well have lit himself up in neon."

"It gets better. She's standing out on the sidewalk screaming bloody murder but took off on a fast trot when the cops appeared. She left something behind in the car that might interest you."

"I'm all ears, Mercer."

"A perfectly healthy little girl, around nineteen months old. She's got a gold locket around her neck, engraved with the name Ana."

I was out of bed, reaching for my clothes. "They get the driver, or did he run too?"

"He's sitting in the station house, waiting for you. It's your friend Ethan Leighton."

FORTY-ONE

The child was sound asleep in a portable carrier that had been brought in from the car. A young policewoman was watching over her in a quiet corner of the detective squad room on the second floor of the Thirty-third Precinct station house on Amsterdam Avenue.

I noticed them before I saw the congressman sitting at a desk in the corner. He looked even more drawn than he had yesterday in the park, now dressed in a black-and-gray argyle sweater. Over his shoulders, he had one of those all-weather jackets with corduroy collars that made him look ready to embark on an early morning hunt from Balmoral Castle.

"This is the last thing I expected to happen during the night, Ethan."

"Hello, Alex."

I could barely hear him, even though I was only several feet away.

"This is Mercer Wallace. He's a detective from the Special Victims Unit."

Leighton nodded. "Am I being held here in custody?"

"Not as I understand it."

"Free to leave?"

"We have some questions we'd like to ask you. We'll wait till Lem gets here."

"I haven't called Lem."

Leighton was staring at the floor. I looked over at Mercer and shook my head. "I'd better do that."

"You don't need to."

"Actually, I do."

"I fired Lem Howell."

"You what? You couldn't have a better lawyer. When did you do that?"

"Late last night. I'll be representing myself." Ethan Leighton picked his head up and looked at me. His eyes narrowed to dark slits, hooded by heavy lids. "What do you want to know?"

The cops who brought the congressman into the station house had not charged him with any crime, even before they had identified him. The car was registered to his father, he didn't appear to be intoxicated, and the screaming woman who had attracted police attention didn't wait around long enough to make a complaint to them.

Mercer nodded at me to start asking questions. "Why don't you tell me where Ana has been since the night you were arrested? Who the woman was making a scene up here in the middle of the night?"

Leighton put his jacket on and started walking toward the baby in the carrier.

"Not the baby, sir."

"What?"

"You can't take the baby with you."

"Don't be ridiculous, Mr. Wallace. She's my child."

"Right now we don't know who she is."

"I'm telling you who she is. She's my daughter." Leighton turned to me. "Tell him this is my child, Alex. Doesn't he read the newspapers?"

"No need to raise your voice, Ethan. You don't want to talk to me, so just head off into the night and we'll take good care of Ana, I promise you."

"Has your daughter ever lived with you?" Mercer asked, even though he knew the answer.

"No. But she's going to live with us now."

"In your wallet, sir, do you have any kind of identification for her? Any medical card, for example? A photograph?"

"I don't have any forms, any cards. I—I'll have to get those. Her mother's been killed, Detective. Have a heart."

There was a slight tremor in Leighton's hands when he reached for his wallet. "At my office, I've got results of a DNA test that established my paternity of Ana. Obviously, I wasn't married to her mother. You can pick it up from my secretary on Monday."

Someone had done a banner business in faking paternity tests. Leighton must have caved to Salma's demands when he saw the report that even an amateur could have forged, with the indecipherable markings of a DNA match.

"Who was the woman in the street, Ethan? The woman who was screaming at you?"

He pretended not to hear me as he stalled for time, for a way to resolve this potentially explosive incident. The tabloid feeding frenzy would crush any hopes he had of disposing of his drunk driving case.

"Who was the woman in the street?"

Leighton glanced at the sleeping baby but didn't answer. The tic in his eye was getting more pronounced.

Mercer stood up from a nearby desk and took his worn leather badge case out of his pocket. From behind the flap, he removed an old photograph of Logan.

"This is my son, Mr. Leighton. He's a little older than Ana. He's home safe in his bed, where he should be at this hour, surrounded by all his favorite things. And I'd be right there with him if you hadn't interrupted my night."

Leighton almost whispered. "I'd like to take her home with me."

"Not a single photograph in your wallet of that beautiful little girl? I can't imagine it," Mercer said. He was getting to Leighton in a way that I could not. "You want to tell me how you expect to get legal custody of Ana? What your wife says about all this? Hell, Claire hasn't even been cleared as a suspect yet."

Ethan Leighton turned and walked back to his seat.

I wasn't ready for this enormous curve ball that had been thrown at me in the middle of the night. I was shocked to think that Leighton had known about Ana's whereabouts all week, puzzled that he'd had the bad sense to toss Lem off his case, no less walk into this bizarre situation on the street. I was unprepared to be the one to tell him—in the dingy confines of the squad room—that he was not in fact the biological father of this little girl.

"Suppose I leave here without taking Ana?"

"You can do that."

"What happens to her now? I mean, where does she go?"

The ugly truth was that Ana was likely to be placed in the care of the city's children's services agency until her identity could be sorted out.

"I wasn't expecting any of this, Ethan. It won't be my decision."

"The woman who's been caring for her is a good person. If you'd assure me that Ana can stay with her, I'm willing to step back until things are settled."

"Then you've got to tell me who she is. Nobody's going to let this child go off in the night with a stranger on your say-so. Give us a chance to fight for the baby."

"Drag her into a police station? You're punishing me, not the child. I don't think I can do that."

"What's her name?" Mercer asked again.

Ethan Leighton got to his feet and began pacing across the room.

"She's called Anita. Salma named the baby for her, in her honor."

"That's a good start," I said. I was thinking that the baby was most likely Anita's child, given the name for that reason. "Her last name?"

"Let me think about whether I want to do this."

"Maybe I can move you along," Mercer said. "Salma must have been very close to Anita, right? Trusted her a great deal?"

Leighton was still reluctant to talk. He took his time answering. "Yes, she did."

"Is Anita also Mexican?"

He nodded.

"Did she come here illegally? I can help her with that if you'll let me. We're not going to do anything to hurt her."

"They were very dear friends, Detective. Anita took care of the baby when Salma needed help. They've been through a lot of things together. Things you couldn't begin to understand."

Try me, I wanted to say. "How much time have you spent with your baby?"

"Very little, Alex. I told you that. It's been a very complicated relationship. I—I wasn't even sure the child was mine until recently. I've been trying to do the right thing by both of them, okay? I'm financially capable of giving the child a good life. Claire—my wife—is an incredibly strong woman. She's willing to take this on with me."

"There are many more issues to be considered than just your wishes. I don't think anyone's going to leave that decision up to you and Claire."

"What the hell is this? A social work office or a police station? Somebody pass a law I don't know about that I can't raise my own kid?" Leighton was suddenly raging like a gored bull.

"Calm yourself, down, sir. Alex is right. The family court will have a look at the paternity tests. They'll establish the maternal link, too, what with Ms. Zunega dead and unable to be party to this."

Leighton swiveled around and swept a few volumes of a detective's penal law books off the top of the old wooden desk.

"They'll take my word for it, goddamn it. I'm a congressman, for Chrissakes."

I didn't want to get any more specific with him, give him any more bad news, until I checked with Lem Howell to see if his representation had really been withdrawn and we were all in a more private place.

"It's five o'clock on a Sunday morning, Ethan. You know nothing is going to be settled today. If you want Ana to be well cared for, tell me how to find Anita."

"And you'll give her the baby?"

"I'll recommend that she be vetted to take custody in the short term. You know there's been a manhunt for this child, all over the country, for days now."

Leighton dropped his head again and nodded. "The baby's been perfectly safe. They've hardly left their apartment for a minute since the news about the murder. Anita's only fear is that Salma's baby will be taken from her, in the event that I'm not granted custody."

"You mind telling me why your friend Anita was standing on a street corner at three o'clock in the morning, causing such a commotion? Running off without this child she loves so much?" Mercer asked.

Leighton shuffled uncomfortably. He wasn't making eye contact with any of us. "Anita's been difficult since last week, when she heard the news about how sick Ana was, and then about my accident."

"What was she screaming for? Doesn't she want to help you?"

"She doesn't want anything from me. She's hysterical right now," Ethan Leighton said, mopping the sweat on his temple and smoothing back his hair. "Anita's full of crazy ideas. She thinks I'm the one who killed Salma."

FORTY-TWO

I stepped out into the hallway and called Mike on his cell.

"Yeah?" he asked. "Wassup, Coop?"

"Returning the favor. Sorry for the early wake-up call. I'm in the Three-three with Mercer. We think we have the baby that Salma borrowed to put pressure on Ethan Leighton."

"Alive and well? When did you get there? Why are you only calling me now?"

"Because Mercer didn't know what he had when he was on his way uptown." *Because I thought I could handle things without getting you out of bed*, is what I wouldn't say out loud. "And we're about to have breakfast with Leighton himself, in case you want to join us."

"Give me twenty minutes and I'll be there. The baby and her mother okay?"

"Baby's sleeping through the whole thing. Like a baby. Patrol is combing the 'hood for Mama."

"Hold tight. See you soon."

Mercer had sent one of the uniformed officers out to pick up sandwiches and coffee. We had turned the discussion around, explaining to Leighton our fears for Anita's well-being, alone on the streets at this hour of the morning, and the importance of finding her before she was hurt.

While the congressman took a few minutes to eat, I went downstairs and asked the desk sergeant to get in touch with ACS—the Administration for Children's Services. This time, baby Ana would be examined at a hospital and placed with a good foster home until the circumstances of her parenthood and living conditions could be determined.

Leighton was beginning to understand that there was no possibility that the child would be released to his care at this point in time. It wasn't clear that he trusted us, but he seemed to get the fact that we needed to look for Salma's friend.

We learned from him that her name was Anita Paz, and that she was twenty-two years old. She had not landed in quite the kind of luxurious lap that had cushioned her friend Salma recently. She shared an apartment with a distant cousin on the Upper West Side, in the vicinity of Columbia University.

"When did you meet Anita?"

He was gnawing on a toothpick. "Why does that matter?"

"Maybe something you say will help us find her."

"I met her when Salma came back from Texas with the baby. She lived in the apartment for a while, sort of helping out until she got her own place. She was so grateful to Salma for getting her out of—you know—the business, and the way she could repay the kindness was by taking care of Ana."

It was becoming more and more obvious to Mercer and me that Anita was the likely birth mother, loaning her child to Salma in order to blackmail the congressman.

Leighton had been ringing Anita's cell number every fifteen minutes. It went right to voice mail and she hadn't returned any of the calls.

"She'll cool down and get back to me."

"Mind if I try her on my phone? The number's blocked so she won't know who's calling."

"Suit yourself," he said, extending his hand to give me the phone.

I made note of the number and dialed it. The voice mail message was in English. I left her my name and number and told her that I was a friend of Salma's who wanted to help her.

"How does Anita support herself?" I asked.

"It's not what you think, Alex. She's not in the sex trade anymore. She's—she's just an escort. Very occasionally. Nothing sexual, just conversation and company."

Put that in the category of wishful thinking.

Mercer and I were both trying to restore ourselves with hot coffee. "Now, why would Anita go and accuse you of hurting Salma?" he asked, as though the thought itself was the height of absurdity.

"I can't fathom it myself. She knows how good I was to her."

"That little display you put on, throwing the law books around, is that typical for you?"

"Not at all. I'm—I'm just horribly frustrated by what's going on tonight. I want that child to be safe. I'm prepared to take whatever legal steps are necessary to have her with me."

"Like Alex says, you're free to leave. The baby goes nowhere."

When Mike walked into the squad room, Leighton stood to greet him but I took him aside first and told him what we'd learned.

He and Mercer picked up the conversation while I sat a few desks back, out of Leighton's line of vision. They were going to do the "guy thing," persuading him to open up about his relationship with Salma and her circle of friends.

Mike started the conversation and I pretended to busy myself in paperwork. He was at his most proper and polite, trying to get into the low-down sex life of Ethan Leighton.

"Look, Ethan," Mike said. "We're going to find Anita and we'd like to do it sooner rather than later. What happened tonight, huh? What's this all about?"

He rambled for minutes before telling the story. "After I heard about Salma's death, I knew Anita was out of control. And I knew she had the baby and that I had to reach out to her."

"Didn't Lem think that was dangerous?"

"I didn't tell Lem. My father keeps a suite of rooms at the Waldorf that he uses to entertain business guests from out of town. I told Anita to move in to one of them for the weekend. To bring Ana there."

"Because of your concern for her well-being and the baby, or because you were worried about how she was spinning things?"

"Both. Fair to say it was both."

"More worried about yourself—your reputation—than about her?" Mike asked.

"Anita's made of tougher stuff than I am, Detective. I also needed a place where Claire could go to meet the baby," Ethan said, dropping his voice. "I mean, in case she was willing to do that."

"And did she go?"

"No. Not yet. She—uh—she wasn't ready for that."

Score one for Claire Leighton.

"Did Anita actually move into the hotel with Ana?"

"Yes, she did."

"Did you visit them there?"

"Briefly."

"You didn't think that was stupid, I mean in the event the paparazzi sniffed it out?"

"My family is well-known at the Waldorf. No one would think twice of my coming or going there."

"So was the purpose of your visit to see Anita, or—?"

"Anita went out for a while. I gave her some cash so she could shop for some things she needed. I hope you understand this, Detective. I have to get to know my daughter, spend time with her. Let her get used to me."

"Let me figure this," I said. "Even though Anita suspects you had something to do with Salma's murder, she left you alone with her—with the baby?"

"Not alone. She left her cousin there, sort of babysitting, in case I needed help."

"A cousin?"

"Yes, a seventeen-year-old named Luci. Anita lives with Luci's family."

"What do you know about Luci?"

"Well, she comes from a good stock. Decent people. Hardworking. Her mother's a nurse's aide at one of the hospitals on the West Side."

"I'm missing something here," Mike said. "How'd you wind up in this dogfight on Edgecombe Avenue tonight?"

No answer.

"The stork drop the baby out of the sky?"

No reaction.

"Let me tell you something, Mr. Leighton. This is a neighborhood where the men are men and the women don't have teeth, okay?"

The congressman's head jerked up.

"A pretty young thing like Anita on the loose here in the middle of the night—well, it doesn't always have a happy ending. I'm going out for a spin around the block. Kinda like looking for a needle in a very rotten haystack, so anything you can do to make things a little easier for me would be greatly appreciated."

Leighton reached for his cell phone to see if there were any messages. "Anita lied to me."

"Story of my life, Mr. Leighton. Everybody lies to me. Deal with it."

"I thought she had gone home for the night to be with her family, like she told me she planned to do. About one o'clock this morning I got a call at my apartment from the front desk at the hotel. Anita's cousin was in the lobby, with the baby. I raced over there."

I wondered where Claire stood with this mess that must have turned her life upside down.

"What'd she want?"

"Anita had gone out around eight o'clock. Said she'd be home by midnight. When she didn't show up, her cousin called her cell. She said Anita answered but was crying hysterically. Told her to have the desk find me. She doesn't have our home number, but she wanted to get the baby to me so Ana would be safe."

"Safe with you? Have you ever freaking diapered a kid?"

"That's the least of my problems, Detective. I can pay any idiot to do that. I was in the hotel suite with her cousin, whom Ana adores."

I stood up from the desk and moved closer to Mike and Mercer. "Did you call her? Did you speak to Anita on the phone?"

"She finally answered about the third time I called."

"What did she tell you?" Mike asked.

"She was only worried about the baby. She was afraid someone was going to try to take the baby away."

"Someone specific?"

"Yes. A man. She wouldn't tell me who."

Maybe it was the guy who had shown up at Salma's apartment earlier on the night she was killed—the guy who claimed to be the father of the baby.

"She asked me to meet her. To pick her up and bring her back to the hotel."

"So that's what you did? And you took the baby with you?"

"I had no choice, Chapman. What was I to do? Leave Ana in a hotel room with a seventeen-year-old who doesn't speak the language? Whose address I don't have? I made Luci walk me to the hotel garage and put the child in the portable carrier she'd brought. Then I sent her back to the room to wait there in case Anita called."

Mike yelled out to one of the uniformed cops who was standing by for a possible assist. "Get downstairs and tell the desk sergeant to get on the phone to the Waldorf security office. Tell them to sit tight on the Leighton rooms. Get a scrip on the broad in the suite, okay? Order room service for her, whatever she needs. Just make sure she doesn't move."

"What am I telling him?" the cop asked. "How long you want her?"

"Till the Seventeenth Squad finishes shining their shoes and gets over there. Till mañana and the day after that. Think for yourself, will you, kid? I'm occupied." Mike turned around to Leighton. "Where'd you find her? Your friend, Anita?"

"She'd been working, Detective."

"In this shithole of a precinct? Rough trade up here. A girl could get hurt."

"Anita got in over her head is what it is. Salma said she took too many risks."

"On her back? She got in over her head while she was on her back?"

I could hear crying from the far corner of the room. The baby had awakened and was beginning to wail as the policewoman picked her up. She was talking softly to Ana, going to the refrigerator to take out a bottle of milk that had been put inside, I guessed, when Leighton had been brought upstairs.

The congressman looked helplessly across the room.

"Don't even think about it," Mike said.

"It's some kind of private club, Chapman. All I know is that Anita was supposed to have dinner with a gentleman who belonged to some kind of club. He paid her a lot of money, just to spend the evening with him. That's what she told Luci when she left the hotel."

It was Mike's turn to raise his voice. "You know what kind of clubs they got up here, Mr. Leighton? You serious? They got clubs you can buy every kind of street junk ever cooked up by a dealer. Clubs you can find every kind of whore except a clean one. Clubs you can drink and snort and smoke in till you're blind and crazy. They've got no book clubs. They've got no supper clubs. And they sure as hell have got no gentlemen's clubs."

"I'm telling you what I know."

"Sounds a little bit too much like your own club. Like your father's tontine, with your two-faced buddies like Donny Baynes."

"What's Donny got to do with this?" Leighton rubbed his eyes with both hands. "If he told you about the Tontine Association, he also told you it was disbanded years ago."

I thought for a moment that Mike had hoisted Ethan Leighton on his own petard, that the slick politician had dangled a piece of misinformation in front of us, not realizing that Baynes had tied himself in knots too. I'd hoped Mike connected tonight's events to Moses and Ethan Leighton, Donovan Baynes, and perhaps Mayor Statler himself.

"Did Anita tell Luci anything else about this man she was meeting—or about the kind of club it was?"

"Only that she said she felt safe when she went out tonight, because the guy who asked her to do it was an old friend," Leighton said, pausing before he remembered another fact. "Yes. Yes, there is a name. The club is called Sub Rosa. It's all very discreet like that. That's what she told Luci."

"Sub Rosa," Mike said. "I get it. Secret, confidential, private."

"You don't get it at all. Go for the literal translation, Mike," I said. I thought of the small tattoo—the property stamp of the snake-head, the trafficker—that was on the bodies of our Jane Doe #1 and on Salma Zunega. That might have been part of Salma's bond with Anita. "Doesn't that expression mean 'under the rose'?"

FORTY-THREE

" 'Under the rose' it is," Mike said. "The nuns who taught me would have been proud of you. I didn't think your Latin was that good."

"Just the basics. I don't know why it means what it does."

"It's a practice from the Middle Ages." Mike's parochial school education had served him well. "In medieval days, a rose was hung over council chambers if the proceedings were to be kept secret. *Sub rosa.* You should come to church with me more often. A lot of times you'll see roses carved into the confessionals, for exactly that reason."

"That's my point," I said. "Find Anita, find the friend who set her up tonight, and we'll have the bastard behind all this misery. We'll learn why these girls are the property of the rose."

"Where did you locate her?" Mike asked Leighton.

"On Edgecombe Avenue. I really don't know this area. It was just before two A.M."

"Edgecombe and what? You want to see her alive, or don't you care?"

There was an urgency in Mike's voice now that Leighton caught too.

"Yes, I care. A Hundred and fifty-sixth Street, maybe a Hundred and fifty-seventh. I'm not certain. As I drove along, Anita ran out into the roadway. There was a park on the right. I remember that."

"High Bridge Park. I hope to God she isn't in there."

I'd handled scores of cases that had occurred in the long strip that stretched north from 155th to Dyckman Street, with rugged topography and a treacherous slope that ran down from Edgecombe to the Harlem River Drive below it.

"She was waiting for me, sort of hiding behind a tree until she recognized the car."

"Was she okay? She wasn't hurt when you got there?" I asked.

"No, no she wasn't. Just scared."

"Did she get in the car with you?"

Leighton hesitated.

"There's no time for you to even blink right now, man, so don't start with censoring your answers," Mike said. "Did she get in the car?"

"That's what we were fighting about. She refused to get in. She wanted to take Ana with her."

"Take her and go where?"

"I don't know. Don't raise your voice to me, Chapman."

"Make sense, then. Why didn't Anita get in your car? Where was she planning to go in that neighborhood with the baby, in the freezing cold?"

"That's what we were fighting about. She told me her friend was waiting for her. That he'd take care of her."

"The guy who did the dinner fix-up?"

"I guess. I wouldn't give her the child, and she wouldn't come with me."

"Why do you think that is?"

"Because she's still all mixed up about Salma's death."

"While she was standing in the road, arguing with you, was Anita yelling?"

"Yes, yes, she was. Then she saw the patrol car coming. She accused me of calling the cops on her. That's when she flipped out and started to run."

"Into the park?"

"No, no. The other way. She ran west, but I don't know those streets."

"And she left this child with you?"

"Yes." Leighton practically whispered the word.

The baby had stopped crying and seemed to be drinking her bottle, so Mercer came back to join us. "Where are the clubs around here, say, west of a Hundred and fifty-sixth?" Mike asked.

"Amsterdam Avenue, mostly," Mercer said. "A few on St. Nick."

"What's she wearing, Leighton? What does she look like?"

"Medium height. Long dark hair."

"Skin color?"

"White. Brown eyes. She had on black slacks and a jacket—it looked like fake fur, almost iridescent. A short fur jacket."

"I hope to God it glows in the dark. Give me your car keys."

"What?"

"The Jag. Let me have the keys," Mike said, holding out his hand. "Every mope in this part of town can make a department Crown Vic. At least I'll look like we're hustling for drugs in your father's wheels."

Ethan Leighton reluctantly handed over the keys.

"You want to ride with me, Coop?" Mike asked, walking away from the morose congressman to discuss our plans. "Mercer, why don't you take your car, and we can tag-team to see who's walking the streets. Back us up."

"You start going into clubs in this neck of the woods, we'd better ask for a detail to hang out in case there's trouble," Mercer said.

"I got a different idea. Let's take a gander at Jumel Terrace."

Mercer's scowl disappeared. He slapped Mike on the back and

reached for his jacket. "Just a ways up from a Hundred and fifty-sixth, and a block in from Edgecombe. I like it."

"What's Jumel Terrace?" I asked. "What's there?"

"The oldest Federal house still standing in Manhattan. The Morris-Jumel House. It's a mansion, Coop. It's a fine-looking old mansion, with a well."

FORTY-FOUR

Mercer was in the beat-up Toyota he used to drive to work. Mike was adjusting the seat and the steering wheel in the steel gray Jaguar that he had commandeered from Ethan Leighton.

We left Leighton in the station house. He would not have need of the car for hours. By the time the children's service agency workers finished talking to him, he'd be wishing that Mike were conducting the interrogation.

We pulled out of the parking space on West 169th Street. There was a Yankees baseball cap on the dashboard. "Put it on, kid. That ponytail I ragged you about the other day? Do it again. I need you to look like a nineteen-year-old aching for coke, in case we run into any locals."

I took a rubber band from my jeans pocket and followed Mike's orders. "What took you so long to remember the mansion?"

"'Cause that's not how I think of the place. It's got a military significance to me, not a social one."

"Why? What is it?"

We were moving at a snail's pace down Amsterdam, each of us looking into doorways and alleys, on fire escapes and in parked cars. The cold spell and the early morning hour had most people off the streets. In the rearview mirror, I could see that Mercer was giving us plenty of lead time.

"The house was built by a British colonel in the 1760s—Roger Morris. About one hundred acres, on this hilltop, just east of here. An amazing setting, when you think about it."

"Like Gracie."

"No, no. Even more spectacular. You just see east and south from Gracie Mansion. This gave you all that, plus the Jersey Palisades and up the Hudson River. So in the fall of 1776, George Washington seized the place and made his headquarters here. That's when he forced the British retreat at the battle of Harlem Heights."

"You've been here before? Is it restored?"

"The general's digs? Sure, I have."

"Slow down. See that woman walking?" I asked.

Mike braked gently as someone came out of the shadows between two brownstones.

"Nope. Sorry. Ratty fur jacket," I said. "But it's a man. Who's Jumel, then?"

"Your kind of guy, Coop. Stephen Jumel was French. A wine merchant. One of the wealthiest men in New York when he moved here. He married an American woman named Eliza," Mike said, snapping his fingers. "And you know what? Rumor had it she'd been a prostitute before she married him."

"Must have sounded like the right place for a tryst to Anita."

"The more I think about it, the more it has to be connected to the boys who ran the old tontine. When Jumel died, Eliza actually married Aaron Burr. Didn't last long, but she married him just the same."

"Aaron Burr? Who killed Hamilton in a duel."

"But before that was co-counsel in the murder of the woman in the well."

"Gracie Mansion, Hamilton Grange, and this place," I said.

"The only three Federal houses that still exist in Manhattan. What's the hook between them and our case?"

Mike made a left turn onto West 160th Street, and then a second quick left. "Jumel Terrace, Madam Prosecutor."

The street was only two short blocks, and as Mike glided to a stop at the curb, I looked up the hill at the most unusual sight.

In the heart of this struggling neighborhood, full of tenements and bodegas, brownstones and crumbling old churches, stood a Palladian mansion. Its elegant white lines contrasted against the starless black sky. It was framed by a monumental portico supported by four enormous white columns.

"Nice place for a gentleman to take a girl to dinner, huh?" Mike asked.

"It looks like a movie set."

Mercer parked across the street and came over to the car.

"You bring a flashlight?"

Mercer patted his back pocket.

"Why don't you call the sarge and see if they've got a spare key for the joint? Ask him to send a patrol car over."

"Why would they have a key?"

"The house is open part of the week as a museum. Military buffs like me and house-and-garden babes like you come to visit. The precinct has security responsibility the rest of the time." Mike said as he got out of the car. "Let me have your flashlight, okay? You wait with her."

"Where are you going to do?" I asked.

"I wasn't kidding. I'm going to check the well."

"There are lights on in the house, Mike. In the center hall, on both floors."

"My peepers are working fine, Coop. I can see that. I imagine they're kept on all night," he said. "I'll be right back."

"Follow him, Mercer. It's awfully dark out there."

"I'm with you, Alex. He'll be fine."

Mike focused the light on the approach to the old mansion. He climbed the staircase to the front door, and tried unsuccessfully to open it. He retraced his steps and went off the pavement, disappearing between two sturdy evergreen bushes that were to the left side of the house.

It was quiet on the narrow street around us, and I could no longer track the beam of Mike's light.

"You see him?" I asked Mercer, getting out of the car.

"Not yet, Alex. Just give him a minute."

Then came a sudden noise that echoed off the hilltop, like the sound of a door slamming.

"There, Mercer. Look there!" I said, pointing off the right rear of the mansion. A tall, slim figure, silhouetted against the sky, was running down the slope, away from the house, as fast as his legs would carry him.

FORTY-FIVE

"Get in the car and lock the doors," Mercer said.

We could both see Mike jogging back to us.

"I got Coop," he said. "You want me to try to run that guy down?"

"Nobody needs to 'get' me. Do what you've got to do." I was in the front seat of the Jaguar, shaking ever so slightly. It was not the most vigorous protest I'd been known to make.

"What about the well?"

"There's a solid cap on it. Doesn't look like it's been touched in years. Take off, Mr. Wallace."

Mercer got into the Toyota and sped off out of sight, turning right at the end of Jumel Terrace in the direction of High Bridge Park.

Just as he made the turn, the RMP pulled in behind us and two uniformed officers got out.

"Sorry to pull you here, guys," Mike said.

"That's okay," one answered. "You got a problem?"

"I'm not sure. We'd like to go in and have a look."

"The lieutenant said to tell you that your man left the precinct."

"Whaddaya mean?" Mike asked. "Not the congressman?"

"Yeah."

"Damn it. Nobody watching him?"

"Curb your annoyance," I said. "As long as he didn't take the baby, we had nothing to hold him on."

"The baby's safe, ma'am. She's doing fine."

Mike slammed the flashlight against his fist. "So Ethan Leighton is roaming the streets like a loose cannon, and we've got his old man's car."

"C'mon, Mike. He wasn't any help. He'll catch hell on the other end when he gets home."

The second cop leaned against the window to say hello. "Hey, Counselor. Remember me? I had that domestic with the baseball bat last spring."

"Yeah. Sure, I do."

"You know this place is haunted," he said, opening the door for me.

"Actually, I had no idea it existed."

"The ghost of Eliza Jumel," he said, laughing at me. "That was one unhappy hooker. The folks say she stands up on the balcony and bays at the moon. At least it keeps all the neighborhood kids away. Regular ghostbusters, they are."

"When you guys aren't doing comedy, you have time to help me with this?" Mike asked.

"We've only got three cars on patrol this tour for the whole precinct. We'll stay as long as we can."

"I'd like one of you to come in with me," Mike said. "The other waits here. Coop? You in or out?"

"I'm with you."

Three of us made the approach to the elegant old house. "This place get a lot of use?" Mike asked.

"Just functions. It's open two afternoons this time of year. More in the summer. But there's people in and out some. Doesn't give us any trouble."

"Not a fixer?"

"No need," the cop said. He meant that the mansion was never made a "fixed post" patrolled by the department, like many sensitive security sites had been. "It's got some kind of fancy trust that runs it. They come and go on their own."

We were at the front door, and the cop was working the set of keys that opened the two locks.

"So you drive by at night and see lights on inside, it's not unusual?"

"Nah. They got dinners, they got parties. They got ladies' lunches and garden tours. Like I said, they got functions. That's what my boss tells me. That's the word he uses, supposed to cover everything that goes on in the place," the cop said. "Here we go. Let me just disarm the alarm code."

The door swung open and Mike pushed it wide, stepping inside. The officer followed him and pressed the keypad. "Whoever was here last didn't reset it. The alarm's not on."

Mike glanced at me. "Figures. Could be our guy, Coop."

"Or ghosts," I said.

It was like stepping back into another century to come in the house. The light I'd seen from outside was a wall sconce that illuminated the entrance and hallway. The Federal Period furniture—an ornate crystal chandelier, an elegant grandfather clock, settees, and sofas—had been carefully restored and beautifully maintained, just as in Gracie Mansion.

The officer led us off to the left, into the dining room. The polished surface of the table gleamed in the dim light, but gave no sign of a recent dinner party. To the rear of the first floor was a large room, shaped like an octagon.

The back door of the house, probably the one that we'd heard slam, was in the octagonal room. Mike turned the knob and the door gave easily. He pushed it closed and locked it.

Then he doubled around and came to the staircase. I stayed

behind him, with the cop trailing me. The floorboards creaked but that was the only sound beside our voices.

"Well, hold on," Mike said, waving me into the master bedroom.

An elaborate antique sleigh bed was centered beneath reams of powder blue silk drapery and lace trim that almost shrouded it from view. But I could clearly see that the spread had been removed, the linens had been disturbed, and it appeared someone had left the room in disarray.

"I can't say if it's Eliza Jumel, or Mama and Papa Bear," Mike said. "But I can tell you one thing, Ms. Goldilocks—someone's been sleeping in this bed."

FORTY-SIX

"Lock it up and set the alarm, will you?" Mike asked the cop as he let us out.

We walked down the front steps as Mercer pulled in and parked behind the Jaguar.

"You want Crime Scene to take the sheets for DNA?" I asked.

"Yeah, I'll send somebody over to voucher them tomorrow," Mike said. "Process the room for prints."

Mercer rolled down his window. "Hope you did better than I did. Came up empty."

"Any sign of the guy who ran out of here?"

"I don't think so. Everything's shadows and branches blowing in the wind. My eyes were playing tricks on me. How about the house?"

"Well, if this is where Anita spent her evening with a gentleman, there was a very light dinner served. But the bed saw some action."

"Guess she's up to her old tricks," Mercer said.

"You didn't happen to see the congressman on the prowl?"

"Leighton?"

"Yeah. The uniformed guys tell us he got bored waiting on his wheels. Walked off into the night. Keep an eye out for him. I think he's getting desperate."

"He probably knows more about where Anita might be than he told us. And stupid enough to be trying to find her."

"I think Coop's right. It kills me to go through Tim Spindlis on this," Mike said, "but we need to understand those phantom funds Kendall Reid set up."

The sky was beginning to lighten as dawn eased into the city.

"What are you thinking?" Mercer asked.

"There are only three Federal Period mansions still standing in Manhattan—this one, Gracie, and the Hamilton Grange. Reid's phony operation was snagging cash for the Grange, right?"

"And they're the places that were used when Moses Leighton staged his private dinners," Mercer said. "The Tontine Association."

The uniformed cop nearing the end of his night shift loped down the front steps of the old house.

"But that association was retired," Mercer said. "Too many boys with bad behavior."

"Let's talk it out over bacon and eggs," Mike said. "I'm thinking, what if Kendall Reid took a page out of Leighton's book. I mean, the old guy was his mentor. Taught him everything."

"Like he re-created the gentlemen's club?" I asked.

"Maybe they look like gents but they're scoundrels instead. *Sub rosa*—the secrecy symbol of medieval councils."

"And Reid's in the council," Mercer said. "It's got possibilities."

"Every one of these fabulous houses stands empty. Even Gracie Mansion," Mike said. "The mayor doesn't sleep there. No mayor has been in residence there since long before Bloomberg took office."

"So you're saying forget the dinner, and rent out the bedroom to the highest bidder. Pay for play."

"Like a tontine, with scads of cash being raised from its members, going to import these young women from wherever the cargo is most readily available. Mexico, Asia, Eastern Europe."

"History, politics, sexual intrigue," Mercer said. "It's a heady mix."

The cop in the RMP was calling out to his partner. He started the engine and turned on the red emergency light.

The second officer picked up speed and hurried to get into the car.

"Where's the fire?" Mike asked. "What's your hurry?"

"High Bridge Park. Sector Charlie just called in. There's a woman down."

"What happened? Have they ID'd her?"

"Not yet. A couple of dog walkers found her beneath the bridge. Looks like she screwed up a suicide attempt. The bus is on the way to take her to the hospital."

"She's alive?" Mike asked.

"Barely. She's still breathing," the cop said. "Likely to die."

FORTY-SEVEN

It took less than three minutes for Mike to race up Amsterdam Avenue to West 174th Street once he floored the Jaguar.

The bridge was at one of the widest points in the park. It was difficult to navigate the rocky terrain and scramble down to the area where EMTs and cops were trying to put the woman's body on a stretcher.

Mercer had followed us. He and Mike were the first detectives to arrive on the scene.

There was little doubt in my mind that the woman, who appeared to have fractured her skull and both legs, was Anita Paz. She fit the vague physical description Leighton had given us, and she was wrapped in a cheap synthetic fur jacket.

"She don't have time for you, Detective," the head EMT said as Mike put his hand in her jacket pocket to look for identification. "We don't get her to Columbia Pres in minutes, she's goin' out of the picture."

There were four men on the team. Two lifted the stretcher with Anita Paz strapped into it while the other two tried to clear the brush for the steep climb back up to the roadway. The great hospital was mercifully close to our location.

Two men, each holding a leashed retriever, were talking to the pair of cops.

Mike and I approached them, while Mercer scoured the ground for things that might be related to the woman's fall.

"You see any of this?" Mike asked, after displaying his badge to the men.

"No, sir. We meet every day, same time, to walk our dogs down here by the river. I never saw nothing like this. I thought for sure the girl was dead."

"Who called it in?"

"Me," the same guy answered. His walking buddy looked like he was going to be sick.

"A suicide?"

"I said it could be that. Could be just an accident. You know that bridge is very dangerous, Detective."

"I know. It's the oldest bridge in the city. It's been closed for fifty years."

"Bad way to go," the cop said.

"Find a note?" Mike asked. "Anything to suggest a suicide?"

"You kidding? Not here. Paper would have been blown away by this arctic air."

I guessed the temperature was in the teens, but the wind chill made it feel like single digits.

"There's a guy who was up in the squad for a couple of hours, might be able to ID her. He ran out of there a little while ago. You know the congressman who got collared for DWI last week?"

"Seen that scumbag's pictures in the papers," the cop said. "Think he was messing with this broad too?"

Mike didn't answer.

"You know who the jumper is? That would solve half my problems, if she don't wake up too soon."

"Run the name Anita Paz. Leighton knows her. She's been missing for a couple of hours."

"Did you see anyone else in the park before you got to this point?" I asked. "Or jogging away?"

The dog walkers looked at each other. The same one spoke for both. "Just the regulars. Maybe a few less runners and people out for exercise. A little chilly, no? We're only out because the dogs have to be."

"But you didn't hear people fighting with each other? Shouting? Nobody running through the park?"

"Nothing. We didn't see nothing unusual."

"Crime Scene on the way?" Mike asked the cops.

"After the triple homicide in Brooklyn and a gang rape in the Bronx. They want us to cordon off the area and they'll deal with it by afternoon."

"Keep an eye open for that Leighton weasel, pal."

"You think he's dangerous?"

"I know he's self-destructive and angry. Don't know what he's liable to do."

"I'll put it out on the radio."

"Good man," Mike said. "C'mon up top, Coop. Let's see what it looks like."

My driving moccasins and Mike's loafers were not the best shoes for managing the rocky incline, which in places was coated with ice. It took us almost ten minutes to climb from the edge of the Harlem River up to the Manhattan end of the High Bridge, which connected the island to the Bronx.

Mike tried to distract me as we made our way up. He knew me well enough that my first thoughts were about the baby, who was probably this woman's child. Mercer brought up the rear.

"What if she's Ana's mother?"

"Steady as she goes, Coop. Don't go there yet. You hear that guy? This is the oldest bridge in town."

"Older than the Brooklyn Bridge?" I asked.

"Way. It was built in the eighteen forties as part of the system bringing water to New York from upstate. From the Croton Reservoir. It's the very first structure that linked Manhattan to the mainland. To the rest of America. Don't you remember what that lady told us when we were in Poe Park?"

"That when Edgar Allan Poe lived in his little cottage in the Bronx, while his wife was dying, he'd console himself with long nocturnal walks across the river. On this? The High Bridge?"

"You got it."

We were directly beneath the series of vaulted arches that held up the span on this side of the river.

"You know, I would think that if Anita was going to jump— going to really try to kill herself—she would have gotten farther out on the bridge, to the middle, so she'd land in the river. That's the sure way to a suicide."

"Yeah. But the condition of the walkway is such a mess up there, it may not be easy to get out that far," Mike said. "Whether she jumped or got pushed, the boulders she landed on are pretty unforgiving."

"Mind if I catch my breath?" I asked, stopping as we neared the top.

"I can pull you the rest of the way," Mercer said jokingly, grabbing my hand. "You got the wind at your back."

"I feel like I've got the wind everywhere. It's brutal." The bitter cold made the landscape even more stark and miserable. "Was the bridge ever used for carriages or cars?"

"No. Just pedestrians. It was always a walkway."

"Why was it closed?" I asked.

"Some morons threw rocks off the bridge. Almost killed several tourists on the Circle Line boat."

"And it never reopened?" We had almost crested the grade.

"No. The aqueduct was replaced by the underwater tunnel system you got to know so well," Mike said, reminding me of a case we had worked a year earlier. "This bridge hasn't been used to carry water to us for a hundred years. So nobody's ever invested the money to open the walkway again."

The three of us stood together at the walled-off entrance to the crumbling span and looked across at the stone masonry piers and arches. "It really does look like a Roman aqueduct," I said.

"That's the ancient principle they used to bring water here from the mountains, Coop."

I had learned the hard way, through a murder case, that Manhattan had no natural water supply of its own.

"Wait a minute, Mike," Mercer said. "High Bridge, right?"

"Yeah. A low one would have been cheaper to build, but they needed the height so that boats going through to the Hudson could get under it."

"But it was built as an aqueduct, you said."

"Yeah."

"That's one of Kendall Reid's fake funds," Mercer said, warming his ears with his gloved hands. "That's one of the phantom charities Tim Spindlis named at the press conference. Save the Aqueduct Bridge."

"Dead on, Mr. Wallace," Mike said, processing Mercer's logic. "Reid should have patched some holes in this bridge instead of stuffing his cash in shoe boxes and cargo ships full of immigrants."

"Time for a wake-up call to your pal Spindlis, Alex."

"All Battaglia's horses and all his men may not be able to put Anita's cracked head back together, Coop. Get on the phone and tell him to give us everything he's got."

FORTY-EIGHT

It was only six thirty on Sunday morning. I didn't have Tim's home number programmed on my cell, so I called the cop on duty in the lobby of the DA's office and asked him to reach out and have Spindlis return my call.

"Maybe somebody gave Anita a boost up to get over this," Mercer was saying to Mike as they examined the stone wall blocking off the old walkway, fronted by an iron gate. "Makes it a lot more likely she wasn't out there planning to jump if she didn't go onto the bridge alone. If she was pushed, then whoever did it found the perfect place to mimic a suicide."

"Coop? You off the phone? See if you can get a toehold on that wall. Put your Pavlovas to good use."

I stuck the phone in my pocket and walked to the imposing gate. Weeds had broken through the brickwork on the path and cracks were everywhere. I put one foot on the guardrail and hoisted myself up.

"It's not hard to do. The question is why she would have agreed to go out on the bridge with anyone," I said.

"Well, she either trusted the guy enough to follow him, or he had a gun to her head."

"Follow him where, Mike?" I asked.

"Leighton said Anita told her cousin that it was an old friend who had set her up for the night. It must have been someone she could count on to lead her around up here."

"Why would you say that?"

"Well, she trusted him more than Leighton, 'cause she wouldn't even get in his car, baby and all."

"So maybe the guy—this friend of hers—tells her that he's parked in the Bronx," Mercer said. "It's just a short walk across this old bridge. That's the Bronx, right at the end of the footpath."

"I get it. So if anything illegal was going on at the mansion—prostitution, at least—then the police wouldn't even see this guy's car anywhere near the Jumel House. The car wouldn't actually be in Manhattan. Could be a useful escape route, especially if this friend was already in trouble—say, a guy like Kendall Reid."

I peered over the top of the wall at the surface of the bridge. Just below me, stored on the other side, were four large wooden barrels.

"Take a look for yourselves," I said, as I jumped down.

Mercer lifted one of his long legs onto the railing iron and looked over the wall. "Easy enough, Alex. You're right. Up over the top. Climb down onto the barrels. And assuming there are more like those on the other end, you'd be home free."

"Interesting idea," Mike said, positioning himself beside Mercer to look for himself.

"Are we going to stand out here in the cold and debate this, or do something about it?" I asked.

"Your lips are turning blue, kid. Why don't you wait in Leighton's Jag? Get comfy," Mike said to me, then turned back to Mercer. "Let me call the lieutenant and see if he can get Bronx Homicide to do a plate check on the cars parked around on the other side. See if anybody was ticketed during the night. Someone could have led Anita out on the bridge to her death, and there'd be no trace that he'd even been in Manhattan."

"That's true," Mercer said. "If your perp was smart enough to have planned all this—worried about getting caught—then he'd know that even a check of EZ pass plates would show he left Manhattan by bridge or tunnel the night before, and never came back."

"See what I mean? And all the time, he's just a hop, skip, and walk across the bridge away from the action in the Jumel Mansion."

The two uniformed cops were approaching us. They must have taken all the information and sent the dog walkers on their way.

"We're just going back to the street to get some tape to block off the scene," one cop said to Mike. "You guys need anything?"

"Take Ms. Cooper with you, okay? My little hothouse flower looks like she's about to freeze her ass off."

"I'm not going to the car, Mike. I'm with you two until you figure out what's next."

"The park rangers opened up the tower for us this morning," the cop said.

"They around to give us a hand?" Mercer asked.

"Are you kidding? Rangers on a frigid Sunday morning in January? We had to call to get them over here. They said they'd check back in before too long. Want me to tell them to be available if you need them?"

"Please."

"It's warm in there. Go on in and make your calls."

The graceful granite water tower, almost two hundred feet high, was just a few yards away from the end of the bridge, much closer than the street where Mike and Mercer had left their cars. It was octagonal in shape, like the unusual room in the Jumel Mansion. It looked like a Renaissance church tower that had been lifted from the Tuscan countryside and planted on a Manhattan hilltop.

"Good idea," Mike said to the more talkative cop. "You got enough tape with you so we can rope off the gate at the entrance to the bridge?"

"No problem. I'll be back with it in a few minutes."

The two cops led us toward the tower. Mercer walked on ahead. "Yeah, it's open. Thanks."

Mike was explaining that when water was originally pumped across the Harlem River over the High Bridge, it coursed through two iron pipes that still ran up the interior of the handsome structure, to equalize the pressure in the nearby holding reservoir.

"And now?" I asked.

"Just decorative. The tower's got views from the top that you wouldn't believe. You can practically see Paris."

We went inside and even though the building wasn't heated, it was a welcome shelter from the morning's fierce winds.

"Hey, Loo?" Mike said, talking into his phone. "Time to rise and shine, Boss. Let me explain what's happened since last night."

Mercer and I listened while Mike tried to tell Peterson what had developed, and enlist his help in getting detectives from Bronx County on board to help.

"Yeah, and the congressman went AWOL. Don't know. Maybe he's getting the picture that the kid isn't his. Maybe he had something to do with the scene on the bridge. He's off the charts."

"I've never been in here," Mercer said. "But at least somebody spent a few nickels restoring this beauty, which I'm glad to see."

"I didn't even know about it."

The redbrick walls in this small lobby were punctuated by twenty-foot-high windows on each of the eight sides. Running up from the basement below were the two iron pipes that had once carried all of Manhattan's drinking water from upstate—painted a shiny black—and surrounding them was a wrought-iron staircase that twisted in a narrow spiral to the top of the tower.

Mike was still arguing with Peterson. "I appreciate how hard it is to get anyone to help at this hour of the morning, Loo, but we can't cover the territory ourselves. There's a lot going on, okay?"

"Want to check it out with me?" Mercer asked, as he craned his neck to point above us.

My shoulders shook with chills. "You know how much I hate heights. I trust you'll tell me about it."

"Even if it is Kendall Reid, he didn't run this operation himself, Boss. Mercer and I need reinforcements, that's what you've got to tell Commissioner Scully," Mike said. "No, no. Battaglia doesn't know she's here with us. We'll dump her at home on the way downtown."

Mike flipped his phone shut

"Dump me?"

"Your teeth are chattering so loud, Coop, I can't hear myself think."

"I'm warming up in here," I said. "This helps a lot."

"What did Peterson say?" Mercer asked.

"He gave me a firm *no* to letting us go to Mayor Statler's home to knock on the door and question him again. We can't touch Kendall Reid until we bring Battaglia and Spindlis in on what we've got." Mike paused to smile. "Peterson doesn't miss a trick. Asked me whether I'd heard the rumors about Spindlis. Says if this whole thing has to do with hookers and escorts, maybe there's fire behind that smoke. Maybe that's why the DA jumped so fast on the Reid indictment, to clamp everybody down so Spindlis's name didn't come up."

"Leave me out of that brainstorm," I said. "Tell the lieutenant he can raise that errant thought with Battaglia because I sure as hell won't."

"Peterson also doesn't want us to do anything about Donny Baynes unless the feds are part of it. He doesn't have the manpower to have guys tracking down Ethan Leighton as well as sitting on Moses twenty-four/seven. Everything's a friggin' manpower issue in the department."

"I'll take the weight for bringing Alex out in the middle of the night," Mercer said. "That was my idea."

"Nice. You're both making it sound like I'm a liability to you guys. Thanks a million. I'm looking forward to being dumped. I'm sure I can get somebody to drive me home."

"The lieutenant's bent out of shape 'cause your car got tagged Friday night," Mike said. "He's just soft for you."

"I'm delighted to know I still have one fan."

"Does he have anybody for us?" Mercer asked.

"The day tour starts in an hour. He says he'll round up whoever comes in and send three or four guys over here to give us a hand."

"Excellent."

"Yeah. Might as well get going on the bridge. And I'd like to get the guys into the mansion to see what's been going on there."

The uniformed cop who had gone to the car to get yellow crime-scene tape returned. "Why don't you start with this roll?" he asked. "If you need more, I'll call the house and they'll bring it over."

"Thanks," Mike said. "You going down by the riverbed where the body was found?"

"Yeah."

"Mercer and I will work up on top, at the entrance to the bridge. We'll tape it off first. And then, we'll go over the wall and try to position ourselves directly above your spot, where you found the body. See if we can figure out where she dropped from. You mind spotting that with us?"

"Glad to do it," the cop said.

"Okay if I wait here?" I asked.

"I told you it was comfortable, right?" the cop said.

"That's the best advice I've had in days."

I watched through the tall paned glass window as the teams separated to stake out the scene. The two cops dropped out of sight as they maneuvered down the steep incline, while Mike and Mercer were visible off in the distance, headed for the gated entrance to the rotting old bridge.

My cell phone vibrated in my pocket. I reached in to remove it but the thick material of my gloves got in the way. As I withdrew it, my fingers fumbled and the cell dropped on the floor and skidded across the room.

When I picked it up, I saw that I had missed the return call from

Spindlis. His number had been captured, though, so I flipped the cell open to reply.

"Tim? It's Alex. I apologize for the hour, but I think we really need to sit down together. It's rather urgent."

I could barely make out his answer.

"You're breaking up," I said. "Give me a minute."

I walked a few feet to the north side of the lobby, around the spiraling black staircase, and planted myself against one of the windows. I held the phone to one ear and plugged my finger in the other so I could hear him.

"Of course I'll tell you everything that's happened," I said. My skin crawled just talking to him, as though I didn't really know him at all, despite ten years as colleagues working for Battaglia. The cheap rumors rattled around my head as I thought about how much to tell him.

"Yes, this is much clearer. We didn't mean to set you off about Kendall Reid. Mike only wanted to talk to him about our case, not yours. The murder and the—well—possible prostitution ring."

My normally laid-back and spineless colleague was agitated about our drop-by interview yesterday of his perp. He wanted to unload his annoyance on me and the least I could do was listen.

I stared out the window at the breathtaking view of the Hudson River that stretched for miles to the north.

"We got a lot of good stuff in the last twenty-four hours, Tim. Lieutenant Peterson thinks we should all meet and put our heads together. That we might be able to solve some of this."

I was so absorbed in the tongue-lashing that Spindlis felt it necessary to deliver that I was oblivious to my surroundings.

"If you don't want to come up here to the station house today, I understand. We can be in your office first thing tomorrow," I said. "Yes, Tim. I promise we won't question Kendall Reid again unless you're there."

I flipped the phone closed and smiled to myself. *We won't question Reid unless we find him clearing the dirty linens in the Jumel Mansion.*

Or sitting in his car alongside the Harlem River, in the Bronx, watching how the cops handle Anita's tragic fall.

I didn't know there was anyone else in the water tower until I felt the icy metal rim of a gun bore against the skin behind my right ear.

My body seized with fear as I tried to turn my head to see my attacker, but he gripped the back of my neck firmly with his left hand.

"Stay calm, Alexandra. Stay calm and don't move a muscle. Don't even shiver."

I tried to place the familiar voice but too many terrifying thoughts were racing through my brain.

"Now you're going to listen to me carefully, 'cause you know what they say, don't you?"

It was Rowdy Kitts, the detective assigned to bodyguard the mayor. The detective whose perjured testimony had cost my victim her case several years ago. The detective who'd been among the first people on the beach the morning the *Golden Voyage* hit the rocks.

"Panic kills, Alexandra. First thing they teach you at the academy. Stay really still," Kitts said to me, whispering in my ear. "Don't you forget that panic kills."

FORTY-NINE

"The first thing we're going to do is lock this door," Kitts said, pushing me to the entrance of the great tower so that he could secure the bolt from the inside.

"Chapman and Wallace are—"

"Right down at the bridge. I heard that. I was in the basement, just hanging out with the water rats, when you so rudely decided to make yourself at home here. But they've got their hands full at the moment, what with the blood, the bits and pieces of brain matter they're going to find."

My stomach churned at the thought of what Kitts had done to Anita Paz.

"All we need is a few minutes to get you taken care of so I can be on my way."

"What do you mean—?"

"Just have to get you up these stairs," he said, nudging me toward the twisting staircase with his gun. "We'll create a little diversion. If you're half as smart as Chapman thinks you are, you won't get hurt."

I was replaying the words that Mike had used to explain the

deaths of the victims who'd washed ashore. He and Stu Carella were the ones who said that panic kills.

"I'll walk out of here with you, Rowdy. We'll walk out together and you can just leave me in Mercer's car and take off."

"Damn, I wish it were that easy, Alex. Get you outside and if I put a gag over your mouth, it won't look quite right to folks we pass along the way in the park. And if I don't gag you, you might just scream. Then Chapman would jump for you like he always does, like his pants are on fire."

"I won't scream. I promise you."

"Just climb, Alex."

His strong, lean body pressed against mine as he tried to move me forward. He was dressed in ski clothes, his slicked-back hair revealing his sharp features—steely gray eyes, a pointed nose with a few ridges that made it appear it had been broken once or twice, and thin lips that drew tight into a menacing grimace when I didn't comply with his orders. He was likely the figure I'd seen running from the Jumel Mansion half an hour ago.

"The guys will come back and find the door locked and call emergency services to break it open."

"It'll take an awfully long time to get a response from ESU just to come to the water tower. There won't be any reason to think you're here."

The sight of the gun in the hands of someone as vicious as Rowdy Kitts, someone who despised me so intensely, terrified me. He was just as liable to shoot if Mike or Mercer interrupted his plans to get away. He was only likely to keep me alive as long as I might be viable to him as a hostage or a bargaining chip.

"That reminds me, Alex. Take off those gloves." When I did, he grabbed them and tossed them across the room. "Sounded to me like Chapman was anxious to get rid of you. Open your phone for me."

I did exactly as he said.

"Show me the screen. Good. Now bring up Mike's number and text him. I'm watching. Just text like I say. 'Rangers here. Taking me to the Three-three to get warm.'"

Rowdy Kitts dictated and I typed. He gave me no chance to insert any other message into the phone.

"Hit Send. Now give me your cell. By the time Chapman finishes what he's doing and reads this, he'll think the park rangers got you out of his hair and locked up this tower. Buys us a little time together."

Then he let go of the phone, and I heard it clanging against the basement steps, echoing throughout the chamber as it bounced off one of them along the way and hit bottom. "So sorry, Alex. It just sort of slipped."

Here, only hundreds of feet away from Mike and Mercer, Kitts was cutting me off without a lifeline.

"Start moving."

"I can't do it, Rowdy." I tipped my head back and looked to the crown of the tower. The endless parade of metal steps—hundreds of them—curved above me, tapering off at the very top in a dizzying swirl of wrought iron.

"Climb, Alexandra. Step lively. Your life may depend on how fast you do it."

"You don't understand," I said, placing my foot on the first platform. "I get vertigo. I get sick from heights. I'll never be able to climb this."

"You get queasy on my watch it could be fatal to you, girl," Kitts said, wrapping his arm around my neck and pulling me back to him, whispering into my ear. "I just need to tuck you away up there so I can do what I've got to do. It's not my plan to make you sick."

Did he only want me to mount the staircase so he could throw me over from the top? Make it look like I had fallen while trying to see the view?

"Two suicides won't work, Rowdy. No one will believe Anita

went out on that bridge and jumped. You didn't think about a note, did you?"

"Sure I did," he said. "She was so despondent about her girl-friend Salma being killed. Worried that she'd lose her baby once her story came to light. Give the kid a better life and all that. Got the saddest little note she wrote right here in my pocket. Now I just need to get it to her house."

Rowdy Kitts was half pushing, half lifting me up the steps. I gripped the banister tightly and paid attention to my footing.

"Is it money? You want money?"

"I'm drowning in money, Alex. Never knew what a grown man would pay to have sex with a beautiful girl."

"I've got a pretty good sense of that."

"Well, you should have told me a whole hell of a lot earlier, then. Could have quit this damn job ages ago," Kitts said with a laugh. "You never took to me from the first time you met me, Ms. Cooper. You were always so high and mighty 'cause you didn't like me sniffing around those girls in your office."

He kneed me in the back and I edged up. He kept talking. "Or maybe you were just jealous."

There were no landings along the staircase. It continued to wrap itself around the slick black pipes, the steps getting smaller and smaller and closer together. We had circled at least twenty feet up, maybe thirty. I couldn't bear to bring myself to look down at the distance to the cement flooring.

"I didn't make you for a snakehead, Rowdy. I've seen the crimes committed by the lowliest bastards on earth. I've witnessed every kind of pain and torture that a man can inflict on a woman, but trad-ing in human lives—there's nothing more despicable."

"You don't like to hear that some of those girls actually enjoy what they do."

"Maybe when you hold a gun to their heads like this, that's what they tell you," I said. "How many young women have you done this to, Rowdy? How many have you had to kill? Or is that all *sub rosa*, Detective Kitts? Is that all a big secret?"

Rowdy cracked the gun against my shoulder blade. I dropped on one knee, banging it against the edge of the step. When I straightened up I briskly climbed away from my captor, closing my eyes and revolving around the spiral.

"So you got the sub rosa bit, huh? Is that what Anita told Leighton last night? I had her all set up with a really high roller—"

"At the Jumel Mansion?"

"She threw away a good deal, Alex. She was still all spooky about Salma. Never gave the man a proper chance. I promised to help her. No need to call the fat cat with the Jaguar."

How many young women were there who'd been subjected to this treatment? It was impossible to guess the extent of his network, in the city and well beyond.

"I saw the tattoos on their thighs. I knew Salma had been trafficked. I just didn't know whose property she was. I didn't know where to look first to find the rose." I was several steps higher than Kitts and had rotated my body a bit to face him, gripping the banister with all my strength. "You were standing next to me in that makeshift morgue on the beach when I spotted the tattoo on that girl from Ukraine. I never liked you, Rowdy. I just didn't take you for that much of a lowlife."

He was coming toward me, and I backed myself up several steps. "I guess I got lucky, Alex. I was afraid you were more clever than that. I was actually afraid that morning that you and your first-grade dicks were going to figure it out about Jane Doe."

"Figure what?"

"You're all shaky, Alex. You got to hold on tight, 'cause these metal stairs can get slippery."

Kitts was reaching out to touch me again and I turned away from him. I turned away from his gun, his outstretched hand, and the sick leer on his face to climb higher, fighting my fear and my nausea.

"Figure what?" I asked.

"The girl you call Jane Doe. The one who washed up on the beach."

"Stabbed in the heart before she was thrown overboard to die," I said, recalling the ugly circumstances of her death. "A knife, a sharp instrument—"

"An ice pick, Alex."

How could he possibly know what had happened to her on the ship, unless some other snakeheads were on board?

"How'd you wind up with her makeup, Rowdy?"

He stopped in his tracks and I raced on ahead, daring to look back to see that I had surprised him.

"She had nothing to do with the *Golden Voyage*, Alex. The girl was never on that ship. Tell that to Chapman next time you see him."

The entire disastrous seascape appeared in my mind's eye like I was still standing on the windswept beach.

Rowdy Kitts, rogue cop who had worked for the disgraced and indicted former police commissioner. Rowdy Kitts, who owned a piece of a small marina near the site of the wreck of the shipload of slaves. Rowdy Kitts, who'd killed a still-unnamed young prostitute with an ice pick, and thrown her in the ocean, hoping she'd be counted as one of the lost souls of the tragic accident. Rowdy Kitts, the mayor's bodyguard who knew as much about Gracie Mansion—and City Hall—as anyone with that kind of daily exposure to those places could.

"It was *you* who approached the ship in the middle of the night, flying the NYPD colors in your own speedboat so the authorities would leave you alone while you unloaded your cargo. Making the landing arrangements for your trafficked goods," I said. The picture was coming together for me. "But you were late—"

"The damn mayor doesn't keep regular hours, Alex. Can't please everybody."

"And some of the passengers went crazy when they finally saw your boat approach, 'cause they thought it really *was* the cops, coming to board them."

Rowdy Kitts had been right under our noses since the first hours we stood on the beach, watching the bodies come ashore.

I flashed to the image of the Ukrainian interpreter who had been with me at the morgue when two male passengers viewed the body of the girl we called Jane Doe. I'd been annoyed when he injected his own opinion that she was too pretty to have been forgotten if those men had ever seen her. He'd been right, of course. She had never been on board the *Golden Voyage*.

"Human gold, Alex. And it all went up in smoke."

"But that's not why you killed the girl," I said, clutching the banister to keep my balance as I tried to stare him down. "Who was she, Rowdy?"

"She was nobody, Alex."

I started to tremble uncontrollably at his coldness, his calculation, his utter disregard for human life.

I was mad at myself for having missed the obvious. The girl on the beach had had a rose tattoo, like Salma and Anita Paz. But the others just coming to America—the girls like Olena, whose tattoo was a green dragon, her last owner's mark—hadn't yet been stamped with the small red rose. They wouldn't become Rowdy Kitts's property till he got them safely ashore, till he took control of their lives. Of course the beautiful young woman we called Jane Doe had not come on the *Golden Voyage*. She'd been Rowdy's property long before last week.

"The girl had a name, Rowdy. Give her that much."

"Now, don't get all upset about it. She was just one more pitiful story, that's who she was. I took her in with me too. Eugenia was her name. She was living on my boat, being treated pretty good the last six months," he said. "But she was threatening to make trouble with the new girls. She was going to warn them off the life, before I even got them sorted out and signed up."

"So you killed her, just to shut her up?" I was frozen in place, practically halfway up the tower.

Rowdy Kitts reached out with his left arm and grabbed my ankle. I started to kick but he clamped my foot down on the step and smiled. "It's not the worst way to go, Alex. If I had a little better luck with the tides, Eugenia would have had a proper burial at sea."

FIFTY

"May I make a suggestion, Alex?" Kitts asked with saccharine-like concern for my condition. I was sitting down, halfway up the tower, trying to quell the nausea that swept over me whenever I opened my eyes. "You can get the rest of the way a lot quicker if you just hold tight and put all those bad thoughts about me out of your head."

"Don't you see I can't move? Take off, Rowdy. I won't do anything to stop you."

He stood in front of me, stroking the barrel of his Glock. "Me and my friend, we'd really like to get out of here. Just need to secure you up top."

"What's there?" I asked.

"Seems like I left my cuffs in the car last night. Wasn't very smart of me, but we'll just take off your socks and make a nice tight knot. Give you something to do for the next few hours."

Rowdy stuck the gun in his waistband, at the back of his slacks, and removed my moccasins. He pulled at the soft wool knee-highs that had kept my feet so warm, stroking my legs as he bared them.

"You'll have a hard time getting to your car," I said, "with Mike and Mercer out on the bridge."

"How so?"

"You left it in the Bronx, didn't you? Save the Aqueduct Bridge and all that phony politicking that Kendall Reid did to give you money to traffic in the girls."

Before I could finish the sentence Rowdy Kitts had slapped me across the face. His whole mood changed. "Walk, you damn bitch."

"It's way too big an operation for you to have pulled off alone, as good as you think you are." My cheek stung and I was as angry as I was frightened. "You were in charge of the Eastern Europeans, I'd guess. Kendall Reid has what—the Mexicans, or the Asians? How many snakeheads does it take to feed the perversions of all your clients?"

He pulled me to my feet and grabbed the hood of my jacket, pushing against my back to move me upward.

"You'd be surprised at how efficiently we work, Alex. A few ex-cons, some of the friends Kendall left behind in the ghetto, a bunch of hungry guys willing to scratch their way out. You'd be surprised."

"Did Eugenia leave her makeup on your boat, Rowdy? Is that why you had to get rid of it? You were such a good Samaritan to let the cops use the boat that night, after you'd taken it out first and killed her. They didn't know they were covering up most traces of both you and Eugenia."

"What do you know about her makeup?"

"Let me stop," I said. "Let me sit down."

I couldn't tell whether he was poking me with his finger or the gun, but I got the point.

"We found Eugenia's makeup in the ditch in front of City Hall," I said, pausing to steady myself. The spiral was so tight now that we were practically facing each other as the curve narrowed.

"You're lying."

"They got her print off the mascara. And they got yours off the plastic bag." Maybe the second half of what I said would be proved true by the end of the day. Touch DNA might be the nail in his coffin, if we could shut that lid before he slammed mine. "Your best girls got Chanel makeup? Salma, Eugenia—how many others? Should have just thrown it overboard with the ice pick."

"Hard to do, Miss District Attorney. Eugenia left it in the glove compartment of my car. It wasn't on my little boat. I didn't remember that till I got to work the other morning. Just tossed it away with all those old bones."

"You were getting sloppy, Rowdy." I was tired and light-headed and didn't think I had much to lose.

"You know what they say about the end of the tunnel, Alex. Look ahead and you can see the sun rise."

The dark interior of the tower opened onto a small platform about ten feet above me.

"Were you part of Leighton's Tontine Association?" I asked.

"Another minute or two you're going to be eating one of your socks, young lady," Kitts said. "I'm going to stuff one right in that busy mouth."

"Is that where you got the idea for a gentlemen's club?"

"Those rich boys didn't want me anywhere near their dinner parties. But when the operations they ran went to the dogs, when that all broke up, I had me an idea for a little something else."

"A bit more like an escort service," I said. "Young girls, high prices, fancy settings. Who better to know when the mayor isn't going to be at home?"

"You'd be surprised how many gents fantasize about a night in the Lincoln bedroom," Rowdy said, taking one of my socks in his hands and twisting it around. "Hell, what I had to offer here in Manhattan wasn't so bad."

"You transformed the Tontine Association into another kind of club. And you renamed it Sub Rosa. Sleazy, Rowdy, and I should have been the first to figure you for something sleazy."

"It wasn't such a bad idea. Archibald Gracie really did belong to a dining club called Sub Rosa. You ought to tell Chapman to bone up on his history. Maybe he would have brained it out by now," Kitts said. "Sit yourself down and give me one of those hands, Alex."

We had made it to the top. Daylight poured in through the windows and the brightness hurt my eyes as we emerged from the dark climb.

"Is there really a tontine, Rowdy? Somebody in line to get all the money in Salma's shoe boxes?" My hands were deep in the pockets of my jacket.

"That was just seed money to ship in the precious cargo." He was motioning for me to give him my right hand. "It's a small club, Alex. Last man standing's going to be able to set himself up for a nice life anywhere he wants to go. Now, give it up, girl."

"The mayor?" I was trying to clear my head, sitting on the lacy metal fretwork and trying to meet Kitts in the eye, instead of looking all the way down.

"Clean as a hound's tooth. I don't think Vin Statler likes the ladies."

"Donny Baynes?"

"He might like to be a player, but he just doesn't have the cash. It's probably what keeps that boy honest. Same with that loser Spindlis."

"Ethan Leighton?"

"Like father, like son. That gene pool must have been really screwed up." Kitts liked the sound of his own voice. He clearly relished telling me about his ability to outsmart the richer, more powerful men who surrounded him. "Those boys play rough."

"Who tagged me, Rowdy? You do it yourself?"

He frowned as he tugged at my hand. "I don't usually have to do this kind of shit myself, Alex. I got men. I got people I pay to do things for me. You know how that is, don't you? I need you to just hold out your hand."

Kitts wrapped one end of the smooth cashmere sock around my wrist, doubling the knot until I winced in pain. I was trying to think of any word that applied except *panic*. That had consequences I didn't want to accept.

"I'm surprised you missed the signals, Alex."

I couldn't make up my mind whether to look out at the bright blue sky, praying for a miracle, or watch Kitts tie the other end of the long sock to the banister.

"You hear me?"

"What signals?" I asked.

"Jeannie Parcher. That paralegal I got messed up with. She wanted to talk to you so bad. She threatened me that she'd go see you for advice. What to do when I got nasty."

Mike had guessed right about that. Jeannie had tried to tell me about her experience—Mike had asked me if Rowdy had gotten rough with her—but I didn't pick up on what terrified her about this hideously evil man.

"What did you do to Jeannie?" I asked softly.

"Nothing you want to hear right now," he said, sneering at me. "You ought to give her a ring sometime."

The arm that Kitts was tying up jerked so badly that he grabbed my shoulders and started to shake me.

When he let go, I realized for the first time that he had bound me securely to the iron rail. I'd been so fearful of falling throughout the entire climb that it was almost a relief to be anchored to something that wasn't going to move.

"It's too tight, Rowdy." I was still afraid of what he might do to me before he left.

"I don't really think you're in a position to be calling the shots, Alex. Shit, there's always the Civilian Complaint Review Board." He was laughing as he balled up the other sock between his hands and leaned over to stuff it in my mouth. "You can take up all your problems with them."

I recoiled as he came at me. I clutched the banister as tightly as I could, almost chained to it as I was. Both of my knees came up between us, almost reflexively. I kicked my legs out in front of me with all the power I could muster and struck Rowdy Kitts squarely in the gut.

I screamed as I watched him fly backward over the railing, shouting my name, falling through the middle of the spiral staircase until his body hit the floor of the water tower, several stories below me.

I covered my eyes with my hand and tried to make myself breathe.

FIFTY-ONE

"I'll tell you what it's going to take, Loo." Mike was talking to Peterson on his cell, standing at one of the windows. It was more than an hour after I had pushed Rowdy Kitts to his death. "Go to the Bronx Zoo, get yourself the kind of tranquilizer gun they use on elephants. She's not coming down that staircase unless you pump her full of that stuff."

Mercer had untied me and was massaging my wrist, trying to stop the tremor in my hands. The two of us were sitting on the floor of the tower's platform, leaning against the wall while we waited for backup.

"Coop's not going anywhere unless you put a bag over her head and have somebody carry her down. She can barely open her eyes up here. Vertigo, smertigo—I'm not cleaning up after her if anything happens. I draw the line at my assignments."

"I can't move. I don't feel steady enough to stand."

"Did you hear that, Loo? Tell you what. I'll lower down a bucket. Maybe you can fill it with a few Bloody Marys to loosen her up. No, I'm not kidding. Hurry along."

"I just killed a man."

"Correction. The murdering son of a bitch got a faster exit than he deserved. Me? I would have plucked out all his finger- and toe-nails, then I would have gouged—"

"Enough, Mike," Mercer said.

"I would have tortured him. I would have taken pleasure in it. What does that say about me? He bought his own ticket out of here, Coop. You know how many lives he ruined, how many girls are dead because of Rowdy Kitts? Think forward—think of the women you've saved. Those can't be teardrops, are they? You'll lose me if you start to cry. I'll abandon you right here."

Mercer wouldn't let go of me. "You do anything that makes you feel better."

I bit the inside of my cheek and checked my emotions. There would be plenty of time for all this to settle over me when I was safely at home.

Mike was circling the small platform, checking every crevice and jiggling the bricks, as though to see if they were loose.

"Can you please be still? You're making me dizzy again."

"Rowdy didn't say what he was coming up here for?"

"I didn't ask. I just assumed it was to get rid of me."

"No offense, kid, but it's not always about you. He took a real gamble on this climb. Turned out to be his death gamble."

Another chill went through me. "He couldn't get out of the basement as long as I was keeping warm, waiting for you in the lobby."

"Yeah, but why was he in here in the first place? Why did he waste all that time forcing you to climb to the tower? He could have just cold-cocked you and kept heading for the highway. There must be something up here he wanted."

Mercer looked away from me for the first time and got to his feet. I closed my eyes. Mike's idea had piqued his interest.

"Rowdy thought we'd have caught him because of the first Jane Doe on the beach. Did I tell you that?" I was rambling, but I couldn't remember which parts of the story I had repeated to Mike and Mercer when they found me.

"Hindsight's a wonderful thing, Alex. My mother used to say she could tell when I was being bad 'cause she had eyes in the back of her head. Would have saved me a lot of lives if I could have stopped perps before they got started." Mercer extended a hand. "You want to try standing?"

I shook my head. "What's happening downstairs?" I could see flashes of light that reflected off the shiny black paint of the stair rail.

"Crime Scene's finishing up with photographs. There's a bus ready to take the body out. We'll head down after that."

"Seriously, I don't know how I'm going to move."

"We'll get you down."

Mike was on his tiptoes, running his fingers around the rim of the fancy trim that topped the brickwork. "You've got a few inches on me, Mercer. Help me out."

"Will do." He tossed his head in my direction, expecting I wouldn't catch the body language—his request that Mike do some hand-holding for a while.

"What'd we miss, blondie?" Mike hovered over me while he talked. "This Eugenia was also from Ukraine?"

"Yes, but more than six months ago. She was living with Rowdy, but threatening to blow the whistle."

"So I should have noticed nails bitten to the quick? Half the girls on the boat were like that, their nerves shot to hell. The jogging bra? Is that so very American?"

"The rose tattoo. I should have figured that wouldn't have happened to the girl until she was firmly the property of her trafficker."

"Don't beat yourself up. Could just have easily have been done before she set sail. Did he admit to tagging your car with the GPS?"

The flashes of light had stopped, but now from below I could hear voices. Someone was talking about a body bag. Another guy warned his companions not to step in the blood.

"I'm talking to you, Coop. Did Rowdy say he tagged you? Don't listen to what's going on."

"He talked about guys who did the dirty work for him and for Reid. Guys he'd locked up, street thugs."

"Who better to have access to a GPS than Rowdy? Probably walked into headquarters and told them the mayor's detail needed a few. Queered the numbers off them so they'd be impossible to trace."

"This what you think Rowdy was after?" Mercer said.

At the point where the crown molding touched the edge of the ceiling, almost seven feet above the landing, Mercer had dislodged and removed a loose brick. He reached in, retrieving a small plastic folder, not much bigger than a wallet, with a zippered top.

"What have you got?" Mike asked, walking away from me.

"Your idea, Detective. Take a gander." Mercer stepped around him and reached out for me. "On the count of three, you're on your feet. There's still some life in those eyes of yours, isn't there? You've got to be a little bit curious."

I clutched the stair rail with one hand and grabbed on to Mercer with the other.

Mike had unzipped the pouch and was scanning the documents inside. "This is why Rowdy was risking so much to climb up here, and why Anita was willing to come with him."

"What are they?" I was standing, surprising even myself, sandwiched between my two friends.

"These two are American passports. One for Salma Zunega and one for Anita Paz. The letter enclosed with them says they were obtained from the office of Congressman Ethan Leighton."

"That means they might even be legit. Passports and potholes—that's what most congressmen do half the day. No wonder there were no papers kept in Salma's apartment. That's one of the holds, one of the controls, Rowdy kept on his girls. He hung on to the only proof they had that made them legal," Mercer said. "What's that other one?"

Mike unfolded the cream-colored paper. I could see that it was headed in fancy calligraphy, bore a seal of some kind, and had the print of a tiny foot inked on it.

"It's the birth certificate for Ana."

"Oh God. What will become of the child?"

"Don't buckle now, Alex," Mercer said, resting his hands on my shoulders.

"Says she was born to Anita Paz in Brownsville, Texas. Gives the name of the hospital and date of birth."

"Paternity?" I asked. "Did she—?"

"Yeah. According to this, Ana's father is Kendall Reid."

Mercer's low whistle blew into my ear. "No wonder Rowdy was so bound and determined to get up here. Fine piece of blackmail that is. Any question between them of who gets whatever cash is still hidden away, Rowdy Kitts would have been holding the golden key to unlock the moneybags."

"Reid's baby. Ethan Leighton's beloved protégé duped him into thinking the kid was his own."

"You're assuming Reid knows the truth," I said.

"There's a gift to put right in the lap of Tim Spindlis. That'll let him tighten the screws on Reid."

"So now this baby has no mother, and her real father's about to be a convicted felon, once my office finishes with him."

"You can't do all the world's worrying, Coop. Maybe Anita's aunt really is a decent, hardworking woman. ACS will look into that. I'll make you a promise here and now. We'll sit on that one, with you, to be certain Ana's taken in—eventually adopted—by the kind of family she deserves. Hell, anything's better than the way she's been treated till now."

I looked at Mike quizzically. He didn't make pledges lightly.

"You have my word."

"Chapman?" a deep voice called from below.

"Yeah?"

"All clear here. You can start on down."

"Thanks. We're on the way."

"Where's my Bloody Mary? I think I need it."

"I'll spring for a six-pack when we get you home."

"How am I going to do this?"

"You're going to trust us, Alex, like you always do," Mercer said. "I'll go first, just one step ahead of you. Mike will be right behind. You need to hold on to me? You do that."

"But if I trip, you're the one who'll get hurt. What if I knock you over?"

"You're more surefooted than that. I'm not the least bit worried."

Mercer put his foot down one step and I forced myself to the edge of the landing. I picked my chin up and looked out the window for the first time from the top of the stately tower.

The sky was a crisp, clear blue. The clouds that shrouded the skyline in a wintry mist the last few days had passed through the city. I thought of all the victims of the shipwreck, and how the turn of events of the last few hours could speed their clearance through the system and let them get on with their lives.

My gaze caught on the promontory where the mayor's elegant mansion jutted out into the East River. I had met the deadly fury that is Hell Gate head-on.

Mike put his hand on my shoulder gently, to reassure me that he was right there with me. "Enough with your sightseeing, Ms. Cooper. It's not every day I offer to buy the first round of cocktails."

FIFTY-TWO

"Good morning, Alex. I'm Elizabeth Arrington. How do you feel?"

Two days had passed since my terrifying confrontation with Rowdy Kitts. Mike, Mercer, and I were in a conference room at the federal courthouse on Pearl Street where Arrington, an assistant United States attorney, was about to appear before a magistrate judge for the arraignment of Kendall Reid on trafficking charges.

"I'm okay, thanks."

"Don't worry, Liz," Mike said. "She cleans up a hell of a lot better than this. Give her a month or two."

I was sitting at the end of a long wooden table. Mercer had planted himself as close to me as physically possible, his chair catty-corner to mine, staring like a family member watching a critically ill patient in an intensive care unit. Mike was leaning against the windowsill, impatiently waiting for the magistrate.

"You understand that I'll be handling Reid's case?" Arrington asked. "I'm sure you know that Donny Baynes has recused himself."

The feds had taken jurisdiction of the trafficking investigation that stretched halfway around the world at this point, and it would doubtless grow as more victims were uncovered by cooperating witnesses. For once, Battaglia didn't battle to keep the case, in large measure because my involvement would have made his efforts futile.

"I'm very glad it's in your hands," I said, hoping my smile looked as sincere as it was meant to be. Liz Arrington, a short feisty brunette, had done a brilliant job as second seat to the lead prosecutor in the trial of one of the most notorious terrorists—a blind sheikh who had masterminded the planning of bombings at several landmarked buildings but was caught before the acts were completed. "You've got a great reputation."

"You'll get your cred back, Coop," Mike said. "People find out you can drop-kick a killer like Rowdy Kitts, they'll forget you needed a team of Saint Bernards to get you down from the tower."

"Mike," Mercer said, pointing a finger at his good friend. "Save it for another day."

"Why? She didn't lose her sense of humor, too, along with her cell phone and her sanity?"

"What do you need from me, Liz?" I ignored Mike, even though I knew that teasing was his way of trying to nudge me from the morose state that I'd found myself in since my Sunday-morning encounter with death.

"I've tried to get myself up to speed with the facts. Donny sat me down and gave me a crash course, but I've still got questions."

"Is he—?" I wondered whether his close relationship with Ethan Leighton and his membership in the Tontine Association had derailed Baynes professionally.

"He's good, Alex. Donny will help with anything he can. He's asked for a transfer to the appeals bureau till we see how this all shakes down."

"We've spent a lot of time trying to puzzle this out, Liz," Mercer said, taking the lead in his calm, mannered style. "Let me help. You trying to keep Reid in jail?"

Kendall Reid had surrendered to the feds on Monday evening,

just a little over twelve hours before. His lawyer would use that voluntary move as a basis for requesting release on his own recognizance, so that he wouldn't have to come up with money for bail. The cash he'd been stealing from the council's phantom funds was no longer at his disposal for personal use.

"Absolutely," Liz answered without a moment's pause. "The magistrate will want to know exactly which crimes he played a role in. I'm hoping you can guide me the rest of the way. Donny admits he had blinders on to much of what the Leightons were doing, and to Kendall Reid too."

I had been in Liz Arrington's shoes. I knew she had to immerse herself in a complicated series of facts—criminal conduct that stretched back over years, from one continent to another, with laundered money from illegal human slave trading stashed in shoe boxes and other places not yet imagined. I needed to shake off my own dark thoughts and concentrate on helping her get the job done.

"The dead girl," Liz said, looking down at a sheaf of notes she had put together. "I'm looking for her name. Sorry—give me a minute."

"Salma Zunega?" Mercer asked.

"No, no. Eugenia, the girl who washed up on the beach. It was Rowdy Kitts who killed her?"

I lifted my head to look at Liz. "That's what he told me."

"He actually admitted that?" She seemed somewhat skeptical, or else I was too sensitive to the way everyone was looking at me. "I mean, Kitts talked to you about Eugenia?"

"Rowdy wasn't going to let me live, Liz. He was making that climb up the tower to get his insurance, his blackmail material—the baby's birth certificate. And once done, I had no doubt he was going to get rid of me too," I said. The coffee was cold and tasteless, but I took another sip. "He delighted in seeing the terror in my eyes when he told me that Eugenia was worthless to him. That she'd been trafficked in long before the *Golden Voyage* grounded here, lived with him for a while, and was ready to blow the whistle so the new girls wouldn't be subjected to his personal form of torture."

"Did he talk to you about Salma?" Liz asked. She was looking for another murder confession and I couldn't give it to her.

I shook my head.

"Coop gave him the boot before he got that far," Mike said, turning his back to lean on the sill and stare out the window. "The lab handed us the rest. Twist Kendall Reid's testicles and he'll paint the whole picture for you."

Liz looked to Mercer for help. "Touch DNA? Someone can explain it to me this week, I'm sure. I've never handled a case with that kind of evidence."

"Alex will make it crystal-clear for you. She's done the forensics before juries more times than you can count, and the team at the lab is the best in the business. They've got Kitts on the murder weapon in Salma's apartment, and from the satin trim on the blanket she was wrapped in."

"Yeah, and that nubby white wool is even stuck in the threads of a sweater we recovered from his apartment yesterday," Mike said.

"Can you help me with *why* Kitts killed her?" Liz wanted answers from all of us. "I mean, why the spoofed phone calls before the murder?"

"Think big picture, Liz," Mercer said. "Let me get you there. This trafficking scheme has tentacles that are going to take you deep and wide, so back up to that. Rowdy Kitts and Kendall Reid are just two of the snakeheads at the top of the pit. An operation as big as this, as well-funded? It takes a village."

"So was everyone in the Tontine Association involved with the trafficking business?"

"None of us believe that," I said. "I think the perps counted on the reputations of guys like Donny Baynes to give them cover. They built the social club around that. And then the bottom feeders got to work."

"The judge is going to ask me about Ethan Leighton, Alex. I don't want to go on the record and make him a target if we don't believe he's mixed up in anything worse than last week's accident."

"Of course not."

"Tell Liz about the house call you had," Mike said, crossing his arms after he passed me a bottle of water. "That coffee'll rot your gut."

"The district attorney dropped by my apartment on his way home last night. To check on me, make sure I was okay."

"Nice." Liz smiled at me.

"Bullshit. Battaglia did the drop-in to make sure she wasn't holding back anything," Mike said. "And toadying along beside him was Tim Spindlis."

There was a knock on the door and Liz Arrington's assistant started to come in. She held up her hand and told him to step back. "Tell the judge I need some more time."

"Will do. Sorry. And some of Ms. Cooper's friends are here."

My prosecutorial posse, no doubt. I almost let myself relax.

"They'll have to wait," Liz said. "What about Spindlis?"

"Battaglia wanted me to hear right from him—"

"She means right from the mouth of the jellyfish," Mike said.

"Battaglia wanted Spindlis to tell me himself that he had never played any part in Leighton's introduction to prostitutes. The two had been close enough for Tim to come to realize—long before Claire caught on—that Ethan Leighton had an addiction that no one seemed able to help him control."

"So Ethan was a client of Rowdy Kitts all along?" Liz asked, taking notes while she listened to me talk.

"You'll have to meet with Tim Spindlis for more details. He told me Salma wasn't the first."

Mercer leaned forward and picked up the story. "We can point you in the right direction, Liz. Rowdy and his partners—Kendall Reid, some other politico riffraff, and a slew of ex-cons—they put together this Sub Rosa operation. They grew and grew it, in part

from the money Reid was stealing from the City Council, and fueled by the appetites of rich men like Ethan Leighton, who were
willing to pay through the nose for these women."

"Look at the hold it gave these guys on Leighton," Mike said.
"Not just now, but for what they saw as his powerful political
future."

"So you don't think the paternity scam was dreamed up by the
girls—by Salma and Anita?"

Mike answered before I could open my mouth. "Rowdy Kitts
all the way, Liz. Remember Kitts had a role model for bad behavior.
He cloned himself from Bernie Kerik, the corrupt former commissioner. Hell, Kerik almost became the head of homeland security—
a presidential appointment—before he got nailed for his crimes."

"So why kill Salma?" Liz asked again.

"Reid'll turn on a dime," Mike said. "He'll tell you why, if you
sweeten his deal."

I raised my head. "Sweeten nothing. We'll help you build a
case."

"Yo, blondie," Mike said, clapping his hands as he did a double
take. "The phoenix is rising, Ms. Arrington. You'll get her back in
the game."

"I don't want to see any deal for Kendall Reid, Liz. Once you
meet some of these victims and see the lives he's destroyed, I think
you'll understand."

"I'm sure I will."

"Claire Leighton thinks Salma signed her own death warrant,"
I said. "She confided in Battaglia yesterday. Salma fell in love with
Ethan, or at least thought she could make a run for the whole pack-
age. Without the baggage of the baby."

"So their argument the night of the car accident?" Liz asked.

"It was about Ana's fever, to start," Mercer said, filling in from
what I had told him. "But Salma wanted Ethan to leave Claire, and
she was tired of the charade about Ana being their child. Truth is,
she didn't want anything more to do with the baby."

"That means Rowdy Kitts was about to lose the goose that laid the golden egg," Liz said. "His blackmail ammunition to follow Leighton for life, up the political ranks."

"Kendall Reid knew," I said. "How cold-blooded can he be? That's his very own baby. It's unthinkable."

"He certainly knew part of his seed money was stored in Salma's closet," Mercer said. "And since Rowdy was holding on to her papers, she had no choice but to sit there with it. She had nowhere to run."

"And a rich sugar daddy to give her whatever she desired," Mike said, folding a sheet from a legal pad on the table. "Salma didn't want for cash."

Liz walked toward Mike. "You think Rowdy went to Salma's apartment intending to kill her?"

"Yeah, I do. Check the phone and e-mail action between Kendall Reid and Rowdy Kitts all day. That's the whole plan behind the spoofing."

"What kind of plan?"

"I gotta say, I was wrong. Coop called it on the spot. Spoiled my dinner, but she was right. She didn't know about the murder, but she figured the idea behind the spoofing."

I glanced at Mike—it was so rare for him to give me credit for anything—and Mercer patted my hand, winking at me.

"Those repeated nine-one-one calls did just what they were supposed to do," Mike went on. "We haven't tried to make a match to the woman who actually made them for Rowdy—voice print technology will help us do it—but you can bet she's one of the young Mexicans trafficked in by him and by Reid. Setting Salma up as an out-of-control hysteric, Rowdy Kitts knew exactly what would happen."

I picked up the thread. "The responding cops told Salma that they wouldn't come back the next time she called. That's what prompted me to fuss about going there with Mercer in the first place. Salma didn't want detectives snooping around, but didn't think she was in any danger with Kitts coming over. And he knew that even if things got out of hand when he attacked her, the next nine-one-one call—the one she tried to make from her cell phone before he killed her—would be ignored by the cops, who thought she was acting irrationally all through the day and evening."

"The spoofed calls set the scene for Salma's murder," Liz said. "Now I see it. Let Kitts get the job done and gave him time to dispose of the body. The precinct cops had washed their hands of her."

Another rap on the door and a federal marshal pushed in without waiting for an invitation. "Fifteen minutes, Ms. Arrington."

She scowled at him. "I get it. We'd like some privacy."

"You, Counselor," he said, pointing at me. "You've got a fan club."

Mike tossed the paper plane he'd been crafting in my direction. "Coop never travels light. Those girls are loyal, I'll give her that."

"More like a stage-door Johnny," the marshal said as he backed out.

"What is it, Coop? Didn't trust us to get the job done? Call in the French Foreign Legion?"

Mike turned his back to me and looked out the window again.

I was thoroughly confused. If Luc had chosen this moment to surprise me, he had picked the wrong time. "I didn't call anyone."

"I did," Mercer said. "I thought it would be good for you right now. Blame me for this one."

"Capitaine Luc Rouget," Mike muttered. *"Légionnaire extraordinaire."*

"What am I missing?" Liz asked. "The French authorities are involved?"

"Yeah. French toast and French fries. Truffles and foie gras. Detective Wallace is clearly of the view that too many cooks don't spoil the broth." Mike started to pace around the table. "Really professional, Coop. Spare me the courtroom hand-holding, okay?"

Mercer stood up and Mike came to a stop. "I'll explain this to you, Liz."

"I'm beginning to get it."

"You want us standing by in here during the arraignment?"

"Yes, please, Mercer. The judge may ask something I can't answer without your input. You think Ethan Leighton is looking at a collar?"

"Down the line, yes. Depends how deeply he got himself entangled with the trafficking, by design or unintentionally," I said. "There's so much to be done before you've got all the answers."

"And Liz has the troops to do it, Alex," Mercer said. "You get to take a break."

"Look, I'm going to help you and Mike." That seemed far more important to me than entertaining Luc, no matter how far he had traveled. Something about the timing of his arrival felt all wrong to me, especially after my flirtation with Mike at Mercer's house on Friday night.

Mike barely met my gaze as he waved me off. "There'll be plenty for you to do next week. Give it a rest, Coop."

"Have you made any decision about what becomes of all the passengers on the boat?" I asked.

Liz Arrington smiled at me. "This may be a first, Alex. We're going to ask Washington to give amnesty to everyone on board. We'll do some more background checks to make sure we haven't got any young men with criminal records who slipped on in Ukraine, but I think the attorney general wants to use the Golden Voyagers as a public lesson about the trafficking problem."

"*The United States of America against Kendall Reid*," Mike said. "Sounds a hell of a lot better than just the *People of the State of New York*. Got the whole nation going against him in this court. Wish Kitts had lived long enough to hear the clerk say that with his name in bold print."

Liz gathered her papers and jotted the last few notes on the file. "Can you give me a few hours today?"

"Of course," I said.

Luc would understand this was the place I needed to be, the

work I had to get done. Tonight, I could put thoughts of the prosecution aside and unleash the flood of emotions that were bottled up inside me.

"Hey, Coop," Mike said, pulling out a chair to sit on my other side. "I'm sorry if I was rough on you. I was just trying to keep things light."

"Got it. Nothing to apologize for."

"You were right about Rowdy from day one, from years ago. You've got good instincts."

"Bottle that, Alex. Two apologies and a compliment all in one week," Mercer said. "I don't think I've ever had the pleasure of getting either from him."

"Tell you what. We'll give you ten minutes with Luc in the jury room for a quick reunion. Then he can buy lunch for us. Sound good?"

"You break the news to Luc," I said, laughing despite myself. "Luncheon for four, after flying all night to get here 'cause Mercer thought I need some shoring up. How very romantic."

I watched Liz Arrington stand up, smooth out her jacket, prepare herself to face the magistrate judge and argue for Kendall Reid's remand without bail. I liked her style.

"You ready to let go of the case, Coop?" Mike asked. "It's not yours anymore."

"Done," I said, with an exaggerated brush of my hands.

"I think I need to keep on Ms. Arrington's tail this time. She's a little too intense already."

"You have such a winning way with the ladies, Detective Chapman," I said. "Just stay out of her path and let her nail the bastards for me. You owe me that."

"We're talking debts now? I seem to remember some promises I'm due to collect on."

"Ready when you are, Mike. Ready anytime."

ACKNOWLEDGMENTS

The raging currents in the narrow straight east of Manhattan known as Hell Gate made it a watery grave for scores of men and women for centuries. A magnificent bluff that overlooks that deadly passageway was the site of a merchant's summer home built in 1799, which eventually became the city's mayoral residence, rich with its own history and intrigue.

The great public institutions of our large cities are well-known and often well-used. But it is a handful of the oldest private homes in New York City – still standing – that captured my imagination as I set out to explore the nature of some of the political scandals that have become so shockingly commonplace in recent times.

The Historic House Trust of New York City brilliantly preserves many of these buildings – the simple cottage that was the last home of Edgar Allan Poe, or the elegant Morris-Jumel Mansion, a Georgian masterpiece that George Washington seized to use as his headquarters in 1776. My favorite of these is the magnificent Gracie Mansion, operated by the Gracie Mansion Conservancy, a member of the trust.

I am grateful to Susan Danilow, director of the Conservancy, who

ACKNOWLEDGMENTS

so graciously and warmly introduced me to the treasures of Gracie Mansion, and to the assistant director, Diana Carroll, for whom no inquiry was too insignifi cant. Although evil things occur around the mansion in this book, they are entirely imaginary and would never happen under the loving eye of the Conservancy, nor during the administration of Mayor Michael Bloomberg, whose generosity is evident throughout the stunning restoration of 'the people's home'.

Of great interest and help to me were the books *New York City's Gracie Mansion: A History of the Mayor's House* by Mary Black, and *Gracie Mansion: A Celebration of New York City's Mayoral Residence* by Ellen Stern. As always, the archives of *The New York Times* proved invaluable in my research of the city's history.

I'm thrilled and honored to be at Dutton; thankful to Brian Tart for his patience, persistence, wisdom, and good friendship. Ben Sevier, my editor, has used his strong hand to make this book better, and I look forward to many more volumes together. Christine Ball has already proved to be a smart partner in crime, and Melissa Miller is holding my fingers to the keyboard. I like it here.

David Shelley, Hilary Hale, and their great team at Little, Brown UK have been steadfast and loyal through all of Coop's capers, and so I thank them all again.

Esther Newberg is first and foremost my great friend. That she has also been my agent, guiding me through professional waters every bit as treacherous as Hell Gate, is one of life's great bonuses. And to Kari Stuart and Allie Green, who I lean on constantly, thanks to you. A shout-out to Katie Cion, who offered me her name to create a fine new character to hang with Mike and Mercer.

Family and friends, as always, are my supreme joy and encouragement.

Welcome, beautiful Isla. And Alice Maude, my precious heart, you are always with me.

My fiercest literary critic – and my most devoted fan – is my great warrior, my husband, Justin Feldman. These books are all for him. And this one is especially dedicated to the women and men who do the very difficult work of special victims investigations and prosecutions – sexual assaults, domestic violence, and child abuse. They have been my colleagues in the New York County District Attorney's Office and the New York Police Department, and they will always be my heroes.

ABOUT THE AUTHOR

Linda Fairstein is America's foremost legal expert on crimes of sexual assault and domestic violence. She led the Sex Crimes Unit of the District Attorney's Office in Manhattan for twenty-six years. Her eleven previous Alexandra Cooper novels have been critically acclaimed international bestsellers, translated into more than a dozen languages. Fairstein lives in Manhattan and on Martha's Vineyard.